Praise for *What You Leave Behind*

"A single-sitting read! Morris brilliantly explores family ties, community injustice, and haunting grief all in one fell swoop. This is the kind of thriller that keeps you thinking long after the last page."

—Lisa Gardner, #1 *New York Times* bestselling author

"Wanda M. Morris's *What You Leave Behind* is a propulsive and unforgettable thriller that paints a haunting picture of a homecoming gone wrong. Readers will ride along with Morris's protagonist, Deena Woods, as she uncovers a deadly mystery that could ruin her Georgia hometown—and her entire life—in a story that spotlights Morris's deft characterization and razor-sharp plotting. *What You Leave Behind* is a one-of-a-kind novel that will keep you guessing."

—Alex Segura, bestselling author of *Secret Identity* and *Alter Ego*

"With an engrossing plot that evokes the work of John Grisham, *What You Leave Behind* cements Wanda M. Morris as one of the most exciting thriller writers working today. You can't help but root for Deena as she deals with personal issues, professional struggles, and a haunting encounter with a stranger that sends her down a dangerous path. *What You Leave Behind* is the perfect mix of mesmerizing thriller and emotional exploration of the question if you can ever go home again."

—Kellye Garrett, award-winning author of *Missing White Woman*

Praise for *Anywhere You Run*

"*Anywhere You Run* had me hooked from the first page. Wanda Morris brings 1964 to vivid, richly textured life and populates it with unforgettable characters. It's a novel both tender and ferocious—an absolute stunner."

—Lou Berney, Edgar Award–winning author of *November Road*

"The immensely talented Wanda M. Morris delivers an unflinching exploration of the pain and injustice of the Jim Crow South, a moving tale of sisterly devotion, and a riveting thriller all in one stellar novel. Morris writes with empathy and keen insight about the choices we make when we're out of choices, and about how, when we dig deep, we find a strength and resilience we didn't know was there. Wise, riveting, and full of surprises, *Anywhere You Run* will keep you up past your bedtime and stay with you long after the book is closed."

—Lisa Unger, *New York Times* bestselling author of *Secluded Cabin Sleeps Six*

"Evocative, heartbreaking, and utterly life changing. With the groundbreaking *Anywhere You Run*, Wanda Morris blooms into literary fiction, bringing readers a chillingly knowing and brilliantly upsetting novel of the sixties. With no holds barred and no emotion unplumbed, the talented Morris writes a tale of two sisters that's unflinchingly raw and passionately authentic. We cannot turn away from the story, or from the immersive settings, or from Morris's skilled depiction of tragedy, triumph, and the struggle to love and survive."

—Hank Phillippi Ryan, *USA Today* bestselling author

Praise for *All Her Little Secrets*

"*All Her Little Secrets* is a brilliantly nuanced but powerhouse exploration of race, the legal system, and the crushing pressure of keeping secrets. Morris brings a vibrant and welcome new voice to the thriller space."

—Karin Slaughter, *New York Times* and international bestselling author

"Wanda M. Morris hits all the right notes in *All Her Little Secrets*, a taut, sleek thriller that's also a searing story about the secrets we can never manage to leave behind. A stunning debut."

—Alafair Burke, *New York Times* bestselling author

"It's hard to know just how far you might go to protect yourself *and* your secrets . . . but it's remarkably easy to get swept up into this razor-sharp workplace thriller. At times deeply disturbing and all the while gripping, *All Her Little Secrets* is a refreshing whodunnit that will keep you guessing—and second-guessing—from start to finish."

—Zakiya Dalila Harris, *New York Times* bestselling author of *The Other Black Girl*

"Wanda M. Morris's *All Her Little Secrets* is that rare debut novel that doesn't miss a beat—expertly plotted, beautifully written, and so compelling I read it in one sitting. Fans of Attica Locke and Celeste Ng, take note!"

—Wendy Corsi Staub, *New York Times* bestselling author of *The Other Family*

"*All Her Little Secrets* is a truly remarkable debut—an expertly paced thriller with terrific twists, as well as depth, heart, and conscience . . . not to mention the smart, complicated Ellice Littlejohn, a protagonist who kept me turning pages well into the night."

—Alison Gaylin, *USA Today* bestselling author of *The Collective*

WHAT YOU LEAVE BEHIND

ALSO BY WANDA M. MORRIS

All Her Little Secrets

Anywhere You Run

WHAT YOU LEAVE BEHIND

A Novel

WANDA M. MORRIS

wm
WILLIAM MORROW
An Imprint of HarperCollins*Publishers*

This is a work of fiction. Names, characters, places, and incidents are products of the author's imagination or are used fictitiously and are not to be construed as real. Any resemblance to actual events, locales, organizations, or persons, living or dead, is entirely coincidental.

HarperCollins books may be purchased for educational, business, or sales promotional use. For information, please email the Special Markets Department at SPsales@harpercollins.com.

FIRST EDITION

Designed by Diahann Sturge-Campbell

Title page and part opener image © Jeff Holcombe/Shutterstock

Library of Congress Cataloging-in-Publication Data has been applied for.

ISBN 978-0-06-332221-9
ISBN 978-0-06-335973-4 (hardcover library edition)

24 25 26 27 28 LBC 5 4 3 2 1

This one is for my guys,
Anthony, Mitchell, and Ashton,
for always making me feel safe, protected, and loved

A good man leaves an inheritance for his children's children,
but a sinner's wealth is stored up for the righteous.

—Proverbs 13:22

Part I
DAYCLEAN

The island was ours and we roamed everywhere except for one place.

Dunbar Creek.

Some folks believed it was haunted, filled with mystical unseen spirits. Other folks called Dunbar Creek "the end of the world."

It very well could have been too after what happened there. Way back in 1808, the government passed a law that declared that there were to be no more ships transporting our African people to this country to turn them into slaves. But evil men with no hearts or souls continued to work in clandestine ways, even after the slave trade had been outlawed for years. Those mongrels on two legs anchored their boats on quiet creeks and rivers along the Georgia coast. Small ships that left lands and broke family bonds it would take their cargo generations to knit back together.

One blue-black night just before dawn peeked over the horizon, a small schooner called the York *slinked along Dunbar Creek to unload a cargo of West Africans known as the Igbo people of Nigeria. The old folks told us how the Igbo rose up and took over that ship. They were dirty, tired, but still strong enough to drive their captors overboard. But other vile men waited for those brave souls when the boat hit the shore. Men ready and waiting to get them to plantations across the south. After they were taken off the ship, they were shackled once more. Chained together, with freedom slipping from their grasp, the Igbo ancestors knew what lay ahead and decided in that moment what their future would be.*

They chose freedom.

Together, they walked into the water, shoulder to shoulder, their chains still intact. The farther they walked, the closer they came to freedom. When the final ripple of water erased the last trace of them, they were free.

Some folks say the Igbo people drowned themselves deliberately by walking into Dunbar Creek. But not me. I think those brave souls walked into the water and flew home.

Imagine it. A person could be so disgusted with the thought of living in bondage that death seemed a better option.

Like the Igbo people, perhaps there is a better option for me, and one day, I'll fly home too.

CHAPTER 1

Dead people don't talk to the living.

It should have been like any other drive out to the island to hear her voice. Simply get in the car and ride and ride until the tears blurred my vision, making it impossible for me to see and forcing me to pull over to the side of the road. On really bad days, I'd drive for over an hour, sometimes winding up in a different city or town. Street signs and landmarks shifting in the periphery as I went chasing after someone I couldn't see or touch. Once, I drove all the way to Savannah from Daddy's house in Brunswick. But I never once went to the cemetery where she was buried because, to me, she wasn't in some dark hole in the ground. She was with me. I needed to believe that or else I would die too.

Depending on the day, sometimes I'd go to a park to sit and listen to the brief voicemails she'd left on my phone. I only had a few because it was rare that I didn't pick up a call from her. Even if I was in a meeting, I picked up her calls.

Now, I relied on the soft fragments of brain tissue that conjured up memories and the deep well of despair in my heart to connect me to the woman I cherished more than anyone else in the world.

Elizabeth Wood.

Libby to her family and friends.

Ma to me.

Her death had landed like a boxer's blow inside my chest, sweeping away my breath and bringing me to my knees. A year later and I was still having a hard time navigating the indescribable grief because the person who usually helped me through any heartache I ever had was now the source of it.

Shortly after she died, I'd swear I could still hear her voice. The cadence of it as she talked about some church gossip or giggled at some joke Daddy had told her. It was silly, I know. Maybe it was some sort of grieving mechanism to get me through. When you're a grown woman and you lose a parent, people expect you to power through the grief. You have a job, responsibilities. You're an adult. You're supposed to know that death is a part of life. And if you looked at me, on the outside, I was all that. But on the inside, I was a broken mess.

And if losing Ma wasn't enough, that imaginary boxer hit me with a one-two combo. Six months after Ma's death, Lance came home one night, quietly ate dinner with me, and then proceeded to tell me he was filing for divorce. He told me I wasn't the same since Ma's death. Who is after you lose someone you love? The truth of the matter is that Lance was *exactly* the same. Things I had stupidly tolerated before as a small ripple in our marriage—flirtatious interactions with restaurant waitstaff, women we encountered in a store who were unusually comfortable with him—became a tsunami. The sudden appearance of receipts for jewelry I didn't own and dinners at restaurants I'd never been to became ground zero for the ugly destruction of a marriage that had been a fragile structure from the start. Much of what happened between us, I still hadn't told anyone, including Daddy.

Perhaps that's the way life is. You don't just deal with one bad thing at a time. Life throws a stream of adversities at you with no break in between. Ma used to call it a season. A job loss follows a death in the family. A cancer diagnosis comes right before a car accident. It's like a nonstop battle with the universe to see if you're strong enough to fight your way through the layers of misfortune and heartache. But Ma always said, seasons pass.

With no real home of my own and my life in tatters, I left Atlanta and moved back to the house in which I grew up in Brunswick, Georgia. The prodigal daughter returned home with a divorce settlement and a set of emotional baggage heavy enough to kill a decent-sized bear under its weight.

I needed what the old folks used to call a "dayclean." A new day. A fresh start.

Today, I drove for over thirty minutes before I wound up on the island. I pulled my Audi A6, a remnant from my previous life in Atlanta, up to a small band of trees and leaned into that old familiar feeling of grief and failure. I'd driven so far out on the island I wasn't even sure where I was. But it was quiet, and I was alone. I could listen for Ma.

This time, instead of sitting in the car, I decided to walk. I cut the engine, took off my heels, and slipped on a pair of black and white Skechers I kept in the back seat of my car. I stepped outside and closed my eyes for a moment. The salt-tinged ocean breeze that kissed my cheek and the sound of rushing water calmed me like a healing salve. The April air was uncomfortably warm for so early in the season. It felt more like June and a threat of summer's early arrival. The land was empty, and some parts of the ground were soft and muddy, remnants left behind by the recent rains.

The morning fog had lifted and offered a straight view across open land that rolled down onto a sandy shore and out into the teasing blue sparkle of the Atlantic Ocean. When you looked beyond the emptiness of it all, this place was stunning. A large swath of land covered by huge live oak trees with low thick branches that dipped and rose in chaotic beauty. Many of them draped in Spanish moss, like ghostly old women stooped and covered in green lace.

Back at the turn of the last century, the Vanderbilts, Rockefellers, and Morgans built winter homes here. Their grand estates that still stood as pricey villas for vacation rentals. My parents and their friends used to talk of how the wealthy built their fortunes on the backs of working-class whites and built their winter retreats on the backs of Black laborers right here on the Georgia Golden Islands. Things hadn't changed much since wealthy people still continued to own vacation homes here in the Golden Isles. The thought that some people owned several homes, and I didn't even have one, was like the sharpened end of a rod that constantly poked at my psyche.

I stood beneath an oak tree, closed my eyes, and listened. Waiting for Ma's voice.

A few seconds later, I felt a light tickling at my ankles. I opened my eyes and looked down. A small dog, a brown shaggy terrier of some type, with a bright shot of white fur over one eye, sniffed at my shoes. The dog wasn't wearing a collar. A stray out here in the middle of nowhere like me. I looked around and that's when I spotted it. A few hundred yards off in the distance was an old, rusted trailer. I squinted, trying to make out exactly what I was seeing. Did someone live out here?

I looked back at the dog. "Hey! Is that where you live, little guy?"

The dog raised one scruffy ear, bent his head, and stared at me. Then, I heard a loud bang.

A flash of panic bloomed inside my chest. The ringing in my ears lingered as a group of birds noisily flapped off into the sky. The dog took off like a shot.

A firecracker?

A gun?

I snapped to. My only thought: I have to get out of here. I dashed from behind the tree where I was standing, heading for my car. As I did, my foot caught on the gnarled tree roots jutting up from the ground. I spun and tripped, hitting the back of my head against the roots.

And everything faded to black.

CHAPTER 2

When I blinked my eyes open, the first thing I saw was the irregular pattern of a brown water stain. Somehow, I was leaning back and facing ceiling tiles. I was inside a room, small and dimly lit. Maybe my eyes had suffered from the blow to the back of my head. I smelled bacon and my head was pounding.

Where the hell am I?

I blinked a few more times before I leaned forward. That slight motion sent the room into a revolution and spikes of pain radiated through my head from ear to ear.

I gotta get to my car.

A man's voice slipped from the darkness beside me, southern drawl, deep-throated, and raspy. "Why'd they send *you* out here?"

I blinked again and peered around the room. I was sitting beside a table on a hard upholstered bench. Worn, brown linoleum spread from beneath the bottom of my Skechers, which were now covered in mud and moss. In front of me was a kitchenette, the light coming through a small window just bright enough for me to see a frying pan and a thick coating of dust and grease across the stove. Now, the pain swirled and filled my head like thick smoke rising from a fire. When I tried to get up, my vision blurred for a moment.

"Stay still and answer my question." The man again.

I still couldn't see him, his voice coming from somewhere beyond my view. I rubbed the back of my head. "I was just driving around, looking for a quiet place to think."

"I've warned y'all."

"Can I at least see who I'm talking to?" Speaking to some voice without a face was unnerving.

The man slowly walked out from the shadows and stood squarely in front of me. A Black man, early seventies if I had to guess. I couldn't be sure because the only thing I focused on was the rifle he held with hands that looked like two large knobs of thick veins. Thankfully, he didn't point the gun at me, but he had it at the ready. He was a tall, haggard-looking man with deep brown, leathery skin and a scruffy gray beard. Maybe I could make a run for thc door. I ran high school track back in the day, but he had a gun and I couldn't outrun a bullet.

Shit! Where is the door?

"Where am I?" I peered back at the man. "Who are you?"

"I'm asking the questions."

I glanced around the room. The small, tight quarters. The dirty kitchenette. The tattered brown banquette I was sitting on. I remembered the trailer I'd spotted. *I must be inside the trailer.* I tried to remember every detail of this place for recounting back to the police if I made it out of here alive. I looked down at my shoes again, at the muddy sand and moss covering them. The old man had dragged me in here. I tried to unmoor myself from the bench.

"Uh-uh." He tightened his grip on the rifle, holding it across his chest. "Don't move. Not until you tell me why they sent *you* out here this time."

I slowed my roll. Old men and guns are a dangerous combination. This guy was obviously in a fight with someone and now I might become a casualty of his determination to win. "I'm sorry, sir. You know what? Apparently I made a mistake. I shouldn't have stopped here, Mr. . . . ?"

"You're the third person that's been nosing around here in the last few months. Like I told those other two, my mama and daddy left this land to me and my sister, Delilah. Y'all can send as many letters as you want. I'm not leaving."

"I'm really sorry. I don't know what you're talking about. Let me just leave, okay?"

"Not until you tell me why they sent a Black woman this time."

A Black woman this time? I didn't know what the hell this guy was talking about. Maybe I could finesse my way back to my car and hightail it back to Brunswick.

"I'll tell you the same thing I told the others. I'm not interested in selling. This property's been in my family for generations. I was born here and I'll die here."

I kept staring at the barrel of his gun. No one knew I was out here. This man could shoot me at any moment. If he hurt me, how would anyone find me? I had to get out of here.

"Sir, I assure you, I didn't know this was your property. I recently lost my mother and I guess I'm not handling it very well. Sometimes I drive around to clear my head. I was just looking for a quiet place . . ." I watched him loosen his grip on the gun. "There must be some sort of mistake."

"You damn straight there is." The man gripped the gun tightly again. "Now get up." His voice was quiet but firm.

What is he going to do?

I struggled to my feet. The room spun again, and I grabbed the edge of the table. The back of my head throbbed. But I wasn't about to pass on the only chance I might have to get out of here alive. He pointed me toward the door at the front of the trailer. I got my bearings and stepped outside into the blazing sunlight with the old man right on my heels. The sun was searing and worsened the headache I was nursing. I shielded my eyes with my hand to knock off some of the brightness. The dog I'd spotted earlier came over. He raised the one hairy ear again, sniffed me, then looked up at me.

"Now I'm going to walk you back to your car. And you're going to leave and never come back. Are we clear?"

"Yes, sir."

"Come on, Trooper," he called to the dog. The dog sniffed me again before he ambled over to the old man. "I don't know why they keep sending people out here. I'm never gon' sell it. You're the first Black person they sent. I guess they thought you could sweet-talk me out of my land. I warned them other two just like I'm warning you. *Stay away.* The next person to come out here uninvited is gonna catch a bullet right between the eyes. The only reason I didn't shoot you is . . ."

He didn't finish his thought. Maybe because I was Black too? A woman? So, the old man was at odds with someone trying to buy his land. He must have mistaken me for someone associated with his adversary.

"Well, I appreciate you not shooting me." I smiled slightly, trying to lighten things between us. He returned my effort with a solemn expression as if his face were etched in bronze on a museum bust. Again, old men and guns.

"Do you mind if I ask your name, sir?" I would need it when I called the police.

He stared at me for a moment, like he was debating whether to answer me. "Holcomb. Holcomb Gardner. Same name on all them damn letters y'all sending."

"Mr. Gardner, I'm sorry. Like I said, I was just driving around looking for a quiet place to think. I didn't mean any harm."

We walked in silence for a few moments before we finally arrived at my car. I stared up at the old man. "Where's your sister?"

He hesitated for a beat before he took in a deep breath. "That's none of ya business. Now, why don't you get in your car before I change my mind about shooting you." He patted his rifle.

I climbed inside my car and started up the engine. He tapped the window with the butt of his gun and made a gesture for me to roll the window down.

"Yes, sir?"

He leaned in toward the car window. "Please tell them folks you work for, I don't take kindly to them sending people out here. This here is Gardner land. Always has been, and it always will be. The next person they send out here won't be as lucky as you. Now, get off my property."

I peeled off without another word. In fact, I sped off so fast, I nearly hit a black car headed onto the old man's property. I jerked the steering wheel. The driver blared his horn and swerved widely to avoid a T-bone crash. I never slowed. I never stopped. A few seconds later, I glanced in my rearview mirror. The same black car made a U-turn in the middle of the road. Within a minute, the car was right on my tail.

"What the fu—"

I thought about pulling my car over to the side of the road so it could pass me. But it was right on my bumper. If I tapped my brakes in the slightest, it would rear-end me. I floored the gas pedal, trying to get some distance between us. The engine revved as I watched the speedometer climb to eighty-five. The car behind me never let up. My head was pounding from the fall and my ears started to ring from fear. I gunned the gas to ninety and prayed for a police car to catch us in this dangerous chase. Nothing. The grassy marshlands whizzed by in a blur. I finally raced toward the causeway headed to Brunswick. Soon, there would be more cars. Maybe I could lose this nutjob in traffic. I peered in the rearview mirror and watched as the car finally slowed before making a right turn onto a side road and disappeared. *What the hell was that?! Road rage?*

I blew out a deep sigh of relief, grateful to be out of the crosshairs of some crazy psycho nutcase fueled by anger and vengeance. I promised myself I would never drive back out here on the island, no matter how much I needed to be close to Ma.

CHAPTER 3

I turned off the causeway and onto the Golden Isles Parkway. My pulse was slowing, and the fear was falling away. Traffic was light. To me, traffic was always light here in Brunswick compared to Atlanta. Atlanta was a lifetime ago and leaving that city felt like a soft curtain falling on my sad little theater of pain. First Ma, then Lance. And I still hadn't told anyone about the other stuff that happened back there. All anyone needed to know was that Lance and I had decided to divorce, and I came back home for a while to clear my head. Everything else that had happened back in Atlanta would remain exactly what it was—a hellish nightmare tucked away as a shameful secret.

I suddenly realized in my frenzy to get away from the crazy old guy with a gun and the crazy road rage dude, I'd forgotten about Ma. For a fleeting few minutes, Holcomb Gardner and some guy with an axe to grind had washed away the fog of grief. My only thought back then was to live. My next thought was to call the police. But I was the trespasser in that situation. Besides, he hadn't harmed me. He scared the crap out of me, of course, but I was still in one piece. If people had been on his land before, I guess he had his reasons for the gun. But who was the person headed to the old man's property and why had he followed me like a bat out of Hades?

I made a mental note to be more mindful the next time I went out driving.

By the time I made it back to work in Brunswick, my pulse had returned to normal. Most people were buzzing around the break room when I arrived at Medallion Company's office, or "the Old Victorian," as everyone called it. Beau Walsh, one of Medallion's partners, had ordered a breakfast spread from Jupiter's around the corner—bagels, sausage sandwiches, muffins, and coffee. Nothing lured a group of dull and lackadaisical coworkers away from their desks faster than free food in the office break room. Half the meetings I attended in the office offered candy and snacks. Always something to drive traffic since work ethic and collaborative spirit were never enough.

Medallion's offices were located inside a huge, stately teal-blue Victorian mansion in the SoGlo section of Brunswick. The front porch with its narrow spindles and the curved turret at the side of the house made it stand out from all the other houses on the street. Something about it was grand and inviting. I loved old houses like this one, with its creaky hardwood floors and original tin ceilings. Every door turned with a glass knob that had been touched by hands long dead and gone.

The house had been renovated to accommodate the twelve of us who worked there on a regular basis, with room to spare. Inside, the large foyer held a half circle mahogany desk where Jennie, the young receptionist, sat and greeted visitors. The large staircase behind her desk led to management's and the engineers' offices upstairs, seven former bedrooms that were decorated with expensive office furniture. The parlor to the left of the reception desk held an impressive array of bookshelves, a fireplace, and soft seating, like a small library of sorts. The former dining room to the right had been converted into a conference room with a long oak double pedestal table and soft upholstered chairs around it. Beyond the dining room was a large butler's pantry and the former kitchen, now serving as an oversized break room. And off this, down a narrow hallway, were a bathroom and two small rooms. I imagined these were the former servants' quarters. One room held three small desks and housed the HR manager, the IT guy, and some woman who was never in the office with enough regularity for me to figure out what she did for the company. The other room, smaller than the first, was my office. Yes, my office was inside a former maid's bedroom. My guess, considering where we were, here in Georgia, was that maid had probably been Black like me. I was just grateful I didn't have to share an office with anyone else.

As I passed through the break room, Jennie, the receptionist, gave me a forced smile as if she were about to deliver bad news. She leaned in close and whispered, "Joe wants to see you," as if I were an errant child, now in trouble with a scolding parent.

I already knew what was coming. Another lecture about my being late and how important face time was around the office. The world had gone through a two-year pandemic. No one worked in the office five days a week anymore. No one except the people who worked at Medallion.

"Thanks." After I dropped my bag in my desk drawer, I headed up the back staircase to Joe's office. I didn't even knock, just stepped right inside.

"Hey, you wanted to see me?"

Joe was hunched over his desk, about to take a bite out of his sausage and egg sandwich. He'd tucked a napkin inside his collar and spread it across the front of his shirt like a kid's bib. Joe was a short, muscular guy. He could have easily been mistaken for a gym rat on the days when he didn't wear a suit and tie. He was in his mid-fifties and worked as a real estate attorney before he joined Medallion. He had both an engineering degree and a law degree, which made him a double tight-ass.

When I had returned to Brunswick, I was unemployed and desperate. My life had spun out of control in the months prior. A change of scenery from Atlanta, the sanctity of my parents' house, and a new job seemed like what I needed to get my life back together. I made a good impression on Joe, and he didn't ask me for any references. Two days later, when Joe offered me this job, I jumped at it.

He sat his sandwich down and wiped his mouth on the end of the tucked napkin. "Look, I'll get right to the point. Deena . . . you're smart, but . . ."

Oh God. I prayed this man wasn't about to fire me. I couldn't take another blow from that imaginary boxer's fist.

"But what, Joe?"

"Close the door."

I stared at him for a few seconds before I closed the door and returned to his desk.

"Beau is at it again. He thinks we ought to clean house and fill the place up with a bunch of independent contractors."

"So what are you trying to say?"

"Look, Deena. I like you. I like you a lot. Hell, I hired you. But you have to understand what's going on around here."

I already understood what was happening. They'd hired me and then realized they could get a paraprofessional to do my job. Now they had to figure out what to do with me. Fire me outright or slowly paper my personnel file and "performance manage" me out the door. Either way, I smelled another dismissal in the air.

Most people thought of lawyers as high-flying leaders, hustling into court or presiding over executive meetings or quietly whispering into the ear of their powerful clients during congressional hearings. But there was also this dark underbelly of boring, brain-numbing legal work that was little more than glorified tasks that needed a sign-off from a living body who had passed a bar exam. I was working in one of those jobs. My official title was legal consultant. What I really did was review form contracts and pull permits from government offices. I used to be a litigator in Atlanta with a major law firm. These days, I was doing busywork to earn a paycheck every two weeks.

Joe cleared his throat and waited, obviously dreading whatever he was about to tell me.

"Look, Clare told me your mom died last year. That's tough. My mom's been gone for ten years now. It's hard. I know. But . . ." He sighed deeply. "You come in late. Leave during the middle of the day. No one knows where you are. You're outta here by five o'clock sharp. Sometimes before."

"But I always get my work done. You've had no complaints, have you?"

"No, but you gotta put in the face time. You know how Beau is. Just be present, okay?"

"Okay."

"Okay," he mimicked. "You know Clare likes you too. She told me to make sure you're working on the big projects."

So Clare was trying to save my job. *Thank God for Clare*. Clare Walsh was the managing partner of Medallion and Beau's aunt. She founded the company and brought in Beau to give him something productive to do instead of his usual get-rich-quick schemes. She was one of the first female civil engineers in the state of Georgia, back in the late seventies, when there was no such thing as STEM for girls or a proliferation of women engineers. Every day, thousands of people drove across bridges between the islands that she'd had a hand in building. Clare spent the bulk of her time out drumming up business. She left the day-to-day operations of running Medallion to Beau. I adored Clare. Beau, not so much.

"Besides, you know Beau. He's an asshole. Hell, if he had his way, I'd be on the chopping block too. Just make sure you're pulling your weight and keep your head low. If you wanna stick around, you gotta be on time and in here. Ass-in-chair. No more disappearing act in the middle of the day. Where do you go, by the way?"

I shrugged. "Just getting a bit of fresh air."

"Well, do less of it," he said before he went back to his sandwich.

I left his office. At least I wasn't getting fired.

Not yet.

* * *

MY LIFE WAS a dumpster fire, and this dead-end job was stoking the flames. I was *losing* brain cells in this role. But I needed the job. Mortgage companies had this pesky little requirement about proof of income. Even though I'd been outbid on my first two attempts at buying a house, I would keep at it. I couldn't keep living with my father and his new bride.

I left Joe's office and headed to the kitchen, aka the break room, for a cup of coffee. I needed to focus, to be on my game. I pulled a dark roast coffee pod from the canister and dropped it into the Keurig machine. The coffee maker gurgled for a few seconds before the liquid dribbled into the Styrofoam cup. I heard someone else enter the kitchen behind me. I didn't turn around because I wasn't in the mood for conversation.

"Well, well, here's surprise sighting I didn't expect to see."

A man's voice. *Shit.*

I nodded. "Good morning, Beau."

Beau Walsh was a tall, thick guy with a ruddy complexion. He always reminded me of a lumberjack in a suit and tie with a lazy southern drawl.

He strolled over to stand beside me. "Oh, is it still morning? Sometimes, we don't see you until after lunch."

I chose to ignore his comment. I was smart enough to know he wanted to get a rise out of me, get me to say something that he could use in his effort to fire me. Maybe accuse me of being insubordinate. Not today. I edged away and picked up a coffee stirrer and a sugar packet.

He leaned against the sink. "Now, how long have you worked for us?"

"A little over three months."

"Hmm . . . and in all that time, I don't think I've seen you more than a few times."

I didn't respond. I stirred the sugar into my coffee without a word.

"Maybe we don't keep you busy enough. Perhaps, if we give you more work, you'll spend more time in the office. Or maybe we should have hired you as a part-time paralegal to get our money's worth out of you."

I tossed the coffee stirrer in the garbage can. "I'm always here when you need me."

I smiled and walked out of the break room before he could make another wisecrack or before I actually abandoned my reserve and told him to go to hell.

I sat inside the broom closet that pretended to be my office and thought about Ma. Her daughter being a lawyer was her greatest achievement, the successful result of her first and only pregnancy. Even though Ma was ten years younger than Daddy, she told me she had a rough pregnancy and an even rougher childbirth experience, which probably explained why I was an only child. She said all her late nights of worrying when I was sick as a baby or when I'd missed curfew in high school had been worth it because her daughter was a lawyer. Ma used to tell me there was a special reason I was in the world. But now, she wasn't. I closed my eyes, straining to hear her laugh. But all I could muster was the vision of Ma's casket draped in white roses.

My eyes began to sting with the first inkling of tears. To distract myself, I pulled up the internet web browser on my laptop. On a whim, I typed in "Holcomb Gardner." It yielded several hits for landscaping companies, but none of them specifically related to the old man who'd run me off his property with a gun. I did a search for his sister, Delilah Gardner, in Brunswick. The first thing to pop up was an obituary from Murray Brothers Funeral Home. I clicked on it. Delilah Gardner had lived in Brunswick and died six months ago. No mention of Holcomb Gardner. I did another quick search and located the last known address for Delilah, jotted it down, and closed the browser.

I sat at my desk, my stomach growling like crazy. Pride wouldn't let me go to the break room to rummage through cold, picked-over breakfast remnants. A couple minutes later, I heard the floorboards outside my office pop and creak with footsteps right before Peg Nelson stepped inside. Peg was a dumpy-looking woman with a loose turkey neck that shook whenever she got excited and talked fast.

She told people around the office that she was forty-five years old. The last forty of them she must have spent living hard because I thought she had to be sixty.

"Hey, Deena."

Peg's voice had a loud, slightly annoying quality to it, like cheap jangling bracelets in a quiet room. In the few short months I'd worked for Medallion, I was starting to get used to it. But every now and again, she'd startle me just by saying "good morning."

Before she could say another word, the old metal steam radiator in the corner of my office began to clang. A hard, uneven knocking noise that rattled the windows. She walked over and kicked a valve. The noise subsided.

"Why the heck the radiator clangs in the middle of spring when the heat isn't on is beyond me," Peg said.

I shrugged. "Old houses make lots of noises."

"Maybe, but it's creepy. Listen, Joe wanted me to remind you that he needs you to go through some boxes in the attic to make sure there's nothing in there we need to keep. He wants me to put a destruction order on them and send them out to be shredded." She pointed a crooked finger to the ceiling. "A little cost-saving measure from Beau."

"Yeah, okay."

She walked out.

Obviously, the IT guy who worked for Medallion wasn't nearly as savvy as the IT people I worked with back at my old firm in Atlanta. Nearly every file there was digitized. It was the way the world worked. But here at Medallion, it was all paper and gusset files. This place was hopelessly rolling around in the dark ages.

I had been avoiding those boxes for weeks now for two reasons. First, digging through a bunch of old boxes looking for legal documents was not legal work. And second, I hated going up in that attic. The only other time I'd been up there to retrieve a box, it was hot and dark with its creepy brick walls. And it always smelled like cigarette smoke. Clare was adamant that no one was to smoke or light candles anywhere in the Old Victorian. Probably because the place was so old it would turn into a flash fire at the sight of a match. I bet whoever was catching a smoking break up there would be fired on the spot if Clare Walsh found out.

I slid a stack of files toward me and began sifting through them for some licensing information and fought off the urge to fall asleep. Each time I tried to focus, my mind always wandered back to the old man—Holcomb Gardner. Crazy as it was, I couldn't stop thinking about him. Even more bizarre, I couldn't figure out *why* I kept thinking about him. Some old guy who'd scared the crap out of me, whom I hadn't talked to for more than ten minutes, was at the top of my mind.

CHAPTER 4

By lunchtime, I was feeling restless again. I decided to head home for a quick bite and to ask Daddy something. I turned the corner onto Campbellton Street, where I grew up and where Daddy still lived. Where we all lived. On the days when I gave a damn, I was flooded with embarrassment that I was thirty-nine years old and living back in the bedroom where I'd grown up. I told myself it was just temporary since I was looking for a place of my own. Telling myself that I was back home to help Daddy was utter nonsense because he'd moved on from Ma's death and married her friend Ruth a mere six months after the funeral. He was doing just fine. A part of me still hadn't forgiven him for the betrayal.

I hadn't lived here since I graduated from high school. But home didn't feel like home anymore. I was what the Geechee folks called a bit of *from-ya* and a bit of *come-ya,* which meant I was both from here and a visitor as well. I didn't belong in Brunswick, and I didn't belong in Atlanta either. Daddy had Ruth here in Brunswick. Lance had all our friends and a new fiancée back in Atlanta—the twenty-four-year-old *child* who used to be his assistant at his company.

And my efforts to find my place in a home of my own had failed. The first month after I returned to Brunswick, I put in an offer on a small bungalow located not too far from Daddy's house. Someone outbid me with a huge all-cash offer that I couldn't compete with. The second time I put in another offer on a house, the same thing happened. I was frustrated but took it as a sign that maybe Brunswick might not ever be home for me again. The one thing I wanted most—to find a home—kept slipping away from my grasp.

The neighborhood where I'd grown up had changed. Everyone was either moving slower or moving out. The closest casualty was Eddie "Pee-Wee" Lincoln, Daddy's next-door neighbor. He used to own Pee-Wee's BBQ Joint around the corner. After the third robbery in a year, he closed the restaurant for good. A year after that his daughter packed him and the entire house up and moved him to Indianapolis to live with her. They sold the house and it sat unoccupied for almost a year. The folks left behind tried to look beyond the blight that a boarded-up, empty house created in the neighborhood. But everyone knew it was only a matter of time before those abandoned houses attracted a certain criminal element who would leave the residents in fear or scrambling away from the neighborhood. This was usually the first step in the downward spiral of a community.

My parents' house sat near the middle of the block. A one-story redbrick structure with a blue and white awning to shade the porch from the south Georgia sun. The yard was tidy, and Daddy always kept a colorful array of seasonal flowers in the beds. This house was the first and only piece of property my parents owned. They'd spent their lives caring for and pampering it. Back before Daddy's knees got bad, it wasn't unusual to see him up on a ladder painting the windowsills or cleaning the gutters. Always puttering around the house. Now, he still puttered around fixing this or that. He just did it at a slower pace.

As I started to climb the stairs to the front porch, I noticed a dark

Ford Escape parked in front of Mr. Lincoln's house next door. I hesitated for a moment because it looked exactly like the car I'd nearly hit trying to run away from the old man out on the island. Before I had a chance to pull my phone out and snap a picture of the license tag, the car sped off and I missed my opportunity. Okay, maybe I was freaking myself out. Or maybe I wasn't.

When I stepped inside the house, Ruth was crocheting and watching *The Price Is Right*.

Even though Ruth was Daddy's new wife, I refused to call her any iteration of *mother*, step or otherwise, as she had asked me to do. She even tried to get me to call her by her nickname, Roo, like everyone else did. Nope. By marrying her, Daddy had replaced his wife, not my mother.

Admittedly, Ruth was pleasant enough, a small brown woman with mousy little features, a keen nose, and slightly buck teeth. She was no beauty like Libby Wood, not by a mile. I was feeling some kind of way when Daddy called me six months after Ma died and told me he was thinking of getting married again. And when he told me it was Ruth he was planning to marry, I wanted to reach through the phone and slap some sense into him. It was like Ma's body was barely in the ground before he went off sniffing behind another woman and at his age too. Of all the women in the world to marry, why pick Ma's friend? Why pick any woman at all so soon after she died?

Ma and Ruth had been friends for decades too. They both sang in the church choir and worked on the Helping Hands community project together. The thought that Ruth was standing shoulder to shoulder with Ma and secretly eyeing Daddy made me sick to my stomach. I sometimes wondered whether he had been cheating on Ma when she was alive, and Ruth was simply waiting in the wings.

Daddy had always been devoted to Ma, but who knows why Daddy and Ruth found each other.

Crazy too that they wound up together since Ma and Ruth were so different. Where Ma had always been the life of the party, laughing and singing, Ruth was shy and timid. Ma was forward-thinking about life and people. Ruth, on the other hand, still held on to some of the old Gullah-Geechee ways, sometimes slipping into a hint of an accent and the Gullah Creole dialect whenever she was anxious or excited. I appreciated my heritage but with Ruth, she took it to a whole other level. She always talked of hexes, bad juju, and "putting roots" on people. Some older people, like Ruth, believed in what they called the haints—evil spirits—and burning roots and carrying amulets with herbs and trinkets to ward off ghosts and bad omens.

After she married Daddy, she had him paint the front door of the house cobalt blue. A tradition in the Gullah-Geechee culture. She said it would ward off the evil spirits. She covered the branches of the small myrtle tree in the backyard with soda bottles, telling Daddy that any haints that tried to get into the house would get caught up in the bottles and burn in the morning light.

I remember one time, Ma told me she'd gone to the front door and there was a pair of men's boots on the porch that didn't belong to Daddy. She said Ruth told her it meant a ghost was trying to get in the house and Ma should sprinkle red pepper all around the perimeter of the house and inside the boots. Ma laughed it off and tossed the shoes into the garbage can.

Ruth was baptized in fear and paranoia instead of the Holy Spirit. I sometimes wondered what Ma would think if she knew Ruth was burning roots in her house instead of getting on her knees to pray. Maybe it was her feeble attempt to manipulate the things she couldn't control or understand. God bless her. Ruth's talk of evil spirits and bad juju made her the polar opposite of Ma, but somehow, despite all their differences, Ruth had found a way to become Daddy's new wife. What kind of friend did that?

I stepped inside the living room, the screen door squeaking closed behind me.

"Hi, Ruth."

"Deena! This is a pleasant surprise. What are you doing here in the middle of the day?"

"I just thought I'd come home and have lunch with you and Daddy today." She grinned from ear to ear. "Where *is* Daddy?"

"He's out in the backyard pulling up weeds. Come on in the kitchen and let me fix you something."

I tossed my purse onto the sofa, and we walked to the kitchen at the back of the house. The room was small but spotless, the way she always kept it. The way Ma had kept it too.

"Sit down at the table. We've got some leftover jambalaya and rice from dinner last night, or I can make you a turkey sandwich. What sounds good to you?"

"The sandwich."

"Alright, then. A turkey sandwich it is."

I knew she was happy to have an excuse to busy herself in the kitchen. And my little comment about coming to visit *her* and Daddy had set her mood on high. I watched her pull turkey and mayo from the refrigerator before she lifted a loaf of wheat bread from the bread box at the end of the counter.

Ruth had two grown kids, a daughter and son, both several years older than me. They lived somewhere in Pennsylvania, but they never called or visited. Daddy said he'd only met them once when they were teenagers. I didn't attend Daddy and Ruth's wedding and he told me her kids didn't either. Maybe they felt the same way I did about this marriage business between Daddy and Ruth.

"How's work?"

A pinch of guilt hit me. I hated my job, and I hoped I was masking it well. "Work's good."

Daddy walked through the back door. "Hey there, baby girl! What are you doing here in the middle of the day? Your boss know you goofing off?" He chuckled and patted my shoulder.

Daddy didn't know how close to right he was with his last question. I rubbed his arm and smiled. He was a tough one. He'd beaten cancer twice, but you could see the toll it had taken on his body. He was much thinner, and his hair had grown back in silver after the chemo. But his eyes still lit up whenever he looked at me. I loved him but I hated that he had betrayed Ma.

"Jimmie Lee Wood, you are tracking dirt all through my kitchen!" Ruth said.

The comment set my teeth on edge. This wasn't her kitchen. It was Ma's kitchen. She was just a fill-in.

"Alright, woman, don't get yourself all wadded in a knot. Baby girl, let me go change out of these overalls and then we can have a proper visit."

"Okay, Daddy."

Ruth placed the sandwich on the table in front of me and then sat in the chair beside me.

"Oh, I forgot to tell you. Guess who stopped by yesterday before you got home?"

"Who?"

"Howie!" she squealed.

"Howard Lawson stopped by here?"

Howard Lawson's parents and my parents had been friends since before Howie and I were born. The two couples always held out hope that someday I would become Mrs. Lawson. But a lot had happened since we were kids.

"Yes, and he asked about you too." Ruth smiled in a mischievous way that let me know she was thinking bridal shower and wedding bells. Once again, Ruth picked up every single thing Ma did and tried to run with it. But she was out of her wheelhouse with this. And getting married again? I wanted to do that about as much as I wanted to stand in the middle of Golden Isles Parkway butt naked.

Howie and I had this crazy way of moving in and out of each other's lives. We were the worst poster children for a rom-com. He took me to the eighth-grade dance and I thought we were going together until I found out he was secretly kicking it with LaShonda from across the street. As soon as she found out I knew about them, she dumped him. She'd only wanted him because I wanted him. We were back together by the time I was in the eleventh grade and Howie was a senior. I stayed close to home and went to Savannah State while Howie was in Boston for college. Holidays and summers weren't enough to hold the relationship together despite all the pledges and effort we made to keep it going. For a period of time, we went through the "we're just friends" stage. Stupidly, I assumed we'd find a way back together someday and pick up where we left off until the summer after I graduated from Emory Law School. Howie showed up at my parents' annual summer crab boil with a date.

I'll never forget: Ma had just lined the long picnic table in the backyard with newspaper. Daddy and Uncle Duke unleashed a huge stockpot of crabs, shrimp, potatoes, and corn across the paper. I watched Howie walk in with her. She was of the false lashes and acrylic nails variety. As he introduced her to people, I remember thinking she had to be from some place other than Brunswick because she wore a black bandage dress and four-inch stilettos to a backyard cookout. She was definitely *come-ya*. After he introduced us—describing her as "a friend"—I ignored the two of them for the rest of the cookout. I was pissed and embarrassed but Howie and I had drifted apart so he had a right to bring anyone he wanted. Ma told me I needed to break up their little friendship since he'd only brought her along to nudge me back to him. She said men sometimes did stupid things when they didn't know how to do the right thing. I didn't take Ma's advice. A few years later, when I heard they'd gotten married, I cried for two days.

I hadn't talked to Howie since he attended Ma's funeral. I decided to shut down whatever thoughts Ruth was thinking. "Howie, huh? Did you ask him how his wife is doing?"

"I sure did and guess what he said?" She leaned across the table and grinned. "He's divorced. Has been for a while now."

Damn. I couldn't believe this woman was giddy at the thought that someone's marriage was dissolved. Was this how she reacted when she found out Ma was sick, and that it would open up an opportunity for her with Daddy?

"And guess what else?" she said.

"Ruth, I'm not interested in Howie Lawson. Do you have some Tylenol around here? I have a headache." The repercussions from my fall out on the island were still lingering but at least the knot on the back of my head was going down.

"Oooh, he's still just as tall and handsome as ever," Ruth said as she hustled over to the kitchen cabinet where we kept the antacids and cold medicine. "He works for Welburton and Harley. That law firm downtown."

"Wait. He's moving back here?!"

She returned to the table with a glass of water and the Tylenol. "Oh, he's been back ever since his divorce. Isn't that something?" She grinned. "I told him you were divorced too! Who knows, maybe you two can get together for lunch and catch up on old times."

"Ruth! Why'd you tell him that?! You had no right to do that."

Ruth's smile melted. "I'm sorry. Deena, your daddy and I just want you to be happy. I know it's what your mother would have wanted too."

"And you think . . . Ruth, don't. Just don't."

We both got quiet. She had no right to be in my business about who I dated, as if a man was ever the key to happiness. I shook two Tylenol from the bottle and gulped them down with the water.

After a couple minutes, Ruth chimed up all cheery again. "I was thinking maybe you and I could go over to Savannah on the weekend. You know, make a girls' weekend out of it. Go to the beach, a little shopping, have a few good meals."

"I'm sorry, Ruth. It's not a good time."

I bit into the sandwich. How did she know Ma always cut my sandwiches in a diagonal? Ugh, I was acting like a child.

She gave me a weak smile. "That's what you said when I suggested we do something a few weeks back. Is there ever a good time?"

"Maybe during the summer."

I placed my sandwich on the plate and stared at Ruth. Surrendering, she got up from the table and retreated to the kitchen sink. I felt like a monster. She was a seventy-two-year-old woman trying to be nice. And I pushed away every attempt she made to do so. I slid the sandwich away. I wasn't hungry anymore. Before either of us said another word, Daddy was back in the kitchen.

"Jimmie, you want a sandwich?"

"That'll be fine, Roo."

She busied herself with the second sandwich. I watched her for a bit as I wrestled with my guilt. Ma had raised me better than this. And being mean to Ruth wouldn't bring Ma back. I'd figure out what to say to her later.

"Listen, Daddy, I came by because I wanted to ask you something."

"Ask me what?" He'd changed into a pair of jeans that hung off him like wet laundry limply hanging from a clothesline. His "Savannah Sea Lions Softball" T-shirt was worn and just as drapey on his thin frame. He headed over to the refrigerator and pulled out a can of Coke.

"Do you know a man named Holcomb Gardner?" It was a long shot, sure, but Daddy knew nearly everyone in Glynn County, Black and white. He'd worked in a number of jobs around Brunswick after he was honorably discharged from the air force. Daddy had always loved the water and once he found a job working on the port docks, he never worked anywhere else until his retirement.

"Holcomb Gardner?" Ruth repeated. She shot a look at Daddy.

Daddy gave an apprehensive look back at her, then smiled at me. "Well, yeah . . . I knew of some Gardners lived over off Union Street. But that was years ago, back when Black folks still lived over there. Why you asking about Holcomb?"

"Did he have a sister named Delilah?"

Daddy hesitated for a beat. "Uh . . . yeah, Delilah Gardner. She died about six months ago, some kind of accident."

I saw Ruth shoot another look at Daddy before she placed his sandwich on the table and walked out of the room. Odd, because usually she always lurked around, hanging on every word Daddy spoke. Now she'd eased out of the room like she didn't want to be a part of the conversation.

He sat down at the table. "Why you lookin' for Holcomb and Delilah?"

"Well . . ." I didn't want to tell him that Holcomb held a gun on his only child and threatened to shoot her for trespassing. "I met him over on the island. He said he owned some oceanfront property over there."

"Say what?"

"He didn't look rich to me."

"That is pretty high cotton out that way. I didn't know a Black man owned any of that land out there." Daddy gave a long cat whistle. "If he ever decides to sell it, he could make a fortune."

"That's just it. He told me he'd never sell it. But I get the impression someone must be trying really hard to get him to sell."

"So what's all this got to do with you?"

"I don't know. I was just wondering why he would be living out on the island in a trailer."

"A trailer?"

"Yeah. I think he lives out there to keep away people trying to buy it. Crazy, right?"

"There you go again. All up in other folks' business." Daddy shook his head like he pitied me. "You've always been a nosy child. And what have I always told you?"

"That I need to keep my nose on my face."

"And . . ."

"And that one day, I'm going to stick my nose in something and not be able to pull it out."

"Exactly. Don't go digging around in that man's business. Grown folks live grown lives. He don't need you poking around in his affairs."

This was new for Daddy. Ever since I could remember, whenever I brought something to him that even closely resembled gossip, he'd be all over it. Now, he was practically avoiding the topic and advising me to stay out of it. And Ruth had scooted off from the kitchen like she had some emergency crochet project to attend to.

I decided not to argue. "Yeah, Daddy, maybe you're right."

They knew something about Holcomb Gardner. But whatever it was, they didn't want to share it.

Deena asked her father about Holcomb today. She's onto something. I can tell when that girl gets on a scent, she won't let it go. And that's exactly what I want her to do. Of course, Jimmie disagrees. He doesn't want her digging around in all that business out on the island because he knows it might expose everything we kept secret for years. I wonder if she knows what happened with this house. That this is my home. It always has been. They just didn't know it. But they will soon enough. People underestimate me. Always have.

I've watched Deena ever since she moved back and stepped foot inside this house. Deena is back in Brunswick for a reason.

She is what the ancestors prayed for. Those angels with scars who still to this day lean close to whisper in our ear to give us courage and tell us we are strong. Some folks only think of us by the beautifully woven sweetgrass baskets they buy at outdoor markets. Or when they sit down to a plate of shrimp and grits or gumbo. Or maybe they don't think of us at all. But Gullah-Geechee is so much more. We are the strength of the iron that seeped into our blood from the shackles of ships that brought us to this country. We are tanned bronze and beautiful from the sun that baked our skin as we toiled the land and built this country. We are in the words and dialect that the ancestors cobbled together from a dozen different African tongues just so they could communicate with each other when buckra brought us to this land. We are love forged and nurtured from the broken hearts of the ancestors.

Deena, you beautiful child, you are all of us. Keep digging. Keep searching.

CHAPTER 5

I was tired by the time I pulled into the driveway after work. All I wanted to do was eat and go straight to bed. My new routine—work, eat, sleep, rinse, and repeat—since moving back to Brunswick. The pace of this town was slow enough for a woman whose life was upended to find a way back to normal. The people here in the Low Country were friendly, concerned about each other without being meddlesome. Pride in the Gullah heritage was like a fragrance in the air, something akin to the smell of salt water in the marshes. Geechee folks worked hard, loved the land, and cherished their roots that sprang from it. But the Gullah-Geechee community was dying out, along with the language, the stories that had been passed down, and, most importantly, the land that was ours.

Being in Brunswick was different from Atlanta. There I was constantly chasing the next big case or eating at the latest trendy restaurant. Here, I could heal and forgive myself. Things were slower here and I had the chance to heal in isolation. And just to make sure people didn't become too concerned about the pace of my healing process, I gave empty platitudes whenever anyone asked how I was doing. *I'm fine since the divorce . . . My mother is in a better place . . . She's with the angels*. The truth of the matter was that I was always a blink and a memory away from breaking down in tears. It was as if I carried my hurt and grief around with me like a string of rosary beads that I needed to count and massage to assuage my pain.

Here, at home, I simply waited for the day when the pain didn't hurt as much.

I gathered up my bag and keys and stepped out of the car.

"Hey, Deena!"

I heard her calling from behind me. I tried to pretend like I didn't. Since moving back home, whenever I ran into someone I knew from high school, I pretended not to see them or feigned forgetfulness when they tried to jog my memory. It was bad enough that I was living like I was back in high school. But I'd be damned if I would start hanging out with people from my past and acting like a teenager. Besides, all my friends I had amassed from my youth in Brunswick were like me and had moved away after graduation. I was the only one who was back, if I didn't count Howie.

"Deena, wait up."

I'd despised this woman since the fourth grade, when her mother married Mr. Duncan and they moved into his house across the street. LaShonda Graham was what Ma used to call a "shit starter," someone who always started a bunch of trouble. She was the kind of little girl who was always tangled up in a bunch of chaos—fights at school and around the neighborhood or stealing candy from Mr. Sylvester's store on the corner. As a teenager she graduated to mean girl gossip and pettiness that caused other people to fight because of something she'd said or done. Now that she was a full-grown woman, nothing had changed. As a youngster, whenever I had a run-in with LaShonda, Ma used to tell me to ignore her because she was jealous of me. I remember coming home from school one day in tears because LaShonda had called me ugly. Ma said, *Have you looked at her? Deena, your ass would make a Sunday face for LaShonda.* I laughed so hard, I forgot all about LaShonda's comment.

"Hey, girl. Slow up. I need to talk to you."

I watched LaShonda hobble across the street toward me. She was wearing some kind of orthopedic boot on her left foot. I never liked her and the boot did nothing to drum up my sympathy for her. LaShonda was a tall, light-skinned woman with lots of bosom and belly, all of it clamoring for attention when you looked at her. She was the same age as me, but she looked ten years older. I always thought she'd be a lot prettier if she didn't armor herself in the fifty-dollar lace-front wigs and fake nails she always wore. But how she presented herself to the world was none of my business. LaShonda had four kids by three different men, and she, her kids, and her mother all lived in the house across the street. Maybe I wasn't as bad off as I imagined myself to be. I'd moved back home but at least I hadn't dragged four babies to Daddy's doorstep.

"Hey, LaShonda," I said without an ounce of emotion. I didn't say more or ask about her foot because I didn't want a conversation. I just wanted to get in the house and keep avoiding her like I'd done since I'd moved back home three months ago. There was a time I would have stood out on the sidewalk and asked a thousand questions. *What happened to your foot? Are you alright? What are you going to do now?* Unloading my arsenal of questions on the unsuspecting, as Daddy would say. But now, I'd lost Ma and my marriage. I didn't have much interest in what was going on with other people, especially LaShonda.

"How you doin', girl? I heard you moved back. This is my first time seeing you where we can talk. You always driving in and out."

"Yeah, been busy. New job."

"Ooh, I like your hair."

My hair was pulled back in a nondescript ponytail, so LaShonda was either lying or squirming around for something to say.

"Thanks."

"You've always been a pretty girl. You remind me of Beyoncé if she was heavier and wore khakis and a ponytail and no makeup all the time." She smiled as if she really believed that was a compliment. "You still a big baller lawyer?"

Ugh, this woman. I decided I'd given her enough time. I hit the key fob and locked my car doors. "Yes, I'm still a lawyer. Gotta run." I started for Daddy's front porch.

"Wait, I wanted to ask you something." She hobbled closer to me. "Well . . . I thought since you were a lawyer and everything, maybe you could help me."

"Help you how?"

"It's my house." She pointed across the street like I didn't know where she lived. "You know my stepfather died a few years back. It's just me and my mother and the kids. Anyway, my stepfather had some kids with his first wife. Mama thought the house was ours lock, stock, and barrel. But turns out, it's not."

"I don't know how I can help you," I said.

"One of his cousins . . . or one of his grandkids . . . I'm not sure which but one of 'em said he owned part of our house and he sold his part of the house and now they trying to say we gotta move."

"What?"

"They say if we can't come up with thirty-five thousand dollars we gotta move. We ain't got that kind of money. That just doesn't seem fair, you know? We been living here all this time with no problems. How can somebody that don't even live here sell our house out from under us?"

I softened. That entire house was barely worth thirty-five thousand dollars. Besides, no one deserved to be kicked out of their home. "I'm really sorry to hear that. So, your stepfather didn't have a will?"

"Nah."

"It sounds like you might have an heirs property situation—"

"What's that?"

"It's kinda complicated but it means if you own property and you die without a will, other people related to you can inherit a portion of your property, even if they don't live on the property or pay the taxes. That means they can also sell their portion too."

"Well, I was thinking since you're a lawyer, maybe you can sue him for us."

"I'm sorry, LaShonda. I don't practice that kind of law. Maybe I can put you in touch with a lawyer who specializes in property law."

"Can't you just sue him for us? We ain't got no money for some fancy, expensive lawyer."

I decided to ignore her assumption that I wasn't a *fancy, expensive lawyer.*

"Have you tried contacting Legal Aid? They have attorneys and they won't charge you. Your issue needs someone with expertise in property law and estate planning."

"See, I don't even know what all them words mean. That's why you should help us."

"I'm sorry. I can't. That's not what I do. Like I said, maybe I can help you find a lawyer who can help you."

"Oh." I saw the hopefulness fade from her face. The same way it had when she learned a fight she had instigated with a bunch of lies over some silly boy would not materialize. "Well, never mind, then."

"I'm really sorry."

"Whatever," she said quietly. "Tell your daddy and Miss Roo I said hey."

I watched her hobble back across the street and up the steps to her porch. She sat down on the kitchen chair that doubled as her outdoor seating. I caught her eye when she sat down. She stared at me for a moment before she rolled her eyes and focused on a passing car. I felt horrible and I wasn't quite sure why. Maybe because I knew what it was like to be kicked out of your home and I wasn't doing a thing to help her avoid that fate. In that moment I remembered what Ma used to tell me whenever I felt sorry for myself. *Deena, we are all connected and there's always someone worse off than you. You wanna feel better about yourself, help one of those souls.*

God, I missed Ma so much.

But here I was, divorced, working in a dead-end job, and living back in my childhood bedroom. My life was a shit show on steroids. I couldn't even help myself. Who was I kidding to think I had the capacity to help someone else?

CHAPTER 6

It had been a week since I'd stumbled onto Holcomb Gardner's property, and he ran me off with a gun. And during that week, I'd managed to heed Joe's warning. On time for work. No wandering off during the day. But not a day went by that I didn't think about Holcomb Gardner and his dead sister, Delilah. I found it odd that he'd spoken of his sister in the present tense as if she were alive. *My mama and daddy left this land to me and my sister, Delilah.* Even odder, she was dead and there was no mention of him in her obituary.

A week ago, I'd never heard of Holcomb Gardner. And now, he was all I could think about. He must have been troubled in a huge way to sleep in a trailer out in the middle of nowhere with one eye open and his finger on the trigger of a gun. Even though the guy had threatened me with a gun and sent me speeding away in fear for my life, I couldn't get him out of my head. And for some inexplicable reason, I had the craziest thought that I needed to protect him. According to Ma, we were all connected, so maybe I was supposed to help him. Or maybe it was like Daddy said and I was just being nosy. Either way, Holcomb Gardner lived rent-free inside my head. I decided there was only one way to put him out of my mind.

I walked into the kitchen in search of coffee before heading off to work. A couple minutes later, Ruth walked in, her hair still in pink curlers and her blue bathrobe tied tight against her small frame.

"Oh, Deena baby, I overslept. I should have made breakfast. I'm sorry."

"Daddy's still sleep?"

"He left outta here at the crack of dawn. Said he had to go check on something."

Ruth had stepped inside Daddy's house and tried to fill my mother's shoes with her ability to act as a homemaker and wannabe surrogate mother to me. I had to get past whatever was bugging me about this woman. But every time I tried, I became more defiant that she would not replace Ma. No one could. Not even Ma's friend and choir mate. Even still, I was being a bitch to a woman who hadn't done anything to me. Ma used to say, *If you know better, you ought to do better.*

"Ruth, I want to apologize."

"Apologize for what?"

"About the trip to Savannah. It's just that I'm new on this job and . . ."

"No need to apologize, honey." She patted my arm lightly. "But think about it, okay? It might be good for the two of us to get away."

I tried to smile. "I promise. I'll think about it."

"Now, let me make you something to eat."

"No, that's okay. I'll grab something on the way. I don't want to be too late." I didn't want to put Ruth through any trouble or maybe I just didn't want to eat another omelet or a couple of scrambled eggs that she prepared exactly like Ma. I left the house and promised myself I would drive straight to the office. No more wandering off trying to chase away my grief. No more encounters with gun-toting strangers. Ten minutes into the drive, I found myself driving toward the Sidney Lanier Bridge, headed back to the island, almost as if I were possessed.

If Daddy knew what I was doing, he'd tell me to keep my nose on my face. Whatever. I decided to drive over to the island. I'd still be on time for work if traffic was on my side. Maybe Daddy was right—I was a little on the nosy side. Probably a bit impetuous if it was something I really wanted. But sometimes it was better to ask for forgiveness than for permission. Daddy and Ruth had acted strangely when I mentioned Holcomb's name. I wanted to find out why.

I'd go back to the island to talk to Holcomb Gardner. And maybe I'd find out who was in that black car that was headed for his property. Sure, he'd threatened me with a shotgun, but he didn't shoot me. If he'd really wanted to shoot me, he would have done it the last time I was out there. He didn't because he was looking for information from me. *Tell me why they sent a Black woman this time.*

Several minutes later, I pulled up to the edge of the island property, the same spot where I first saw Holcomb Gardner's trailer. Holcomb, his dog, and the trailer were all gone. Nothing there except an empty stretch of land. And posted at the edge of the property was a huge sign that read:

AVAILABLE
For Sale
For Commercial Development
Call Empire Realty
932-555-6527

CHAPTER 7

So, what happened to Holcomb Gardner?

The man who said he'd never sell his property had suddenly put it up for sale and vanished into thin air. How could a man and his entire home, such that it was, disappear off the face of the earth in a few days? He'd held a gun on me and threatened to shoot because he thought I was there to take it away. It didn't make sense. And why did Daddy and Ruth act so suspiciously when I asked about Holcomb and his sister?

By five o'clock, the time I would normally fly out the door of the Old Victorian, purse on my shoulder and car keys in hand, I was still sitting at my desk. But just because I was there didn't mean I had to keep doing Medallion's grunt work. My curiosity about what had happened to that old man got the better of me.

I opened my laptop and searched for Empire Realty. It was a real estate company located in Dallas, Texas. They specialized in residential properties. That didn't make sense either because the sign on the island property stated it was being sold for commercial development. There was no real internet presence for the company other than the homemade-looking website with a phone number and some weak marketing verbiage. They weren't on any of the social media platforms either—no Facebook, Instagram, or Twitter.

I decided to poke around a little. I clicked the land records web page for Georgia and typed in "Empire Realty." A list of transactions popped up. I clicked on the first one. It was for the purchase of a parcel of land with a church on it, located in Darien. Another was for a tract of land in neighboring McIntosh County, and two more for smaller properties I knew were near Daddy's house. On it went. Empire Realty of Dallas, Texas, was on a buying spree all over Georgia.

Next, I clicked over to the Glynn County tax records site and searched for any information under Holcomb's name. His name popped up as the owner of a piece of property located at 7200 Eaves Street in Brunswick. Nothing under his name for the island property.

I pulled up the Georgia Department of Revenue and clicked over to the online portal for property records in Glynn County. I typed in the address of the land parcel on Boden Road where I'd encountered Holcomb Gardner. The cursor blinked for a few seconds and then the screen bloomed with information. I scrolled to the section titled "Value Information." The land was valued at $1.5 million. Holcomb Gardner owned property valued in the millions?! How did a man in his seventies and living in a trailer afford the taxes on such expensive real estate?

I scrolled a bit further. Empire Realty was listed as the owner of the island property. The date of the purchase was over a month ago. But Holcomb had been adamant that he wouldn't sell the land—as if the sale hadn't occurred. Maybe I wasn't the trespasser, but Holcomb was.

I clicked off the web browser. *Go home, Deena.*

I grabbed my keys and purse, along with a file I'd promised Joe I'd leave on his desk before I left for the day. It was after six o'clock and I had the Old Victorian all to myself. The hardwood floors were over a hundred years old, and they announced their age through a series of grunts and groans depending on which floorboards you stepped on. The Old Victorian was a "talking house," with its creaking stairs and noisy pipes. In the evenings, when this old house was empty and quiet, it was ominous. As if it might tell all the secrets of its previous owners if you leaned in close to the walls. I always found houses like the Old Victorian or Daddy's house stable and secure. Their noises a testament to their ability to still stand despite the march of time.

I eased up the front stairs, past what had formerly been the main bedroom suite of the house, now converted into a large office for Clare Walsh, the founder. Joe's office was two doors down, where all the engineers' offices were. At the end of the hall, past their offices, was a staircase leading up to the attic and another, back staircase down to the kitchen.

I slipped inside Joe's office. I figured since I was here, it couldn't hurt to snoop around a little on his desk too. Joe knew a slew of commercial real estate brokers. Maybe I could find something about Empire in the files in his office. Joe didn't usually give me access to all the details on what he knew or what he was working on for the company. He always joked it off and pretended like the higher-ups were keeping secrets from him, as if the two of us were kindred souls. I knew better.

The windows in his office overlooked the parking lot below so I could keep a look out if someone came back for a forgotten file or bag. The top of Joe's desk was spotless as usual. No files, no books, not even a paper clip. That was because Joe specialized in moving work off his desk, out of his office, and onto other people. I dropped the file I'd brought on top of the desk. I peeped toward the doorway before I quietly slipped open a couple drawers and flipped through the files. Nothing beyond a few memos about some recent projects that were stalled because of permits or some other city bureaucracy. Maybe they really did keep Joe in the dark too. Before I pulled the next drawer open, I heard the soft whispers of a woman talking. Was she singing too? I leaned in to listen closely. A small ping of alarm rose inside me. I'd thought I was alone in the office. The whispers stopped. No more singing. *My imagination.*

I opened another drawer. Inside was a joint and an unopened condom. Yuck! The thought of why he had these items at work and with whom he was sharing them was enough to shut down my snooping expedition. I hustled out of his office and hurried toward the back staircase.

Before I could reach the stairs, I heard my name.

"Deena?"

Clare.

I stopped in my tracks and spun around. "Hey, Clare," I said, suddenly feeling guilty for rummaging through Joe's office.

"What in the world are you doing around here so late? Shouldn't you be at home by now?"

Clare Walsh was a silver-haired, impeccably dressed force to be reckoned with. She didn't take any crap and everyone within a two-hundred-mile radius of Brunswick knew it. She was the type of self-made woman who could slice a person with a single look in one moment and in the next nuzzle a baby like a doting grandmother.

"Oh . . . just dropping off a file for Joe."

"I thought I was the only one working late tonight. I like it when it's quiet like this. No calls. No noise. Not a peep. Well, as long as you're here, come in my office and have a seat. I haven't seen you in forever."

As I entered her office, Clare motioned for me to sit in the chair in front of her desk. Her office was an interior decorator's magnum opus. The tall ceilings and blush-pink paint of the room made the space seem cavernous. A Plexiglas desk and soft upholstered chairs and pillows gave the room a clean and intimate feel. But more than anything, Clare's office was inviting because she was so interesting and always easy to talk to. Occasionally, Clare talked of her political ambitions. She was convinced the country had gone off the rails and needed more centered leadership. I could very well see her as a politician. If I'd had to guess, I'd say she leaned moderate Republican. I wasn't sure I'd vote for her, but I'd wish her well.

Clare pushed away the papers on her desk. "Now, how many times have we talked about you spending your evenings doing some self-care or maybe a fella instead of hanging around here?" She smiled at me sheepishly.

I smiled back. After my panel interview with Joe and a few other Medallion managers, Clare had met with me alone. We'd hit it off when we landed on the topic of our respective divorces. She was the kind of person every newly divorced woman needed in her corner. She was always egging me on to get back out there. Somehow when she did, it was different from when Ruth did it. Clare didn't make me feel like a rapidly expiring crone too old to find love again. Clare's theory was that I needed to create Deena Wood 2.0. To carve out a new and better Deena.

"I've told you before, Deena, you're pretty damn lucky. You made it out of a bad marriage with youth and beautiful skin that still glows."

"Youth?! Don't remind me. I'll be forty on my next birthday. I'm hardly young."

"Oh my God, to be thirty-nine again. You're a baby! Talk to me when you're sixty-seven years young. Listen, I bought this really expensive antiaging cream a couple months ago, but it makes me smell like fried liver and onions. I would stop using it except lately I've been getting a lot of compliments on how dewy my skin looks."

She mockingly held her head high and batted her eyelashes and we both giggled.

"Seriously, you can start all over again. Go find whatever it is that makes you feel alive. Don't be like me. The only thing I have going for me is this business. Unless I decide to do something else." She gave me a wicked smile. "I'm seriously considering jumping into the deep end of the pool."

"Politics?"

She grinned and nodded yes.

"I think you should do it. You'd be great."

"I've been traveling all over the state, talking with some people. I've gotten a lot of great support from some important people, some big donors."

"That's fantastic."

"I think so too. Surprisingly, Beau agrees with me for a change. Usually, he is against any idea I have for running the business. Speaking of . . . I know I've been out of the office quite a bit lately. How's my nephew treating you folks these days? Do I need to rein him in on anything?"

"He's fine." I didn't want to come off like I was tattling on Beau because he was prodding Joe for more face time from folks. I guess that was in his purview since Clare had left him in charge of running the business. Clare spent the bulk of her time out schmoozing business clients over expensive lunches and golf course tee times, and now, drumming up political donors. Even though Beau was supposed to be in charge, it couldn't hurt to put a little bug in Clare's ear about his latest initiative. “Peg told me he’s putting in some new cost-saving measures.” I waited for Clare to bite.

“Cost-saving measures? The company’s doing fine. I had to bust his chops about his ideas of expanding the business, whatever that means. Ugh.” She shook her head, shuddering at the thought.

“Expand it how?”

“Who knows with him. I believe when you’re good at something, you stick to that thing. Venturing out, doing all kinds of crazy stuff is not the way to run a successful business. I’ll keep my eye on him. Beau’s ideas can sometimes be bigger than the brains he puts behind them. Just between us, Beau can be a piece of work, but he’s my brother’s child. Family.”

I smiled.

“And as for you, learn from me. I’ve made mistakes by working and not building a life for myself. Don’t make this job your life.”

I nodded and continued to smile. Clare didn’t have a clue how far this job was from being the center of my attention.

“Don’t think I’m not grateful,” she said. “I fought tooth and nail to get where I am. This business didn’t build itself. Back in the days when I started, there were very few female engineers and men held all the power. A woman running an engineering contracting firm was unheard of.” She gazed out the window with a faraway look before she turned back to me. “I’ll be damned if I give away what it took me a lifetime to earn. Even to my own nephew. But enough of that.” She narrowed her eyes and scoped me for a few seconds. “Seriously, how are you?”

“I’m fine.”

Clare stared at me. “This is me you’re talking to. Be honest.”

I had only mentioned Ma’s death once in passing. I didn’t like talking about Ma with people who didn't know her. I couldn't fully comprehend how much she meant to me and how her death had swallowed me whole. So how would I even begin to talk about her to someone who didn't know her?

"Seriously, I'm good."

Clare always seemed to have some sixth sense about me. It was almost like she could tell how much pain I was trying to cover up and she just wanted to massage my grieving soul. She didn't have enough skill to do that no matter how much business acumen and intuition she had.

"Listen, you've suffered two tremendous losses back-to-back. The loss of your mother *and* a divorce." She slowly shook her head. "You must have the strength of Job. But you've got to rebuild your life. I'm telling you, Deena, do not get swallowed up in the loss of what you used to have. Take some time to find yourself among the ruins. You'll be surprised at what you discover."

I smiled again. Clare was wise beyond her sixty-seven years.

"By the way, I'm thinking of hiring a new law firm. I'm not happy with those curmudgeons over at Jesse's firm. I want you to meet the new guys I'm thinking about hiring. You know I'm on the board of the Coastal Georgia Food Bank. Really sad how much food banks are needed since the pandemic." She shook her head. "Anyway, I met a great lawyer through the organization. I might consider using his firm."

"Sounds great."

"I've asked Beau to include you in the meeting. Let me know what you think of them."

"Of course."

Then she stared at me with a half smile. "Seriously, Deena, you let me know if anyone gives you any shit around here. And that includes Beau. We girls gotta stick together. Now, go home and soak yourself in a hot bath. You know what? I think I'll take my own advice tonight. Let me gather up my things. We can lock up and walk out together."

CHAPTER 8

It was almost seven o'clock by the time I pulled into the driveway of Daddy's house. Early evening activity fell over the street. A few neighbors sat on their front porches trading details of how the day had unfolded. I heard the *thump-thump* of a basketball and laughter as a couple teenagers shot hoops in the driveway a few houses down from Daddy's. I cut the engine and sat inside the car for a few minutes.

I needed this time to myself. The stress of working in a dead-end job, failing to live up to my full potential as a lawyer, and fighting off Ruth's efforts to replace my mother—all of it was like the burden of a second full-time job. Sometimes, I felt like I was coming apart at the seams. As if all the emotional joists and pulleys precariously holding my life together were working in reverse and splintering—my smiling when I wanted to cry, laughing when I wanted to scream. All of it working to make me fall into a million little pieces at any moment. Clare was right. I needed to find a way to take care of me.

When I stepped inside the house, everyone was in their usual spots. Everything the same. Ruth in the kitchen fidgeting around. The evening news on TV and Daddy dozing off in his recliner in the corner. The same channel on the television and the same walls covered in sepia-toned pictures of the elders. My déjà vu reality of being back home again except I was almost forty years old, and instead of my mother in the kitchen it was Ruth, trying to replace her. College. Law school. Atlanta. Those seemed to be the lost years. How could I be right back where I started? When I moved back to Brunswick, Daddy had convinced me to save the money I'd pay for rent to invest in my new home. Not an unreasonable idea, but now, I was really leaning toward getting an apartment until I found a house to buy. My independence and sanity were more important at this point. I had to find my way back somehow.

"That you, Deena? You hungry?" Ruth called from the kitchen.

"It's me. I'm good." I tapped Daddy on the top of his balding head. "A little hard to watch the news from behind your eyelids."

He blinked himself awake. "Hey there, baby girl. How's our little lawyer?"

Every time Daddy called me a lawyer, it conjured up feelings of being a fake and a fraud. Sure, I had a law degree. But for all intents and purposes, I was working far below my potential. And he didn't have a clue what happened back in Atlanta.

I sat down in the recliner next to Daddy. Ma's chair. Now Ruth's chair.

Daddy glanced at the TV screen. "Ugh! That guy!"

I looked at the television. Charlie Lester, a city commissioner, was on the news blathering on about something.

"With that guy, a little bit of his gravy goes all over my plate! All those politicians are crooks, especially Charlie Lester."

Against my better judgment, I decided to ask Daddy about Holcomb again. "You remember that man I asked you about the other day?"

Daddy picked up the remote and lowered the volume. "What man?"

"Holcomb Gardner. You told me his sister died in an accident."

Daddy lowered his head, almost as if saying a quiet prayer for her. "Oh yeah, Holcomb. What about him?"

"Something weird is going on."

"Weird like what?"

"I went back out to the island this morning—"

"I thought you were going to stay out of this."

"Listen to me. I went back out there, and Mr. Gardner's gone. No trailer. Nothing. And there's a For Sale sign in front of the property."

"Say what?" Daddy leaned forward in his recliner. "Well, baby girl, maybe he changed his mind."

"I don't think so. He was pretty adamant." I didn't dare tell Daddy I'd stared into the barrel of Holcomb's gun. "I just have a feeling he wouldn't ever sell it. He said he was born on that land, and he was living in a trailer out there to keep people off of it. Something's not right. So, I did some digging. From what little I found out, the company that's selling the property is located in Texas."

"So why does a company in Texas come all the way out here to Georgia to buy property?" Daddy asked.

I shrugged. "They've bought a lot of property all over the state. That's what makes this all so weird."

"Hmm . . . Maybe Holcomb just realized the fortune he can make on the sale. But I'm telling you, Deena, stay out of it."

"I was thinking maybe Uncle Duke could help me find out a bit more?"

"Deena . . ."

"Maybe I'll go over there and ask him about Holcomb."

"Why is it so important for you to go digging into this man's affairs? Leave it be."

"Daddy, that man disappeared into thin air and his property is up for sale just a few days later. I'm telling you, something's not right about all this."

"Then that's his family's concern, not yours."

I stared at Daddy. He was determined to keep me from looking into Holcomb's disappearance. The strangest part of all this was that it ran counter to how Daddy normally behaved. Daddy knew everybody and he'd give the shirt off his back to help someone else. Now a man he said he knew had disappeared and he didn't have the least interest in finding him. I had a feeling something else was going on. Something involving Holcomb and Daddy. After a couple minutes of sitting in silence, he relented.

"Since you're not gonna let this thing go, I'll ride along with you."

Daddy walked into the kitchen. "Roo, me and Deena are gonna ride out to Duke's. We'll be back in an hour or so."

I watched Ruth give Daddy the same look she'd given him the first time I mentioned Holcomb. She'd probably been listening to our conversation from the kitchen. What did they know about Holcomb that they weren't telling me?

He grabbed the keys to his pickup truck and turned to me. "Let's ride."

I watch Jimmie when he's with Deena and my heart aches. I wonder what might have been if she had been my daughter instead of the one I had. She's such a pretty woman with an inquisitive mind. Jimmie thinks she's nosy. I think she's smart. There's never anything wrong with a smart woman who asks the right questions.

Deena has started digging around trying to find out what's happened to Holcomb. She is Geechee through and through. We don't give up.

She is home for a reason—to make things right. This is where she belongs. These sacred and hallowed grounds are hers just as much as anyone else's. Native Americans had nurtured this precious land until it was ripped away from them. After that, Black people had toiled and worked the land to build wealth for the whites with little or nothing to show for our labor.

Land is wealth. Why else would men and entire countries fight over it?

When I was younger Papa told me about how our people who were enslaved on the sea islands forged a life for themselves despite living under the bondage of the buckra. Slave owners didn't venture onto the islands for long periods of time because of the harsh conditions. The swampy marshlands and grueling heat made the islands a haven for all sorts of bugs that didn't just bite. They spread disease and sickness. But the bugs were nothing compared to the venomous snakes and alligators that could take you out if the bugs didn't. In those days, the island was reserved for those with a sturdy constitution and an unshakable will to live. Gullah-Geechee. We were strong and resilient. Still are.

Papa said because the plantation owners left them alone for most of the time, the ancestors grew their own produce and raised their own livestock. They crafted sweetgrass baskets and cast nets, fished, and hunted.

Their isolation allowed them to hold on to a lot of the things we brought to this country from Africa—the things we made, the stories we told, and our connection to the elders who had passed on before us. The ones we turned to for help and wisdom.

The Geechee people had been so isolated during slavery that, after, the island was essentially ours anyway. After the Civil War, and without our people to work the land, buckra figured it was better to sharecrop the land, which was simply glorified slavery. Others deeded some of their property to former slaves.

Our people loved the land and were deeply connected to it. Papa used to say, "De land we, we de land." So, when given the chance, the ancestors bought land for all those to come after them. But buying land is not enough. We must hold on to it. Something that I was unable to do. I don't think I truly realized the value of owning property until I lost it.

And now, malevolent forces are taking our land and trying to force our people from the homes we've known for generations. If Deena is the strong young lady I know her to be, she'll make things right. Deena is asking all the right questions.

She and Jimmie are going to Duke's barbershop. I don't know how Jimmie will react when everything comes to light. And it will. It's just a matter of time. I know he's trying to discourage Deena from looking into all this business because he's trying to protect me and our secrets.

But he doesn't need to do that anymore. He doesn't know it, but I want Deena to know the truth. It'll be for the best. I hope she continues to dig and uncover every little secret.

Her curiosity will free us all.

CHAPTER 9

The pink-orange glow of sunset settled across the city. The bustle of traffic was now reduced to the hum of a few passing cars every so often. We rode in Daddy's Ford pickup. A big red thing that he'd bought as a present for himself when he retired from the port docks. Daddy was usually low-key, but something about this truck and the pride he took in it made him act differently when he drove it.

"You don't have to escort me over to Uncle Duke's."

"And you don't have to go digging into this man's business."

I didn't respond.

"You got some vacation time coming up?" Daddy asked.

It took me a few seconds before I realized why he was asking. "I told her I would think about it."

Daddy nodded. If I was lucky, he'd consider his task done and tell Ruth as much.

"I think we've got some time to spare. I wanna show you something. Let's take a little detour."

Fifteen minutes later, we were driving down a gravel road on the outskirts of town. Daddy pulled the truck up to the front of a house that was barely standing. Weathered siding hung from some spots along the side of the house, a couple of windows were boarded up, and weeds as high as my hip covered the front yard.

"What's this?" I said.

Daddy climbed out of the truck, and I followed him. We both stood in front of the boarded-up property. It appeared to be the only house for miles.

"This is what's left of Roo's house."

"What?"

"Hurricane Michael came through here back in 2018. Wiped out a lot when it did." Daddy pointed at the house. "You see that line that comes up just above the front window?"

"Yeah."

"That's about where the water stopped after the rains. She lost nearly everything she owned. She couldn't repair it so she had to leave."

"Oh my goodness. What about government assistance? FEMA offers money to help people who suffer losses after natural disasters like hurricanes and tornadoes."

"She couldn't get help from the government because she couldn't prove the house is hers."

"I don't understand."

Daddy put his hands in his pockets and leaned against the truck. "Roo was born in this house. Her mama was too. The house passed down through her family." Daddy pointed behind the house. "The property goes out to the edge of that marshland. Almost seven acres. But she ain't got any paperwork that says it's hers. What's it called . . . FEMA? They turned her away."

This reminded me of Holcomb living on property that had been in his family for generations.

"The deed's in her grandparents' names and Roo's folks didn't have a will either. A lot of folks around here don't. By the way, thank you, baby girl, for helping me with mine so this doesn't happen to you one day. I ain't got much, but what I got I'd like us to keep."

We were both quiet for a moment.

"You were born here. You know how it is. We don't live like the rich folks do, which means we don't have all the things that rich folks have, like lawyers and accountants and big trust funds. They got everything in place to protect themselves. We don't."

I thought about LaShonda and her relative and the lawyers trying to take her house across the street. I hadn't thought about heirs property this much since Property Law class in my first year of law school. Now, I was surrounded by it. Folks who toiled over land they didn't own and when finally given the opportunity to buy property, they didn't have the resources to keep it. Such an injustice.

"So, what is Ruth going to do?"

"Me and Duke come over here whenever we have some spare time to make repairs. It'll all get done eventually. God always works things out. I drove out here so you can understand Roo's not your enemy."

"I know that, Daddy."

"She lost everything. Her kids don't call or visit." He stared up at the house. "There but for the grace of God. You understand what I'm getting at here?"

I nodded. "I understand."

"Come on. Let's get over to Duke's place."

We climbed back inside the truck. I stared at the dilapidated structure as we pulled off. The weight of my guilt stilled me. Ruth was not my enemy.

* * *

Thirty minutes later, we were sitting in front of Duke's Headliner, a barbershop in the Dixville section of town. Dixville is the only known, and still intact, Black community in Brunswick developed by formerly enslaved Americans. The hand-painted sign out front with the red, white, and blue barber pole that no longer spun or lit up was the preview of what was on the other side of the door.

Inside, the first thing you noticed was all the brown wood paneling. Four solid walls of it. The shop was small and the dark walls didn't help. There were two barber chairs, a small counter, a large mirror, and a poster of men's haircut styles circa 1995 on the left side of the room. On the opposite side of the room above a row of four plastic chairs hung a trio of pictures—Martin Luther King Jr., President Barack Obama, and, perched between them, a portrait of Black Jesus, eyes looking to the heavens and hands clasped in prayer.

Uncle Duke, the proprietor, was Daddy's younger brother and one of the funniest people I knew. He opened this barbershop back in the eighties. I doubted he ever had enough patrons at one time to fill up all the chairs in the shop. This shop used to teem with men looking for a haircut, a shave, and a place to share a tall tale. These days, most Black men were looking for a barber who doubled as an art designer, someone who could cut patterns and fades with flawless precision. Others had given up on haircuts all together, preferring braids or locs. Uncle Duke always joked, "Those fancy styles are trending now, but them cats will be back." Now his customers usually consisted of his and Daddy's friends—a group of old heads that sat around the shop talking trash. On most Friday nights, there was a loud game of bid whist or poker going on in the back room.

I could count on one hand the number of times I'd been inside the shop. When I was growing up, Daddy never let me come in here. He said it was unseemly for a young girl to hang around a venue with a bunch of rowdy men. But LaShonda from across the street always hung around the shop with her brothers. Not surprising.

We stepped inside. Tonight, the two barber chairs were occupied by a couple men I'd never seen before and neither of them was getting a haircut since Uncle Duke was hoisted on a tall wood stool laughing and talking when we arrived.

"Butta! I didn't know you were stopping by." "Butta" was Daddy's nickname around the old neighborhood. Everybody in the old community had a nickname. People started calling Daddy Butta when he was young because he could smooth-talk his way into or out of anything, the implication being that he was as smooth as butter. "And is that my beautiful niece with you?"

Uncle Duke hopped off the stool and pulled me into a bear hug. He was a big barrel-chested guy with arms like oak branches and I sank into him. He always smelled like Barbicide and barbecue sauce.

"Hey, Uncle Duke. You look great."

"Well, look who's taken up lying as a side hustle." He roared back in laughter and his gold tooth shimmered in the light of the shop.

Everybody in the shop laughed along.

I giggled. "I'm serious. You always look great."

"Well, that's nice of you to say, sugar. I guess I'm not doing too bad for an old dude. Y'all come on in. Butta, you know these cats. Red and Thumb."

Daddy exchanged pleasantries with the two men. I glanced down at the hands of the man he introduced as Thumb, looking for a missing appendage. Both thumbs were intact, so who knew how he came by the nickname.

Both men rose to their feet. The one named Thumb offered his chair before they both begged off and gave reasons why they needed to leave—early morning business to attend to, wives who might be wondering where they were. Uncle Duke walked them to the door, then locked it and turned the sign to indicate Duke's Headliner was closed for business, whatever that meant, considering he didn't have much business.

"What brings y'all over here on a weeknight?"

Daddy sat in the barber chair beside mine. "Deena's looking for some information, so we came to where everybody gets their information."

Uncle Duke laughed and scratched behind his ear. "I'm not sure what you're tryin' to say, but you ain't lying."

Daddy chuckled. "You got something cold around here to drink?"

"There's some Old Milwaukee in the fridge in the back room."

"Can't you ever get the good stuff instead of that cheap crap you buy?" Daddy said.

"Listen, I may be broke, but I ain't cheap. Broke is a state of being. Cheap is a state of mind. There's a difference. Now, go around the corner and see if Winn-Dixie will give you a *free* beer."

Both of them busted up laughing before Daddy walked off to the back room.

"How you doin', sugar?"

"Fine, Uncle Duke."

"Are you really?" He paused for a moment. "Everybody around here still miss Libby. Your mama was something special. Her and your aunt Cree. I loved that bossy old woman. She was my wife but now she's one of God's angels."

Everybody had lost somebody. I guess I had been wearing my grief like a weathered old coat and people kept trying to help me slip out of it. First Clare, now Uncle Duke.

"I'm fine, Uncle Duke."

"Alright, 'cause you know I got your back if you ever need anything."

I smiled. "I know you do."

"Did your daddy ever tell you about the time right after that bastard kicked you outta the house?"

I didn't respond. Shock and embarrassment roiled through me like an electrical current. How did he know Lance had kicked me out? I hadn't even told Daddy. I didn't tell anyone except my friend Bridget because she let me sleep in her spare room for two months as I tried to put my life back together before I moved to Brunswick. I fought back an urge to either cry or run.

"Well, me and ya daddy thought about rolling up on . . . what's his name? Lester?"

"Lance."

"Yeah, whatever. We had a little something for that bastard. But Roo talked us out of it. She told us you was smart and strong and you didn't need anybody to save you." Uncle Duke leaned in closer to me and whispered, "Even though y'all ain't together no more, it ain't too late for us to drive up there and whup his ass."

We both laughed. I tried to tamp down my embarrassment about Lance demanding that I leave *his* house and the fact that my dad and my uncle both knew about it. Every time I was reminded of Lance's cruelty, it made me want to scream in frustration that I'd been so stupid to pick a man like him as a life partner.

"It's nice to know how much you care, but that's not necessary. Business kinda slow today, huh?"

"Business is always slow when the fellas go fishing." Uncle Duke laughed. "Sweetie, I ain't had no real customers around here in years. I keep the lights on, and the door propped open for folks that just wanna talk and kill some time. Ever since Cree died, this here shop gives me something to do besides miss her."

"Uncle Duke, why didn't you ever remarry after Aunt Cree died?"

He smiled and got a distant look in his eyes. "I used to joke around when she was alive and tell her that I'd never remarry because women were too much to handle. Turns out it wasn't a joke after all. I loved Cree like nobody's business, and I didn't wanna give up my heart like that to another woman again, as if it was possible. And to love a woman less than the way I loved Cree would be unfair to that woman."

"Aunt Cree was special."

"Yes, she was. Besides, I'm not the type that ever needed a woman to cook and clean for me. I can do all that for myself. But some men need that. And ain't nothing wrong with that. Your daddy is like that. When Libby died, I didn't know if he'd make it without her. I don't mean just cooking and cleaning. I mean he was broken. Me and the fellas couldn't help him none. But Roo stepped in and made sure he didn't throw himself into the sea. She saved his life."

"I guess," I said.

"I think Roo has loved your daddy since the day she laid eyes on him, back when we all used to hang out at Club 115. But she loved your mother more and she wouldn't do a thing to come between your mama and daddy. Cut her some slack. Them kids of hers ain't shit. They don't call. Don't visit. I suspect she needs the same thing as your daddy—a purpose. A reason to get up in the morning. All of us are just a bunch of old people trying to live out these last precious days the best way we know how."

Daddy walked back in the room and snapped the top on a can of Michelob. "I found your personal stash in the bottom drawer of the refrigerator. Holding out on me, huh?"

"That was my last one too," Uncle Duke said with a chuckle.

Daddy raised the can in a mock toast and took a sip. "Listen, what can you tell us about Holcomb Gardner. Nosy Rosy here is looking for some information."

I shook my head at Daddy's moniker.

"Hmm . . . let me see," Uncle Duke said. "I know he had a sister, Delilah Gardner. Ooh, she was fine as wine back in the day. I couldn't get no time with her or her friend Ophelia. The finest women on the block. Butta, you remember. I think you had a little crush on Delilah before you went in the service, didn't you?"

Daddy gave me a sheepish look and peered back at Uncle Duke. "Man, just tell the girl what she wants to know."

Uncle Duke and I cracked up laughing.

"Seriously, did you know about them owning some property?" Daddy asked.

"I guess you really did forget everything, Butta. Them Gardners lived in that big house with the funny roof. And Holcomb used to own that gas station over by your place until his wife, Gracie, died about ten years ago. Big, tall, lanky guy."

Daddy scratched his head. "I think I vaguely remember something like that. Deena says Holcomb mighta owned some beachfront property out on the island. And now, he's gone missing. Tell him, baby girl."

I chimed in. "I met Mr. Gardner." I hesitated for a moment, guarded about how much I wanted to share about that meeting. "He was living out on the property in a trailer. When I met him, he told me he'd never sell his land, that he and his sister, Delilah, would never do that. But when I went back to the property, he was gone. So was his dog and the trailer."

"Shut yo mouth. Really?" Uncle Duke rubbed his chin. "You

know his sister was killed in a hit-and-run accident. Damn shame how somebody just left her to die in the street," he said.

Daddy stared out the window. Silent. Another odd reaction at the mention of the Gardners.

"I saw a copy of his sister's obituary, but it didn't mention that she had a brother. No mention of Holcomb or his wife."

"Really? That's strange."

"Did they ever find the person who did it?" I asked.

"Not as far as I know." Uncle Duke leaned against the doorjamb to the back room. "What I do know is that Holcomb was always a bit of a loner. Especially after his wife died. He wasn't the same. Stopped running the gas station. He all but disappeared. Might explain him living out on the island in a trailer. He never was much on church or clubbing. Some folks say they see him in the grocery store sometimes. But not much else."

"Do you know if Holcomb and Gracie had any kids? Somebody who would have inherited his land?" I asked.

"No, it was just him and her. The two of 'em never had kids. Gracie used to come over to the church some Sundays. She was pretty friendly too. I never saw Holcomb at church much. So, you say he's gone missing, huh?"

"Yeah, but it doesn't make sense. He was adamant he wouldn't sell his land. And now, he's vanished and the property is up for sale."

Uncle Duke eased up from the wall and started to shut the lights down in the shop. "Let me put some feelers out and see what I come up with."

CHAPTER 10

The next morning I was up, out of the house, and on the road before Daddy and Ruth woke. I wanted to check out the addresses I had jotted down from my search of the tax records. Now that Beau and everyone else at Medallion was eyeballing my every move, I didn't want to be late.

I usually tried to get moving before Daddy and Ruth so that I was in and out of the bathroom and out of their way. Daddy's house was comfortable, but it was small—three bedrooms and only one bathroom. I needed my own place so desperately. I wanted my own home. Not the one I used to live in in Atlanta and not Daddy's either. I wanted a place that was mine.

I hadn't had a place of my own since before I married Lance. But even after we married and I moved in with him, it wasn't my home. It was *his* condo that he'd purchased before we got married. Spacious, beautiful, but his—not ours. He paid all the household bills and frequently told me how lucky I was to live so well. Whenever I talked about us finding a new home, something we'd both own, he dragged his feet. I found out why when the marriage fell apart. Six months after Ma's death, around the same time Daddy announced his upcoming nuptials with Ruth, Lance asked me to pack up my things and leave *his* condo. He literally kicked me out. Why would I allow a man to kick me out of my marital home?

Stupidity or maybe I was so broken from Ma's death that I didn't have any fight left in me. Uncle Duke's mention of that whole saga dredged up memories I'd spent a vast amount of energy trying to forget.

Nothing in my life made sense anymore—my family, my career, my living situation. It was like everything had been upended and was spinning out of control. And it was all my fault too. I had been so slow and obtuse not to recognize Ma was sick. Maybe I might have gotten her to a doctor earlier and saved her if I hadn't been so caught up in digging through receipts in Lance's wallet when he was in the shower and plowing through his cell phone for evidence of what I already knew to be true. Maybe if I'd been able to get pregnant when we were trying. Deep down, I knew I didn't want a child with Lance. But maybe if I had, he might not have felt the need to seek out someone else, someone younger. Or maybe it wouldn't have made a bit of difference. Maybe I ruined my whole life because I wasn't smart enough to ever make the right decision.

All my life, Ma and Daddy's house had felt like a sanctuary for me. Even after I left home and went off to college, I always had somewhere that felt safe and constant. But now, I felt out of place here. Ma was gone. And I was almost forty fucking years old and living back in my childhood bedroom with my father and his new wife. I didn't have a home. I had a room in my dad's house. "Baby girl" was Daddy's affectionate pet name for me, but now I had become the living embodiment of it.

"AHHHHHHHHHHHH!!!!!" I screamed out loud, inside the car, windows rolled up. I drove down the street, screaming and banging on the steering wheel. Then the screams turned to tears. And the tears turned to sobs. I had a full-on meltdown driving down Altama Avenue at forty-five miles per hour because I had screwed up my life. I was a stupid and broken mess, and I didn't know how to fix me.

A few minutes later as I got closer to my destination, I managed to compose myself. The tears subsided and I was able to tamp down all the pain. So much pain.

I double-checked the addresses I'd found for the Gardners. Even though Daddy told me I should stay out of it, I figured it couldn't hurt to take a quick look. Maybe the old man was safe and living with relatives. Once I confirmed that, I'd drop this whole matter.

My first stop, Holcomb's address. The first time I drove down Eaves Street, I couldn't find it. I made a U-turn and drove back up the street. Still no house with the street number 7200. On my third drive-by, I finally figured out that the house would have to be on the corner of the street according to the numerical order of the addresses. I drove back to the corner. And there it stood: 7200 Eaves Street. But it wasn't a house. It was an old, abandoned, and boarded-up gas station. The two gas pumps in the front sat weathered and caked over in rust like two squat statues from another era. Somehow, Holcomb's tax records had listed for his address a location that must have been boarded up for years.

A dead end.

I drove off and headed for Delilah Gardner's house. She'd lived in an old, established Black neighborhood that had held up well despite economic downturns and political efforts to squeeze its residents out of their homes. Delilah's house was near the end of the block. A small tan stucco ranch with green shutters. I sat inside the car for a few minutes debating whether to go up and ring the doorbell or to shift the car into drive and speed off. Daddy's words echoed in my head: *Why is it so important for you to go digging into this man's affairs? Leave it be*. But something inside me couldn't let it go.

I tried to mentally practice my introduction. *Hey, I'm Deena Wood. A strange man threatened me at gunpoint so I'm here looking for him.* Nope. And what if Holcomb Gardner answered the door? If he did, I'd just tell him I was concerned about his well-being, and I wouldn't bother him again. He obviously had his reasons for changing his mind and selling. He had 1.5 million reasons.

Anyway, once I confirmed that he was alive and well, I'd go back to my pathetic, lonely little life of living in my childhood bedroom, missing Ma, and doing grunt work for Medallion Company.

I paced up the short path to the small front porch. Even through the closed front door, I smelled food cooking. Something spicy. I rang the doorbell. No answer. I rang again. A few seconds later an attractive, young, brown-skinned woman peeped through the sidelight window of the front door.

"Yes?" she said, through the glass.

I didn't blame her for not opening the door. She didn't know me.

"Hi, I'm Deena Wood. I'm a lawyer with Medallion Company and I—"

"I'm not interested in selling!"

"No. I'm not here for that reason. I wanted to talk to you about Holcomb Gardner."

"I don't know any Holcomb Gardner," she said.

"What about his sister, Delilah Gardner?"

Her eyes grew wide. A few seconds later, she opened the door. That's when I saw her in full view: long micro braids, dressed in a T-shirt and a pair of jean shorts that could easily have doubled as an oversized thong with ample butt meat showing. I was right. She was young. Twenty or twenty-one, maybe. But her face was serious. She looked like everybody's homegirl and nobody's fool.

I smiled. "Like I said, I'm a lawyer. I met Holcomb Gardner a few days ago. I wanted to speak to him about the sale of his property out on the island."

"Who?"

"Holcomb Gardner. He mentioned he had a sister named Delilah. Do you know her?"

"Delilah Gardner is my grandmother. But who is Holcomb Gardner?"

"I think he may be your grandmother's brother. At least, that's what he told me. I guess that makes him your great-uncle."

"I'm sorry, my grandmother didn't have a brother. I don't know any Holcomb Gardner."

"What? Are you sure?"

She stared back at me like she was annoyed. "Yes, I'm sure. My grandmother didn't have any siblings. What did you say your name was again?"

"Deena Wood. Uh . . . I'm sorry to have troubled you. I must have the wrong person. Sorry."

The young woman closed the door without another word. I stood there for a few seconds stunned and slightly embarrassed by my mistake. Maybe I'd gotten things all twisted about Delilah Gardner, where she lived, and whether she was related to Holcomb Gardner. Maybe I had the wrong Delilah.

I climbed inside my car and tried to quash this insane compulsion I had to find Holcomb Gardner.

* * *

It was a little after two thirty and I was finishing up lunch at my desk. I heard the telltale creak of the floorboards outside my office just before Joe peeped his head in the doorway.

"Hey! Ya busy?"

I wrapped up the remnants of my sub sandwich and put it back in the bag. "Just finishing up lunch *at my desk*." I raised an eyebrow at him when I said it. I tossed the bag of garbage in the waste can and gave Joe my full attention.

"Noted." He walked in. "Beau and I just finished up a meeting with a couple people from a new law firm and one of the attorneys says he knows you. I told him I'd escort him here to your office."

"Hello, Deena."

I nearly fainted. Howard Lawson. *Howie*. All six four of him. His smile, smooth mocha skin, and deep brown eyes were gorgeous enough. But all that coupled with the slightest hint of a five-o'clock shadow literally made me sweat. No lie, I felt perspiration forming under my arms. He was gorgeous. Howie always had this aura, a way of walking into a room and commanding attention by his posture, his gaze, his mere presence. I'd swear he'd been that way since the eighth grade.

I'll kill Ruth for blabbing to him.

When we both lived in Atlanta, we'd sometimes bump into each other in some of the legal circles we both traveled in. We were cordial but his glances at me always lingered a little longer than was necessary for two platonic friends at a work event. I'd hate myself too because I couldn't stop thinking about him for weeks after. Once, I'd joined him and a group of other lawyers for drinks after a panel presentation we'd all attended. Howie and I were the last ones left at the table. The conversation turned slightly flirtatious. We were both still married to other people. When he suggested we go to another bar, someplace quieter to catch up, I hightailed it out of there. I had enough strength to pass on a couple drinks. I wasn't sure I was strong enough to resist what might follow. Before I left Atlanta, his company hired my firm to handle their litigation work.

But these days, I wanted no part of Howie Lawson because he'd betrayed me—a second time.

"Well, I'll let you two get caught up. Howie, it's great to meet you. We'll be in touch." Joe and Howie shook hands before Joe walked out.

I hadn't seen Howie since my mother's funeral. And now, he was at my job, of all places.

He strolled over to my desk with that smile, and I promised myself I would be cool. He was just an old boyfriend from high school. That's all, just another guy from another time. In the next second, I was embarrassed. I didn't want him to see me here, in *my element*, surrounded by a rattling radiator and an office that looked like a broom closet with a desk and a window.

"How are you?" Howie said. His deep baritone voice nearly took me out until I remembered that I wasn't supposed to like him. Not after Atlanta.

"What are you doing here?"

"Nice to see you again too," he said with a smirk.

I took a deep breath to control the snark in my voice. "Howie—I mean, Howard, let's not pretend we're something that we aren't. Why are you here at my job?"

He shook his head sadly. "Now, when did we get so formal? This is me."

He casually unbuttoned his jacket before taking a seat in the guest chair and I caught a whiff of him. Sweet mother of mercies, he smelled like heaven in a pinstripe suit. Whatever cologne he was wearing I wanted to drift off to sleep with it on my pillowcase at night. Howie had always taken care of himself. Worked out. Ate healthy. And here I was ten pounds heavier since the last time he saw me, wearing a pair of chinos and a blouse I'd bought on sale at TJ Maxx a few years ago. I needed to start putting in more of an effort. Just because I didn't like where I worked didn't mean I had to dress like it.

"You still didn't answer my question."

He leaned back in the chair like he owned the Old Victorian. "I work for Welburton and Harley. Medallion is thinking of hiring my firm. I just came over to meet with Beau Walsh and the team. I was hoping I'd see you in the meeting."

Damn. Beau didn't include me in the meeting with outside counsel as Clare said she'd tell him to do. I'd mention it to her later. Right now, my focus was on Howie.

"What happened with Haynes Corp in Atlanta? What brought you back to Brunswick?"

"It's a long story. Let me take you to lunch and I'll explain it all."

"You conveniently pitch my company for firm business and show up at my job, huh?"

"Are you trying to say I'm stalking you?! That I would do something so cunning as to get a client assignment to be close to you?" He jokingly clucked his tongue. "I'm offended." Then he laughed.

"You're not funny."

"Yes, I am. It's one of the things you love about me. Come on, seriously, Dee, I just want us to be friends again. I wish things hadn't turned out the way they did back in Atlanta."

"Stop calling me that. My name is Deena. We're not back in middle school. And we're not friends anymore. Friends don't stab each other in the back. Look, I gotta get back to work."

"Just let me explain. We've known each other since we were kids. Let's just talk. Have dinner with me."

I stared at him for a moment. "I thought it was lunch you wanted."

"I'll take whatever I can get."

I shook my head. "Howard—"

"Look, if I can't call you Dee, you can't call me Howard. Deal?"

I just glared at him.

"By the way, I was sorry to hear about you and your husband."

I didn't respond.

"Seriously, divorce isn't easy. I've been there, done that. I wouldn't wish it on my worst enemy."

I still didn't say anything although a small part of me wondered what happened to him and his wife. Did he cheat on her like Lance did to me? I didn't ask because it might dredge up a conversation I didn't want to get into with him.

"Come on. It's just dinner." He stared at me with those eyes, and I didn't even trust myself for what I was thinking. "I'll explain everything. And then if you tell me to stay away, I will. I promise."

My cell phone buzzed. Howie didn't budge or beg off. He nodded toward the phone. "You gonna answer that?"

I frowned, then picked up the phone. "Hello."

"Deena, it's me, Lois." I recognized her twangy southern drawl without her having to say her name. Lois was my real estate agent. "I found a great little house over in Old Town. I think it'll be perfect for you. You got some time to take a look today? I think we'll have to jump on this one quickly."

"Uh . . . sure. After work okay?"

"Great. It's not even listed yet, so if you like it, maybe we can snap it up before it hits the market."

"Okay. I'll see you after work," I said before I hung up.

Howie looked at me and grinned. "Now, how can you make plans with someone else tonight when we have dinner plans?"

I sighed. "*We* do not have plans. Come on. I'll walk you out."

I rose from my chair and Howie chuckled. "So, is there someone else?"

"That's none of your business. Let's go."

He smiled at me. We walked through the Old Victorian and out to his car in the parking lot.

He grabbed the door handle, then stopped and looked at me. "We really should talk. Just think about dinner, okay?"

"Sure, I'll think about it."

He leaned over and kissed me on the cheek. I caught another whiff of his cologne. *Damn, he smells as good as he looks.* He climbed inside a shiny silver Lexus sedan, and I watched him pull off. There would be no dinner or anything else with Howie Lawson. We had too much history. He was the first man I ever loved, the one who deflowered me.

And the one who got me fired from my job back in Atlanta.

CHAPTER 11

After work, I drove over to the house in Old Town to meet Lois. I didn't believe my eyes as I pulled up to the front of the house. A colorful array of petunias and tall purple salvia led up to the most adorable white cottage with dormers and black shutters. A black iron fence surrounded the house and gave it a picture-perfect border.

"What do you think, hon?" Lois said, standing in front of the house. Lois Blackwell was this huge personality tucked in a slim frame of sheath dresses, long box-dyed red hair, and four-inch stilettos.

"It's gorgeous."

"Wait until you see inside. Come on."

The house did not disappoint. Hardwood floors throughout. Three spacious bedrooms, including one with an en suite bath. A bathroom of my own. A place where I could sit my bath salts and lotions on the counter. No more darting in and out of the shower to avoid hogging the bathroom while Daddy and Ruth waited. I'd be able to take long baths with a book and a glass of wine. I'd have someplace that belonged to me. As Lois walked me through the house, I kept telling myself, *Do not fall in love, Deena*. I'd been outbid on two houses before. It could happen again.

"It's a pocket listing. That means it hasn't gone on the market yet. The owners are friends of my uncle. As soon as they said they wanted to sell, I immediately thought of you. As you can see, they've recently renovated the kitchen, even though it's a little on the small side. But a new five-burner gas stove, stainless-steel appliances. You a big cook, hon? Ya like to entertain?"

"Not really."

"Well, then. This kitchen will be just perfect for you."

I eased back through the living room like a six-year-old inching through a toy store. Every room offered a surprise I could barely believe. Right off the living room was a sunroom with a long window seat that overlooked a huge backyard, big enough for a garden. "Why are they selling such a lovely home?"

"They're retired. Decided they want to be closer to their kids and grandkids in Florida. Now, if you like this, we need to jump on it quick, sweetie."

"I love it!"

"Yay! I recommend you go in at full asking price to keep 'em from waffling. It's priced right so give 'em what they want."

"That's fine. Can I ask you something . . . unrelated?"

"Sure, sweetie. Anything."

"Are you familiar with a company called Empire Realty?"

"You mean the agency that keeps outbidding me on sales, including the last two offers you made?"

"Wait, Empire was the agency on those offers?"

"Yeah, and it ticks me off too. But this house isn't on the market officially, so maybe we can snap it up for ya before they get wind of it."

"How much do you know about Empire?"

"Not much. They're kinda squirrelly. You know what I mean? They run a low-key operation out of Texas."

"So you don't know any of the agents that work for them?"

"Nope. They popped up a few years ago with a couple sales in McIntosh County, then they started showing up here in Glynn County. I'm not sure how they do it, but somehow, they get in early on the new listings and they always bring cash offers. I wouldn't be surprised if they've got some kind of corporate backing."

"What do you mean by that?"

Lois started walking back through the house to shut down the lights so she could lock up. "Some of these big companies come into areas and buy up real estate, then turn it into corporate housing to lease to their employees they transfer into the area."

"Oh . . ."

"Shame too 'cause it makes it tough for first-time buyers like you to get into the market. They price ya out."

"Have you ever known companies like that to buy large parcels of land, oceanfront maybe?"

"Hmm . . . I don't think so. Let me go out to the car and get my laptop. We can write up the offer now."

Lois had given me something to think about. Maybe Empire was connected to some corporate giant. Although that still wouldn't explain why they scooped up Holcomb's oceanfront property if there was nothing for them to lease.

CHAPTER 12

The next morning, I felt hopeful again as I drove into work. I opened the sunroof and took in the spring air. Spring was my favorite season of the year with all its signals of something new to come—bright crocuses, blooming trees, sunny days. I had an offer in for a home of my own. This was my first step to finding my way and living like a grown woman again. Maybe I could get back what I'd lost through the divorce, my peace of mind.

I parked my car in the lot on the side of the Old Victorian. That's when I noticed a Georgia Natural Gas truck parked in front of the house. Peg told me the day before that she smelled gas occasionally throughout the day. Old houses. Thankfully, I never smelled it, probably because I had always been leaving in the middle of the day so I was never there long enough to smell much of anything.

Inside, things were quiet. Jennie was on the phone at the reception desk and threw me a quick wave when I walked in. The smell of coffee permeated the place. I headed to my little hovel at the back of the house. The only redeeming quality of this cramped space was that it overlooked a spectacular garden of flowers and dogwoods. If given the chance, I'd sit back here for hours just to stare out the window. If the angels were on my side, I'd soon have a view like this from my own home.

A few minutes later, my landline buzzed. Jennie was calling from the reception desk out front. I hit the speaker button.

"Yes?"

"There's a woman here to see you. She said her name is Rae."

"Umm . . . sure. I'll be right out." I didn't know anyone named Rae.

I walked up the hall to the reception area. And there she was. The same young woman I'd talked to the day before who denied ever knowing Holcomb Gardner.

She rose from the leather club chair in the foyer when I walked up to the front desk. This time she was dressed in a pair of black jeans and a white silk blouse. Her long micro braids were neatly tucked behind her ears and underneath an Atlanta Braves baseball cap. She gave me a long gaze from head to toe when I approached her, as if she were sizing me up for some stealth assignment. This woman was twenty-one, twenty-two years old, tops. But in that moment, with that look she gave me, she made me feel like an awkward kid.

"My name is Raynell. Everyone calls me Rae. I found something, you know, about that man you told me about, Holcomb Gardner."

I glanced at Jennie, who sat behind her desk smiling at us. I smiled back at her, then turned to Rae and nodded toward the front door. "Why don't we go outside."

We stepped onto the front porch. Jennie was still staring through the large glass window of the door. I guided Rae down the steps and out onto the sidewalk. "Why don't we stroll down to the corner and talk."

"Was my coming here a problem?"

"Uh . . . no."

She gave me that suspicious sweeping look again. "You act like it is."

"I work around a lot of people with big ears and even bigger mouths."

"You told me you were a lawyer for Medallion. I thought maybe that man you're looking for had something to do with your job."

"No worries." I decided to get her back on track and off me. "You said you found something?"

"Yeah, about that man you asked me about. You said you thought he was related to my grandmother. I found this in my grandmother's Bible." Rae reached into her cross-body bag and pulled out an old Polaroid. She handed it to me. "That's my grandmother when she was younger."

I looked down at the picture. A young man and woman standing side by side in front of a house. Neither of them smiling. Late teens, early twenties, perhaps. The man in the photo looked like a younger version of Holcomb Gardner—tall, lean, and strikingly handsome. Instead of the bearded scruff he bore in the trailer, he wore a neatly trimmed mustache along with a denim bell-bottomed suit that draped his body like it was handmade for him. He held his head back and struck a fig-leaf pose like one of those action movie actors from the 1970s. The young woman in the picture was tall and extraordinarily attractive, with a big Afro. She wore a red halter top, a black miniskirt, and matching platform shoes. Her large hoop earrings framed a beautiful face that was both regal and defiant. Delilah Gardner was stunning.

"You see what's written on it?" Rae said.

Written across the white border at the bottom of the Polaroid, in faded ink: *Delilah and Holcomb in front of Mama's house, November 1969.*

"The first time I found this picture, right after she died, I just assumed he was an old boyfriend. Do you think that could be the man you're looking for?"

I looked at the picture a beat longer. "I think that's him."

"If my grandmother had a brother, she never told me about him. Gran never talked about having brothers and sisters. And Gran told me everything. Why are you trying to find this man? Is he a relative of yours?"

"No, I met him, and I'd just like to talk to him. Perhaps your mother knows more. Do you think she might know him?"

"My mother is dead."

"Oh my gosh. Rae, I'm so sorry. I . . ." I didn't know what else to say. She shrugged. My heart sank and I wondered how she could be so nonchalant at losing her mother.

"If my grandmother didn't want to talk about her brother—and that's *if* she had one—she must have had a good reason. I wanna know the real reason why you were looking for my grandmother. Are you some kind of detective or something?"

"No. I didn't mean to pry. I was just following up on a hunch I had about Mr. Gardner."

She gave me another side-eye once-over. "What kind of hunch?"

"I don't know. I think he may have disappeared under mysterious circumstances. I'm not even sure why I'm looking for him."

Rae stared at me with the strangest expression, as if she was trying to mentally calculate something. "You're looking for a man who's gone missing and my grandmother is dead. But . . ."

"But what?"

"You think that man is dead or something?" she asked.

"I don't know."

"Hmm . . ."

"What is it?" I asked.

"My grandmother. She died after a hit-and-run accident. They said a car hit her as she was crossing the street. The couple times I called to ask them what's going on with the investigation, I got the runaround. They told me they have no witnesses or leads. I finally stopped calling. Do you think my grandmother's death and that man's disappearance are connected?"

"I'm not sure."

She folded her arms. "Don't lie to me. Why are you looking for this Holcomb Gardner person, and what do you know about my grandmother?"

This girl was young, but she was tough. "I don't know anything about your grandmother. But I think Mr. Gardner might be in some trouble because of some land he owned. He said he owned it with his sister, Delilah, and that they would never sell it. But now he's missing and someone else has the land."

Rae's eyes widened. "What? You're telling me you think my grandmother had a brother and they owned land together?!"

"I'm not sure about any of this."

"We have to find this Holcomb guy. Maybe he knows what happened to my grandmother."

"Wait a minute. This is none of my business. I think you should go to the police."

"It was *your* business when you walked up on my front porch yesterday asking about him. Besides, I just told you, the police aren't hard-pressed to find out what happened to a seventy-three-year-old Black woman who was run over and left to die in the street like an animal." Rae stared at me again. "If you know so much, why haven't *you* gone to the police? Did you report this Holcomb guy missing?"

"No. I'm not really sure it's my place to go to the police. Maybe as a relative of his, you can go to the authorities. I just thought if Mr. Gardner was related to your grandmother she might know where he was, and I could put my mind at ease. I was simply concerned, that's all."

This time, Rae stared at me so long it started to get awkward. She finally cleared her throat, like she was about to say something. She didn't. But I saw tears welling in her eyes.

"Look, Rae, I'm really sorry about your grandmother . . ." I heard myself talking and it sounded hollow. She was right. Yesterday, I was bold enough to walk onto the front porch of a complete stranger looking for Holcomb Gardner. I never should have gotten involved this much.

"Yeah, okay," Rae said.

"Here's your picture." I held out the Polaroid to her.

"Keep it. I hope you find what you're looking for." She rolled her eyes at me and headed off down the street.

I watched her until she rounded a corner and was out of sight.

I looked at the picture again.

Delilah and Holcomb in front of Mama's house, November 1969.

* * *

I'M CONVINCED THAT working in a dull, dead-end job is far more exhausting than working in one that isn't. I'd worked in both. It takes extraordinary skill and stamina to make it through the workday while playing a game of "don't watch the clock." Or trying to appear interested while sitting in a meeting and then realizing you've spaced out at least ten times and lost track of what's going on around you. The worst part is getting to payday and facing the fact that the paycheck you earned doesn't fairly compensate you for the herculean effort you exerted just to keep from telling your boss to kiss your ass and walking out.

Every day as I walked into the Old Victorian, I told myself my job was the first step to braiding the pieces of my life back together. My mother was gone, and my father had a new wife. My marriage was over. I had to find my independence again. Now that I had an offer in on a house, I needed this job to demonstrate proof of income so that I could qualify for a mortgage and move out of Daddy's house. I needed to keep my ass in the Old Victorian no matter how bored I was.

I was right in the middle of a game of "don't watch the clock" when I glanced down at my phone. I lost again. It was 4:53, four minutes since the last time I looked. I decided to hell with it and shut down my computer. I'd ask for forgiveness tomorrow rather than permission today. I grabbed my purse from the bottom drawer, clicked off the desk lamp, and headed for the front door.

I would do better tomorrow.

Jennie waved goodbye as I passed the reception desk. She was sweet, not nearly as judgmental as Peg or some of the other support staff who worked around here and thought it was in their job description to monitor my comings and goings.

I stepped out onto the front porch of the Old Victorian. As I did, I noticed a black Ford Escape parked out on the street in front of the house. The same car that had nearly forced me off the road out on the island. The windows were tinted so dark I couldn't make out who was inside. This was the third time I'd seen that car. First at Holcomb's property, then outside Daddy's house, and now here at my job.

Someone was following me.

I hustled down the stairs. The car pulled off before I got close enough to make heads or tails of the driver, or even get a license tag number.

Shit.

I raced to my car, turned the engine, and sped off. This time, I was chasing the black Ford instead of the other way around. I peeled out of the parking lot and straight up the street. A car pulled out of a driveway in front of me. I raced up behind the car, trying desperately not to lose sight of the black Ford. A few yards later, the car in front of me graciously allowed another car to switch lanes in front of him. *Damn it.* Now there were two cars between me and the black car. I was barely able to keep track of it. I switched lanes and sped up, trying to go around the cars in front of me. The light changed. The black Ford made it through the yellow light. It was red by the time I got to it. I screeched to a stop. *Shit.* I watched the Ford speed away. By the time the light turned green, the black car was gone. I sped up to the next intersection. No sign of the Ford.

Who the hell is following me?

I made a U-turn and started for home. A flash of Holcomb Gardner's dog and his trailer eclipsed my brain.

Let it go, Deena.

The Polaroid of Holcomb and his sister, dressed to the nines.

Do not get involved.

I closed my eyes as a sudden wave of guilt washed over me. A Black woman was dead under mysterious circumstances. A Black man was missing, also under mysterious circumstances. And now somebody was following me. If what Ma used to say was right—*we are all connected*—then I might already be involved.

Fifteen minutes later, I was standing on Rae's front porch. Again.

CHAPTER 13

I sat in Rae's living room. Even though I'd never met the woman, the whole house had *Grandma Delilah* written all over it. A peach floral sofa with two matching chairs, a framed print of a pastoral scene on one wall. Two brown wood veneer end tables bearing matching gold lamps rounded out the living room furnishings. My guess from looking around was that Rae either had no interest in changing things since her grandmother's death or she'd simply chosen to hang on to the memories. Perhaps she was too overwhelmed for a dayclean. Either way, she put up a good front for someone who had suffered so much loss. Both her mother and her grandmother were with the ancestors, as Ruth would say. She had some fortitude too, continuing to live in a house with so many memories. Sometimes the mere act of walking into Daddy's bedroom, where Ma had once slept, was enough to bring me to tears.

"What was your grandmother like?"

"Gran was my day one. Always there for me. The sweetest person I've ever known. I guess everybody says that about their grandmother, huh?"

I smiled. Rae was lucky. I wished I had known my grandparents. My mother's father was the only grandparent I had a memory of and even that was vague.

"And oh my God! She was so beautiful. She never left this house without her makeup, nails, everything tight. She really took care of herself." Rae opened her cell phone, clicked a couple times, and pulled up a recent picture of Delilah. "See."

I took her phone and gazed at the picture. It showed the two of them standing on a deck with the beach and the ocean in the background. Rae was right. Delilah was beautiful, and she still bore that regally defiant look from the Polaroid. The only thing that had changed was that she wore a short silver Afro and a few crinkles around her eyes. Time had been kind to her. She was a striking woman, or least she had been, even into her seventies.

"And she never mentioned having a brother, huh?" I asked.

"Never. I can't ever remember her talking about family. The few times I asked her about her family, she'd just say me and my mother were family enough for her. Whatever that means. What makes you so sure you have the right Delilah Gardner anyway?"

"That picture you gave me, for starters."

Rae pinched her face into a frown. "Gran told me everything! Why wouldn't she tell me she had a brother? Even if they didn't get along." Rae hesitated for a moment. "Gran raised me. My mother was kinda in and out of my life. Drugs. I never knew my father. When I was twelve, my mother almost overdosed on heroin. Gran moved me in here with her. My mother finished what she started a couple years later."

"I'm so sorry, Rae."

Rae shrugged her shoulders. And it dawned on me that her shrugging at her mother and grandmother's deaths wasn't nonchalance. It was a coping mechanism. It was like my smiles and utterances that I was fine when people asked me how I was doing since Ma's death. Like me, Rae had found something to soothe the pain in public. It was a way to keep standing when you wanted to fall apart.

I handed the phone back to Rae.

She gazed at the picture for a moment before she clicked the phone off. "Gran wanted me to go to college. She said nobody she'd ever known had gone and she wanted me to be the first. But sitting up in a classroom with my nose in a bunch of books wasn't me. I wanted to go to culinary school. Didn't matter since there was no money for either one. I guess working as a cook over at Soul Food Station is the closest I'll ever come to being a chef." She stopped talking and stared out the window for a moment. She looked back at me. "Anyway, what did this Holcomb guy tell you about my grandmother?"

"Not much. Just that he had a sister, and they would never sell their land. He claimed he owns a large parcel of land out on the edge of Glynn County."

"And what makes you think he's missing? Maybe he just doesn't want to be found."

"I guess that could be true. He just seemed adamant about his land. Did you ever get a copy of the police report for your grandmother's accident?"

"Yeah. Hang on." Rae walked over to a buffet in the dining room. She pulled out an envelope from one of the drawers and returned to the living room. She handed me the report. It looked pretty dog-eared, which told me she had pored over it more than a few times before I wandered onto her front porch. "Essentially, the police have told me it's not likely they'll ever find who killed Gran."

I read through the paperwork. According to the police report, a man out walking his dog found the body but didn't witness the accident. No tire tread marks left at the scene. No cameras out in that section of the island. All of it made the likelihood of finding the driver slim to nil. It wasn't until after I read the officer's comments that I went back to the top of the report and read the box marked "Location of the Incident." My heart raced—Delilah's body was found at the edge of Holcomb's property on Boden Road!

"Rae, your grandmother's body was found out on the island?"

"Yeah."

"You didn't mention that before. According to this report, it was found near the property that Holcomb said he owned."

"Wait! Really? So maybe she was out there to see him?"

We both stared at each other. And then I thought about the black Ford Escape that chased me off the island. Maybe there was some connection.

"So, Holcomb told you he owned some land with my grandmother. You think somebody killed Gran and kidnapped the old man to get their land?"

"I'm not sure, but I don't think any of this is a coincidence," I said.

Rae looked back down at the police report in front of me. She got up from the sofa and disappeared into the kitchen. She returned a couple minutes later with a can of Red Bull, a Diet Coke, and eyes that blinked back tears.

"You look more like a Diet Coke type to me," she said as she handed me the can of soda.

"Thanks, and that stuff will eat a hole through your stomach."

"The alternatives are a lot worse."

"True." I snapped the soda can open before I took a long sip. "Do you know if your grandmother went out to the island very often?"

"Sometimes. She and her friends would go out to the island to have dinner. But most times, she didn't go too far from home. To the grocery store, church, shopping. The night she died, she said she and a friend were going to the island to have dinner and she'd be back in a couple hours. She never came home. Police showed up at my door the next morning."

"Did she say which friend she was having dinner with?"

"No."

"Did your grandmother have someone she might have been close to? Maybe somebody she talked to regularly?"

"Well, there's Miss Ophelia. Ophelia Ealy. She and my grandmother have been best friends since the 'early days,' as they used to call it. They met at the diner where they used to work. Used to go out to dance parties together back when they were young. I always loved sitting around listening to them tell stories. I suspect they were probably something else back then. Miss Ophelia is getting on now. She's been sick off and on, but they still talked almost every morning until Gran died." Rae shook her head wearily. "I feel bad that I haven't talked to her since the funeral."

"You think she might be willing to talk to us?"

"Us?" Rae said with raised eyebrows.

I smiled. "First things first. Let's just find out if your grandmother's death and Holcomb's disappearance are connected. If they are, then we should have enough evidence that the police will have no choice but to take this seriously and look into everything."

"Miss Ophelia will talk to us, but what do you think she can offer?"

"I'm not sure, but women have a way of sharing things with their best friends. Maybe your grandmother shared something with Miss Ophelia that she didn't feel comfortable telling you."

Rae polished off her Red Bull. "It's worth a shot."

CHAPTER 14

Ophelia Ealy lived in a small blue-and-white bungalow with a pleasant-looking flower bed and an inviting front porch that held two rockers. Birds chirped noisily in the surrounding trees. The whole scene was almost idyllic but for the fact we were here to question Miss Ophelia about her dead best friend and her friend's missing brother. Rae rang the doorbell and we waited.

"She moves slow," Rae whispered.

A minute later, a small Black woman with bright eyes and a big smile appeared at the screen door. She was leaning on a cane, the only hint that she might be infirm in any way. Miss Ophelia was probably in her seventies, a contemporary of the Gardner siblings and just shy of five feet tall. The first thing I noticed about her was the bright pink velour track suit she wore and her immaculately manicured red fingernails. Seeing her nails reminded me of how Ma and I would go get mani-pedis before she got sick. And in that moment, it took every ounce of strength in my body not to break down in tears. Grief can be a sneaky little bitch like that, cutting your heart open in the most unlikely places, and each slice as fresh as the first.

"Rae! Is that you?" she said in a high-pitched squeal of a voice. She opened the door, reached up, and hugged Rae. "I haven't seen you in a month of Sundays. Lord Jesus, where you been, girl?"

"Yes, ma'am. It's me," Rae said. "And I brought along someone I want you to meet. This is Deena Wood."

"Well, nice to meet you, Deena Wood. Y'all come on in."

We stepped inside the living room. Everything matched. Blue walls matched a blue floral sofa and chairs, which matched floral print pictures on the walls, which matched the blue hydrangeas in a vase on the coffee table. This house was almost a replica of Delilah's house, except in blue. Ophelia and Delilah were definitely friends.

"Sit down and rest yourself," she said.

Rae and I took the sofa and Miss Ophelia sat in a large high-back Queen Anne chair that emphasized how petite she was by the amount of room left in the chair after she sat down. She could almost fit a whole other person in there with her.

"I'm so glad you dropped by to see me. I sure do miss your grandmama. She was my heart."

"I'm sorry I haven't been by to visit sooner. Just busy with work and stuff."

"Oh honey, don't you waste another minute with an apology. You young folks got busy lives. I was young once." Miss Ophelia winked at us and giggled. Rae and I smiled back. "I was just thinking about Delilah this morning. I remember how we would go over to Club 115 on Saturday nights. Ooh wee! The place would be crawling with folks. And the men! All of 'em elbowing one another to try to get me and Delilah on the dance floor."

Rae and I looked at each other and smiled again. I imagined the miniskirted, Afro-laden Delilah out on the dance floor. It reminded me of Daddy and Uncle Duke talking about Club 115, the 1960s watering hole for Blacks out on the island.

"Delilah had something about her that men couldn't resist. And most times she half liked them. She'd give a guy hope and then drop him the next day. I think that's why neither of us ever married. Too many good-looking men out there." Miss Ophelia cackled in a high-pitched voice. Then she grew solemn. "Delilah should be here."

Rae and I sat quietly. My heart tugged for the woman who had lost her best friend. It must be hard to grow old and outlive your loved ones. I thought about my friend Bridget back in Atlanta. We always hung out like we'd have forever to live. But one day, one of us would end up like Miss Ophelia.

"Yes, ma'am, she should be here. That's why I stopped by with Deena. We're trying to find out what happened to Gran out on the island the day she got hit by the car."

Miss Ophelia leaned forward in her chair and looked at me. "Are you a police detective or something?"

"No, ma'am," I said, a bit embarrassed that I was meddling in this whole affair.

"Miss Ophelia, did you talk to Gran that morning? Did she tell you where she was going that day?"

"Well, we talked the day before. She said she was going over to Winn-Dixie. Said she planned to bake a pie and she needed some apples."

"Okay, but there isn't a Winn-Dixie out on the island. Did she mention why she was going out there? Who was she going to see?" Rae asked.

Miss Ophelia turned away from Rae's stare.

"Miss Ophelia, did Gran know anybody out that way?"

The old woman glanced at Rae, then at me before she stared out the window. "I promised I wouldn't tell a soul."

"Tell what?"

"Your grandmama was seeing someone."

Rae's eyes widened in shock. "What do you mean *seeing someone*?"

Miss Ophelia pressed her hands together. She glanced at me and suddenly I felt like I was eavesdropping in on a family secret I had no business knowing.

"She had a friend," Miss Ophelia whispered.

"Like a *boyfriend*?!" Rae said.

"Don't say it like it's a disease or something. Your grandmama was a beautiful, vibrant woman."

"Gran had a man?!"

"What makes you think she couldn't have a man in her life? That's what wrong with y'all young folks. You think love and sex is reserved for everybody under thirty-five. You'd be surprised how good sex can be when—"

"Okay, okay, Miss Ophelia. I don't need details." Rae held up her hands and shook her head like the thought of Miss Ophelia and her grandmother being anything other than kindly old women would make her sick. I was thirty-nine and I had to admit the thought of who'd love me when I was in my seventies wasn't at the top of my mind either. "Do you think she might have been going to see her *friend* when she was killed?"

"Yes. She said they were going out to dinner on the island. Sometimes they would go driving out on the island or go for a walk along the beach. He's real sweet to her and handsome too."

"Wait," I chimed in. "She had her car the day she was killed?"

Rae and Miss Ophelia both nodded yes.

"So why was she walking at the time of the accident? Where was her car?"

"The police said they found it in a nearby park," Rae said. "They seem to think she left her car to take a walk and became disoriented.

Couldn't find her way back. I'm telling you, none of this makes any sense. Gran didn't get disoriented. She was sharp."

I turned to the old woman. "Did you tell the police this, Miss Ophelia?"

"What police? The police didn't talk to me. Besides, I wasn't supposed to tell you two. I certainly wasn't going to tell a complete stranger even if they asked." Miss Ophelia laid a hand on her heart. "I sure hope Delilah will forgive me. God rest her soul."

Why wouldn't the police talk to Delilah's best friend?

"What's her friend's name?"

"Leave him out of this. He's just trying to live out the rest of his days in peace. He didn't have anything to do with this. Let him have his privacy."

"Miss Ophelia, it's really important that we know everything. Did you know Gran had a brother?"

The old woman froze, her eyes widening in surprise before she turned to stare out the window. "How did you find out?"

Rae and I looked at each other again.

"You *knew* Gran had a brother? Why didn't you tell me?" Rae said.

"Because that was Delilah's secret to tell, not mine. I feel awful telling it now."

"Why did she keep it a secret all these years?" Rae asked.

Miss Ophelia sighed deeply. "Goes back decades. She and Holcomb always had issues. They never did get along. Always squabbling about one thing or another. I think it was because they were both so much alike. Both of 'em stubborn as a swollen mule."

"What kind of issues?"

"The kind that always breaks up families, sweetie. Money."

Rae leaned forward on the sofa. "What money, Miss Ophelia?"

"Some stuff happened a long time ago. Between Delilah and Holcomb. They weren't rich, but their daddy was big on owning property. He worked as a porter for the old Carolina Limited rail company. When their parents died, they left the house to the kids. Big, pretty house too. It was just Delilah and Holcomb. Holcomb was married to Gracie by then, so Delilah continued to live in the house for years. But she never was good with money. A few years back, she either sold it or lost it. I don't know which. But when Holcomb found out, he was hellfire mad. They argued and never talked again. Nothing could bring them two together."

"I never knew that," Rae said quietly.

"Most folks didn't. Delilah was ashamed of what she'd done. She never talked about any of it. Felt like she'd messed over property that she could have passed on to you and your mother. She used to tell me, if she had kept that house, maybe she could have kept your mama out of trouble and away from that crowd she ran with. But that wasn't Delilah's fault. Kids gonna do whatever they got a mind to do. Anyway, when you came to live with her, she put all her attention on you and tried to put it all out of her mind. You can't blame her for nothing. She did the best she knew how."

I finally chimed into the conversation. "Do you know about land they might have owned over on the island?"

Miss Ophelia nodded slowly. "They argued about that too, but by then Delilah had just thrown her hands up and left Holcomb to do whatever he wanted. She said she was tired of arguing about it. I think it always made her sad that they could never find a way back to each other, the way brothers and sisters ought to be."

I watched Miss Ophelia wrestling with secrets and memories she probably thought were long buried. It made me hesitant to pry deeper, but I had to know. "Did you ever tell Holcomb that his sister was killed?"

She stared back at me with tears welling in her eyes. "I wanted to, but we didn't know how to find him."

"That's why we're here, Miss Ophelia," I said. "Holcomb's missing and we think it might have something to do with that land they owned. Maybe if we can find him, we can find out what might have happened to her."

"You mean you think Holcomb killed his own sister?"

"No . . . no. Nothing like that. I think maybe someone wanted their land. Holcomb's been missing for over a week, and we just want to make sure he's okay."

"Well, the last I heard, he was living out on Old Farm Road. Delilah said it was the only blue house out there."

"Thank you."

The old woman turned to me. "Listen, when you find Holcomb, tell him his sister really did love him. She made a mistake. That's all. It was just the two of them left. She really was hoping they'd make up and be brother and sister again."

"We'll tell him," Rae said. She leaned closer to the old woman. "Now, please, Miss Ophelia, can you tell us her friend's name? Maybe he can help."

Miss Ophelia hesitated for a moment. "The city commissioner. Charlie Lester."

CHAPTER 15

Rae and I were back in my car, headed out to Old Farm Road. The bright sun of the late day and the confident male voice of my GPS directing us made it seem as if we were off on some wonderland adventure. The unfamiliarity of this section of the county heightened the experience of finally finding some answers. The road was surrounded mostly by farmland dotted with a random McDonald's or a gas station. Rae stared out the window in silence. Part of me wanted to pepper her with more questions, but her silence seemed heavy, laden with thought. I turned on the radio and a jazz station popped up.

"You can turn to something else if you like," I said to her.

She leaned over and turned to a station out of Jacksonville. A rap song blared through the radio. I didn't recognize it, but the lyrics hit like a sledgehammer to the ear. I didn't necessarily consider myself a prude, but every other word explicitly referenced sex or was completely bleeped out. Rap had come a long and scary way from the Snoop Dogg and Puff Daddy songs that I bopped to back in the day. Rae went back to staring out the window. She'd been more talkative on the way over to Miss Ophelia's house. Now, she was different.

I turned down the radio volume. "You're quiet. You okay?"

"Yeah," she said, watching the landscape whiz by.

I didn't say anything else. Maybe I'd pushed too hard. She'd lost her mother, then her grandmother. Now, I'd showed up blathering about some great-uncle she never knew she had. It was a lot to process.

Finally, she turned to me. "I don't understand."

"Understand what?"

"What would you do if you found out your mother or father had been keeping secrets from you?"

"What do you mean?"

"Why wouldn't she have told me about her brother? Lots of people in families have falling-outs. My friend Tenesha said her aunts don't speak to each other, but at least she knows about them. Gran had this whole other life she never talked about—a brother, a boyfriend. Damn, who was she?"

"Everybody keeps a little part of themselves hidden from the world."

Rae stared back out the window. "I wonder what other secrets she had."

"Like Miss Ophelia said, maybe your grandmother was embarrassed."

"Hmph. Whatever."

"Our parents and grandparents are people too. Sometimes we tend to think of them in the context of when we met them."

She looked back at me. "What does that mean?"

"Just that she's always been Gran to you. You only knew her as the older, more settled, wiser Gran. You didn't know her when she was Delilah Gardner. Nobody's mother or grandmother. Just Delilah. Young and working at the diner with Miss Ophelia. Dancing on Saturday nights with all the boys crowding around her. Did you look at your grandmother in that picture, in that miniskirt? Like, seriously!"

Rae smiled.

"Parents, even grandparents, are like everybody else. They're sexual beings too. After all, that's how we all got here."

Rae giggled and shook her head.

"Everybody makes mistakes when they're young."

"She wasn't young when she started dating the city commissioner guy. Why didn't she tell me that?"

"Remember your reaction when Miss Ophelia told you about him? I thought you were going to gag up a lung. That might have had something to do with your grandmother keeping it a secret."

"You got all the answers, huh?" Rae said with a smirk.

"Whatever. Okay, I see a couple houses farther up."

I slowed the car as we approached some small sign of civilization. By the time I pulled the car up closer, Rae and I both went silent. Three shotgun houses stood side by side. And just as Miss Ophelia said, there was only one blue house. But the house was in rough shape. The grass in the yard was overgrown. The weathered blue paint looked more gray than blue. The windows were boarded up and the hole in the roof made the house look as if it had a black eye. It was obvious Holcomb hadn't lived here in a very long time.

And planted in front of his house, a sign:

AVAILABLE
For Sale
Call Empire Realty
932-555-6527

There was that real estate company again. The same one with the sketchy online presence. The same one that had outbid me on a couple offers for houses I tried to buy. I cut the engine and eased out of the car.

"Hey! Where you going?" I heard Rae yell from behind me.

"Just stay in the car. I'll be right back."

A few seconds later, I heard the car door open and slam shut. Rae was hardheaded. I didn't say anything. I walked up to the edge of the front porch and heard Rae scramble up behind me.

"Well, it doesn't look like he's here," Rae said. "Can we go?"

Suddenly, I heard a noise. "Shh . . ."

"What?"

We both stopped and waited. This time we both heard it. There was a loud thumping noise coming from the back of the house.

"Go get back in the car and lock the doors," I whispered.

"You're not going back there, are you? You got a piece on you, or you just big and bad enough to go up in there unarmed?"

I ignored Rae and walked around to the back of the house. Rae ignored me and followed. We both treaded carefully over the broken concrete path that led to the back of the house. Overgrown grass brushed against my legs, and I prayed there were no snakes lurking in it.

A few moments later, we found the source of the noise. The back door was swinging on its hinges in the breeze. I climbed the three short steps on the back stoop.

I glanced back at Rae. She folded her arms across her chest. "I know you're not going in there, right?"

"I'm just gonna take a peek through the door. I told you to go back to the car, remember?"

"He's not here, so what are you looking for?" she said.

"I don't know. I just wanna see if he left anything behind that might help us find him."

I peeped inside, but I had a hard time focusing with the glare of the sunlight pouring in from the back door.

"Do you see anything?" Rae said.

I didn't respond. I stepped inside.

"Deena!"

I didn't say a word. I knew she wouldn't listen if I told her to wait outside. I was right too because a few seconds later, she followed me into the house.

Inside, the kitchen was empty except for newspapers scattered across the linoleum floor and an old dirty stove, the oven door missing, sitting in the middle of the room. Two cupboards were barely hanging on the wall, and they held a few broken dishes inside. I glanced down at the newspaper. It was the sports section dated two years ago. Had that been the last time Holcomb had lived here?

I walked through what must have been the bedroom as the house grew darker, the boards blocking all but a few slivers of daylight from the windows. Just before I made it inside the living room, two large rats raced in front of me and down a vent on the side wall. Rae and I both screamed.

"Let's go, Deena! There's nothing in here."

There was an old dresser in the living room. Several drawers were missing. I slid open one drawer and at least four spiders crawled out. I jumped and nearly knocked Rae down in the process. The drawer was empty.

"Now can we go?"

I clapped dust from my hands. "Yeah, I guess you're right. There's nothing here."

"Thank you."

We climbed back inside the car and closed the doors.

Rae turned to me. "So, what now?"

I sighed. "I don't know, but I still have a feeling something's not right. That real estate company, Empire Realty, is the same company that's selling Holcomb's land out on the island. Land he swore he would never sell. And they're also selling his home too? Doesn't make sense."

"Maybe he's selling all his stuff to get a fresh start somewhere else."

"I don't think so. We need to find out who's behind Empire Realty." I started up the car. "Come on. Let's go."

CHAPTER 16

I dropped Rae back at her house and headed home.

Home.

I dreaded going in. When Ma was alive, I couldn't wait to sit beside her at a dinner table or a restaurant and listen to her regale us with stories of the days when she and Daddy were younger, how they met at church, the parties they gave. Tonight, I'd have to sit through dinner listening to Ruth badgering me about dating. And I still needed to get her straight about blabbing to Howie about my divorce and where I worked. I don't know whether it was a matter of trust or flat-out dislike for her, but whatever this thing was I had about Ruth, I had to get over it. Daddy's little excursion out to her house was his way of telling me to be more patient with and sympathetic to her. I would try. She was Daddy's new wife. This was her home, not mine anymore. And not Ma's either.

I swung by the mailbox and retrieved the mail. There wasn't much there. A few utility bills, a catalog for Macy's—Ruth loved to shop. Whose money was she spending, hers or Daddy's? And the last thing in the mailbox was a flyer printed on bright yellow paper.

WE BUY HOUSES
GREAT PRICES!!!
QUICK CLOSINGS
CALL 932-555-7283

Daddy had been getting this same flyer for months now. Most of the neighbors had. And then I heard the uneven clop-clop sound of feet behind me.

"Deena!"

LaShonda.

I turned around and stood face-to-face with her.

She cut daggers at me with her eyes. "Thanks to you, I gotta leave the only home I've known since I was nine years old."

"Excuse me?"

"I know you hate my ass. But I wouldn't let somebody kick you outta your daddy's house if you asked me for help. You a lawyer but I guess you only help the big shots. Forgot where you came from, huh?"

"What are you talking about?"

"They're gonna sell my house! Where me, Mama, and the kids supposed to go?"

"LaShonda—"

I heard a small boy yell "Mommy!" from across the street. We both looked in the direction of LaShonda's front porch.

"Mommy, I'm hungry."

I completely forgot to find the name of a lawyer to help her with her house situation. I felt awful. I simply stood there, looking at her.

LaShonda rolled her eyes at me and hobbled back across the street. "I'm coming, baby."

She was right. I definitely didn't care for her, but I didn't want to see her thrown out of her house. No one deserved that. I watched her as she grabbed the little boy's hand and walked inside. I promised myself I'd dig out the phone number of an estate lawyer and leave it in her mailbox. That was the best I could offer her.

I headed inside the house. I handed the mail to Daddy.

"Hey there, baby girl. Roo's got the table all set. You hungry?"

I smiled. "I am."

Ruth walked into the dining room from the kitchen holding a casserole dish of gumbo in one hand and a bowl of rice in the other.

"It smells good, Ruth." I'd try to meet her halfway.

"Why, thank you, Deena." She stood grinning at me for a moment. "Come on. Let's all sit down," she said.

This was Ruth's house now, not Ma's. I couldn't bring my mother back by being mad at Ruth. I missed my mother, and I didn't know how to open up my heart to anyone else who Daddy loved. But I'd try. Besides, there was no point in ruining everyone's dinner by sulking at the table like a twelve-year-old. Why should I make everybody miserable because I was?

I washed my hands at the kitchen sink before we all sat at the dining table to eat.

We bowed our heads and Ruth said the blessing. "Bress 'n nyam," Gullah-Geechee for "bless and eat."

"Guess what?" I said. "I put in an offer on another house."

"Hey! That's great, baby girl. Where is it?"

"It's in Old Town, not too far from my job. And my real estate agent said it's not on the market yet. So maybe I won't get outbid this time."

"Third time's a charm," Daddy said.

"Well, that calls for a celebration," Ruth said sweetly. "Oh, I think we've got some sherry up in the cupboard. I'll go get it."

To my surprise, the entire dinner was pleasant. Daddy and Ruth told stories about the old days, with Ruth filling in the holes where Daddy's memory fell short. They talked of how they all had danced and dined at Club 115.

"Why was it called Club 115?" I asked.

Ruth laughed. "Whit Hawkins owned the club. He said he was tired of going to juke joints and back rooms to party. Back then, there wasn't a lot of places we could go and eat and dance. Anyway, Whit use to say if he ever hit the number with the Bolito Man, he was gonna open up a club. You remember that, Jimmie?"

Daddy nodded in agreement. "And he did too. He said his wife dreamed they were on a boat with the number 115 painted on the side of it. He played that number and hit. So he opened up the club and slapped a sign over it—Club 115."

"It was the only place we could go that was like a real club. He served food and brought in different singers from all over." Ruth giggled.

"Roo, you remember that time Junior Walker and the All Stars came to town? Man, you could hardly get through the door of the club."

Ruth nodded and beamed, but never interrupted the stride of Daddy's story.

"Me and Duke knew the bartender and he slipped us in through the back door. The place was but so big. After all the folks jammed in, there was barely enough room left for all the sweat and tall tales that floated around in there." Daddy chuckled. "The whole place was jumping. The dance floor was packed. As soon as the All Stars' set was over, a couple cats got to shouting and talking trash. Before we knew it, chairs and bottles got to flying. The next thing I heard was sirens. Duke took off in one direction and I took off in the other."

"So, what happened?" I asked eagerly.

"Well, I made it outside, but I didn't see Duke. Once I heard the cops busting through the front of the place, I took off running. I was running so fast I lost my left shoe. A brand-new pair of Florsheims. I'd spent the whole summer casting nets and pulling oysters to afford 'em. Hated that too. I loved them shoes."

Ruth and I cracked up. This was the first time I'd ever heard that story. It was also the first time I'd heard of Ruth being in his little circle back in the day when he was younger. I knew they all grew up on the island, including Ma, but Ma was ten years younger than Daddy, so I imagine she was too young to be in the clubs back then. I'd always thought Ruth hadn't entered my parents' lives until later, but apparently, she and Daddy ran in the same crowd when they were young. So, she'd been eyeing my father for decades. I wondered what other little secrets they shared.

Daddy leaned back in his chair and laughed. "Yeah, baby girl, I bet you didn't know your old man could dust it up when he needed to, huh?" Then he got a faraway look in his eye. "Hmph . . . I haven't thought about that night in a long time." He shook his head in disbelief. "I wonder what made me remember it tonight." He looked at Ruth. She smiled sweetly, as if she knew but had decided to keep it between the two of them.

Ruth stood from the table. "I'd better get these dishes done before my TV show comes on."

"You made dinner. I can clean up the kitchen," I said. Daddy's stories had put me in a lighter mood.

"We can do it together," Ruth said with a big smile.

The doorbell rang. "I'll get it," Daddy said.

We started to clear the dishes from the table. After my years of begging, Ma had finally agreed to get a dishwasher, although she rarely used it when she was alive. Ma said gazing out the window while washing dishes gave her the opportunity to think and dream. That was another difference between Ma and Ruth. Ruth didn't mind using the dishwasher because she hated doing dishes. I had to admit, I was on Team Ruth when it came to dishes.

"Deena," Daddy called from the living room. "Come here for a minute."

I handed a spoon and bowl to Ruth and headed to the living room. Uncle Duke was standing beside Daddy. Both men wore a solemn expression when I entered. Unusual, especially for Uncle Duke. No uproarious laughter or a silly joke.

"Hey, what's going on, Uncle Duke?"

Both men glanced at each other before Uncle Duke spoke up. "Holcomb Gardner, the man you said was missing . . ."

"Yeah?"

"I got a buddy works over at the county morgue. He said they brought in a John Doe. Black man. Seventies."

"What?! Oh my gosh, do you think it's Holcomb?"

"I'm not sure. My buddy works the night shift. I don't know if you're up for it but he says he can slip us in through the back if you wanna take a look."

"Now, wait a minute, Duke," Daddy interjected. "Ain't nobody said nothing about looking at no dead bodies. Deena, you don't even know this man. This is something for the police to handle."

"Daddy, I don't know if we can rely on the police. I met Delilah's granddaughter, Rae, and she said the police aren't doing anything to find out who killed Delilah. Think about it. We all know, to the police, to the media, Holcomb and Delilah are just two old Black people who are dead. Nobody's gonna put in any real effort to find out what happened to them."

"And what's your grand plan?" Daddy asked.

I didn't have one so I didn't respond.

"Besides, we don't even know if it's Holcomb. Let the police handle this, Deena. Tell her, Duke."

Uncle Duke gave a wary look at Daddy but said nothing.

"Uncle Duke, would you drive me over there?"

Daddy stared at me. No one said anything for a moment. Daddy finally shook his head. "We'll both drive you over there," he said wearily.

CHAPTER 17

It was after nine o'clock. Dark. Quiet. I'd never been a fan of the darkness. I didn't like the unknown. And what was darkness but a manifestation of the unknown. Perhaps it was the reason I usually asked so many questions. Always trying to see my way out of a situation with information.

Ma told me that when I was little, I would refuse to sit on the porch at night unless they turned on the porch light. To me there was nothing more frightening than a pitch-black night in Low Country Georgia. All the hissing and clicking noises of animals you cannot see. The warm and humid air that crawled against your skin made the darkness seem like something you could see and feel. Now, I wished there were some switch to light up the sky and offer a way to see past this black night.

When Daddy's truck quietly rolled across the black asphalt of the parking lot, my nerves jangled. We pulled up to the side of what looked like a small loading dock with a long ramp, near a door marked "Employees Only." The entire area was illuminated by a single light from the side of the building and a solitary lamppost. Lighting just dim enough to cast the surrounding trees in a sinister-looking silhouette across the parking lot.

Uncle Duke pulled his cell phone from his pocket, filling the cabin of the truck with blue light from the screen. He sent a short text to someone. I was impressed that Uncle Duke had the wherewithal for texting. Most people his age shunned texting in favor of a phone call. A few minutes later, the "Employees Only" door opened. A young Black guy—tall, thin, with shoulder-length locs—waved his hand, motioning us to come in. We slipped out of the truck and followed him inside.

"Hey, what's up, youngblood," Uncle Duke said in a hushed tone. "This is my brother, Butta, and his daughter, Deena." The man nodded. "This here is Monty, Thumb's grandson. We appreciate you doing this for us, Monty."

"No problem, Unc," Monty said. "But we gotta make it fast, the supervisor is on a thirty-minute meal break."

We followed the man down a long narrow hallway until we reached a set of double doors. Despite my initial demands back at the house to chase down the missing Holcomb Gardner, I wasn't quite sure I was ready to see a dead body. I didn't know what kind of shape Holcomb's body might be in, how he'd died or how long ago. Ma's body was the last one I saw, and I was still messed up by that. We passed through the doors and into a huge room with two metal tables. Everything in the room was white, glass, or stainless steel. A metal scale hung from the ceiling between the two metal slabs. For some reason, I looked down at the floor, as if I expected it to be covered in blood and body parts. It was spotless. Suddenly, I didn't want to do this. I shouldn't have insisted that we come here. I wanted to run back to the truck.

"Wait here," Monty said before he walked to the other side of the room and disappeared behind a heavy door. As much as I wanted to break into a sprint and run away, fear locked my feet to the floor. My body tensed, and I stuffed my hands deep into my pockets. Funeral homes and cemeteries terrified me. Now I'd add morgues to the list. A couple minutes later Monty was back, pushing a metal table. On top of it was a blue body bag. Silently, I prayed that Holcomb Gardner wasn't inside of it. If he wasn't, then I'd be free to go back to grieving Ma and trying to figure out my life. I could pretend he was still alive somewhere out there with his gun and his little dog. But if he was in that bag, everything would be different. I just knew it. Deep down inside, I had this feeling that if that old man was dead, my life would be weirdly different.

Monty wheeled the table up to me, Daddy, and Uncle Duke.

We stood silent, watching him slowly open the body bag. The rip of the zipper and the crunch of the hard plastic filled the cavernous space and grew louder as the sounds bounced off the stainless-steel surfaces. Finally, the zipper stopped, and Monty folded back the flap of plastic.

It was him.

Holcomb Gardner.

I stepped closer. The same gray scruff on his face. The same deep-set eyes. The same leathery brown skin, with a grayer hue now.

Daddy put his arm around my shoulders. "God rest his soul," he said.

"What happened to him?" I asked, still staring at his lifeless face.

"That's for the coroner to figure out," Monty said. "But when they found him, he had a needle in his arm."

"Drugs?" Uncle Duke shook his head. "You sure, son?"

Monty nodded.

"But that doesn't seem like the man I met." Then I realized how foolish I sounded. I'd talked to Holcomb for all of ten minutes before he ran me off his property. How would I know what Holcomb did in his private life? A widower who lived alone in a trailer and kept people off his property with a shotgun. Who knew what he was capable of?

"Granddad told me some of these old heads like him came back from the Vietnam War and were hooked on heroin and stuff," Monty said.

"Butta, Holcomb didn't serve, did he?"

Daddy nodded no. "Not as far as I know."

"And you're sure this is the man you met?" Daddy asked.

"Yes."

"Where'd they find him?" Uncle Duke asked.

"Found him near the marshes, over by Coffin Park. Some guys on a cleaning crew found him."

"Was there a dog with him?"

"A dog?" Monty looked at me like I had asked him to grow wings and fly out the nearest window. "Uh . . . I don't think so," Monty said, shaking his head as he started to zip the bag back up.

"What happens next?" I asked.

"The coroner performs an autopsy. If no one comes forward to ID him, they cremate him, and the remains are buried in a potter's field."

"Thanks, Monty," Uncle Duke said. He reached in his pocket and peeled off a fifty-dollar bill and handed it to Monty before we left.

Back in the truck, the three of us sat quiet for a few minutes.

"Baby girl, none of this sits right with me. It's time to go to the police."

"I agree with your daddy," Uncle Duke said.

"But . . ."

"But what?" Daddy turned in his seat to face me.

"Think about it. I think Holcomb has been living out on the island in a trailer for at least two or three years. I went by his house on Old Farm Road—"

"Deena!"

"The house looks like it has been boarded up for years. It's also up for sale by the same realty company selling his island property."

"Fine, the man has decided to tap into some of his wealth."

"He taps into his wealth and then goes out to a park to OD? Somebody killed him and wants it to look like an overdose."

Daddy looked past me and stared at Uncle Duke.

Uncle Duke casually shrugged. "She might have a point, Butta."

"Think about it. If he lives isolated out on the island, why would he come back into Brunswick to shoot up? His sister was killed out on the island near his property. Whoever did this wouldn't want a second body out on the island. It might connect the two deaths. Besides, how many seventy-year-old men do you know who shoot up? Something's not right about all this. Somebody killed this man and threw him away like trash. Just like they did his sister. It's not right. It's not fair."

"You ought not climb into harm's way with this thing, Deena. Leave it alone. Holcomb and Delilah's kin can pursue all this. Didn't you say she has a granddaughter? Let her look into this."

"Delilah's granddaughter is young, and she didn't even know Delilah and Holcomb were related. I think she's already suffered enough losing her mother and her grandmother. This is another blow.

"Ya daddy's right. Best thing for you to do is go to the police. But when you do, don't mention our little visit here tonight. Monty wasn't hired to give morgue tours for cash. We need to keep this one between us."

"But they'll cremate him and all the evidence will be gone with the body. This is exactly what someone wants to happen. Two old people no one cared about. Dead and thrown away while their property is sold off."

Uncle Duke scratched his head. "Sweetie, I'm sure if there's some type of crime involved, the police will keep any evidence they need. But that's not your concern."

"Duke's right. Listen to me, Deena. Whether Holcomb sold that land, or someone stole it from him, do you think anything will change by your digging around in this mess? Maybe you should just keep your head low and let this thing play out with the police."

There it was again. The warning for me to keep my head low. Joe telling me to keep my head low to save my job. Lance telling me to play small to make him look big. And now, Daddy telling me to turn a blind eye even though two people were dead.

Ma's words slipped into my head again. Just as they did when LaShonda asked me to help her with her stepfather's house.

There's always someone worse off than you . . . help one of those souls. That's when God can use you best.

Two innocent people dead. Both of them owned land worth millions.

Who would help them if I didn't?

CHAPTER 18

Holcomb Gardner's dead body stretched out in a blue bag became a still-life portrait effortlessly painted in my brain. I had a hard time falling asleep after we got home from the morgue. But I must have finally dozed off at some point during the night because when I opened my eyes, the sun bathed the entire room in searing bright light. I lay there for a few seconds. I was fuzzy from the lack of sleep. *What day is it? Sunday? No, Thursday.* I had to go to work. Then it occurred to me that it was too bright outside. I glanced at the clock.

Shit.

It was after eight o'clock, an hour after the time I should have gotten up. I'd be late for work. I'd left work early yesterday to go see Rae, and now I'd be late this morning. Joe would have his henchman, aka Peg, standing in the foyer, tapping her watch as I arrived. I unplugged my phone from the charger and checked the local news websites for any reports of an unidentified Black man found dead. Nothing. I tossed the phone on the bed. Who was I kidding? Of course there'd be no reports because nobody gave a damn, especially the media. I jumped out of bed and got ready for work. The cotton dress I wore probably could have used an ironing, but I didn't have time for that. Unless Howie was going to drop by the office again, I didn't care what anyone thought of what I wore to work.

By the time I made it to the kitchen, Ruth was clearing away the breakfast dishes.

"Good morning, Deena. Can I fix you a plate? Me and your Daddy just finished eating a few minutes ago. Everything's still warm."

"Uh . . . no. I overslept. I'll just grab a muffin."

"Are you sure? It's really no trouble."

"I'm sure. Is there coffee?"

"Yes. Let me grab a travel mug for you. You like it black with sugar, right?"

"Uh . . . yeah. Thanks."

I pulled a blueberry muffin from the package in the bread box and watched as she poured my coffee into the travel mug. She poured just the right amount and then added a single teaspoon of sugar. Just the way I did. *Damn*. Ruth watched everything and she missed nothing.

"Listen, your daddy told me where y'all went last night. Ahh, the debble workin' overtime agin' us ooman."

Of course he would tell her. He probably told her everything. And she'd slipped into the Geechee dialect, which told me that the conversation had made her anxious. Now, here was one more person ready to tell me to lie low, to stay in my place. As long as I lived in my childhood bedroom, people assumed it gave them the right to treat me like a child.

Ruth stirred the coffee and placed the lid on the mug. She handed it to me. "You do whatever *you* think is the right thing to do. Those people meant something to someone. They were loved by somebody. If you can figure out a way to make it right, I know you will."

She rubbed my arm softly before she left the room.

I wanted to cry. I was lost. I missed Ma and now Ruth was trying to replace her with advice Ma probably would have given me. The one person I cared for the least was the only one giving me the advice I most wanted to hear.

I thought about Holcomb and Delilah. I didn't have siblings, but I always wished I did. When I was little, I wanted someone to share nighttime secrets with. A sister to share clothes with or a brother to play sports with. Ma told me how difficult it was for her to get pregnant. She used to call me her "almost not a baby" baby. She'd had several miscarriages before she got pregnant with me. Even though Ma was younger than Daddy, she said it had been hard for her to bring babies into the world. So, I fully understood my parents' decision or fate's intervention to make me their only child. But every so often, I wondered what it would have been like to grow older with a sibling. How often did Delilah and Holcomb wonder about their estranged relationship? Maybe Delilah had been attempting to mend fences when she was killed out on the island. Did Holcomb die never knowing his sister was killed just a few feet away from his trailer? It was truly sad the two of them lived a few miles from each other but were still unable to conquer the divide that money and property had caused between them.

There had only been a few times in my life where I felt like I was in over my head: finding out Ma's cancer was terminal, the fiasco at my job with the law firm back in Atlanta, and now. Creeping into the county morgue to identify the body of a man I didn't even know, snooping through his life and rummaging through his family secrets, made me feel like I owed the Gardners something.

The least I could do was find out if the property they owned became the motivation for their murders.

Deena's doggedness has paid off. She found Rae and I couldn't be more pleased. Deena also found Holcomb. Poor Holcomb. I'm so sorry she had to find him like that. I can tell Deena is confused. I'm asking the good Lord and the ancestors to show me how to reach Deena. If I can get her to trust me, then I can show her how to stop those monsters.

And things are moving along as I had hoped. Jimmie told her about Club 115. He talked about the night the fight broke out. It was good to hear that story again. And I understood why he didn't tell her the whole story. He's still trying to protect me. He didn't tell her what we did that night. No one's ever known, not even Duke. For now, it's okay if it's just our secret. But eventually he will have to tell her. It's the only way things will work out and we'll all find peace.

Hope ent neba nutt'n long as oonah mean fa good.

Hope is never in vain.

CHAPTER 19

Peg was Joe's eyes and ears around the office. And she was on task by the time I got to the Old Victorian. She'd walked past my office twice since I'd arrived, probably checking to see if I was "ass-in-chair." Not once did she stop inside to chat or even say hello. She didn't know what time I'd gotten in since I bypassed her when I slipped in through the back door in the break room. Whatever.

My office started to warm with the midmorning sun pouring through the window. I turned to the corner of my desk where I normally kept a small desktop fan. It was gone.

Hmph.

I looked around the room and spotted it on the bookshelf by the door, its electrical cord clumsily falling to the floor. *Who the hell moved my fan?* The cleaning crew Medallion hired was lazy as hell, barely emptying the garbage cans. Not likely they did it.

Peg had told me that someone around the office had been pulling pranks lately and moving things about—staplers found on the windowsill, files moved to the break room. Folks yuck-yucked it up that the house was haunted. I usually tried to send the very unsubtle message that I didn't like pranks and to stay out of my office. Clowns.

I moved the fan back to my desk and plugged it in. I took a sip of coffee from my travel mug and thought about Ruth encouraging me to find Holcomb. Maybe she wasn't as bad as I kept trying to make her out to be. But thoughts of Daddy's and Uncle Duke's warnings rumbled around in my head: *Go to the police . . . That's not your concern . . . You ought not climb into harm's way . . . Leave it alone.*

Maybe they were right. I was ill-equipped to investigate the murder of two people. Maybe If I told Rae about Holcomb being in the county morgue, she could go to the police. But she'd never seen Holcomb before so she wouldn't be able to identify him. She was as nosy as me, so I'd have to tell her where I saw Holcomb's body and I didn't want her to spout off to the police that we were in the morgue looking at a dead body for fifty bucks. Perhaps I did need to manage this whole thing to avoid getting Daddy, Uncle Duke, and most especially Monty, our morgue tour guide, into trouble.

I checked the internet again for any reports of Holcomb Gardner being found. Again, nothing.

Everything was a mess. And all of this was complicated by the fact that someone was following me, lurking around in my life. For that reason alone, I should go to the police.

To hell with it.

I grabbed my keys and purse. I made up some excuse to Jennie about doing some research outside the office and left.

* * *

I STEPPED INSIDE the Brunswick Police Department, a brown-and-tan-colored, nondescript brick building. A young female officer sat behind the information desk. She perked up and gave me a smile composed of metal braces and baby-pink lip gloss. Between the lip gloss on this girl and the booty shorts Rae wore, I was starting to feel ancient. Was I old, or did everyone just look much younger these days? I told the officer that I wanted to file a missing person report. She directed me to wait, and I watched her as she called someone on the phone.

A few minutes later, a stout older man with a gray beard walked up to me. He was dressed in a pair of khakis and a blue button-down shirt, his sleeves rolled up to the elbow. He looked like Santa Claus in business casual.

"Hello. I'm Detective Brian Mallory."

We shook hands. "I'm Deena Wood."

"I understand someone you know is missing?"

"Well, sort of . . ."

He looked at me quizzically. "Why don't we step back here." I followed him down the hall to a small bland room with a table and two chairs. He closed the door and I took a seat.

He smiled. "Now, tell me what's going on," he said as he sat in the chair across from me.

I took a deep breath. "Well . . . I don't exactly know the person . . . I mean . . ."

"Why don't you start at the beginning. Who's missing?"

"Last week, I took a drive out on the island. I sometimes do that to clear my head. I parked and got out to look at the ocean. While I was there, a man . . . he said his name was Holcomb Gardner . . . he told me to get off his property. He said he owned the land, and he wasn't going to sell it. I guess he thought I was working for someone that's trying to purchase it."

Detective Mallory nodded as I spoke. Then, he removed a notepad and pen from a small drawer on his side of the table. He jotted a few notes as I spoke.

"Anyway, a few days later, I went back out to the property, and he was gone. The trailer he was living in, all of it, gone. And there was a sign in front that Empire Realty was offering it for sale. And . . ."

"And what, Ms. Wood?"

"I think something may have happened . . . I think . . . he was murdered."

He stopped writing. "Murdered? Why do you say that?"

I remembered my pledge to Uncle Duke to keep everyone out of it, especially Monty, who worked at the morgue. I didn't want him to lose his job. "I just have a bad feeling. I was wondering if you could check the morgue for a John Doe."

The detective placed his pen down on the table. "Why are you so sure this man is a John Doe in the morgue?"

"He was living out on the island in a trailer alone. I just thought if he's alone . . . If anything happened to him . . ."

"I'll tell you, Ms. Wood, that's an oddly specific request." He hesitated for a beat then smiled at me. "But I guess it's not the oddest thing I've ever been asked to do. But why are you so sure he was murdered?"

"I think his death might be related to his sister's death six months ago."

"Who was his sister?"

"Delilah Gardner. She was killed in a hit-and-run out on the island."

"Hmm . . . I'll check with the Glynn County Police Department. If she was killed out on the island, that would be their jurisdiction. They would be investigating it, not us. Did you know Delilah Gardner? Are you related to her?"

"It's more like I knew of her. A friend of a friend kind of thing."

"I see." He stared at me for what seemed like an eternity. Maybe he could tell I was keeping some information close. Or maybe he was just being a cop and that's what cops do. "Okay. Can you tell me what Holcomb Gardner looks like?"

I described him.

"I'll check it out. Let me get your contact information."

I provided it and he jotted it down on his legal pad.

"There is one other thing."

"What's that?"

"The day Mr. Gardner ran me off his property, a car followed me."

The detective leaned in closer. "I don't understand."

"As I drove away, someone in a black Ford Escape started following me. I later saw that same car in front of my house and at my job."

"Okay, that's not good. Did you get a license tag number?"

"No, and the car windows are tinted so dark I couldn't see who was driving."

"When was the last time you saw the car?"

"Yesterday. The car was parked outside of my job. I tried to get a tag, but it was gone too fast. I don't know. Maybe I'm imagining all this."

The detective smiled. "Or maybe you're not. Here, take my card. If you see the car again, call me. In the meantime, I'll see what I can find out about Mr. Gardner."

I thanked him and left. By the time I got back inside my car, I had a feeling this would probably go into some black hole of police department filings. As nice as the guy seemed, I didn't think he'd put in any extraordinary effort to find out what happened to Holcomb. When had the police ever cared about a missing seventy-something Black man? But I'd done my part. I'd reported it to the police as Daddy and Uncle Duke insisted. I had helped someone else as Ma would want me to do. As for the car following me all over the city, I'd chalk it up to my sleep-deprived imagination.

Maybe now, I was done with the Gardner murders.

* * *

When I got back to the Old Victorian, Jennie handed me a note. Clare wanted to see me in her office. A few butterflies fluttered in my stomach. Had Beau convinced her that I wasn't working as hard as he thought I should, and they'd decided to fire me? But Clare wouldn't do that. Beau was the asshole and he'd reserve that pleasure for himself.

When I arrived in her office, Clare was behind her desk wearing a pair of bright red reading glasses that matched her red dress. I'm sure it was some fancy designer brand. She took a trip to New York City twice a year just to shop for her clothes. I bet she couldn't spell *TJ Maxx*. I didn't necessarily succumb to designer clothes. It was one of the things Lance would frequently point out, telling me I'd make a better impression on people if I put more effort into my appearance. Good gracious. How desperate was I to have married such a jerk?

"You wanted to see me?"

Clare removed her glasses. "Deena! Come in and close the door."

I took a seat in the chair in front of her.

"Soooo . . . ?" she said.

I was confused. "Excuse me?"

"Oh, don't play coy with me. What'd you think of the new law firm? And I'm especially interested to hear what you thought of Howard Lawson." She laced her fingers together and placed them under her chin with this eager look in her eyes.

"Well, I can't tell you much about the meeting. Beau didn't invite me. He and Joe held the meeting without me."

Her playful smile melted like icicles in the winter sun. "What?! How did that happen? I specifically told Beau I wanted you there. How the hell do you hold a meeting with prospective outside lawyers and not invite the one lawyer who works for us? I had to go over to Savannah or else I would have been there."

I shrugged.

"Deena, I am so sorry. I've been away from the office quite a bit lately, but I'll get to the bottom of what happened. I was really hoping to get your take on what you thought of them. There's a really handsome one who works there—"

"Howard Lawson. Yes, I know him. Joe brought him to my office *after* the meeting was over."

Clare looked at me quizzically. "You know him?"

"I do. He grew up here in Brunswick. We ran in the same circles as kids."

"Do tell," Clare said with a sly grin.

"It's nothing like that. We're just old friends."

Clare raised an eyebrow. "Keep an open mind. He's pretty impressive. There's something else I wanted to ask you. I managed to get an afternoon tee time at the club. Come with me. We'll chat and have a little girl time together."

"Oh . . . sure. But you know I'm not much of a golfer."

"Then this will give you a chance to get in some practice. Tuesday at three o'clock. You know how to get there, right?"

"Yes." Clare lived in The Dunes, a gated golf-residential community out on the island. You couldn't get in a house in that place for under two million dollars. "Well, I'd better get back to work."

"Well, well, what kind of hen party are you two up to?"

I turned in my chair and watched Beau strut into Clare's office.

"That's disrespectful, Beau," Clare said sternly.

"It's just a little joke."

"I'm glad you stopped by. I'd like to know how the meeting with Welburton and Harley went."

Beau darted his eyes between me and Clare.

I knew Clare was setting him up to catch him in a lie. I wouldn't budge an inch to help him. "Perhaps Beau can explain better than I can," I said.

"Beau?"

"Uh . . . it went well. Right, Deena?" he said nervously.

"Let me stop you right there before you dig yourself into a hole. Deena just told me that you and Joe didn't include her in the meeting as I had specifically instructed. What I want to know is why?"

"Look, I'm really sorry. I guess it was an oversight on my part. For what it's worth they're a fine group of lawyers but I wonder about their expertise in property law."

"Damn it, Beau! We've discussed this before. We don't need property law experts. What we need—" Clare stopped mid-sentence, suddenly realizing I was in the room. "Deena, would you excuse us, please. I'd like to speak to Beau alone."

I quickly stepped out of the office and closed the door behind me. Beau was about to get a professional ass whipping and Clare didn't want any witnesses.

A little part of me, deep down, snickered.

CHAPTER 20

When I got home that evening, Daddy and Ruth were in the living room. Maybe I was starting to soften, but this time when I walked in the house after work, I didn't resent seeing Ruth in Ma's chair. They both looked up at me as I entered the house.

"There's our little lawyer," Daddy said.

"You hungry, Deena?"

"No thanks, Ruth. Daddy, you're good?"

"I'm pretty fair for an old man."

I squeezed his shoulder. "I'm going to take a shower. I'm beat." I started for the hall.

"Hey," Daddy called behind me. "I wanna ask you something."

I walked back over to the sofa and sat down. I slipped off my shoes and rubbed my feet.

"Did you call the police like Duke and I said?"

This was the conversation I wanted to avoid. I didn't want to regurgitate my visit to the police or anything else about Holcomb Gardner. I didn't want another lecture.

"I did. Honestly, I don't think anything will come of it. The detective probably thinks I'm nuts, but I told them."

"Good. You've done the right thing. The matter is over and put to bed. Now, I need you to take a look at something." He leaned toward the coffee table covered in his afternoon snacks and necessities—at least three remote controls, a half-empty two-liter bottle of Coke, ginger snap cookies, and a huge canister of cashews. He pulled a slip of paper from the food rubble and handed it to me.

Please Join Us
This Saturday at 3 pm
PINEY GROVE BAPTIST CHURCH

Recently, our neighborhood has been flooded with solicitation attempts to purchase our properties. The Harristown community has stood intact in this city for over a hundred years. We can't let the corporate developers destroy what the ancestors built for us. Come out to express your opinion on this matter. We will have an estate planning expert along with a city leader to help us understand and retain what is rightfully ours. Our homes.

"Reverend Tate and some of the folks over at the church have organized this meeting. We need to make sure we put up a united front to keep folks from selling off."

"Makes sense. Who's the city leader attending?" I asked.

"I'm not sure yet. Pee-Wee's house next door has been empty for over a year. Just like a lot of houses on this side of town. I think those yellow flyers might have something to do with it. I want you to come."

"Daddy, I'm not an estate planning lawyer."

"Reverend Tate's got that covered, but I still think you ought to come. For a different reason. This house is the only thing of any value that I own. I've got a will that says one day, it's gonna be yours. You need to be invested in this neighborhood just like I am."

"Is there something you're trying to tell me?"

"No, no. I'm fine but I'm not immortal. Come to the meeting. This is your home too that we'll be talking about."

"You know who really needs to be there? LaShonda. I told you about the problem she's having with some relative of hers who sold his interest in their house. Mr. Duncan didn't have a will like you."

"That's 'cause he didn't have a smart girl like you for a daughter."

I smiled and rubbed the top of Daddy's head.

"Folks don't realize the legacy they have in these homes until they sell 'em off for a few thousand bucks. I'll tell her about the meeting too."

"Okay, Daddy, I'll be there."

* * *

THAT NIGHT, AS I climbed into bed, I thought about all the dead ends I'd run into trying to find information about Empire Realty. A company based in Dallas, Texas, was on a buying spree in south Georgia. Two people who owned property worth millions were dead and their property was now being sold by that same company. Perhaps the police weren't the only ones that might be able to help me. Against my better judgment, I pulled out my phone and tapped in a text message.

Let's do lunch.

I hit send.

Ten seconds later, a reply:

You sure you don't want to make it dinner and a nightcap?

I left him on read.

Two minutes later, my phone buzzed again.

I'll take whatever I can get

Tomorrow. Noon at Hampton's

I smiled, flipped off the light, and snuggled under the covers.

CHAPTER 21

The next day, I tried to make amends for falling off the face time wagon again. Beau's comment in the break room about hiring a part-time paralegal for my position might have provided a bit of motivation as well. I was in my office at the Old Victorian bright and early. The first thing I noticed: my desk fan had been moved again. Instead of sitting on the corner of my desk where I normally kept it, this time it was on my chair. The cord was twisted and fell haphazardly to the floor. *What the hell?* I picked it up and placed it back in its spot on my desk. This was the second time someone had come in here and touched my things. People in this office played too much with all their corny jokes about the place being haunted and it wasn't funny.

I wasn't in my office more than five minutes before Peg was standing in my doorway. She gave me a weak smile and I immediately knew she was there about those damn boxes again.

"Deena, Joe—"

I raised my hand and stopped her mid-sentence. "I know. The boxes in the attic."

"I'm sorry. I'm just the messenger. I don't understand it either. But you know when Beau gets a bee in his bonnet, he just doesn't stop."

I plugged my fan into the electrical socket. "What do you mean Beau has a bee in his bonnet?"

Peg walked inside my office. "Oh, every few months, Beau complains that this place was once his home and we don't give it the respect it deserves, blah, blah, blah."

I shook my head slightly. "I don't understand. This was once Beau's home? I thought he's always lived out on the island, in The Dunes with Clare."

"Didn't you know?"

"Know what?"

"Beau bought this house years ago."

"Wait. Beau owns this house, not Medallion?"

"No, Beau owns it. Clare moved Medallion's office here after he bought it. They worked out of the first floor and Beau lived up on the second floor. Eventually, he renovated the entire house as they started to hire more people."

Peg looked around the room. "He did a pretty good job with the renovations, but it still needs work." And as if on cue, the radiator rattled. "See what I mean? Who ever heard of a radiator making noise when it's not on?" She walked over to it and gave it a swift kick. The radiator knocked hard a couple times before it hissed and finally quieted. "The ghosts are at it again."

"There's no such thing as ghosts. That reminds me. The office prankster has been in my office twice now. I don't like pranks."

"You heard the radiator. You sure it's not the ghosts?"

I rolled my eyes.

Peg smiled and whispered, "I'll get the word out."

"And I'll take care of the boxes. I promise. Hey, can I ask you something?"

"Sure."

"Have you ever heard of a real estate company called Empire Realty?"

"Hmm . . . I don't think so. Why do you ask?"

"Uh . . . I'm planning to buy a house. Just looking for a realtor. That's all."

"Okay. Don't forget, there's potluck in the kitchen for lunch today. What'd you bring?"

"I'm so sorry, I forgot to stop by the store to pick up something. I won't eat anything since I didn't put in my fair share." As if I had planned to do so. I didn't do office potlucks. I was surprised they were still happening since the chili cook-off potluck took out the entire office with food poisoning. Well, everyone except me and Jennie, who was vegan. We were the only two people who didn't eat at that potluck.

"I'm sure it'll be fine if you eat. See ya at lunch."

When hell freezes over. I smiled and waved as she left my office. I thought about heading to the attic to tackle those boxes, but Holcomb's boarded-up house out on Old Farm Road flashed through my mind. Whoever was behind Empire had to be involved in the Gardners' murders. Empire obviously had a financial interest since they were selling two pieces of property Holcomb owned. I pulled up my internet browser and decided to do some quick research on Empire Realty. Once again, nothing but dead ends. The same phone number that went into a bunch of voice-activated prompts and a voicemail box. And yet, they were selling an island property worth millions and the owner of it was lying in the morgue as a John Doe.

Once I found out who was behind Empire Realty, I'd leave all this alone.

CHAPTER 22

I showed up at Hampton's at twelve noon exactly. The waitress seated me at a table near the window overlooking the sea. Howie had picked this restaurant and probably this table too. Hampton's Restaurant was out on the island, situated against the creamy white sand dunes and their tall green grasses fanning in the sea breeze. The Atlantic Ocean just beyond the dunes with waves and whitecaps scrambling up against the shore. All of it made me hungry for the summer days ahead.

Inside, the restaurant was one of those light and airy places with a coastal vibe—whitewashed wood and shiplap walls everywhere with an open kitchen looking out onto the table seating. I peeked at the menu. Fifty-five dollars for a lunch portion of steak! Howie had picked this place to impress me. But I wasn't interested in falling back into some high school crush. I needed help and right now, he was the best I could do under the circumstances.

Howie was late, not a good look if he was trying to impress me. I'd been waiting so long, the waitress stopped by the table twice, once to refresh my water glass and again to ask if I wanted to order an appetizer. I tried not to get pissed. He had something that I needed. But I was about thirty seconds from grabbing my purse to leave when Howie came hustling up to the table.

"I'm so sorry I'm late. Last-minute fire popped up and I was the only one around that could put it out." He chuckled and leaned down to kiss me on the cheek.

I was suddenly embarrassed, although I didn't know why.

"Did you order for us?"

"No. I thought . . ." Before I could think of something clever to say, the waitress saved me by walking up to the table.

"Good afternoon, Mr. Lawson. Can I get you your usual?"

He glanced up at her and smiled. "That would be great. Thanks."

"Absolutely," she said before she headed to the bar.

"So, you have a *usual* in a place like this? I peeped the menu."

Howie smiled. "Business lunches with the firm. You know how it is." Now Howie looked embarrassed.

"No, I don't know how it is." I swizzled the lemon around in my glass of sweet tea with my straw. "Maybe you'd care to provide some insight."

Howie took a deep breath like he was bracing himself. "Deena, I'm sorry about what happened back in Atlanta. It was all bullshit. We both know it. You didn't deserve that."

I just stared at him before I took a sip of tea. I hadn't discussed what happened with my job back in Atlanta with anyone, not even my own father. But Howie knew.

"Look, I didn't come here to dredge up old *bullshit*, as you call it. I need—"

"Can you just let me explain?"

"Howie—"

"Please. Just hear me out. I didn't know your firm was going to fire you. I didn't find out until after you left. I tried calling you, but if you remember, you wouldn't return my calls or text messages. No one at my company blamed you for the outcome of the trial. I think your firm needed a scapegoat, and you were it. Believe me, I never spoke an ill word about you." Howie smiled. "I used to enjoy telling people you were my lawyer. It was like a little inside joke between us."

I stared out the window. Feelings of being an incompetent failure rushed across me like flames licking a burning house. Getting fired from my old law firm after losing at trial was my great and hidden shame. Ma's pride in her daughter, the big shot lawyer. Daddy's baby girl, the lawyer. I was grateful neither of them knew.

Howie had worked at Haynes Corp, a manufacturing company on the outskirts of Atlanta. My law firm had been hired to defend his company in a manufacturing defects lawsuit. I was the trial attorney. Perhaps I had no one to blame but myself when I lost the case and the plaintiff was awarded seven figures at trial. Ma was sick at the time. Lance was being Lance and screwing other women. I wasn't focusing. I missed some key evidence. If I'd been on top of things, I would have properly evaluated the evidence and persuaded the company to settle before trial. But I wasn't and I didn't. The long and short of it: the managing partner at my firm told me I had three months to find another job. My last day at the firm was also the same day Lance asked me to pack my things and leave *his* condo. All of it on the heels of Ma's death nearly broke me. I slept in my friend Bridget's spare bedroom for a couple months before I moved back to Brunswick to lick my wounds.

"Dee, that firm you worked for was garbage. They always took ethical risks."

"Your company hired the firm. Whatever."

"I know it doesn't help you, but I left the company about a month after you left that firm."

"Why'd you leave?"

"What they did to you was just the tip of the iceberg of the bullshit they used to do. The company that hired your garbage firm was garbage too. They cut too many corners. They'd had three recalls for manufacturing defects. The last one they didn't even make public. The big salaries they paid us were like hush money payments and I didn't like the way it made me feel, and I didn't want to play fast and loose with my law license."

"Oh . . . I didn't know that."

He raised an eyebrow. "You would have if you had answered my calls." The waitress returned with his drink, a glass that held brown liquor and one of those large, block ice cubes embossed with the letter *H* for Hampton's. I didn't have a clue what his *usual* was. He took a sip. "Anyway, I moved back here."

"Why'd you come back to Brunswick? With your résumé, you could have gone to D.C. or New York. Why back to small town America?"

Howie stared down into his drink for a beat. "I guess I had hit a point where I didn't know what I wanted anymore. I'd just come through an ugly divorce. Haynes Corp had me questioning my values. I wasn't sure what to do next. I came home one weekend to visit my mom."

"How is your mom? I haven't seen her since I've been back."

"She's living her best widowed life. She figured a way forward past the grief. Always on a cruise or flying off with her girlfriends. Of course, she's always asking about you . . . and me."

I shook my head and blew off the comment. I wasn't ready to jump into something else and I didn't know when I would be either. Lance had emotionally banged me up pretty good. Howie might have a long wait on his hands if he was waiting for me.

"Anyway, that visit was different somehow. It did me some good. Just walking around town. Talking to folks in the old neighborhood.

Talking to people who knew me before I was Howard Lawson, Esquire. Who knew me as Howie. It gave me some perspective. It helped me see that there's still some work that needs to be done here at home. And I can help. So, what about you?"

"Ha! My story isn't quite as deep and philosophical as yours. I lost my mother, my marriage, and my job all in the span of a year. I needed a soft place to land."

"Sounds like we both came back for the same reason." Howie softly rubbed his forefinger across the back of my hand. A rush of butterflies swirled in my stomach, and I slid my hand underneath the table and onto my lap.

"So, how do you like working at Welburton and Harley?"

"It's pretty good so far. I'm really enjoying the work. And they do a lot of pro bono work for the community. I like that. I feel like I'm giving something back to repay the community that raised me. How about you? How do you like working for Medallion?"

"I don't but that's a long story for another day. The only saving grace is Clare Walsh, the head of the company. We get along really well. She's a hustler. Gets stuff done. But Beau. He's a different story."

"Yeah, I met him when I was over there the other day. He strikes me as the type who's had everything handed to him and still it's not enough, and he even complains about the manner in which it was given to him."

I laughed. "That's a perfect way to describe him. Clare raised him after her brother and sister-in-law were killed in a boating accident when he was a kid. I like Clare but I think she created the monster she's now trying to control."

We both laughed. Then, I remembered why I had agreed to this lunch.

"Listen, Howie, I need your help."

"Sure. Anything."

"Ugh . . . where do I start?"

He looked at me in confusion. "Are you in some kind of trouble?"

"No . . . well, I hope not."

"So what is it?"

"There's a man who went missing after he vowed he'd never sell his land. I just learned that man is in the county morgue as a John Doe. Here's the crazy part. His sister was killed six months ago in a mysterious hit-and-run."

"And you think the deaths are linked?"

I leaned in closer to whisper. "They owned some very expensive oceanfront property out here on the island. That land is being sold by Empire Realty. Have you ever heard of them?"

"No."

"The company operates like a shell. I can't find much information about it."

Howie shook his head in disbelief. "How did you find all this out?"

"That's not important. Right now, I need you to help me find out who's behind Empire Realty. It might explain why those people were killed for their land."

"Okay, but why are you all involved in this?"

"I don't know. It was something about him—Holcomb Gardner—that's the man's name. The first time I encountered him, he told me people had been trying to get him to sell his land. A few days later, everything's gone. Holcomb. His trailer. Even his dog. Everything. I was able to find his great-niece. She's the one who told me her grandmother, Holcomb's sister, was killed in a hit-and-run and she said the police aren't doing much to find out who did it."

“So, how did you find out Holcomb was a John Doe in the morgue?”

I took a deep breath. Howie, with all his sophisticated manner and elite education, would think my family was nuts.

“Uncle Duke has a buddy who works over in the morgue. He let us in, and I saw him. I recognized him. He was the same man who went missing from the property.”

Howie smiled. “Good ole Uncle Duke. So, have you gone to the police? If this man and his sister were killed, the police should be investigating.”

“I talked to a detective about it but I just have a feeling nothing will come of it. The woman’s granddaughter tells me the police are dragging their feet on the investigation of her grandmother’s murder. You’re in that fancy law firm with unlimited resources. Just help me find out who owns Empire Realty. Please.”

I stared out the window again. Maybe I was losing my mind. I was actually sitting across a table from an old lover asking him to climb into the middle of this mess. “Maybe my imagination has gotten the best of me. But something’s not right about all this. I think some innocent people have been killed.”

“Don’t worry about it. We use an investigation firm from time to time. Let me see what I can find out.” He leaned back in his chair. “How is it after all these years I can never refuse you anything?” He winked.

I felt my face go hot. “Where’s that waitress? I’m hungry.”

Something told me I would pay for this. I’d called in a favor and now Howie would use it to wiggle his way back into my life. I’d cross that bridge when I came to it. I needed his help more than his affection. The waitress finally came over to take our orders. The hour passed quickly. I realized this was the first time since Ma’s funeral that I truly felt relaxed and comfortable. We talked about his job, his new condo, and local people we knew in common. We even talked about the house I'd put an offer on. We talked about everything except us.

Damn it. Howie was working his magic again.

CHAPTER 23

After I finished lunch with Howie, I decided to pop in on Rae for a quick chat to tell her about finding Holcomb's body at the morgue and getting Howie to help us. If Empire Realty had somehow illegally obtained Holcomb's property, then they had stolen from her too. His property was her legacy.

I rang the doorbell. No answer. No car in the driveway either. She was young. Maybe she was out having a good time with her friends.

As I started to get back into my car, an older woman stepped out onto the porch at the house next door. "You looking for Rae?"

"Yes."

"I haven't seen Rae in a couple days. I'm a little worried too. It's not like Rae not to come home at night."

"Wait. What?"

"I try to keep an eye out on things since Delilah died. Rae ain't but twenty-five and living in that house all by herself."

Rae looked younger than I'd first guessed. I edged closer to the woman's porch. "When was the last time you saw her?"

"Day before yesterday. I saw you drop her off at her house. I take it you must be a friend of hers."

"Yes, I am."

"I knocked on her door last night when I hadn't seen her all day.

No answer. I still keep a spare key her grandmama gave me. I even went inside and looked around this morning. Her bed hasn't been touched."

My stomach sank as if it were pulled by a lead weight. Rae was gone. This was the third person in the Gardner family who was in danger.

"We have to call the police."

CHAPTER 24

I learned Rae's neighbor was Mrs. Ellen Trainor as I sat on her sofa sipping from a mug of coffee she insisted on making me while we waited for the police.

"I've lived here in Harristown since I married Raiford. He's gone on to glory now."

Mrs. Trainor was a slender, brown-skinned woman. Beautiful in an elegant, matriarchal way. Her hair was pressed and smoothed slick into a bun at the top of her head. Her eyes crinkled when she smiled, and looking at her, I understood what people meant when they said someone's eyes sparkled. That's what they did as she talked about her husband, Raiford Trainor.

"Raiford insisted we live here after we married and moved to Georgia from Alabama. He loved being close to the water. And beloved, let me tell you, whatever Raiford said was it. He was a good man, but I learned to pick my battles with him." She hesitated and stared out the window. "I miss that old bull. He's been gone going on five years now."

"I'm sorry," I said.

"Nothing to be sorry about. He loved me, made a good home for me and the kids. I remember when the kids were growing up, Raiford used to ask them, *Have you made good choices today? Have you done something to make the world a better place?* And I'm proud to say they have too. My son's a college professor and my daughter's a pediatrician. Raiford lived a good life. When you do that, no need for regrets at the end. That's what Raiford told me."

The doorbell rang.

"I suspect that's the police. What's his name again?"

"Detective Mallory." I'd called him since Rae's disappearance might be related to my missing person's report for Holcomb.

"Okay," she said.

Detective Mallory stepped inside. "Have a seat, Detective," Mrs. Trainor said.

We all sat down and Mrs. Trainor opened things up. "We called you about our friend Raynell. We call her Rae."

"Maybe you can tell me why you're so certain Raynell . . . uh, Rae may be in danger."

"Rae's grandmother is Delilah Gardner," I said. "She was the woman I told you about who was killed in a hit-and-run accident out on the island about six months ago. I'm worried whoever killed Rae's grandmother might be involved in her disappearance."

"Hmm . . . I see." Mallory pulled a small notebook from his pocket and scribbled in it. He turned to Mrs. Trainor. "And you said you haven't seen her in a couple days, is that right?"

"Rae is a pretty smart young woman. I've never known her to just disappear for days."

"I see."

"Detective," I said, "everyone in this young woman's family is dead. Her grandmother and her uncle have died under mysterious circumstances. We're worried that she might be in some serious danger too."

"Who's her uncle?"

I hesitated for a moment. "The man I told you about. Holcomb

Gardner. He's Delilah Gardner's brother. Did you find Mr. Gardner's body at the morgue?"

Mrs. Trainor whipped her head around toward me in surprise.

Detective Mallory pursed his lips. "About that. I didn't find the man you described. I've checked the morgue and the local hospitals."

"Are you sure? You checked for a John Doe at the morgue?"

"I did. The morgue does not have any unidentified bodies. Perhaps a family member came forward and claimed the body. I checked the local hospital as well for a John Doe *and* Holcomb Gardner. Nothing turned up."

"Are you sure?" I repeated.

The detective gave me a look of concerned pity. "I'm sure."

"But . . . I don't know how but I think all of this is connected."

"I'm not sure I understand."

"Me either, to be honest. I just know that Holcomb Gardner owned some very expensive property. He's dead, his sister is dead, and now her granddaughter is missing. And their land is up for sale."

"You keep saying Mr. Gardner is dead, but so far, I can't confirm that. Maybe you just stumbled on some homeless guy who fed you a line."

"No . . ." I didn't want to get Uncle Duke or Monty in trouble by confessing what I'd seen in the morgue. "I don't think it's like that."

The detective jotted something else down in his notebook, then looked back at me. "Okay, Ms. Wood, let me go take a look around her house and see if anything looks suspicious."

Mrs. Trainor chimed up. "I have a spare key to her house in case of emergencies. I'd consider this an emergency."

"Fine. I'll take a look inside too in that case."

Mrs. Trainor left to retrieve the key.

"Ms. Wood, how do you know Mr. Gardner?"

"I told you. I stumbled onto his property accidentally. He told me he would never sell it, but now it's up for sale and he's dead."

"But there's no evidence that he's dead. What about the black car you said has been following you? Have you seen it again?"

"No."

The detective stared at me for a moment before he gave me a weak smile. "Don't worry, Ms. Wood. We'll figure this all out."

I started to doubt myself. But I couldn't be imagining all this. I did see that car following me. I did see Holcomb's body in the morgue.

Mrs. Trainor was back in the living room. "Here's the key. Now, this opens the back door, but you have to give it a jiggle."

"Thank you. I'll be right back."

Detective Mallory walked out the door.

"Lord, I pray Rae is alright," Mrs. Trainor said. "And I never knew Delilah had a brother. In the ten years I'd known her, she never mentioned a brother. And you think he's dead?"

As she spoke, my anxiety grew. I didn't have time to explain Delilah's family dysfunction to her. My curiosity finally got the better of me. I stood from the sofa and headed out the door a minute or so behind the detective.

"Where are you going?" she said.

"I'll be back. You sit tight."

I walked outside and around to the back of Rae's house. The detective had left the back door open, but there was no immediate sight of him. I stepped inside and looked around. The kitchen was clean and tidy. By the time I made my way to the living room, Detective Mallory was coming out of the bedroom.

"Did you find anything suspicious?"

"No, but if we're going to find your friend, you need to let me do my job. From what I can tell, nothing looks out of place. But let me get this straight. You told me your friend's grandmother died in a hit-and-run, now her uncle is missing—"

"Dead. I just feel certain of it."

He stared at me for a beat. "If you're right about all this, it's more than a coincidence. Let me dig into this further. Come on, let's go."

* * *

I HEADED BACK to the office. I'd used up my entire lunch hour and then some, chasing down the Gardners. I sped down Altama to get back to SoGlo without being too late. Now, my head was spinning. Rae was missing, and Holcomb was too—from the morgue. How could his body be gone when it was there a few nights ago? My first thought was to call Daddy and tell him what the detective said about Holcomb. But that would buy me another lecture about the separation between my nose and my face. Instead, I dialed Uncle Duke's number.

"That you, Deena?"

Uncle Duke always had the same greeting whenever I called, as if my name on his caller ID was a lie.

"Hey! Something weird just happened. The detective that I talked to about Holcomb, he told me that Holcomb's body isn't in the morgue."

"Say what?! We just saw him the day before yesterday."

"I know. He said the morgue has no unidentified bodies. He seems to think a family member signed his body out."

"I guess that's possible, but who? Maybe the niece you found. Maybe she found out about all that property and she's staking out her claim."

"Maybe."

"Hang on for a sec," Uncle Duke said.

I heard him laughing with someone in the background, then I heard the tinkle of the bell over the door as someone left the shop.

"Alright, sweetie, sorry about that. Had to see someone out. I guess I could call Monty and ask what happened with Holcomb's body."

"If you have his number, I can call him."

"Sure. Hang on."

A minute later, Uncle Duke rattled off Monty's phone number. "Thanks."

I dialed the number.

"Hey, Monty. This is Deena. I don't know if you remember me. I was the woman who came over the other night with my dad and uncle."

"Uncle Duke. Oh yeah. I remember. Y'all wanna see some more bodies?"

Oh good Lord. Either he thought we were nuts or he was looking to make more morgue tour money. "No. I just need some information. The body we looked at, the old man who was a John Doe with a needle in his arm, I understand he's no longer there. I want to know who signed his body out of the morgue."

"Hmm . . . hang on. Let me take a look."

I heard a clunking sound echo into the phone as he sat it down.

A minute later, Monty returned to the phone. "Okay, I got the paperwork here. It looks like a relative signed him out. It says here Dan . . . uh . . . no. I'm sorry. It was Deena Wood. Hmph. Isn't that your name?"

Deena Wood!

I got lightheaded and thought I would pass out when I heard Monty say my name.

"Hello? . . . You still there?" he said.

"Uh, yeah. Um . . . can you tell me the official cause of death?"

"Well, we don't know. Whoever signed him out declined the autopsy. Had him transferred to McGinty's Funeral Home."

"What? When?"

"Yesterday. That's all I got."

I finally found enough air in my lungs to speak. "Thanks, Monty."

I pulled the car over to the side of the road and stared at my trembling hands on the steering wheel. Someone had used my name to check Holcomb's body out of the morgue. When I was able to stop shaking and gathered enough wherewithal to open my phone again, I looked up McGinty's Funeral Home. It was a local mortuary that had been around for decades, but I was hard-pressed to recall them ever handling Black bodies. I checked the website looking for any details they might have about Holcomb's arrangements. There was no mention of Holcomb so I dialed their phone number.

"McGinty's Funeral Home. How may I help you?" A man's gentle voice.

"Uh . . . I . . . I'm trying to get details on the services for Holcomb Gardner. I didn't see anything on your website."

"Please hold."

The man placed me on hold for what seemed like an eternity. No music or ads. Just a long ribbon of silence. My brain was numb from the thought that someone would use my name as the next of kin. First, someone was following me. Now, this.

The silence was finally broken. "Thank you for your patience. Mr. Gardner's family has declined a memorial service. They've requested a cremation."

"Cremation?"

"Yes. The remains have been transferred to the crematory."

"Uh . . . can you give me the name of the family member, please? I . . . I'm an old family friend and I'd like to pay my respects."

"That would be Ms. Deena Wood."

There it was again. My name. My name associated with Holcomb Gardner.

"Do you have an address for her?"

"I'm sorry, ma'am. That information is confidential."

I couldn't speak. I couldn't think. I simply clicked off the phone and drove away.

CHAPTER 25

I slept in late on Saturday morning. Something I hadn't done since right after Ma's death. I was tired. The kind of tired sleep can't fix. Ruth and Daddy were kind enough not to knock on my door or bother me. Maybe they'd gone out shopping.

I laid in bed, listening to the birds chirping outside my window. In that moment, I realized I hadn't gone out driving to listen for Ma's voice since Rae handed me the picture of the young Holcomb and Delilah Gardner. I'd forgotten about my own mother because I'd become so consumed with two people I didn't even know. I felt so guilty I almost started to cry.

Before I knew it, the guilt slipped all over me and sent me careening into the memory of the night Ma died. I'd been home for the weekend, as I was every weekend after her diagnosis. She'd had a marked improvement. She was sitting in her recliner, and we talked and laughed the entire time. By Sunday, she was doing so well that I decided to head back to Atlanta a little earlier than I normally did. I was preparing for trial, and I wanted to get a leg up on some pretrial motions I was preparing. I kissed her goodbye and made the five-hour drive north. I stopped to get gas in the small town of Metter and called home. Ma said how much she loved me and what a great time we'd all had. The last thing she told me before we hung up: *Keep making me proud. I love you.*

By the time I pulled into the garage at Lance's condo, Daddy called. He told me the hospice nurse was there, and that Ma wasn't feeling too good. His voice trembled as he told me that maybe, if it wasn't too much trouble, I might want to drive back home. I made a U-turn in the garage and took the same route back. I didn't even remember driving home. I just kept praying to God to keep her alive until I got there. I prayed that somehow she'd miraculously be up and waiting for me in the recliner, with Daddy apologizing for having called me and worrying me so. I called Daddy at some point during the drive and had him put the phone to Ma's ear. I was crying and pleading with her to just hang on because I was coming back to her. The miles back home disappeared into a blur of tears and sobbing prayers to God to let her live long enough for me to see her again. I wanted to be close to her when she closed her eyes for the last time.

When I walked back inside the house on Campbellton Street, Ma was gone. The nurse was kind enough not to call the funeral home until after I arrived. I slipped into the bedroom and sank to my knees beside her. For the next hour, I cried and begged her to forgive me for not being at her side as she took her last breath. I should have been there, and I wasn't. I don't think I'll ever forgive myself for that.

This was the memory of Ma that I hated most of all because it made me hate myself. I'd prioritized work over her that Sunday morning so I wasn't there for her when I should have been. Work and a job I eventually lost. She was the reason I became a lawyer. She'd raised me to believe that I had the ability to do something large in the world, that I had the power to help other people. And yet, I was powerless to help the one person who meant so much to me.

I realized that if I continued to focus on that awful memory, I was setting myself up for a day full of tears while lying in the fetal position. I threw back the covers and sat up on the edge of the bed. I'd texted Rae twice before I went to bed and still no reply when I checked my phone. I scrolled through the local news station's website to see if there was anything about a missing Black woman. *Stupid*. Rae was neither white nor blond. Not very likely it would be picked up. Much like Holcomb's disappearance and death.

I grabbed my purse from the bedside table. I dug through it and pulled out the detective's card that he'd given me at the station. He didn't pick up when I called, so I left a voicemail for him asking about the status of his investigation into Rae's disappearance and telling him I had some new information. Maybe that might spark him to return my call with some urgency.

And who the hell was posing as me to sign a body out of the morgue?

Finally, I got up, jumped into a pair of jeans, a T-shirt, and my Nike sneakers. I kept an eye on my phone, expecting Detective Mallory to call me back. That was wasted effort. If I thought the police didn't care about seventy-something Black men, what made me think they would care about a twenty-five-year-old Black woman. This was the same town where a young Black man was murdered simply for going out on an afternoon jog through a neighborhood. Tensions had eased since Ahmaud Arbery's death, but some mindsets still had a way to go.

The more I thought about the detective, the more I realized the conversation we'd had at Mrs. Trainor's house was off. I hadn't recognized it at the time, but there was something amiss when we talked to him. Now, I knew what it was. I quickly brushed my hair back into a ponytail and grabbed my keys and wallet.

I was nearly out the front door when I heard Daddy behind me.

"Hey, where are you off to?"

I turned around. He was sitting at the dining room table eating a slice of bacon and reading the newspaper. "What's your rush?"

"Morning, Daddy. I have to take care of something . . . for work." I didn't want another lecture from him.

"Alright, baby girl. But you're still coming to the meeting at the church this afternoon, right?"

"Yep. I'll be there. Promise. Gotta go."

* * *

I PARKED IN the lot for the Brunswick Police Department. As luck would have it, Detective Mallory was walking toward the building. I hustled out of my car and cut him off before he made it inside.

"Hey! Detective Mallory, you got a minute?"

"Good morning, Ms. Wood."

"I left you a voicemail. Anything on Rae Gardner?"

"Unfortunately, nothing yet."

"What have you done so far to find her?"

Mallory gave me a sheepish look. "Trust me, we're doing everything to find her."

"So why haven't I seen anything on the news about her disappearance?"

"I don't have any control over what the news media picks up. But I assure you, we are working on finding your friend."

"If she were white, blond, and blue-eyed, I would have seen you holding a news conference, asking for the public's help. She's missing and her whole family is dead. Why is this not an urgent matter for you?"

Mallory rubbed his forehead and sighed deeply. "Listen, I've seen situations like this before. A young girl has a fight with her parents or her boyfriend, takes off for a day or two to let off some steam. There's nothing to suggest foul play. As for her family, her grandmother's death was a tragic accident. And as for the uncle, there's no proof he's dead or even exists, for that matter. There's not much to investigate. I'm sorry."

"But you have to do something. It's not fair. A few years ago, a white woman faked her own disappearance so she could have an extended booty call with an old boyfriend, while the police turned this country upside down looking for her. She shows up with self-inflicted bruises and claims a couple Hispanic women kidnapped and tortured her. But I can't get you to investigate a missing Black woman whose closest relative was killed under mysterious circumstances? Do you not see the injustice of this?"

"Ms. Wood, I agree the world isn't fair, but . . . I'm sorry. I have to get inside now."

He quickly strode inside the building and I was left standing outside wondering why the Gardner family didn't matter to the Brunswick Police Department.

CHAPTER 26

My conversation with Detective Mallory had been like talking to a doorstop. I was pissed so I decided I'd handle this a different way. I drove straight to Mrs. Trainor's house. She was standing out front with a hose, watering her flower beds. She was dressed in a pair of pink slacks and a loose-fitting floral top. As before, her hair was pressed and her eyes twinkling. She turned off the hose and waved when I pulled into her driveway.

"Hey, Deena. You're back."

"I am."

"I still ain't seen Rae."

I eased out of my car. "She still hasn't answered my text messages either. Do you have a few minutes? I wanted to talk to you. Maybe we could go inside."

"Of course."

She hooked the hose over the spigot and I followed her inside the house. "I was just about to make myself a bit of lunch. You care to join me?"

"No, thanks."

Inside, her whole house smelled like Low Country heaven. I'd run out of the house without eating and I was hungry, but I didn't want to put her through any trouble. And Ma had taught me not to eat out of everybody's kitchen. Besides, she was probably living on a fixed income and the last thing she needed was me hogging her rations.

Inside her kitchen, she walked over to the cabinet before she turned back to me. “You sure you won’t join me? Fish and grits. Come on, sugar. I cooked more than I can ever eat before it goes bad. And I hate eating alone.”

I relented. “Sure.”

Mrs. Trainor smiled. “Good. Sit down.”

She reminded me of Ruth, hustling and bustling around the kitchen. Plates and silverware clattering, her tapping the serving spoon against the pot. She placed a brightly colored plate down in front of me. The fish sat atop a large mound of creamy grits, all of it smothered in a steaming gravy of okra and tomatoes. I caught the whiff of cream and butter and black pepper as my mouth watered. This was my favorite part of Low Country living, which I missed back in Atlanta. The food. It always conjured up feelings of warmth and love and family meals around a big table.

“This looks delicious, Mrs. Trainor.”

“This was Raiford’s favorite. Sometimes, I wake up on mornings like this, you know, when I miss him real bad, and I’ll make his favorite dish.”

I smiled. This must be Mrs. Trainor’s equivalent to me listening for Ma’s voice. Everyone handled grief in their own way.

“It makes me feel a little closer to him. I know he’s still with me. They always are.”

“What do you mean? They’re always with us?”

“Beloved, folks don’t leave you just because their earthly body has been stilled. Their spirit is strong and everlasting. They are always around us. Watching over us. Guiding us.”

I thought about Ma, and I immediately tamped down the urge to cry. I wished I could be as strong as Mrs. Trainor or Rae. They had made peace with their loss, moved past the heartache. But not me. Ma's death was like an oozing wound that wouldn't heal.

Mrs. Trainor made a plate for herself. "You ever have a time when you were planning to do one thing, but you had this overwhelming sensation not to do it? Or maybe you thought of doing something and everything in your logical mind told you it was crazy but you had to do it anyway? Honey, that's your loved one's spirit guiding you toward the right thing. God and the ancestors are always leaning low to hear us, to guide us. You just have to be wise enough to listen."

Mrs. Trainor was describing my persistent need to dig into the Gardners' deaths. But this spiritual realm with ghosts floating around that she talked about wasn't necessarily something I leaned into. Nonetheless, I respected her opinion and nodded in agreement.

I ate a hearty scoop of the fish and grits and it all practically melted in my mouth. Mrs. Trainor, Ma, and Ruth had all graduated from that Gullah-Geechee school of cuisine where you added herbs and spices and allowed them to infuse the food and release the flavor. Nothing more. Nothing less. Just hand-me-down recipes of fresh food and the right seasonings that simmered to perfection. I let the food bathe my senses. The smell. The taste. Even the sight of the golden-brown fish glistening on top of the bounty of creamy grits.

Mrs. Trainor sat at the table, bowed her head, and said a silent blessing over her food before starting her meal. I suddenly felt like a heathen for rushing right into my food, no prayer.

"Have you talked to that detective again?" Mrs. Trainor asked.

"Yes, ma'am. That's why I stopped by. I don't think he's taking Rae's disappearance seriously. The more I think about it, the more I realize there was something about him that doesn't sit right with me."

"What do you mean, child?"

"Well, for one thing, he didn't ask us for a description of Rae. If someone is missing, don't the cops usually ask for a description or a picture or something to go on?"

"You're right, beloved. He didn't ask us for a description of Rae, did he? Maybe he remembered her from the investigation into Delilah's death a few months back? Ooh, just awful, it was." Mrs. Trainor shook her head in disbelief.

"I just cornered him at the police station. He's not even looking for her. As for Delilah's death, he told me the Glynn County police were responsible for investigating it. He wasn't familiar with the hit-and-run accident when I mentioned it to him. Did Rae ever tell you anything about the investigation or the detective looking into her grandmother's death?"

She rested her fork on the side of her plate. "Lemme see. She said she called a couple times and got no answers. I think after that, she kinda gave up on the police. They didn't have any interest in finding justice for her or Delilah."

"Hmm . . . like I said, something about that detective wasn't right. Even when he went inside her house. He didn't look around for more than a couple minutes and then he was out of there."

"Well, what did he say when you went in there behind him?"

"He said everything looked in order. But now he's telling me his experience indicates that Rae has just run off, that she'll be back. He isn't doing anything to find her."

"Oh, beloved, maybe I shouldn't have been so quick to give him the key, huh? I guess I was just concerned about Rae. That poor girl."

We both ate in silence for a few minutes.

Mrs. Trainor finished a bite of food then tapped me lightly on the arm. "I don't know if this means anything but that detective that came to the house, I got to thinking about him after he left. I've seen him somewhere before. But I can't remember where."

"Really?"

"I'm old now and my memory ain't what it used to be."

"Do you remember how long ago it might have been?"

She shook her head with a puzzled look on her face. "I don't. I just know I've seen him somewhere before."

"Can I give you my phone number? Maybe if you remember, you can call me."

"Sure. That'll be fine." She rose and headed to the countertop near the fridge. She returned to the table with an iPad. She flipped to her contacts app before she handed it to me.

"Just put it in here. That way, I won't lose it."

I smiled. "You're really organized."

"My granddaughter and her husband gave me that two Christmases ago. I love it 'cause now I don't have a bunch of little pieces of paper all over the house with numbers on them. I always say, use whatever the good Lord gives."

"Well, that's a good rule to follow," I said as I typed my number into her device.

I finished the last of my lunch. "That was delicious, Mrs. Trainor. Thank you."

"Anytime, beloved."

"By the way, are you going to the meeting at the church this afternoon? The one about the flyers that have been going around the neighborhood?"

"Oh yes. Like I said, me and Raiford bought this house when we first moved to Georgia, and I'll be damned if I'm going to let somebody run me out of it."

"Good for you! Mrs. Trainor, I had another reason for stopping by. I was wondering if you'd let me borrow the spare key to Rae's house. I just want to take a look around. Like I said, I don't think that cop is doing much to find her."

"Well . . . I guess it's okay since you're a friend of Rae's. I'll go get it."

She left and returned a couple minutes later. "You *are* a friend of Rae's?"

I understood her reluctance. "Yes, ma'am. I promise to bring it right back. I just want to make sure there's nothing that looks suspicious."

She handed me the key and I walked next door. Maybe if I got inside Rae's place and looked around, I might stumble on a clue to where she'd gone or, God forbid, who'd taken her. I'd do what Mallory wasn't all that interested in doing.

I slipped in through the back door, which opened onto the kitchen. Everything was clean and tidy. I opened up a couple drawers, but there was nothing unusual inside. Cutlery. A junk drawer. I opened a cabinet. Taped on the inside of it was a green sheet of paper from a steno pad. Written on it was *Gran's Brown Sugar Pound Cake*. I ran my fingers along the paper. Delilah's recipe. A woman I'd never met but somehow felt connected to.

I left the kitchen and headed into the dining room. The china cabinet was filled with a ton of glass figurines, bric-a-brac, crystal bowls, even a few books. Everything in the cabinet was haphazardly placed as if each item had been tucked inside as it became special enough to warrant a spot there. I peered across the contents. Nothing in particular stuck out. Ma used to keep a collection of antique tins. It dawned on me that I hadn't seen them since I returned home. Had Ruth thrown them out? I made a mental note to ask Daddy about them when I got home later.

I gazed across the room. Sunlight beamed through the lace curtains hanging at the window. A bowl of silk flowers sat in the center of the dining room table. And next to them was a small stack of papers. I walked over and lifted the paper from the top. It was one of the yellow flyers offering great prices and quick closings that had been placed in mailboxes all across the neighborhood. I looked back at the bright yellow stack. There had to be at least fifty or sixty flyers. How was Rae connected to the company trying to buy up and gentrify our neighborhood? I pulled my cell phone from my jeans pocket and dialed the number on the flyer. The call rang over to a pleasant female-voice recording: *Thank you for your call. If you are interested in selling your property, we're here to help. At the sound of the tone, please leave your name, your phone number, and the address of the property you are interested in selling. Someone will call you back promptly. We look forward to working with you. Beep.*

I clicked off the phone. As I returned the flyer to the stack, I heard a key in the lock at the front door.

I froze.

Who else had a key to Rae's house?

CHAPTER 27

Deena? Why are you inside my house?"

Rae walked through the front door dressed in those ridiculously short jean shorts, a pair of Doc Martens, and a hoodie. She looked perfectly fine. I ran to her and practically knocked her over as I hugged her. My overactive imagination had conjured up all sorts of horrible things that might have happened to her, including suffering the same fate as her grandmother and uncle.

"Oh my God! Rae, you're alive!"

Rae didn't return the affection. I released her and smiled. Her face was stern and then the whole scene suddenly made sense to me. I had come into this woman's home without her knowledge or permission.

"You wanna tell me why you're inside my house?"

"I'm so sorry. Mrs. Trainor, your next-door neighbor, gave me the spare key. The police didn't—"

"The police?!"

"I thought you'd been kidnapped or hurt so I called the police."

"Kidnapped! What the hell are you talking about?"

"I stopped by, and Mrs. Trainor said she hadn't seen you in two days. Where have you been? Are you alright?"

"First of all, I'm fine, and second, where I've been is none of your business."

"I was just so worried after . . . I mean, a lot has happened and I just thought maybe you were in trouble."

"So that gives you the right to come into my home when I'm not here?"

"You're right. I'm so sorry. I had no right to come into your house. Maybe I should go." I edged toward the door.

"Wait."

I turned around to face her, embarrassed and feeling stupid all at the same time.

"Thank you," she said.

"For what?"

She scoped me again in that way that she did. "For caring." She strolled into the dining room and I followed her. She dropped her keys and tote bag on the table.

"Can I ask why you have all these flyers on the dining room table? You know the whole neighborhood is up in arms about whoever is passing these things around."

"Well, you made yourself right at home, huh?" Rae looked down at the flyers. "Donte's buddy must have left them when they stopped by."

"Who's Donte?"

"That's none of your business either," she said with a smirk.

"Why didn't you answer any of my texts? You had us worried sick, considering what's happened with your grandmother. I don't think it's unreasonable that we thought something bad had happened."

"Y'all do realize I'm a grown-ass woman, right?" Rae shook her head. "And why is Mrs. Trainor passing around the key to my house?"

"Don't blame her. I kinda got her all riled up about you going missing."

"Poor Mrs. Trainor. Ever since her husband died, she has nothing to do but stay in grown folks' business." Rae raised one eyebrow and gave me another smirk. "Looks like she has a partner now."

"I deserved that. So, you know who's behind this?"

"Behind what?"

"Someone is trying to buy up all the houses around here and push us out of our homes."

"All I know is that Donte's buddy says he gets paid a hundred dollars to leave those things around. Just some easy money."

"Who's paying him?"

"I don't know." Rae picked up one of the flyers.

"Whoever he's working for is trying to tear down our community. That means your friend is helping them."

Rae continued looking at the flyer. "Sometimes I think I should sell this place. Too many memories. None of 'em all that good either."

"I guess it's your property but be careful. Whoever is behind all this isn't doing it for our benefit."

"What does that mean?" Rae walked into the kitchen, and I continued to trail her.

"If you sell your home, you give this company—whoever they are, developers or whatever—the chance to buy up the property in our community and price us out of it. Some people in this neighborhood have owned property here for generations. There's a meeting over at Piney Grove Baptist Church this afternoon to discuss it. You should come."

Rae removed a pan from the cabinet and placed it on the stove. "Where do you live?"

"What?"

"You're a big-money lawyer. You live around here? I mean, in this neighborhood?"

"As a matter of fact, I do. I live in Harristown on Campbellton Street. Five minutes from here." For the first time since I'd moved back to Brunswick, I was proud to say I lived in my parents' house.

"Mmm." Rae folded her arms and leaned against the counter. "And you ever live in a place where someone you loved died? Where every day, you have to get up and stare at the walls that used to hold them? Where you walk around in the rooms where they ate and slept and laughed and they're not there anymore? Do you know what that feels like?" I saw tears well in her eyes. "You ever long to hear their voice singing off-key from the other room? Or walk into a room and swear you could smell the cigarettes they smoked or the perfume they wore?"

"I do."

Rae stood upright.

"My mother died last year. I lost my job a few months later, and I got divorced. I had no place to go so I returned back home to Brunswick. I live in my old bedroom. In the same house where my mother lived and now my father lives with his new wife. So yeah, I know what it's like to live in a house where you stare at those walls or long to hear her voice just one more time. I know what that kind of ache feels like."

"Sorry. I didn't know." Rae walked across the room and sat at the kitchen table across from me. "It's not easy. That's why I left and was gone for the past couple days. Sometimes it gets to be too much . . . it's . . . I just think some fresh walls might ease the pain, you know."

"I get that. But I'm not sure selling off your grandmother's property will do it. Look, I can't tell you what to do with your property. I'm just saying get all the facts before you sell. Make sure you're selling for the right reasons and to the right people.

Listen, there's something else. I found Holcomb Gardner. In the county morgue."

"That's pretty much where we thought he'd be, right?"

"They found a needle in his arm."

"An old man shootin' up? The fuck?!" she said with a quizzical expression. "I guess everybody's got something, huh?"

"That's all you've got to say?"

"What do you want me to say?" Rae gave me this stern and unblinking stare.

"What?"

"Forget about it." Rae got up from the table and started rummaging through the cabinets, clattering pots and pans.

"What is it?"

"Nothing. You wouldn't understand," she said.

"So, help me understand. What is it?"

She slammed a frying pan on the stove. "I hate it here! Gran's gone. My mother's gone. And all those people who sat at Gran's funeral and said they would help me ghosted me. I'm all by myself. I'm trying to pay bills and figure out how to keep myself standing up." Tears started rolling down her cheeks. "And then you pop up out of nowhere. Telling me all this stuff about my grandmother. Then I find out she had a boyfriend and a brother she kept in secret. Now, you expect me to cry over some old dead guy I don't even know. I don't know who my grandmother was, and I don't know you! Who are you, really? What's the gag?"

"I'm so sorry, Rae. I guess when I found Holcomb and then found your grandmother, I wanted to find out what happened to them. I didn't mean any harm. I just . . . I was trying to help."

Rae ran the back of her hand across her face to wipe away tears. "I keep telling you I don't know any Holcomb. And to tell the truth

I don't really know you either. I come home and find you rummaging around in my house. What are you really after?"

Skepticism and anger were etched across every frown line in her young face. Hell, I guessed I'd be skeptical of me too if I were in her shoes. Some crazy lady she'd never met before shows up on her doorstep and tells her she's been squandered out of a fortune but the crazy lady's going to graciously help her get it back. Why should she trust me?

"Rae, I don't want anything from you. I was merely trying to help. I only want to find out who killed Holcomb and your grandmother, that's all. I don't think any of these things are by coincidence. I think Delilah and Holcomb were murdered for their land . . . please be careful."

I placed Mrs. Trainor's spare key on the kitchen table. "I'd better get going."

I left the house. She was right to distrust me.

Daddy was right too that I should have stayed out of this.

CHAPTER 28

It was almost three o'clock by the time I walked inside the Piney Grove Baptist Church. Word had spread and produced a pretty good turnout. There were at least fifty people there from the Harristown community and some of the surrounding neighborhoods too. People's voices murmured low and anxious across the sanctuary. The church wasn't very large, a single aisle with pews on either side. This was the church where Ma and Daddy met and were married, I was baptized, and Ma's funeral was held. This church had shouldered the troubles and trials of its Black congregation for generations. I had every confidence that Piney Grove would keep the Harristown community intact just as it had kept its congregation likewise since 1928.

Reverend Tate stood at the front of the church quietly talking with a couple of deacons and a woman I didn't recognize. I didn't see LaShonda or Rae, but Mrs. Trainor was there and I waved at her. I finally spotted Daddy, Ruth, and Uncle Duke sitting near the front. I walked up to the pew and squeezed across a couple people, nodding politely, before I took a seat between Daddy and Uncle Duke.

"Hey! What's happening so far? Did I miss much?" I asked.

"Not much, baby girl. Reverend Tate just introduced that woman,

Sarah something. She's gonna talk about how people can protect their property. Reverend Tate said he contacted the city and they're supposed to be sending someone over to talk to us."

"Did they say who?"

Uncle Duke chimed up. "They haven't told us shit."

"Duke! We're inside the Lord's house," Ruth said as she leaned across Daddy to admonish Uncle Duke.

"Sorry, Roo. But these flyers are all over the neighborhood." He rattled the piece of paper in his hand. "They think they'll come in here and snatch up our property and run off. Well, it's not gonna happen. Not while I've got breath in this old body."

I slid the flyer from his hand. It was the same one I'd pulled from the mailbox the other day and the same one stacked on Rae's dining room table. A fleeting thought crossed my mind when I remembered that stack of flyers: Who was Rae's friend Donte, and what woman would pose as me to sign Holcomb's body out of the morgue? Rae? Before I fully fleshed out the thought, Reverend Tate shushed the crowd. The deacons and the woman at the front of the church took their seats in the front row.

"Alright, folks, let's settle down. We all know why we're here."

"Yeah, so what are we gonna do about it?" I heard a man's voice yell from behind me. There was a roar of agreement from others in the church.

"Settle down, Chapman. As I was saying, we're all here for the same reason. But before we get our danders up, someone has asked to join us to say a few words. I think we ought to hear him out. Commissioner Lester, you have the floor."

Everyone turned to the back of the room and watched City Commissioner Charlie Lester stroll down the center aisle like a well-dressed supermodel owning the catwalk. I watched him and my first thought was of Delilah Gardner. This was her “friend,” as Miss Ophelia described him.

Uncle Duke whispered, “Oh God, not this guy. I’m goin’ home before he cons me out of my house *and* my money.”

I elbowed Uncle Duke. “Let’s just hear what he has to say.”

Commissioner Lester made it to the front of the church. He shook Reverend Tate’s hand before the pastor took his seat next to the deacons. I think I saw what Delilah Gardner might have seen in him. Tall, honey-colored skin, a headful of silver-gray hair, and a neatly trimmed gray beard and mustache. His slender build and dapper clothes told me he’d probably been attracting women like Delilah all his life.

Silence fell across the church.

“Thank you, everyone, for coming out. Your presence here this afternoon demonstrates the power of community. Now, I know you’re all upset about those flyers. I understand. I own a home in this neighborhood too.”

Uncle Duke stood up, and Daddy and I looked at each other and braced ourselves.

“I’m sure you’re here because you’re so concerned about us,” Uncle Duke said sarcastically. “But let me ask you something, brotha. You’re the big shot city leader. What happens when all the people who elected you into office are scattered to the winds by some big company coming in, tearing down our neighborhood, and building homes so big and pricey folks like us can’t afford to live in ’em? What happens to you?”

A low murmur ran through the crowd.

“I’m not sure I understand your question,” Lester replied.

“Well, let’s break it down. We sell our houses, and a few people have already begun doing so. If everybody else follows suit, the developers come in and build all new housing and price it so high that people who look like you and me can't afford it. Do you think those new residents are going to elect you back into office? I would think you'd have a self-interest in making sure we shut down the folks who are behind these flyers."

Commissioner Lester stared at Uncle Duke before he straightened his tie. "In that case, let me ask you something, *brotha*. Are you content to remain in a neighborhood that's being swallowed up by drugs and crime, or do you want to take advantage of the financial opportunity that developers may offer you? Not everyone feels the way you do."

"I think Commissioner Lester is right," said a woman's voice from the rear of the church. We all turned around to see who was talking. I didn't recognize her. "I want something better than what this neighborhood has to offer. And if it's my property, then it's *my* decision whether to sell it or not."

Uncle Duke retorted, "See, it's exactly that kind of thinking that tore apart the old SoGlo section of town. Black families lost big, beautiful homes, land, wealth. We've got to start thinking differently if we're ever going to have a legacy to leave the young folks."

"To hell with legacy," she said. "My sister is trying to hold on to a dilapidated old house over on Delowe Street. It'll take more money to fix it than what she can get for selling it."

"Sis, they got you thinking backward. You'll never have anything substantial if you keep letting folks talk you out of what little you got. If God can't trust you with the little things, how can he trust you with something greater?" He turned to the commissioner. "So, it sounds like you want us to take the money and run. Why should we leave? Why can't you take all your so-called power and *clean up* the drugs and crime in the neighborhood? Isn't that why we elected you?" Uncle Duke waved the flyer at Commissioner Lester. "Why wouldn't you get to the bottom of this?"

"I'm not telling anyone what to do. This is a decision each of you must make yourselves. Do what's in your best interests. Do what works best for your family and your financial needs. But do not feel compelled to stay in a place just because that's where you've always been. Be open to change. Next question."

Uncle Duke wouldn't let him off that easy. "The last time I checked, the taxes we pay couldn't afford to buy you a suit like the one you're wearing. You don't work for anybody in this room because we can't afford you. So, who do you really work for?"

I could tell Uncle Duke's last question really flustered the commissioner. He cleared his throat nervously. I saw the glint of sweat form along his hairline.

"Any other questions?" he asked.

Leona Fisher stood at the back of the church. She had been one of Ma's friends on the usher board. "I have a question." Everyone turned in her direction.

"Yes, sister," Commissioner Lester said with a bit of cheer in his voice, probably glad to be done with Uncle Duke. "Your question?"

Miss Fisher looked around the church before she looked back at the commissioner. "I wanna know why you won't answer Duke's last question. Specifically, do you know who's behind these flyers, and do you plan to sell your home in this neighborhood?"

Commissioner Lester's silk ties and expensive suits had bought him a bag of mistrust from his own constituents, and now they rose at the first opportunity for answers. This time, the previous murmurs of agreement turned into a low roar. Some people throughout the sanctuary repeated Uncle Duke's questions, *Why won't you get to the bottom of this? Who do you work for?*

Reverend Tate quickly stood and tried to settle the crowd. In my peripheral vision, I saw a young white guy hustling toward the front of the church. He was well dressed, much like Commissioner Lester. He scrambled up beside Lester and whispered something in his ear before he yelled across the crowd, "I'm sorry, Commissioner Lester has another engagement." He hastily ushered Lester down the aisle and out of the church.

Uncle Duke turned to me and Daddy. "What the hell?! That guy's got more lies than a Baptist preacher got Bible verses. Trust me, Charlie Lester is up to no good."

Uncle Duke was probably right. If what Miss Ophelia had told me and Rae was true, Charlie Lester may have also been the last person to see Delilah Gardner alive.

* * *

WITH CHARLIE LESTER's hasty departure, the woman sitting with the deacons was quickly ushered to the front of the church. She was introduced as Sarah Wheeler, the director of the Georgia Heirs Property Law Center, a nonprofit organization that provided legal resources to help people avoid losing their property. She was an unpretentious, studious-looking woman, with tortoiseshell glasses, a denim skirt and plain top, and Birkenstock sandals.

She gave us an overview of the important work the center was doing on behalf of low- and moderate-income homeowners who had no access to estate planning services like wills or title actions when they were at risk of losing their property. I listened as she described how the attorneys at the center helped families keep the land and homes that had been passed from generation to generation without a will, working with real estate agents and accountants. Like Daddy said the day we stood on Ruth's property, access to the things rich folks had that helped them keep their property and wealth.

Sarah said, "Every year, millions of dollars of generational wealth is lost through heirs property losses. In Georgia alone, over thirty billion dollars in property has no clear title or owner. Much of this is land and property that belongs to Black and poor white rural residents of the state."

I was so impressed by her presentation that I stuck around after the meeting to talk to her.

"Hi, Sarah. My name is Deena Wood. Thank you for this great presentation. I'm a lawyer and I didn't even know some of the information you shared. I have a question. Is it possible for a person to get their property back if they've lost it through the heirs property process?"

"It is," Sarah said. "But it can be difficult. Many times, it involves court intervention to file quiet title actions to determine who legally owns the property. That's why it's so important that we get in on the front end of things before the person loses their property. Then we can negotiate with other heirs, usually extended family members who are not as invested in keeping the property. We have a small staff of attorneys who do this work, but we have resources through other lawyers who work pro bono with us."

I nodded.

"You'd be surprised how easily it happens. People own expensive property, but they don't have access to estate planning services or legal representation that can help them map out what will happen to their property after they die. They're land rich and cash poor. When they die, every relative left behind—siblings, kids, cousins—may all inherit an interest share in the property. Then someone comes along and dangles a few thousand dollars in front of one of the relatives, who sells. And poof. The buyer can force a partition sale. The people residing in the house can be forced out if they can't repurchase the interest share that's been sold. That's why it's so important that folks get to us *before* they lose their homes."

"What about someone who suffered damage to their property through a natural disaster, but they have no proof of ownership?"

"FEMA has relaxed some rules, but it can still be an uphill battle. We can certainly help."

"I think my stepmother and my neighbor might need your services."

She reached in her skirt pocket. "Here, take a few of my business cards and tell them to give us a call."

"I'll do that."

"You mentioned you're an attorney." She raised her eyebrows and gave me a smile. "We can always use your help."

"Oh, I don't really practice estate planning . . ."

"If you're willing to come help us, we'll train you."

I gave a weak smile. "I'll think about it."

CHAPTER 29

The next day, Daddy, Ruth, and I attended the eleven o'clock church service, then returned home. I changed clothes and crawled into bed with a good book—my version of Sunday self-care.

I dreaded Sunday evenings more than anything. Sunday evening meant Monday morning was coming. That meant I had to go back to work. I had a hard time focusing on my book because everything I didn't want to think about clicked around in my head like moving pieces in a cruel game of Whac-a-Mole. I'd knock down one thing just as another popped up. I'd chase Holcomb Gardner's body to the county morgue, then learn someone had used my name to sign his body out and have it cremated. Rae mysteriously went missing for a couple days at the same time Holcomb left the morgue, and she had a stack of flyers in her house that had the whole neighborhood up in arms. And when I concluded that I was done running on the Gardner family murder trail, then Charlie Lester popped up at the church meeting acting suspicious as hell.

A couple minutes later, I heard a man's voice at the door. Probably one of Daddy's friends. I ignored it and continued reading my book.

"Deena! Come out here. We got company."

Geez. It was probably one of their old friends from church or their days at Club 115. I tossed the book and stood from the bed. I caught a glimpse of myself in the dresser mirror. No makeup. Sweats. My hair piled in a mess on top of my head and house slippers. This was just fine for Daddy's old friends.

I walked up the hall to the living room and nearly fainted when I saw Howie. He stood in the middle of the room looking like a goddamn king in a button-down shirt and navy slacks. Why did he always have to look so good? Why didn't I ever put in any effort?

"Look who came by to see us," Ruth said with the widest smile I'd ever seen on her face.

"Come on, Howie, have a seat," Daddy said as he ushered him to the sofa.

"Hey, Deena," Howie said.

"Hey, Howie," I replied as I tugged at the bottom of my sweatshirt, trying to flatten the wrinkles out of it.

"I thought I'd swing by. I missed your dad the first time I dropped by."

Ruth looked at me and grinned before she patted the sofa beside Howie and sat in the recliner beside Daddy. *Ugh*. Suddenly, the room felt smaller, tighter, claustrophobic. Howie was always doing crap like this, ever since we were kids. When he couldn't get through to me, he sweet-talked Ma, who always responded to his big brown eyes and ingratiatingly good manners with adoring looks and pleas for me to give him a chance.

"So, Howie, you like being back in Brunswick working at one of those big law firms, huh?" Daddy asked.

"Well, sir, it's not all that big, but it does feel good to be back. I've missed home."

The whole time he was responding to my dad, he was looking at me.

"Have you eaten, Howie?"

Ruth was always trying to feed people.

"Yes, ma'am. I'm good."

"Isn't it so funny how things work out. That you and Deena would come back home around the same time. Funny," Ruth said, still beaming.

An awkward silence fell over the room. Daddy chimed up. "Roo, I'm feeling like I need something sweet to eat. Why don't you and me take a drive down to the Dairy Queen and get a couple soft serves."

"That's a great idea," she said with way too much enthusiasm.

Ruth practically bounced out of the recliner, and before I could protest, the two of them were out the front door.

"Well, they're pretty subtle, huh?" Howie said as he looked across the sofa at me.

I shook my head. "I think Daddy has softened in his old age. Back in high school, he would practically sit between the two of us on this sofa. But now, he's flying out the front door like Dairy Queen is giving away a hundred-dollar bill with every soft serve cone."

Howie laughed. "Who knows? Maybe they had a real hankering for ice cream."

I rolled my eyes.

"Sooo . . . I guess we haven't been like this since, what . . . college, huh?"

"That's been a minute. So, what happened with you and Neicy?"

He chuckled. "Nikki. I guess we wanted different things out of the relationship. Whatever I wanted, she didn't—kids, fidelity."

"Sorry."

"What about you and Sir Lancelot?"

I smiled. "Lance wasn't big on fidelity either."

"From what I remember of that clown, he wasn't big on much except himself. I wanted to clock that guy at your mother's funeral. He wasn't there for you. I could just tell."

Howie was right. I couldn't recall Lance ever once consoling me during my mother's illness or after her death. Lance was a manipulator and a cheater. But most of all he was unkind. He had no compassion or empathy. I never knew whether my divorce was a result of losing him to another woman or my inability to see through his bullshit when we dated and the four-carat engagement ring he slipped on my finger. Things had been on a slow slide downhill six months into the marriage. By the time my mother died, we were barely speaking to each other. His attendance at the funeral was perfunctory and gave us an easy excuse to sit next to each other in silence.

"Ruth told me he wasn't very kind to you."

"Ugh . . . Ruth! Did she give you my social security and bank account numbers too?! What else did she tell you?"

I was suddenly embarrassed at the thought that Daddy and Ruth might know about Lance kicking me out. Uncle Duke knew so they probably did too. How they all knew, I wasn't sure. I never told them. I prayed if Ruth knew, she hadn't told Howie.

"Don't blame Ruth. I kinda dragged it out of her. She wants you to be happy. I do too." He winked and leaned across the sofa to softly poke me on the arm. "Besides, she's good for your dad."

"What do you mean?"

"Whenever I'd stop by to see your dad after Miss Libby died—"

"Wait a minute. You stopped by to see my dad when I wasn't here?"

"Yeah. Just like I did when your mom was alive. I wanted to see them, not you." He chuckled.

"Why didn't they tell me that?"

Howie shrugged.

"Anyway, right after your mom died, your dad . . . I'd never seen Mr. Jimmie like that."

I guess I was too lost in my own grief to recognize how painful Ma's death was for Daddy; whenever I called him or came home, he put up a good front. Or, as usual, I was simply clueless.

"You should thank Ruth. She brought him through. I don't know how she did, but it worked."

His comment struck a nerve. I sat in silence. I was so busy rejecting Ruth as a wannabe Libby Wood that I never looked at things from Howie's perspective. Or Daddy's. Ruth wasn't trying to replace my mother. She was trying to help my father.

"Now, if we're through talking about other couples, maybe we can talk about you and me."

"Don't get it twisted. *We* are not a couple. Did you find out anything about Empire Realty?"

Howie gave me a sly smile. "Okay, we'll put a pin in that for now. As for Empire, I don't have anything yet, but I have a guy on it. You look cute."

"What does that mean?"

"It means I like what I see."

"Ugh. I'm talking about a guy being on it. What are you talking about?"

"Just what I said. We have a couple investigators that work with the firm. I've asked one of them to dig around and see what he can find out."

"Did he say how long it would take him to look into it?"

Howie shrugged. "A couple days."

"I hope I have a couple days. Some weird crap is going on."

"Like what?"

"Daddy and Uncle Duke thought I should go to the police and report Holcomb Gardner missing, which I did. The detective said he would check the local hospitals and the morgue. He told me later there were no unidentified bodies at the morgue. I called the morgue, and they told me someone named *Deena Wood* was the next of kin and had the body transferred to McGinty's Funeral Home."

"Wait! What?!"

"Yeah, someone used my name. They ordered a cremation of the body."

"Hmph. Who else knew about Holcomb being at the morgue?"

"Just me, you, Daddy, and Uncle Duke."

Howie hesitated. "Do you think the great-niece . . . what's her name?"

"Rae. I thought about that too. She did go missing for a couple days . . . hmm."

"What?"

"The guy at the morgue said Holcomb's body was signed out a few days ago. Rae disappeared around the same time. I talked to her neighbor. We were both worried, so we reported her missing and then she magically shows up yesterday. She gets angry with me and practically throws me out of her house." I leaned back on the sofa and closed my eyes for a moment, trying to make sense of this whole thing. "But why would she sign the body out and have it cremated before an autopsy was performed?"

"Maybe she wants to get at the island property?"

"But why use my name?"

"Hmm . . . good question. What else do you know about Rae?"

"Not much. She's young, just twenty-five, confused, and hanging on by a thread emotionally trying to deal with the aftermath of her grandmother's death. She lost her mother too."

"Well, somebody clearly knows you're digging around into all this. I think getting Holcomb Gardner's body out of the morgue, disposed of, and using your name is a warning to you. Whoever is behind this wants you to back off."

We both went quiet.

A moment later, Howie grinned and rubbed the arm of the sofa. "I think we had our first kiss on this couch. You remember that?"

I quickly stood up. "You want something to drink?"

Howie chuckled. "Damn, I haven't seen you move that fast since you ran the four hundred meter in eleventh grade."

"I think Ruth made some sweet tea. I'll get us a couple glasses."

Howie followed me into the kitchen. "Now, you know I didn't come over here to chat up your dad or Ruth. And I didn't come over here for sweet tea. I think our parents called it right all those years ago. I've done nothing but think about you since your mom's funeral."

"Howie—"

"Listen to me for a minute. Why did we break up after college?"

"What?"

"Serious question. Why did we break up?"

I leaned against the kitchen counter and tried to think. I didn't remember some big parting conversation or tearful goodbye between us. "I . . . I don't remember."

Howie stood against the fridge. "You know why you don't remember? Because we never did."

I giggled. "What are you talking about?"

"We never broke up. We let life get in the way." Howie shrugged.

"Who knows, maybe it was justified. Law school. Hundreds of miles between us. It was tough to hold a relationship together under those conditions."

"Howie, get outta here with that law school moot court, mumbo-jumbo BS." I chuckled. "I think you showing up at my parents' barbecue with Nikki in a tight dress and four-inch heels might have had a little something to do with it."

"It did not. Get your math right. The two of us had drifted apart a couple years before she came in the picture. Besides, in the years she and I were married, I never felt about her the way I feel about you."

"Howie, the only thing we have in common now is that twenty years ago we used to have things in common. All that's behind us."

"Think what you want. I know how I feel about you."

I didn't like where this conversation was going because it would force me to deal with the hard truth I never wanted to admit: perhaps there was a reason Howie and I were always in and out of each other's lives. Ma used to tell me that everyone had someone out there they were meant to be with. The trick was to find that person, and if the angels were on your side, that person would find their soulmate in you. Once, I asked her jokingly if she was Daddy's one true love. She got a wistful look in her eyes and told me, *That's a complicated question*, before she left the room. Maybe she knew something about Daddy and Ruth all along.

"Howie, I'm not up for a relationship right now. I got a lot going on. Can we just be friends?"

"We'll always be friends. That's baseline. But I'm a patient man. We'll get to where we need to be."

"I'd better get that iced tea. Excuse me."

He moved away from the refrigerator door, and I removed the

pitcher of tea. I went over to the cabinet and retrieved two glasses, then poured the tea. When I turned around to hand one to Howie, he was so close to me, I smelled spearmint on his breath.

He leaned in even closer. "Have you ever thought that maybe there's some reason we'd often bump into each other back in Atlanta? Or maybe there's a reason we both wound up in Brunswick again? Both of us single. I admit it. I messed up big time. I never should have let you go. But I won't blow it this time. I can promise you that." He took the glass from my hand, drank it down in one long gulp, and handed it back to me.

He walked out of the kitchen and straight out the front door.

I stood in the kitchen like a brown-skinned mannequin holding an empty glass. It was then that I realized those weren't butterflies in my stomach. It was a tingling somewhere slightly lower.

Shit.

Poor Deena.

She is lost and afraid. She's still grieving her mother's death. She's still trying to figure out what happened with the land out on the island. And she's trying to figure out how to love again.

She's made mistakes of the heart before. She's afraid of making more. But that's what life is. A series of trying, then failing, then trying and succeeding. Every mistake is a stepping-stone to getting it right.

But leaning into love . . . that is a good thing. I want to whisper in her ear, Do not push away love because it is fragile. *Young people take so much for granted, thinking there'll be another time or another place for love. They don't understand how precious love is and how a single misstep can take it all away.*

I wish I could tell her all the mistakes I made with Jimmie. I want to tell her to accept this man's love now, while she can. If Deena knew about me and Jimmie, and the baby and everything that happened back then, she'd understand why it's so important to hold tight to the love that Howie is offering her.

Be a bettuh ooman den me.

Trust love, Deena.

CHAPTER 30

Daddy called a couple hours after Howie left and told me he and Ruth had decided to get dinner and see a movie while they were out. He jokingly told me Howie and I could have the house all to ourselves for the rest of the evening. Yeah, Daddy had truly softened with age. I had to admit it was kinda nice to have the house to myself. I was still waiting to hear back on the offer on the house in Old Town. If the angels came through for me, maybe I'd have more nights like this in my own home.

I took a nice long bath, even used some lavender bath salts that Ruth had in the bathroom. I stayed in the tub so long my fingers pruned. After, I washed my hair and blow-dried it. I still hadn't found a stylist, so I was doing it myself these days. My hair is thick, 4C texture, so wash day is an hours-long process. Ma always sent me to the hair salon when I was growing up so I never really learned to care for it myself. I wore a ponytail all during college and law school, a French roll updo if it was a special occasion. I added "find a hairstylist" to my mental checklist of things to do.

It was dark outside by the time I finished my hair and slipped into my favorite pajamas. I heated up some shrimp creole and rice that was left over from Saturday's dinner. Ruth was an excellent cook. I thought about Howie's comment about Ruth getting Daddy through what must have been the roughest part of his life. I was ashamed that I'd brushed her off and dismissed her. Then, I laughed out loud at the thought that the two of them were off on a date night while I was single and curled up on the sofa with a plate of leftovers and a cable movie—my version of Netflix and chill.

I was about thirty minutes into some mindless rom-com when I heard a car pull up. Maybe Daddy and Ruth had decided to skip the movie and come back early. After a couple minutes, when they didn't walk through the door, I sat my plate on the coffee table. I clicked down the volume on the remote, walked over to the front door, and peeked through the window blinds. Daddy's truck wasn't in the driveway. But sitting across the street in front of LaShonda's house was a dark-colored Jeep. My heartbeat ticked up when I saw a tall male figure standing beside the car. I couldn't make out the person's face. It was dark outside and the closest streetlamp was two houses down.

I checked the door lock on the front door and then the back door. Next, I headed for Daddy's bedroom. Ruth always liked to sleep with the window cracked open. As soon as I hit the bedroom door, I realized I was right. The window was open. I slammed it shut. As I headed back up the hall, I heard a noise coming from the kitchen.

Shit.

My cell phone was in the living room. I couldn't call the police. My heart started to beat faster and louder, pounding in my ears. I hustled back to Daddy's bedroom and grabbed the baseball bat that Ruth kept on her side of the bed. I turned off the light and slowly made my way down the hall, the bat up and at the ready. That's when I heard the noise again. It was still coming from the kitchen.

My palms started to sweat. By the time I made it back to the living room, the only thing I heard was the low voices coming from the TV and the rushing of blood through my ears. I picked up my cell phone from the table and quickly dialed 911.

"911. What's your emergency?"

I whispered into the phone, "Someone is breaking into my house, 7239 Campbellton Street. Please hurry!"

"Okay, ma'am, I'm dispatching an officer now. Stay on the line with me. Are you somewhere safe? In a closet . . . ma'am?"

I didn't respond. I tried to listen for more noises. I kept the phone to my ear as I crept through the dining room and into the kitchen. The only light on in the kitchen was the small dim bulb over the stove. I glanced at the back door. I saw the silhouette of a tall, dark figure on the back porch. I watched as the person shook the knob on the back door a couple times, but it wouldn't give.

"Ma'am? Are you still there?" the operator asked.

"There's a man," I whispered through panting breaths. "He's at my back door. Hurry!"

A few seconds later, the man broke through the glass of the door with a loud crash.

"Ma'am, police are on their way. Tell me what's going on."

A black-gloved hand reached through the broken window to turn the lock. I dropped the phone and rushed over to the door. I raised the baseball bat over my head with both hands and brought it down on the man's left wrist with all the force inside me. More glass shattered and sprayed from the door window. I heard him groan in pain. I brought the bat down a second time. He moved his arm just before the bat came down hard against the window jamb.

I caught a quick glimpse of the man, wearing a hoodie and mask, right before he jumped from the screened porch and ran around the side of the house. I raced through the dining room and back to the living room window just in time to see him hop inside the Jeep and speed off.

* * *

By the time Daddy and Ruth arrived home, the house was crawling with Brunswick police officers. The crime scene investigation unit was in the kitchen combing the back door and screened porch for evidence. I was sure that was a waste since the guy was wearing gloves. I couldn't even give the police a useful identification of the guy since he was wearing a mask.

"Deena! What's going on?" Fear and anxiety rumbled through Daddy's voice.

"Everything's okay. Someone tried to break into the house. I'm fine."

Ruth rushed up to me and lightly touched my arm. "What's this? You're bleeding! Oh heavenly Farruh, henduh de debble. Let me get something to clean you up." She hustled off.

Daddy sat next to me on the sofa.

"Daddy, I'm fine. It's just a light scratch. The guy is somewhere nursing a broken arm thanks to Ruth's bat."

"Shh . . . just tell me the truth. This has something to do with all that business about Holcomb, doesn't it."

"I don't know."

He looked around the room. "Which one of these cops is in charge?"

"I don't know. Why?"

"Sit tight, baby girl." Daddy stepped outside on the porch.

Before I had a chance to run behind him, Ruth was back with a first aid kit from the kitchen. "Ruth, really it's nothing. Just a couple scratches from the glass at the back door."

"I think you're right but let's get it clean, so it doesn't get infected. Where's Howie?"

"He went home hours ago."

"Oh." She started to wipe at the scratches with alcohol pads. I winced at the sting from the antiseptic. Her touch was light, soothing.

"Listen, Ruth . . ." I was just about to apologize for my abhorrent behavior over the past few months, but Daddy walked back in the house.

"You okay, baby girl?"

"Yeah, Daddy. I told you I'm fine."

"Okay, I'm just checking 'cause the officer outside on the porch, the one who took your statement, just told me you told him some guy in a black Ford Escape has been following you all over town." I could tell by his expression he was both pissed and worried.

"Daddy—"

He raised his hand to silence me. I was thirty-nine years old and he still had the power to quiet me with a look and a gesture. I glanced at Ruth. She gave me a "you know your father" kind of look.

"We won't talk about it now. You've been through a lot tonight. The police are nearly done. I'm gonna get some board from the garage to patch up the window." And he walked off.

Ruth placed a piece of gauze on my arm and taped it down. "We drove up and saw all the police cars. It just gave him a scare. He'll calm down."

"Thanks, Ruth."

Gawd stick by e chillun.

Someone tried to harm Deena. They know what she is capable of, and they are trying to stop her. It won't work.

What people forget is that we are steeped in the elements: water, fire, earth, and air. The water that brought us to the land. The fire in our hearts and bellies to live despite all the efforts to defeat us. The earth that we toiled for so long and so hard that it became a part of us. The air that sustains us to keep going in the face of every adversity.

We do not give up. Ever.

What the enemy meant for evil, God will turn into good. The ancestors will rise up and bring them down.

Their plans will fail. Every single one of them.

CHAPTER 31

The next day, I managed to slip out of the house before Daddy got up. I didn't want another confrontation about my digging around in the Gardners' deaths. Maybe it was a random incident. Crime had ticked up in the city since people had come out of Covid hibernation. But deep down, a small voice told me it wasn't random. Someone out there knew I was digging into Holcomb's death and they knew where I lived.

I was skittish as I drove into the office. In my mind, every black Ford Escape, and now every dark-colored Jeep, held my would-be attacker. All I'd done was mistakenly drive onto some man's property and now I was being stalked, nearly attacked, not to mention being used as a conduit for authorizing the cremation of a dead man I didn't even know.

The workday moved slowly and I was accomplishing absolutely nothing. My mind wandered. What if that guy had gotten in the house? Only God knows what he planned to do to me. Who the hell were these people connected to Holcomb's land? I prayed that Howie's investigator might turn up something soon. When I wasn't thinking about Holcomb and Delilah, I thought about Charlie Lester and his odd behavior at the church meeting. Why would he attend the meeting and encourage people to sell their homes? *Read the room, dude.*

I decided to google him. From what I'd found, he'd had a few near misses with the law, but somehow, he always skirted around them and left everyone else holding the bag. He'd been linked to a bribery scheme and managed to walk away without facing any charges. I learned that he was originally from Jacksonville, Florida, before he moved to Brunswick. But a big gap existed between his leaving Jacksonville in 2005 and his popping up in Brunswick local politics in 2015. For ten years there was nothing.

When I was tired of chasing dead ends about Charlie Lester, I googled the Georgia Heirs Property Law Center. They had a wealth of information that I jotted down for LaShonda and Ruth. LaShonda was aggravating as hell, but nobody deserved to be kicked out of their house. Not even LaShonda.

By the end of the day, I'd managed to avoid doing anything productive for Medallion. I was just about to head home until I remembered those damn boxes in the attic. I looked at my cell phone. It was five forty-five. That meant people in the office would be clearing out soon if they weren't gone already. I could count on one hand the number of times I'd been up in the attic. The last time I was up there, a mouse scampered across my feet and I damn near peed on myself.

I grabbed my purse and headed through the hall and up the back staircase to the attic steps. I'd quickly check the boxes then head home. At the top of the attic stairs, I flipped the light switch on the wall. The beam was barely enough to light my path. The pitched roof of the house gave the attic a tight, claustrophobic feel. The heat didn't help. It was like a sauna on the third floor. There was no air-conditioning up here, which made me wonder why they'd selected it for housing papers. The attic covered nearly the entire footprint of the house. There were three rooms connected by a narrow

U-shaped hallway. One of the rooms housed extra chairs, linens, and other things the company used for receptions and office parties. The largest room, at the end of the hall, was converted into a file room for boxes and business documents. The door to the last room had always been closed and I'd never been inside.

As I stood in the hall, the smell of cigarette smoke and perfume hit my nostrils. Hard. Someone had been up here smoking again. Someone who wore a patchouli-based perfume. Clare would have a fit if she knew.

I walked past the storage room and stepped inside the large file room. I pulled the chain to a bare-bulb light fixture beside the door. Apparently, the renovations to this old house stopped at the bottom two floors. The light bulb beamed onto two rows of shelves filled with bankers' boxes stacked at least five feet high. I looked around and spotted a small stack of boxes with a piece of paper taped onto the top box that read "Deena."

Gee, thanks for the personal touch, Peg.

I opened the first box. It was marked "Building Permits" and full of old permits pulled for various projects around the city that Medallion had worked on. The second box contained the same thing. Again, this was busy work that Peg could have done herself. I wouldn't have been surprised if Joe had told Peg to do it and she pretended it was all legal documents to avoid the chore. Nothing in either box was privileged or confidential or necessarily legal documentation.

By the time I opened the third box, I started to sweat. I'd flipped through a couple folders when I heard what sounded like a woman's voice, low and talking. Or was she singing? My first thought was a ghost, but I refused to buy into the nonsense everyone spewed about the place being haunted. This was simply an old house and

I knew the vent system in this place was lousy. Maybe someone else had stayed late too. I peered into the third box. This one did have some legal memos and a few other papers I probably needed to spend some time going through.

I pulled out the first document. An old memo written about a project that preceded my days at Medallion. As I read through it, the voice coming through the vents grew louder. I stopped. It was definitely a woman's voice. When I focused my attention, it seemed as if the voice wasn't coming from the vents but from the room next door. I sat the folder down and eased back out into the hall. The voice was coming from the room I'd never been in before. This time, the door was ajar, and the light was on.

That light wasn't on and the door was closed when I came up to the attic.

My heart sped up. I walked closer; the voice lowered then stopped. I tapped lightly on the door. "Hello?"

No answer.

"Hey, anyone there?" I pushed the door slightly. It squeaked open. The lights were on, but the room was completely empty. No voice. Maybe it really was the vents or perhaps I had imagined it. I stood at the door listening, waiting for the voice to return. Nothing.

I'd never been inside this room before. The exterior wall was exposed red brick like the walls of the other rooms up here. Sitting on the floor and propped against the wall were old pictures in weathered wood frames. Pictures of historic landmarks from around Brunswick. A picture of the old Bijou Theatre. The Sidney Lanier Bridge. The Old Post Office and Custom House.

But something else caught my eye. Something weird. Several spots on the walls seemed to be seeping. Water was coming through cracks in the brick and slowly creeping down the walls. *What the hell?!* I looked around the room. Clear liquid slowly slid down all four walls. I lightly touched one wall. The bricks were cool, but the water seeping through the cracks in the brick was warm. Warm water on attic walls? I looked up to the ceiling for the source of the liquid. Bone dry.

Slowly the smell of the perfume became stronger and enveloped the room. My first instinct was to run, to get out, but I couldn't move. It was like my feet were anchored to the floor. The heat, the pitched roof, all of it seemed to close in on me. Then, something smooth and soft touched my cheek. It sent a current of warmth through my entire body.

I slowly turned toward the door and spotted another picture propped against the wall. It was a huge black-and-white photograph of a house. The Old Victorian. The fanciful round turret that housed the seating area in Clare's office. The huge front porch with a swing. It looked almost identical to the current appearance of the house except for the porch swing and a terra-cotta-tiled roof, which must have been replaced at some point with the current roof of black shingles. But this older house still had the same thin spindles on the porch banisters and the large windows at the front.

And then it hit me. I'd seen this exact house somewhere else before. The old terra-cotta tiles on the roof. The porch swing. I dug around in my bag and pulled out the Polaroid picture that Rae had given me. I stared at the picture in my hand and the photo propped against the wall.

It was the same house!

Delilah and Holcomb Gardner were standing in front of the Old Victorian. I read the inscription written along the bottom of the Polaroid: *Delilah and Holcomb in front of Mama's house, November 1969.*

Then the lights flickered twice before the entire attic went dark.

CHAPTER 32

Beads of sweat popped up along my hairline as my heart thrummed inside my chest, pounding and fighting against my rib cage. Everything was pitch black. My childhood fears of being alone in the dark came rushing from the deep recesses of my psyche.

I managed to stumble down the attic stairs, feeling along the walls for guidance. As I did, I felt it again. More warm water. After a few seconds, my eyes adjusted to the darkness. I tore down the last few stairs and ran straight out the back door of the Old Victorian. I didn't even bother to set the alarm. I just ran.

I didn't stop running until I got to my car and hopped inside. I locked the doors and leaned back into the seat, panting from fear. I was a sweating, hot mess. Who or what the hell was up in the attic, and why did they shut the lights out on me?

Then the realization set in. The Old Victorian was once Delilah and Holcomb Gardner's home.

I remembered Daddy's words the first day I asked him about Holcomb: *I knew of some Gardners lived over off Union Street. But that was years ago, back when Black folks still lived over there.*

Miss Ophelia: *When their parents died, they left the house to the kids. Big, pretty house too.*

Uncle Duke: *Them Gardners lived in that big house with the funny roof.*

Uncle Duke had argued with the woman at the church meeting, telling her how Black people had lost big beautiful homes in the SoGlo section of town.

And Peg: *Beau bought this house years ago.*

Oh God! Why hadn't I put this together sooner. The Old Victorian had once been the Gardner family home, the one that Delilah and Holcomb argued over. I looked down at my hands. My fingertips were still wet. I didn't believe in ghosts and spirits, but there was a presence in that attic. Something was up there.

I looked back up at the Old Victorian. The entire house was dark. And then, a single light popped on in the attic, in the same room I'd just fled.

I started up my engine and sped off.

Praise the ancestors! Deena knows it's me, Delilah Gardner, and she knows this is my home.

It's not "the Old Victorian" or whatever silly name they call it. This is the Gardner home. Or at least it was before I lost it. Holcomb had every right to be angry at me for losing something so precious—our family legacy. I threw away my daughter's and granddaughter's legacy.

But Deena is a smart girl. She'll figure this whole thing out and she'll make things right for Rae. And in the process, she can make things right for herself. I only pray I haven't caused her so much fear that it drives her away from Mama's house. She's getting closer to the truth now. With help from the ancestors, I can keep her safe and stop them from killing her too.

Although Deena is not my child by blood, she could have been if things had been different. I have loved Jimmie Lee Wood since the first day I laid eyes on him. I remember the times we'd sneak off to the beach at the edge of dusk. Just me and Jimmie sitting alone in the sand, listening to the rush of the water. For us Saltwater Geechees, a love of water has always been in our bones. We used to say, we had one foot on the soil and one foot in the sea.

De wata bring we and de wata gwine tek we back.

Those days that were simple in their joy but complicated by everything going on around us.

I lost Jimmie. I lost my family. And I lost my home. But no more mistakes this time.

Right now, my task is to help keep Deena on track, focused on the right things. Now that she's found Rae and Holcomb, she can do what needs to be done. But she will need to know the truth about me and Jimmie . . . and the baby that came between us.

CHAPTER 33

The next morning, I was terrified of going back into the Old Victorian. Maybe the house really was haunted as everyone joked. The odd noises, the unusual smells, the things that people had found moved when they arrived in the morning. My desk fan.

Stop it, Deena.

All this time I'd worked in the Old Victorian, I thought my office was the maid's quarters. In fact, the entire house had belonged to a Black family. It made me proud and sad at the same time.

I thought about telling Ruth what had happened in the Old Victorian, but she would have blown it all out of proportion, probably insisting that it was some sort of hex and that I needed to wear an amulet to ward off the evil spirits at my job. To tell anyone else would make them think I was nuts.

Whether the Old Victorian was or wasn't haunted didn't mitigate the fact that this house had once belonged to the Gardners. Had Beau benefited from the family squabble between Holcomb and Delilah? Or did he steal it from Delilah outright?

Nonetheless, I decided to time my arrival at work until after a few other people showed up. Everything was buzzing when I stepped inside. Jennie was perched at the front desk. Peg and Joe stood in the kitchen engaged in chitchat with the IT guy whose name I could never recall. I waved and headed straight back to my office. I plopped down in my chair. As soon as I did, my cell phone rang.

Howie.

I didn't want to answer Howie's call. I saw all the warning signs that I was falling back into our old routine. Laughing and talking with him. Thinking about him throughout the day. The only thing left was for him to kiss me. God, he was a good kisser. If I wasn't careful, I'd find myself falling into bed with him. The two of us in a naked sweaty knot of entangled arms and legs. *No.*

My life was a whole hot ass mess right now. I didn't need to drag him into it. Hell, I didn't have room for him in it. When I searched deep down inside, I realized the real reason I didn't want to get into a relationship with Howie, or any other man for that matter, was that I couldn't take another breakup. After Ma's death, my divorce, my termination from the firm, I didn't have it in me for one more disappointment. Howie's call finally rolled over to voicemail. A couple minutes later, it was Howie calling back. Sometimes, he was more persistent than I cared for. This time, I answered.

"Hey, Howie."

"I think I found something you might want to know about Empire Realty."

Howie had piqued my interest. "Okay. What did you find?"

"You should know by now, that's not how all this works. I found the information. The least you could do is treat me to lunch."

"Howie . . ."

"Great! Meet me at our spot."

"*We* don't have a spot."

"Okay, not yet we don't. Just meet me at Hampton's again. Twelve thirty."

He hung up before I could protest.

* * *

HOWIE WAS ALREADY sitting at the same table by the window when I arrived at the restaurant. The place was filling up. He waved me over.

"You look nice," he said.

"You said you found something?"

"I think what you meant to say was 'Thanks for the compliment, Howie.'" He smiled at me, and I sat down at the table.

"I'm sorry. Thank you for the compliment." After Howie had dropped by the house unannounced on Sunday afternoon and caught me looking like a hobo, I decided to put a bit more effort into my appearance. Today, I was wearing a navy plaid pantsuit with a silk shirt. I was a little annoyed with myself for doing so. Was I putting in the effort for myself or for moments like this, hoping Howie might notice?

"I'm just a little rattled by this whole mess," I said.

"Has something else happened?"

"It's a long story. Anyway, what did you find out?"

"I found out who owns Empire Realty."

"Who?"

"Not who. What," Howie said. "The investigator found out that Empire is owned by a hedge fund."

"A hedge fund? As in Wall Street, dripping money, filthy rich hedge fund?"

"Yep. It's a real estate hedge fund. It's called Bellar Strategies."

The waitress came over. "Are you folks ready to order?"

We placed our orders and watched her walk away.

"The investigator told me Empire Realty acts as an intermediary, a broker on the transactions. Empire scopes out the properties, almost always poor-performing ones. They buy up the property, but they don't always sell it right away. A lot of times, the hedge fund bundles up the properties in a portfolio and then sells the entire portfolio. With each sale, the value of the portfolio rises. The hedge fund makes its profit. Meanwhile the homes sit abandoned and the neighborhood becomes blighted."

"Damn. That's really messed up."

"It's happening all over the country. Usually in Black neighborhoods, poor white Appalachian areas as well as poor southwestern areas in Texas and New Mexico."

"Who are they selling to?"

"Real estate developers, property management companies. Corporate entities that don't care about the people that have been displaced."

"That's horrible."

"Right?! A lot of the properties come through heirs property purchases. Apparently, Empire Realty comes in and dangles a few thousand bucks in front of the people left behind after a relative dies. If people are desperate or just don't understand the value of their property, they take the money. It's terrible but that's how corporate greed works. Then, there are the corporate buyers who also take advantage, buying up properties and becoming landlords in some cities, charging rents that far exceed the value of the rental properties. It's a billion-dollar industry."

"But I don't understand. The island property is anything but poor performing. That land is valued in the millions."

"True," Howie said. "That doesn't fit with their model. They must have some other reason for grabbing up the island property."

"So if Empire Realty scopes out the properties, that means

they sought out the Gardners' property, which means whoever is behind Empire might be connected to Holcomb's and Delilah's deaths." We were quiet for a moment, then I continued.

"There's something else. You remember when I told you about Holcomb's body being signed out of the morgue under my name and you told me it was a warning from someone that I should back off?"

"Yes . . ."

"Well, whoever's behind Holcomb's murder sent another calling card."

Howie leaned in with a worried expression. "What does that mean?"

"Someone tried to break into Daddy's house a few hours after you left on Sunday."

"What the hell?! Are you okay?"

"I'm fine but whoever it was is probably nursing a sore left arm thanks to Ruth's baseball bat."

"Deena . . . maybe it's—"

"Please don't tell me to turn it over to the police. I tried that. They don't give a damn. There's something else. Last night, I was working late." I removed the Polaroid from my bag. "Take a look at this." I handed him the picture. "That's Holcomb and Delilah standing in front of their parents' house when they were young."

"Dayumm! They look pretty cool."

"Yeah, but take a look at the house behind them."

Howie studied the picture like he was trying to figure out a quadratic equation. "Yeah, okay?"

"Look again. That's Medallion's office."

Howie stared at the photo again. "What the hell? You're right."

"My dad told me the Gardner family used to live in a house off

Union Street. I found a picture of the Old Victorian in the attic last night. The roof has changed, and the porch swing is gone, but it's the same house."

"Oh, snap . . ."

"Beau bought the house and renovated it. According to Delilah's best friend, Delilah and Holcomb argued over a house their parents left them and Delilah somehow lost it."

"So, wait a minute. You think Beau might be involved in all this?"

"I don't know. It's too crazy to think about."

"I've asked one of the paralegals at my firm to dig into the sales transaction for the island property. I haven't gotten anything back yet. I'm also poking around trying to find out more about that hedge fund too. Bellar Strategies."

"Thanks for all this, Howie. I really appreciate it."

"I know you do. That's why you're paying for lunch."

I giggled nervously. "Okay, but you can't order that fifty-five-dollar steak. My cash ain't as long as yours."

He smiled. "Seriously, you've gotta be careful. Whatever is going on, it's not worth you getting hurt."

"I'll be fine."

"You already are," Howie said with a sly wink.

I laughed. "Is that your best pickup line?"

He laughed. "Hey, I'm a little rusty."

I was grateful for the next hour we spent together. Howie took the edge off, and once again, I felt so relaxed in his presence. Whenever I let myself lean into the moment with Howie, I always had a good time. It had been that way since we were kids. Whether we were hanging out on my front porch or sitting in study hall at school, Howie had this way of making me feel lighter with his corny humor and his endless stories. I was glad we were friends again. I didn't realize until I was sitting across from him like this how much I'd missed his friendship.

Every so often I caught him staring at me. It made me nervous and giddy. And sad too because we'd wasted so much time in and out of each other's lives. I wondered what life we might have had if we'd gotten together and stayed that way.

Was there a chance for that now?

CHAPTER 34

By three o'clock, I was dressed in a white polo shirt and a pair of khaki Bermuda shorts, and had just cleared the security entrance for The Dunes, Clare's swanky golf community.

The grounds provided a sweeping view of the golf course on one side and a separate entrance to the private homes overlooking the island sound and the Atlantic Ocean on the other. I pulled my car into the parking lot for the golf clubhouse.

The Dunes was located in the most exclusive section of the island. I'd only ever been here once before. It was to attend Clare's annual "After Christmas" Christmas party at her house. She said she always threw the party after the holidays to make sure no one had an excuse for not attending because of all their other holiday festivities. And everyone came too, people from as far as Savannah and Jacksonville. It occurred the first weekend after I started working at Medallion, so we were all in the honeymoon phase of my new hire status. I even danced with Beau.

After I got home that night, I was regaling Daddy and Ruth with all that had happened at The Dunes—Clare's extraordinarily huge house, the food, the seven-piece orchestra—when I noticed Daddy and Ruth wore somber expressions. I asked them what was wrong. When they told me, a wave of guilt washed over me like a flood. They told me how Dunbar Creek dead-ended at Igbo Landing, which sat right in the middle of The Dunes. The site where African people were brought to this country to become enslaved but drowned themselves instead was now surrounded by wealth and vestiges of white privilege, barely a speck on the map of an exclusive gated community.

This was my first time back in The Dunes since Clare's party and it made me a little uneasy to drive across the bridge in the subdivision that crossed Dunbar Creek. Just below the tires of my car was the black-bottom river that held the spirits of African bodies, chained together in life and dead by a collective choice to be free.

I should have turned down this invitation knowing what I knew about Dunbar Creek. Now, I tried to put it all out of my mind. This would be my last time coming to The Dunes because I planned to have another job before Clare's Christmas party rolled around again. I walked inside the clubhouse.

"Deena!" Clare called.

Clare was dressed in a pink polo and pink pants. Her gray bob was neatly tucked under her sun visor. We walked outside to a waiting golf cart and loaded our clubs. She whisked me out of the clubhouse and onto the course so fast I didn't have time to do my usual count of the number of women and Black and brown people. There were four, including me, at her holiday party and two of them played in the orchestra.

We knocked off the first few holes without a hitch, if you didn't count my first ball that managed to get a little lift before it rolled clumsily off the side of the green. Or the other ball that was a perfect swing into the sand trap. Clare was a great golfer. I played golf about two times a year and it showed, but Clare was always so much fun to be around that I was never embarrassed. We knocked off two more holes and climbed into the cart for the next hole.

"You know, I think Peg and Joe are having a fling," Clare said with a mischievous giggle.

"Stop! Are you serious?"

"I happened to walk into his office the other evening and the two of 'em jumped a mile apart like I'd caught them in the middle of something. I didn't really see anything, but I know a guilty face when I see one. Right now, they're both scared shitless that I might have seen something. I think I'll leave 'em like that. You're two adults. Get a room. Geez!"

We both laughed as the golf cart bobbled over the grassy terrain. I didn't dare tell Clare about the joint and the condom I found in Joe's drawer when I went snooping through his desk.

"Listen, you ought to know . . . I'm gonna do it," Clare said.

"Do what?"

We hopped out of the cart and grabbed the clubs. "I'm gonna make a run for Congress," Clare said.

"Oh, Clare, that's fantastic!"

"I'm glad you think so. Beau is ecstatic. He foolishly thinks it'll keep me outta his ass. It won't. By the way, when I asked him why he didn't invite you to the meeting with the law firm, he tried to feed me a line about it being an oversight. Don't worry. I chewed his ass out about it. Joe's too."

I simply nodded. Now, I'd be in both their crosshairs for coming off as a tattler. Whatever.

Clare hit the next ball off the tee with such force that it created a smooth, wide, picture-perfect arc clear across the course.

"I'm losing my patience with Beau. He's been up to something lately."

Probably swindling poor old women out of their homes, I thought to myself. Aloud I said, "Up to what?"

"I don't know. That's why I might need your help."

I was confused. "Need *my* help? With Beau?"

"If I'm gonna make a successful run, I'll need to be out of the office drumming up donations and support. I need you to be my eyes and ears. Keep an eye on Beau. Let me know what he's up to."

"Well . . . Clare . . . I don't interact with Beau all that much. I don't know if I can be of any help."

"Of course you can. I'm not asking you to do anything outlandish. Just like you told me about his so-called cost-saving measures, which is a bunch of BS by the way. I'm just asking you to let me know if anything's going on around the office that might impact the business."

"I don't know, Clare . . ."

"I don't fully trust him. Isn't that awful to say about my own family?"

I didn't agree or disagree with her. I simply listened. It wasn't my place to jump in the middle of their family dynamic. It also wasn't my job to become Clare's eyes and ears around the office. Peg had that market cornered.

"I never had kids. I've raised Beau since he was thirteen as if he were my own son. I gave him every opportunity and advantage money could buy. Private school, gap years to find himself, and two different colleges he never finished. Maybe that's the problem. Maybe I did too much. Sometimes, I wonder if I let my brother and sister-in-law down. Or maybe that boating accident spared them from seeing the kind of man he's become."

Clare pulled the golf cart up to the next hole in silence. When she stopped, she turned in her seat toward me. "For the past six months, I can't speak reason to him. I have a real shot at doing something bigger, something in service to this country. And I'll be damned if Beau is gonna screw it up for me."

"Have you ever thought of hiring someone more . . . competent to work alongside Beau, to keep him on the straight and narrow?"

"I should have done that years ago. I guess I was so enamored with our being partners that I looked past all his faults as growing pains. But now, I can see he's . . . Anyway, just keep me posted if he's doing something I ought to know about."

I mumbled something she may have interpreted as agreement.

We played the remaining holes of golf, but her request made me a bit uneasy. However, she was my boss and my friend. And Beau was an asshole.

CHAPTER 35

The next morning, I had to run over to city hall to handle some paperwork on a project. I was grateful for the excuse to get out of the office. As I drove, I was feeling proud of myself that I hadn't made any detours, no wandering off to chase my grief. I was working mightily to keep this job regardless of how much I hated it. I was still waiting to hear back from Lois on whether the owners had accepted my offer on the Old Town house. I didn't dare let myself get excited about it, but sometimes as I was drifting off to sleep or standing in the shower, I found myself thinking about cooking, or rather eating takeout, in that kitchen or reading a book in the window seat of the sunroom or planting a garden out in the backyard.

Do not fall in love, Deena.

And I was getting past my bruised feelings after Rae all but told me she didn't trust me. Of course, I was a bit suspicious of her too. She had a stack of the flyers. And her disappearance was incredibly coincidental to the timing of Holcomb's departure from the county morgue. I still felt bad for her, though. She was young and alone and I hoped she would find her own way. Learning all that I did about the Gardners made me realize that family—good, bad, or otherwise—was all we had. And having a home, a legacy, was the best thing we could do for the ones we leave behind.

And then as if the angels had willed it so, my cell phone rang.

Lois.

Butterflies tumbled through my stomach. Had the third time been the charm, as Daddy said the night I told him and Ruth about the offer? Or had Empire Realty shut me out in the cold again?

"Hey, Lois."

"Hey, Deena," she said in her perky southern drawl.

"Did you hear back on the offer?"

"I did . . . and you got the house!" she squealed into the phone.

I went silent.

"Deena, honey, you there?"

"Yeah . . . I'm here. I'm just . . . I'm speechless."

"Well, congratulations! Listen, I'm on my way to show another listing. I just got the good word and I wanted to share it with you right away. I'll call you later with the details."

"Thanks, Lois."

She clicked off the call. For the first time in a long time, something good had happened in my life. I had something to look forward to. A home of my own. I turned on the radio—loud—and started bopping and singing along to Beyoncé's "Run the World." I would finally have a home of my own. Daddy's nearly forty-year-old baby girl was growing up.

I arrived at Brunswick City Hall and parked my car in one of the spaces in front. It was an impressive structure with its steepled roof, wide turrets, and arched doorways. My plan had been to check on the status of some paperwork for a contract and then head straight back to the office. After work, I'd pick up a bottle of wine to celebrate my good news with Daddy and Ruth.

When I walked inside, City Commissioner Charlie Lester was standing in the lobby talking to the same man who had hustled him out of the church on Saturday when things got tense. Commissioner

Lester's behavior at the meeting was weird and, like Uncle Duke said, maybe he was up to something. Why bother to attend a meeting to discuss the displacement of residents in your district if you planned to encourage them to sell their homes for pennies on the dollar? I didn't know why, but seeing him again got under my skin. Maybe it had something to do with the fact that he was trying to sell out his own people. Or perhaps it had something to do with the fact that he was probably the last person to see Delilah Gardner alive. In the next instant, I found myself marching toward Lester like he had just cashed his paycheck and he owed me money.

"Excuse me, Mr. Lester. May I have a word with you?"

He looked at me with a puzzled expression, probably trying to place me in his district or the last place he'd seen me.

"My name is Deena Wood."

He extended his hand, and I shook it. "What can I do for you, Ms. Wood?"

"I'd like to speak to you." I glanced at the man standing beside him. "In private."

He pinched his brows. "Well . . . I'm on my way to a meeting." He turned to the man. "This is my aide, Kyle Bowen. He'll be happy to set up a meeting for us to talk."

The young man smiled at me, and I shooed him away. "Mr. Lester, this is a sensitive matter. It's about Delilah Gardner."

The commissioner's eyes grew wide. "Uh . . . Kyle, give me a few minutes here."

"But we're supposed to be in the meeting in five minutes."

"Then give me two."

The young man gave me a suspicious once-over before he walked a few feet away.

Lester turned back to me. "As you heard, I'm extremely busy. You have just two minutes."

"I understand you had a personal relationship with Delilah Gardner."

"I don't know what you're talking about. Where'd you hear that?"

"From someone who knows. But that's not important. You were most likely the last person to see her alive. I need to know what you know. First, why was she walking out on the island if she had her car? Did you two argue or something?"

"I don't have a clue what you're talking about."

"I think you do. I know you two had dinner together the night before. Maybe out on the island. So what happened?"

Lester looked down at his watch, then nervously glanced around the lobby.

"Commissioner, you can either tell me, or better yet, maybe I'll just share what I know with the police. I'm sure they'll have more questions than I do."

"Look, I really do have to get to this meeting." He patted his breast pocket a couple times. "Kyle!" The young man trotted back over to us. "Do you have one of my cards?" The aide reached into his jacket pocket and pulled out a business card. "Kyle, write the address of the Beaver Street property on it and give it to Ms. Wood," the commissioner said.

Kyle pulled a card from his breast pocket. That's when I noticed a cast on his left arm. I perked up. The guy happened to have a broken left arm.

"I can't talk to you right now," Lester said. "Meet me at this address tonight. It's a house I'm renovating. I have a commission meeting, but I'll meet you after. Eight thirty. We can talk in private there."

I took the card. "So Kyle . . . is it? How'd you break your arm?" The guy flushed bright red.

"Come on, Kyle," Lester said. The two men walked off.

I looked down at the business card. The address was located near Uncle Duke's barbershop. The card was unusually thick for a business card. When I looked closer, I noticed that it was two business cards stuck together. I pulled them apart and read the second card.

CHARLES EVAN LESTER

Empire Realty

A chill ran straight through me.

CHAPTER 36

Later that evening, I laid across the living room sofa watching TV with Daddy, or rather watching Daddy flip through the channels, lingering on one just long enough for me to get interested in the program before he changed the channel again. Annoying. Daddy hadn't mentioned anything about Sunday night, when someone tried to break into the house, except to ask me a couple times how I was feeling. I didn't mention it either. Daddy was always concerned about my well-being, which made me feel bad for having been so dogged about the Gardners and possibly bringing some lunatic to his doorstep.

We watched TV in silence, and I kept thinking about Lester's business card. He worked for Empire. He was tied to Holcomb's property, which meant he might be involved in Holcomb's death. Possibly Delilah's too since they both owned the island property, and he was probably the last person to see her alive. And what of Kyle Bowen's broken arm? He got awfully nervous when I asked about his cast. All of this was connected, but I couldn't figure out how.

"Did you hear anything else from the police about the break-in Sunday night?"

Crap! So now he wanted to talk about my stalker.

"No, Daddy. But I think Uncle Duke was right about Commissioner Lester."

"Right about him how?"

"I had to swing by city hall this morning and bumped into him. I had found out he was in a secret relationship with Delilah Gardner before she died, and I asked him about it."

Daddy stopped fidgeting with the remote control and sat up to face me. "Say what?! How do you know that?"

"I talked to one of her friends, Ophelia Ealy. Anyway, when I tried to ask Lester about it he told me he didn't have time to talk, but he wants me to meet him at a house he's renovating. But here's the kicker. He gave me his business card. Guess who he works for?"

"Who?"

"Empire Realty. That's the company that has Holcomb's land up for sale. So he was dating Delilah and now he's trying to sell property that belonged to her and her brother. Charlie Lester got real nervous when I brought up Delilah's name."

Daddy sat quiet for a minute. "Delilah and Lester? You sure about that?"

"That's what her best friend told me."

"Well, you're not going to meet him, are you?"

"Of course not."

I don't typically lie to my father. Not unless you count lies by omission. There was lots of stuff I *didn't* tell Daddy. The only time I'd lied outright to him was back in high school, my senior prom. I lied and told Ma and Daddy I was spending the night at my friend Melinda's house after the prom. Howie was home from college and we were still going together so he was my date. We made plans to get into stuff we had no business doing—he was going to be my first. We were en route to a motel when Howie's beat-up old Honda Civic broke down, and he had to call his buddy Kareem to come help. Somehow, Daddy showed up three minutes behind Kareem. Daddy fixed Howie's car and took me home. Kareem swore he never mentioned where he was going. To this day, I still don't know how Daddy found out about Howie's car. My virginity remained intact for the time being. And that was the last time I lied to Daddy—until now. This was different.

"You're gonna tell the police, aren't you?"

"For what good that'll do. Delilah has been dead for months and they've barely lifted a finger to find her killer, according to her granddaughter. You can't seriously think anyone's out there trying to figure out what happened to the Gardners. They don't care about them."

Daddy sighed deeply and scratched his head. "Maybe if you give them this information you just found out about Lester, they'll have something more to go on. Why didn't you mention that Lester and Delilah were together when you filed the report about Holcomb?"

"Honestly, I didn't put it all together until now. I was so focused on reporting Holcomb's disappearance, I totally forgot about Delilah's involvement with Charlie Lester."

"You can't keep something like this from the police. If he was seeing Delilah and now he has her property up for sale, the police need to know that. And you certainly can't go meeting somebody like Charlie Lester in some house of his."

"I'm not. I'll call the detective in the morning."

* * *

DINNER HAD BEEN pleasant again. I told Daddy and Ruth about getting the house, and we opened the bottle of wine I'd brought home to celebrate. In fact, I think Ruth celebrated a bit too much.

She was buzzed after half a glass, giggling like a schoolgirl every time me or Daddy opened our mouths. She was funny in a sweet, drunken sort of way.

After dinner, Daddy, Ruth, and I sat in the living room. Ruth and Daddy watched MSNBC as usual. It was like that channel played on an endless loop. I sat on the sofa reading a book and looking up at the television whenever anything of interest popped up on the screen.

Daddy stood from his recliner and stretched. "Listen, Roo, I'm gonna ride around to Duke's place for a bit. I won't be gone too long."

I shot Daddy a glance and he smiled back at me.

"Okay, be careful," Ruth said.

He picked up his keys and left. Daddy wasn't slick. I knew what he was doing. This was his way of slipping out of the house to try and force me to spend one-on-one time with Ruth.

A commercial came on the screen and the volume jumped twenty decibels. Ruth quickly picked up the remote and adjusted the volume. The room was quieter. I continued reading my book. Ruth picked up her crochet from a basket near her chair. I thought about what Howie said about Ruth helping Daddy through his grief over Ma. Here was my father trying to live his life the best way he knew how. And Ruth was a part of that. I knew I should strike up some conversation. *What are you crocheting? Who do you think will win the mayor's race?*

Ruth spoke up first. "I think I'll have some of that peach cobbler and vanilla ice cream I made for dessert. You wanna join me? Maybe we can turn off all this depressing news and watch a movie instead. What do you think?"

I looked at my watch. It was almost time for me to leave to

meet Commissioner Lester. "I'm sorry, Ruth. I forgot I'm supposed to meet a friend in about thirty minutes. Maybe another time. I promise."

Ruth chuckled slightly but never looked up from her crochet. "That's what you said when I offered to treat you to lunch the other week or when I suggested we drive over to Savannah. You are a very busy lady."

"Maybe we can go to the mall on Saturday. I promise. I'll be back in an hour."

I picked up my keys and bag and left.

CHAPTER 37

I pulled up to the house where Charlie Lester had asked me to meet him. The street was quiet and dark. No neighbors sitting on their front stoops. No passing cars. Nothing. One of the streetlamps was busted and an entire section of the street was plunged into darkness. Small bungalows lined the street, covered by huge trees and a blue-black night. I silently talked myself through the fear rising up inside me.

The house was obviously undergoing some renovations. The front of the house was a sight with a portable dumpster planted at the edge of the yard. Construction debris and a couple McDonald's bags and paper coffee cups littered the yard. I didn't see a car in the driveway, although a light was on in the front room of the house. I was nosy but I wasn't an idiot. There was no way I was going inside the house to meet him. If he was serious about talking to me, I'd wait for him to come to my car.

I was just about to blow my horn to let him know I was outside when I spotted a red pickup truck pull up to the front of the house. Daddy's truck!

Damn it.

I jumped out of my car and headed over to Daddy's window. He rolled it down. "What are you and Uncle Duke doing here?"

Daddy frowned. "I'm here because you're hardheaded. Because you have no godly business out here meeting this guy at night. Do I talk just to hear the noise I make? 'Cause it's obvious you ain't listening. I thought we talked about letting the police handle this."

Uncle Duke leaned across Daddy toward me. "Hey there, Deena baby." He gave me a big cheesy smile. "Now, sweetie, if you think me and ya daddy was gonna let you meet up with some dude that isn't clean enough to hang off the bottom of my shoe out here by yourself, then you ain't as smart as I been giving you credit for. Law school notwithstanding."

"How did you know where to find me?"

"Oh, everybody know that snake is renovating this house. It's creating an eyesore too. Look at that mess in the front yard," Uncle Duke said as he reached under the seat and pulled out a gun.

"What in the world?! Uncle Duke! Put that away right now."

Daddy turned off the truck and reached in the glove box and pulled out a gun too.

Ugh. Old men and guns.

"Are you two insane? Put those things away."

"Let's go," Daddy said.

Both men hopped out of the truck and stood beside me.

"Daddy, I don't think Charlie Lester was expecting me to bring along a posse packing heat."

"Listen, baby girl, Duke's right. Lester is as crooked as a sidewinder in the sand. He's got one dead body attached to him already. You said it yourself. You think he's involved in this. Listen, we'll all go up to the door. You just tell him it's late and we gave you a lift over here. But we're not leaving you here alone. Your call."

This was like a bad comedy movie. *Two Old Men and a Baby Girl.* But there was no use in arguing with them.

"At least put the guns away so he doesn't think we're here to kill him."

They looked at each other and slipped the guns into their waistbands. *Please, God, don't let them shoot off a toe, or worse.*

All three of us trooped up to the front door of the house. I peeked through the window. The room was empty except for a few planks of wood and a sawhorse. I rang the bell but it must have been broken because there was no sound. Uncle Duke knocked hard, and I gave him a stern look.

"Uncle Duke, let me handle this, please."

He raised both hands in resignation.

I knocked this time. Still no answer. "Hmph. He told me to meet him here." I looked down at my watch. It was 8:37.

We all turned and stepped off the porch. That's when we heard a rustling in the bushes beside the house. No one moved. I looked toward the sound. A few seconds later, a young white guy darted from the bushes and tried to run past us. He practically knocked Daddy down but not before Uncle Duke grabbed the back of his hoodie. The guy tried to wriggle free, but Uncle Duke's grip was firm, and the guy was probably half my uncle's weight. Uncle Duke managed to wrestle him to the ground but dropped his gun in the process. Daddy leaped over and pointed his gun at the guy's head. I gasped in horror.

"Settle down before my gun accidentally goes off," Daddy said.

The guy froze.

Uncle Duke straddled him. "Who are you?"

The guy said nothing.

"You little punk, you made me drop my gun. Now, are you gonna answer me, or do I have to get it and beat the hell out of you with it? Why were you hiding in the bushes?"

"Fuck you, old man! Get off me!" the guy said through pants of breath.

"Butta, hand me my gun. Let me show him what an old man can do. Deena, call the police while I work this guy over. We can tell the cops it was self-defense."

My hands trembled as I dialed 911 for the second time in one week.

"Wait! Wait!" the guy yelled. "He told me to come over here and scare the woman who showed up."

"Keep talking," Daddy said.

"He paid me five hundred dollars. Told me not to kill her, just rough her up."

"Who hired you?"

"Get this guy off me. I can't breathe!"

"You might not get to breathe anyway when I'm finished with you. Who hired you?" Uncle Duke said.

"Some guy named Kyle."

"Kyle Bowen?" I said.

The guy squirmed underneath Uncle Duke's weight. "I don't know his last name."

Daddy looked at me. "Who's Kyle Bowen?"

"Charlie Lester's aide. He was with Lester at the church meeting on Saturday."

A few seconds later, I heard the wail of a police car. Daddy quickly picked up Uncle Duke's gun and slipped it in his pocket. His slipped his own gun inside an ankle holster he was wearing. By the time the car pulled up the guy was breathing hard and pleading for Uncle Duke to let him go.

Two big, burly officers jumped out of their squad car and ran over to us, their guns drawn. "Police! Everybody stop!"

Daddy and I put our hands up. The officers held the gun on Uncle Duke.

"Let me see your hands," one officer said while the other called for backup. My heart was pounding so loudly, I barely heard his instructions. The police were actually holding us at gunpoint. The whole scene had this chaotic energy that angered me more than it scared me.

"I called the police. That's my uncle and he stopped that guy from hurting me."

The officers continued the standoff, guns pointed. It was as if they weren't listening to me. A few seconds later, another police car raced up to the house. And a third after that. Now the street was flooded in red and blue lights. Everything was frightening. What if one of these policemen played fast and loose with his trigger?

"On your feet, both of you," the officer said to Uncle Duke and the hoodie guy.

Uncle Duke complied. As soon as he did, the hoodie guy got to his feet with his hands up. And a second later, he took off like a shot.

"Hey!" the officer yelled.

Three police officers took off in pursuit. Daddy, Uncle Duke, and I stood with our hands up facing guns, while the man who'd planned to attack me was chased by the cops.

"Somebody wanna tell me what's going on here?" the officer said.

We put our hands down. I'd never had this much interaction with the police in all my life. I didn't want to drag Daddy and Uncle Duke into the middle of this mess, so I spoke up first. "I agreed to meet Commissioner Lester here. But when we showed up, we found that guy hiding in the bushes. He told us he was hired by Kyle Bowen, Lester's aide, to show up here to attack me."

"All three of you were here to meet with the commissioner?" The officer glanced between Daddy and Uncle Duke suspiciously. Neither of them said a word. They simply glared back at him. Old men that had lived and seen as much as the two of them had probably earned the right to be stubborn assholes.

"They came along to make sure I was safe. The neighborhood . . . ," I said.

"Mmm . . . I see," he said, unconvinced.

"So where's the commissioner?"

"I don't know. I just told you, he sent the guy your colleagues are now chasing." Daddy and Uncle Duke stood staring at the officer with granite faces.

"Why were you meeting with Commissioner Lester?"

"I think he's involved in Delilah Gardner's death. She was murdered out on the island six months ago. And y'all just let a key witness escape."

"Hang tight." He stepped away with a couple other officers to talk out of our earshot.

The flashing lights and activity brought out a few onlookers along the curb. I saw someone filming with their cell phone. A few minutes later, the three officers who had gone off in pursuit of the hoodie guy came back empty-handed. Interestingly enough, no one fired their gun at a young white guy running away from the police. What were the odds that same thing would have happened if the hoodie guy had been Black? Every time I thought there was some iota of justice in this country, this country proved me wrong.

The officer stepped back over to us. "Miss, perhaps you can come down to the station and give us a statement. Maybe all three of you should come down."

Panic rushed through me like a bolt of lightning.

Daddy whispered to me, "It'll be okay, baby girl."

I wasn't so sure it would be.

CHAPTER 38

When we arrived at the police station, Howie was in the lobby. Standing beside him was the tiniest woman I'd ever seen in my life. She couldn't have been more than five feet tall and probably ninety pounds if she were holding a case of beer. Her short gray hair was highlighted with purple tips, all of which ran contrary to the black pantsuit and button-down shirt she wore.

"Howie? What are you doing here?!" I asked.

Before Howie could open his mouth to respond, Daddy piped up. "Now, baby girl, before you get your danders up, I called Howie on the way over here. You can't ever be too careful with the police. I thought maybe Howie should be here in case we needed some help."

"I'm glad you did, Mr. Jimmie. I brought along a friend of mine. Deena, this is Easter Prym. She's a criminal lawyer. Your dad filled me in on what happened. I think—"

"Howie, can I have a word with you . . . alone?"

Easter gave me and Howie a small nod and stepped away.

Howie and I walked to the other side of the lobby.

"What the hell, Howie?" I whispered. "You cart someone down here whose name sounds like she's a stripper and she looks like a punk rocker?"

"You need to get past all that," he whispered sternly. "She's a Duke Law grad and the best criminal defense attorney you'll find in the southeast. Charlie Lester is a dirty politician, according to your dad and uncle and everybody else in this town. But he's also powerful. He put a hit out on you. Twice."

"Obviously, they weren't smart enough to do much damage."

"Until he hires the right one, Deena. Are you even listening to me? He sent someone to break into your house. He sent someone to ambush you. Now, you've accused him of murder. You do not want to go into an interrogation room by yourself. You never talk to the police without a lawyer. You're a lawyer. You know this. You need somebody who can hold their own with the police."

I gazed beyond Howie at Easter Prym. She stood between Daddy and Uncle Duke, giving them instructions. Both men nodded attentively.

"Look, you give them a statement and you're done. Easter will be there to make sure nothing goes sideways."

I released a deep breath. "Fine."

We walked back over to Daddy, Uncle Duke, and Easter Prym.

"Deena, I know you're a lawyer, so I don't have to tell you the basics about answering only the questions they ask and all that bullshit," Easter said. I rolled my eyes at Howie. "Maybe the two of us can step outside and chat for a few minutes before we go inside with the police. I don't like the rooms in here," she said as she looked around the station as if it were infested with life-sized rodents. "I just want to hear from you everything that happened."

"Sure."

"I'll talk to Mr. Jimmie and Uncle Duke," Howie said.

Easter and I walked outside. How in the hell did I wind up standing outside talking to a criminal lawyer under a streetlamp? She reached into her jacket pocket and pulled out a business card. It was then that I spotted a small tattoo of a heart on the inside of her wrist.

"Here's my card. So you'll have my contact information. My first question is . . . how are you doing?"

"Well, it's not the best night I've ever had."

"I understand. I need you to tell me everything leading up to your being at Mr. Lester's house. Everything."

I recited everything that had happened, starting with my stumbling onto Holcomb's property and Delilah's relationship with Charlie Lester. I told her about the Ford Escape following me all over town, the break-in at Daddy's house, the baseball bat, Kyle Bowen's broken arm, and the evening's antics, courtesy of Lester. She nodded, only interrupting when she needed clarification on a point. It was weird, but just talking to her under that streetlamp made me feel at ease after everything that had happened.

"Ms. Prym—"

"Please call me Easter."

"Easter . . . there's something else that might come up. My father, my uncle, and I went to the morgue to verify that Holcomb was dead. My uncle has a friend that works there, and he let us in. I later found out that Holcomb's body was signed out of the morgue by someone who used my name as the next of kin. Charlie Lester works for Empire Realty. That company has the Gardners' property up for sale and they're both dead. I think he's behind all this. The break-in at my house and now tonight."

"Okay. I think I've got a handle on things."

"Can I ask you something?" I was slightly embarrassed to ask my question, but if she was purportedly acting as my attorney, I had a right to ask her questions too. "I know this is weird, and . . . No offense but . . ."

Easter smiled. "None taken. I was named after the holiday because I was born on it, more years ago than I care to admit. Prym is an old English name, or so my dad tells me." She pointed to her hair. "Purple is my favorite color. Anything else?"

"I'm sorry."

"The same way you were thrown off is the same way prosecutors and judges are, especially in this neck of the woods. People underestimate me, which gives me the advantage." She winked at me and smiled. "You ready?"

"I think so," I said.

"Okay, let's get through this and get you home."

* * *

AS IF THE night couldn't get any worse, Detective Mallory strolled into the lobby.

"Ms. Wood."

He sent me, Daddy, and Uncle Duke into three different rooms. We all agreed that Howie should go into the room with Uncle Duke to make sure he behaved himself. Uncle Duke didn't necessarily respect authority figures.

Mallory kept me waiting for what seemed like an eternity. It was so long that a female officer came in and asked me if I was okay and offered me something to drink. I passed. Easter and I sat in silence the entire time. If she didn't trust these rooms, then I didn't either. When the detective finally made it inside the room, I was beyond exhausted. He sat in a chair across from us and Easter slid him her business card across the table.

"Uh . . . Easter Prym? Okay, Easter."

"Officer," she said.

"Actually, it's Detective Mallory."

"Actually, it's Ms. Prym," she replied. She glanced at me and raised an eyebrow. Easter didn't take any shit. Nice.

The detective cleared his throat nervously before he spoke. "Thanks, Ms. Wood, for your time. I don't know if it was necessary to lawyer up. We just have a few questions, but your choice." He stared at me for a beat. "I'd like to ask you about Holcomb Gardner. Last Thursday, you came in to see me and told me he was missing. What I don't understand is why you reported him missing, adamant that I check the morgue, and then you later signed his body out of the morgue. Why?"

I looked at Easter and she nodded.

"I didn't sign his body out of the morgue. Someone else did and used my name."

"Who?"

"I don't know."

"Why would someone do that?"

"I have no idea."

He stared at me again before he spoke. "Okay, I just need to understand what happened this evening."

"I saw the commissioner at city hall this afternoon. I wanted to ask him some questions, so I approached him. He told me he was too busy to talk and asked his aide to jot down the address of his house and said we could talk there. The aide handed me the card and they left."

"So why was it so urgent to talk to Mr. Lester?"

"I already told you when you came to Mrs. Trainor's house. I think he's involved in a murder. That seems to warrant some urgency, don't you think?" Easter nudged my arm, signaling me to calm down.

"By the way, did your friend Rae ever show up?" he asked.

"Yes," I said flatly.

He gave me a sneer of satisfaction as if he were pleased with himself that he didn't lift a finger to find a Black woman and she turned up unharmed. He gloated on his hunch despite having shirked his responsibility to protect and serve.

The detective pinched his eyebrows and stared at me. "Why are you so sure Commissioner Lester is involved in Delilah Gardner's murder?"

I glanced at Easter before I spoke. "He was having a secret relationship with her, and he was probably the last person to see her before she was killed in a hit-and-run accident six months ago. Sound familiar?"

"How do you know Mr. Lester and Ms. Gardner were in a relationship?"

I turned to Easter, and she nodded her assent to share the information. "Her best friend told me."

"I'll need her name."

I was suddenly disgusted with myself for dragging yet another person into all of this. But the police should have spoken with Miss Ophelia six months ago. More and more I became convinced that Lester orchestrated this entire thing, and the police needed to speak with her and anyone else who had information about Delilah Gardner—including her best friend. I jotted Miss Ophelia's name on the detective's notepad.

"I checked with the Glynn County sheriff's office, and they have no leads or any other information that would suggest Commissioner Lester is involved in her death."

My anger whipped and spiked with his statement. "Did the Glynn County sheriff's office know he was involved in a personal relationship with her? Did they talk to him about the last time he saw her, which also happens to be the night before she was killed?

Did anyone bother to talk to her best friend, who knew about the relationship? Did anyone question why Charlie Lester's real estate company has the Gardners' property up for sale and both of them are dead? And just because I have a mild interest, is anyone out looking for the two men who tried to kill me, one of whom you have the name of and the other who got away *unharmed* by your officers despite my seventy-four-year-old uncle holding him down for you? Why is no one doing their job around here?!"

Easter touched my arm, warning me to calm down again. I couldn't. I was livid. Uncle Duke said Lester was a snake, but that was an insult to snakes.

"Detective, my client has given you all the information she knows. Not to mention, you haven't asked her a single question about the man who was hired to harm her. Would you care to ask her about that?"

The detective cleared his throat again. "Can you describe the man who was at the house this evening?"

It took me a few seconds to calm down. "Early twenties, white, dark hair, gray hoodie, jeans."

"Have you ever seen him before tonight?"

"No."

Mallory fumbled through a file in front of him. "I pulled the report from the night your house was broken into. Do you think it was the same man?"

"No. I think Kyle Bowen tried to break into my house. He has a broken arm courtesy of my stepmother's baseball bat. But maybe you should be asking Kyle Bowen or Charlie Lester."

He stared at me, then closed his file. "Why don't you sit tight. I'll be back in a minute." Detective Mallory left the room. Either

Mallory was woefully incompetent or he didn't give a damn. Probably both. I wondered how Daddy and Uncle Duke were faring. I prayed that Uncle Duke hadn't unleashed another tirade about Charlie Lester.

Fifteen minutes later, Detective Mallory walked back into the room. "I think we have everything we need. You're free to go."

Easter chimed up. "There's one more thing we need to discuss. You need to have an officer keep watch over my client. There have been two attempts to harm her and someone in a dark car has been following her."

"We don't have the manpower to provide twenty-four-hour protection. I'll have patrol beef up their presence in her neighborhood. That's the best I can offer."

Easter stared at him. Truthfully, I was surprised Mallory was willing to offer that much.

"Where's my father?"

"Your dad and uncle are waiting for you outside."

Easter and I slid away from the table and walked out.

* * *

OUTSIDE THE POLICE station, the four of us—me, Howie, Daddy, and Uncle Duke—stood around my car in the parking lot after Easter left.

"Baby girl, I don't want to say I told you so, but . . . When those cops pulled up, guns drawn, one of us could have been shot."

"I know, Daddy. I'm so sorry." Ignoring Daddy's pleas to drop this was nothing compared to the guilt I felt for lying to him. And just like in high school, I'd gotten caught again.

Uncle Duke walked up to me and threw his arm around my shoulders. "You gotta understand, sweetie, cats like Lester got no soul. He is used to doing whatever he wants but he won't get away this time. Trust me." Uncle Duke and Daddy nodded at each other.

"Uncle Duke, please don't do anything crazy. Promise me."

"I don't make promises I can't keep."

"Daddy?"

"Come on, Duke. Let me take you home."

Howie and I watched as the two men climbed into Daddy's truck. They sat inside talking, their faces grim and serious. If Daddy or Uncle Duke had been shot, I'd never have forgiven myself. Every time I tried to move forward, I fell ten feet backward. I just wanted things to go back to the way they were before, when Ma was alive and healthy. When I wasn't struggling through a horrendous marriage. When my life was whole, and I was in control. After a few minutes, Daddy started up the engine. Howie and I watched them as they pulled away from the parking lot.

"You okay?" Howie asked.

"No."

"You must be onto something that Charlie Lester doesn't want you poking around in."

"And please don't tell me to stay out of this. Charlie Lester has dragged me into it, so I'm gonna finish it."

"I won't tell you to do anything. I just want you to be careful. If Lester's involved in two murders, and he's hiring people to break into your house and ambush you, then he's really dangerous. I'm worried about you."

We stared at each other.

He pulled me in and hugged me, and I swear I wanted to stay there forever. I just wanted to melt right into him and forget everything that had happened, all the stupid mistakes I'd made, all the messes and missteps. I held on to Howie like doing so would take away every bad thing.

When he pulled back, he looked down at me. "Dee, it's all gonna be okay. Trust me."

He softly kissed me on the top of my head. "Tell me what else I can do to help?"

"Nothing. I'm so sorry I dragged you and Daddy and Uncle Duke into this mess."

"Come on. Get in your car. I'll follow you home."

"You don't have to do that. I'm a big girl."

"I know I don't have to, but it'll make me feel better. Besides, your dad will kill me if I don't make sure his *baby girl* gets home okay."

I smiled.

"Come on, it's late. You need to get home and rest."

As Howie opened the car door for me, Charlie Lester drove up in a huge silver Range Rover. He stopped and rolled down the window.

Howie jumped in between me and the car. "What the hell do you want?"

"I'm sorry I wasn't able to make our meeting this evening, Ms. Wood. Something came up." He smiled and I felt my skin crawl. "I heard there was some commotion at my house this evening. I trust everything's fine now. But a little piece of advice . . . you don't wanna fuck with me." He grinned and drove off.

"Oh my God!"

"Get in the car. Let's get you home safely."

CHAPTER 39

I was punch-drunk tired by the time I got home from the police station. Daddy had dropped Uncle Duke off and pulled into the driveway at the same time as Howie and me. Howie tooted his horn, and we both waved as he drove away.

Ruth was in her bathrobe and up waiting for us in the living room. The soft low light of the lamp on the table gave the room a small, quiet feel. "Jimmie, is everything okay? Deena, you alright?"

I slumped onto the sofa without responding.

Daddy glanced at me and back at Ruth. "Everything's fine, Roo. I met up with Duke and Deena. We had to go by to see somebody. When we got there, we found some guy who meant us no good. We had to go down to the police station to give a statement. Might have something to do with the break-in last Sunday."

"Heavenly Fadduh! De debble workin' overtime."

The concern in her voice stung. She was genuinely worried about my father, and maybe me too. I felt like a monster because it was my bullheadedness that had dragged Daddy and Uncle Duke into this hornet's nest. Tonight could have gone wrong all kinds of ways. Any one of us could have been hurt or worse. If something had happened to Daddy, if I lost him too, I couldn't go on.

"Daddy, please forgive me."

"Shh . . . Charlie Lester is a dirty son of a gun and he's trying to drag you down with him. Right now, you need to rest. There's nothing more we can do tonight."

"Jimmie, how is Charlie Lester involved in this?"

"I'll explain it all later, Roo. It's been a long evening. Why don't we all try to get a good night's sleep."

I nodded agreement. I wanted to crawl into bed and forget this day had ever happened. It had started out so good. I was on the brink of having my own place and ended up with a visit to the police station and my very own criminal lawyer. I never should have played the big bad bitch confronting Charlie Lester and threatening him. Ma used to say, *If you're gonna run with the big dogs, you better be prepared to bite.*

"Deena, why don't you go on and get ready for bed," Ruth said. "I'll bring you a cup of hot tea."

I looked at Daddy and Ruth. They both stared at me with such concern, like I was the only thing that was important. I got up from the sofa and headed into the bedroom. I heard them talking in low voices as I changed out of my clothes. By the time I got out of the shower and dressed for bed, some of the anxiety of the evening was wearing off.

A minute later, there was a light tap on the door.

"Come in."

"Here's your cup of tea." Ruth entered and sat a mug of tea on the bedside table. "Lavender chamomile."

"Thank you."

"How are you feeling?"

I sat on the edge of the bed. "I'm fine. Just tired. Like Daddy said, it's been a long day."

"Of course. Deena, I know it's kinda crazy right now, but you're smart. You'll figure this all out. I know you will."

"No, Ruth. I'm not doing this anymore. I was stupid to get involved in the first place. And every time I think I'm doing some good, I make things worse. Daddy or Uncle Duke could have gotten killed tonight if one of those cops decided to let his finger fall on the trigger."

"But they didn't. And if Lester is going through this much trouble to stop you, you must be mighty close to figuring it all out. Don't give up now. Trust yourself on this, Deena."

"No. The police can find out what happened to the Gardners. Or maybe they won't. Either way, I'm done."

Ruth pursed her lips and stared at me. "But what about helping that young woman, Rae, get her land back? What's that poor girl got now that her grandmother is gone? Can you imagine what it must be like to be her right now?"

"She doesn't trust me. She thinks I'm up to some kind of scam. Anyway, she'll have to figure it out on her own."

"Oh, Deena. Try to understand, Black folks have been robbed of so much for so long. Our freedom, our dignity, and now our future. If you can stop even a little part of that, I think you should. Do you know what a blessing and privilege it is to own property? A piece of land or a structure that is totally yours? Don't leave that poor girl without a legacy."

I thought about the day Daddy drove me out to Ruth's house, totaled by Hurricane Michael. Property that had been in her family for generations. Decimated by Mother Nature and she couldn't even rebuild it because the government didn't believe it was really hers. Ruth was right. *Robbed* was the correct term for what had happened.

Ruth patted my shoulder. "I'll let you rest now. Maybe you'll think differently after a good night's sleep."

"Good night."

She smiled at me before she walked out and closed the door.

My phone buzzed. *Howie*.

Hey, you good?

I replied.

I'm good. Thanks for everything.

A few seconds later:

Sleep well ❤

I took a couple sips from the mug before I pulled the covers back and climbed into bed. I was just about to turn off the lamp when my phone buzzed again. This time it was a text from Rae.

I'm sorry. I was all in my feelings. I appreciate u and everything u doing. Please help me find out what happened to my grandmother ❤

I didn't respond. I simply clicked off the phone and turned out the lights.

I'm really worried now. Deena has run up against Charlie Lester. She's thinking of giving up. That's exactly what he wants her to do. If Deena stops searching, we're all done for. I hate Charlie. I never should have trusted him. Another one of my many mistakes.

She has to help Rae get back what's rightfully hers. She has to help us all.

This is about so much more than her. It's bigger than me or Holcomb. This is about the ancestors and those who will come after Deena. Everything that is happening right now, all the things she is curious about, have been carved from the past and threaten her future. The struggles we endured, the things we built, and all that we've left behind are at risk. One day, time and experience will wrap together and give her what she needs to make sense of all this.

Do not be afraid, Deena. You are stronger than all your enemies.

I need to help her in a much bigger way. I may have already waited too long. I stopped when I should have started. I walked when I should have run. But no more. Jimmie won't like it. But that's not important now.

I have to show her how to stop those monsters even if I have to give up the most precious thing to do it.

CHAPTER 40

The next morning, I woke to the earthy, smoky aroma of something burning. *Ruth.* I tried to ignore it because I knew what it was. By the time I walked into the kitchen, the smell was overpowering. There on the table, in a small bowl, was the source. Ruth was burning some sort of root. The ashes were still smoldering.

"Deena! Morning, honey." Ruth walked in through the back door. The one Daddy had boarded up after the break-in on Sunday until the glass repairman came out to fix it. He'd installed a second dead bolt on both the back and front doors. I hated Charlie Lester with every fiber in my body for what he was putting my family through.

I eased over to the coffee maker on the counter. "What's that?" I said, nodding toward the bowl.

"Just a little something to bring some calm into the house. There's been so much going on around here lately. Dead bodies, bad men with evil motives. It'll keep trouble away and give everybody some peace."

Bless her heart. Ruth still held on to the old Gullah-Geechee ways and part of me had to respect her for it. She knew who she was and she didn't change for anyone.

"Can I make you some breakfast?" she said.

"No. Just coffee for me this morning." I grabbed a travel mug from the cabinet and poured the coffee.

"Oh, that's no kind of breakfast. Let me wrap up a couple pieces of sausage and some toast for you to eat on the way."

"Thanks, Roo."

She stopped, still holding the sausage in the air, and stared at me before she broke into a huge grin. I patted her arm and smiled.

"Thanks for last night. You were right. Rae shouldn't have to navigate this alone. What little help I can offer her helps all of us."

* * *

I GOT TO work on time, but I sat inside my car in the parking lot of the Old Victorian for two reasons. One, I didn't want to go inside. I was bored to tears with that damn job. Surely I could do better than this. And two, the fact that the head of the company wanted to turn me into her personal minion to keep an eye on her self-absorbed partner and nephew only made things worse. There had to be some other purpose for me.

I closed my eyes and listened for Ma's voice. Nothing. That deafening silence overwhelmed me with sadness. It dawned on me that in chasing down a dead man I didn't know, I'd lost my mother. I remembered the things she said, but I longed to hear the *way* she said them. I pulled out my cell phone and scrolled through my voicemails until I landed on the few I had from her. They were all pithy. *Call me, it's Ma. . . . It's me, nothing urgent . . .*

And then I broke down and cried. I missed her so much. I leaned forward on the steering wheel and cried until my head started to hurt. After about ten minutes, I realized this was getting me nowhere.

Enough!

I reached in the glove compartment and pulled out a pack of tissues. I blew my nose, then adjusted the rearview mirror to look at myself. I was a mess. The lack of sleep was starting to show in the dark circles under my eyes. My skin looked dull. Clare would not be pleased. I was not taking care of myself as she had instructed. I blew my nose again and dabbed on a bit of lip gloss. Trying to make a mess better.

By the time I stepped inside the Old Victorian, Peg was standing at the front desk talking to Jennie.

"Oh, thank goodness, Deena! Beau has been looking for you. He wants you to come up to his office. He said for you to come up as soon as you got in."

"Okay," I said as I marched away from her and back to my office.

I was clueless as to why Beau wanted to see me. Maybe he'd caught wind of the fact that I was supposed to keep watch over him and he wanted to set me straight. Good. I didn't want to get caught up between him and Clare anyway. Or maybe he wanted to make more veiled threats about my doing something other than Medallion's work. Whatever it was, he didn't scare me. He wasn't smart enough to intimidate me.

I got upstairs and stood outside his door. "You wanted to see me?"

"Deena! Come on in. I want you to meet a friend of mine."

I stepped inside and peered across the room. Beau was sitting behind his desk and on the leather sofa across from him was Charlie Lester. My shoulders tensed and my stomach coiled into a gigantic knot.

"Deena, this is Commissioner Charlie Lester. Charlie, this is Deena Wood, our ace legal consultant."

I froze as Lester stood from the sofa and extended his hand. "Nice to *formally* meet you, Deena."

Something about the way he said the word *formally* and the leer on his face made my skin crawl. Lester knew exactly what he was doing. He was letting me know that his power and his friendships trumped anything I could possibly do. A physical manifestation of the threat he made last night: *You don't wanna fuck with me.*

But how did he know I worked at Medallion?

"You okay there, Deena?" Beau asked with a chuckle.

"Uh . . . yeah." I finally shook Lester's hand. I wanted to vomit.

"Oh, Deena and I know each other, don't we?" He was still holding my hand. When I tried to pull it away, he gripped even tighter. "Deena is one of my constituents." He patted the top of my hand before he finally released it.

"Is that so?" Beau said. "Well, the good and right commissioner here is helping me out with a little pet project of mine."

Lester grinned. "We could always use a smart lawyer to help us out, isn't that right, Beau?"

Beau laughed. "Hold on there, buddy. I'm afraid we keep Deena too busy around here. Ain't that right, Deena?"

They both pissed me off, discussing how they could make use of me like I was chattel.

"Well, I'd better get back downstairs. All that work that keeps me so busy is waiting." I quickly turned and paced out of the office. Lester had accomplished his mission, to scare the shit out of me and let me know there was nothing I could do about it because he was friends with my boss.

But his threats didn't scare me. They only made me stronger. Now that I was sure he was involved in Holcomb's and Delilah's deaths, I would bring his ass down.

I left Beau's office and headed straight for the attic.

CHAPTER 41

I quietly slipped through the attic door and closed it behind me. I tiptoed up the wood stairs, praying that they wouldn't give me up to anyone who might be listening. By the time I reached the top stair, slivers of daylight slinked through the small dormers of each room, offering just enough light to see. The heat was unbearable. Stifling. The first thing I did was touch the walls. They were dry. No warm water seeping through. An odd sense of peace washed over me as I stood at the end of the attic hallway. It was the most incredible feeling, and I wasn't afraid anymore. Not like last time.

If Lester and Beau were working together and both of them were tied to the Gardners' property—Beau had their family home and Lester had their island property—maybe there was something in the Medallion files that would help me bring the men down. I quickly walked down the hallway. I made it past the storage room at the far end of the attic and then dashed inside the room where I'd spotted the framed photo of the Gardners' home. I flipped through a couple other photos but found nothing. I moved over to an old rolltop desk in the corner and rambled through the drawers. I didn't know what I was looking for, maybe some clue that would help me figure out who had killed Delilah and Holcomb and whether Beau had stolen their property. The drawers were empty. Nothing.

I stood in the center of the room, staring at the framed photo of the Old Victorian. I suddenly felt like I needed to be in this attic but not this room. That's when I felt a light movement on my shoulder. I quickly turned but there was no one there. That same eerie feeling was back. The air around me was thick and heavy as if someone were standing beside me. It was like a presence, something else in the room with me.

Ruth called them haints.

Mrs. Trainor called them spiritual guides.

Ma called them angels.

Someone or something was in this attic. I was not alone. Then, a light brush of air swept over my face like it had that first night I was up here.

I didn't move or flinch. Slowly, the smell of cigarette smoke and perfume enveloped me. This time the scent was almost hypnotic, like standing next to a beautiful woman at a bar, where the scent of her becomes your scent too. Unlike the first night, I wasn't afraid. Not this time. I didn't feel the urge to run. I had no fear. I knew that whatever, or whoever, was up here did not want to hurt me. I simply stood still and waited. Within seconds, it was there. A strange sensation came over me, almost as if I were floating above the room. I closed my eyes and against everything that seemed logical, I leaned into that feeling of weightlessness. I let myself float for a moment. And as quickly as the feeling hit me, it was gone. I couldn't explain it, but I felt like myself again.

Someone was here with me. A gentle unseen presence. *Delilah?* This had been her home. Whoever it was, I knew in the marrow of my bones that they meant me no harm. I closed my eyes and soaked in the calm presence.

I paced back across the hall to the file room and searched through the shelves of boxes. I scanned various names marked on them. All the projects Medallion had been involved in. None of them were familiar to me. At least not until I spotted a smaller box tucked behind a larger one on the bottom shelf. I pulled it out. It was marked "Bellar." The name of the hedge fund Howie told me about. I opened it. Inside were records and documents, each file labeled with a different state—Georgia, South Carolina, Kentucky, New Mexico. They were real estate contracts.

"What the hell?!" I quietly mumbled to myself.

I pulled the files from the box. I wasn't sure but maybe there was something among these papers that might help me find out who killed the Gardners. One thing I did know for sure—there was something in this house that was trying to help me.

"Deena, what ya up to there?"

I jumped and quickly turned around. It was Beau.

"Why are you up here digging through files?"

My pulse pumped. "Uh . . . Joe asked me to prepare some boxes for a destruction order."

Beau gave me a half smile that never reached his eyes. "I see. Why are you doing this and not Peg?"

I didn't respond as I held the files tight to my chest.

"Just make sure you're doing the work we pay you for."

"Uh . . . of course."

"You know, Clare has this theory that when you're good at one thing, you should only do that one thing. Now, she and I differ about her theories when it comes to running a business. But I think in your case, her theory might be correct. You come in late, leave early. We pay you to handle contracts for Medallion. Any little side things you do, that's not part of your job here. People can get hurt when you aren't attentive to your job."

Suddenly, I heard a window slam in the room across the hall. Beau and I both looked in the direction of the noise.

He looked back at me. "What was that?"

I said nothing. Sweat trickled down my back.

"Remember, stick to the work we pay you for. Trust me, you don't want to spread yourself too thin around here."

He turned on his heel and walked out of the room.

I quickly replaced the lids on all the boxes and hustled back downstairs with the files.

Deena trusts me. She is not afraid.

I slammed the window to protect her. And I'd slam a thousand more windows to protect her too.

She is so close now. She is smart and I know she'll put it all together. Her and that young man of hers. I need her to continue to dig and uncover every little secret. Her curiosity will save us all.

There is only one thing that remains. Jimmie must tell her the truth about the baby and what happened between us.

CHAPTER 42

If Empire Realty was owned by a New York City hedge fund as Howie said, maybe there was some connection to Medallion too. It would make sense since Lester and Beau were working together.

I sat at my desk with the Bellar files stacked beside me. I opened the first file, marked "South Carolina." It contained at least a half dozen or so purchase contracts, all made by Empire Realty. All this time, I'd believed the files in the attic held records for projects Medallion had worked on as an engineering contractor. But Medallion was also keeping records for a hedge fund's properties. What in the world was going on around this place?

The purchases were all different. Some of them were for land parcels and some for residential homes, but each bought at bargain prices, all less than ten thousand dollars. A three-bedroom home on two acres was purchased for thirty-five hundred dollars. Another home, same size on five acres, was purchased for five thousand dollars. I opened another file marked "Virginia." Much like with the first, the land parcels appeared to be large and purchased for very little money. This confirmed everything Howie had said about the hedge fund purchasing poor-performing properties. This pattern went on through every file, all states in the southeast and New Mexico as well.

The last document in the file was simply a list of names and addresses and other contact information. I didn't recognize any of them.

I went back to the file marked "South Carolina." I pulled out a contract for the sale of a house in a town called Cuba. According to Google Maps, it was about an hour away from Brunswick. I could drive there and be back in town before the end of the workday.

I tucked all the files in my bag and called Peg. I lied and told her I had a doctor's appointment, and I would be back in a few hours.

* * *

I CROSSED THE Georgia–South Carolina border an hour later. According to my GPS, I was about ten minutes away from one of the properties that Bellar had purchased for thirty-five hundred dollars. This one was purchased from Edward Langley. I turned off the highway onto a two-lane road. Three miles later, I saw a small sign: Welcome to Cuba, South Carolina. I'd never heard of this town. But that didn't mean anything.

I passed a place called the Road Rabbit gas station, and a mile later I turned onto a gravel road that ended in a cul-de-sac. There were four houses. I checked the name and address on the contract again before I pulled up to a modest-looking clapboard house. I was a little surprised when I spotted a small pickup truck in the driveway and saw a light on inside through the front screen door. Someone lived here.

I looked around at the other three houses that sat nearby. None of them were fancy. In fact, far from it. One house had at least four different patches on the roof. Another had a front window patched over with plastic instead of glass. I pulled into the driveway for the house listed on the contract. It was the best-looking one out of all of them. I prayed this wouldn't be another encounter like the one I'd had with Holcomb.

I stepped out of my car, walked up a small set of stairs, and tapped on the screen door. A minute later, a tall, middle-aged woman stepped up to the door. Her blond hair, streaked with gray, was thinning at the edges. The deep wrinkles and age spots on her face told me she had seen a lot of years, most of them spent outside in the sun.

"May I help you?" she said with a deep southern drawl.

"Hi, are you the owner of this house?"

She gave me a suspicious look. "Who's asking?"

"My name is Deena Wood. I was hoping you could help me. There's a company that bought your home along with several other properties. I'm trying to find out if the sales were legal."

She placed her hand on her hip. "Listen, lady, I don't know what you're up to, but I haven't sold my home. This is my house. Been in my family for decades. I've never sold my house."

She started to walk away from the door.

"*Please!* Do you know someone named Edward Langley? I just need some information and then I'll leave you alone. I promise."

She stopped and gave me another suspicious look. "Who did you say you were?"

"My name is Deena. I think there is a company that is essentially buying property and displacing people without them realizing it. You might lose your home. I'm trying to stop them."

"Are you a detective or something?"

"No, ma'am. I'm a lawyer."

She scoped me for a moment, then slowly swung the squeaky screen door open.

"Thank you."

I walked into a small living room. It was furnished with the usual things: sofa, chairs, a coffee table. But what really caught my attention were all the family photos lining the walls. Some of them dated back as far as the forties and fifties, judging from the clothing in the pictures.

"Have a seat." I took a seat on the sofa and she took the chair next to me. "Now, what's this business about Eddie?"

"Do you know Edward Langley? He was the person who sold this house."

"Eddie couldn't have sold this house because he ain't lived here in three years." She hesitated. "He's my cousin. His mama was my aunt, but she passed away right about the time he left town."

"Were you and your aunt the owners of this house?"

"I told you, I'm the owner. My folks left the house to me. And my granddaddy left it to them."

"Did your parents have a will?"

"No, and why you asking all these questions?"

"If there was no will, your cousin and any other surviving relatives of your parents would inherit a portion of this property."

"Uh-uh, Eddie ain't lived here in years like I said. I pay the taxes on this property."

I looked at the woman and my heart sank for her. "Ms. . . . ?"

"Nell . . . Nell Drucker."

"Ms. Drucker—"

"Call me Nell. Everybody around here does."

"Nell . . . I'm afraid if your name isn't on the deed and your parents didn't have a will, everyone they were related to may have inherited a share of this house. That includes any cousins or other relatives you have. It doesn't matter if you paid the taxes, or if they didn't live here. It's a legal process called heirs property. Did your aunt have any other kids?"

"A daughter and the one boy, Eddie. And he was a piece of work too. Always got some get-rich-quick scheme. Has he gone off and done something crazy?"

"I'm not sure. But I have this contract here that says he sold his interest in this house. Have you heard from your cousin lately?"

"No."

"Have you recently received a letter from an attorney talking about buying your house?"

"Wait a minute. I got a couple letters . . ."

She hustled off to the kitchen and returned with two letters in her hand. "I got this letter from some lawyer. I just ignored it because I ain't selling my house. This house is all I have."

"Can I take a look?"

The letter was from an attorney in Charleston, and it explained that his client had purchased a share of the property. But more troublesome was the second paragraph of the letter:

> *Since acquiring a share of the above-listed property, we have determined that it would be in the best interest of all parties attached to this property to sell it and split the proceeds in proportion to everyone's respective interests. In lieu of a public sale, my client is prepared to accept $50,000 as payment for their interest share of the above-listed property. If this offer is acceptable to you, you must respond within 30 days of the date of this letter. If we do not hear from you by then, we will be forced to pursue our options in a court of law.*

At the bottom of the letter in the "cc:" block was the name Bellar Homes.

"Nell, this letter essentially says you have to buy back the interest share your cousin sold or else they will force a sale of the property."

"Wait a minute. What are you talking about?"

"Your cousin sold his interest in the property and now the company that bought it wants to sell it. They can do that unless you can come up with fifty thousand dollars to buy their interest and keep the property for yourself."

"I don't have that kind of money!"

"Did you call and tell them that?"

"I just told you, I ignored that blasted letter."

I looked at the date of both letters. The last one was dated fourteen days ago. "Nell, you're going to have to get a lawyer to help you sort this all out. You only have about two weeks to do so or they may force you out of your home. You can't ignore this letter."

"Did you hear me when I said I don't have fifty thousand dollars to pay someone? I also don't have money for a lawyer. And I am *not* leaving my house!"

I sighed and stared at her for a moment. "I tell you what. Call this woman." I handed her one of Sarah Wheeler's business cards from the Georgia Heirs Property Law Center. "She's in Georgia. She might be able to help and she won't charge you. Because you're in South Carolina, she may have to refer you to someone in this state who is more familiar with South Carolina laws. But either way, it's really important that you call her ASAP. You don't have a lot of time."

She took the card as she looked at me suspiciously. "Okay."

Now, I needed to do one more thing.

CHAPTER 43

I drove back to Brunswick and straight to LaShonda's house. I knocked on the door. I knew she was home because Ruth told me she wasn't working but looking for a job. Again. LaShonda was always looking for a job because she could never hold one for very long. She either cussed out her supervisor or caused a major scrap between coworkers so that her days were always numbered wherever she worked. A "shit starter," as Ma had called her.

LaShonda finally lumbered to the door with her boot intact. She was dressed in a nightshirt and her hair was under a bonnet. It was almost noon and she was still in bed? Ma would have rustled me out of there if I'd ever tried to sleep through the middle of the day. But LaShonda's mother had become full-time babysitter to her four grandkids and she didn't have much fight left in her.

"Deena? What are you doing here? What time is it?"

"I think I found someone who can help you with the situation with your relative regarding the house."

She looked at me like she didn't know what I was talking about. I heard her mother call from behind her, asking who was at the door.

"You told me one of your stepfather's relatives is trying to force you out of your house, remember?"

"Oh, that asshole."

"I noticed that you weren't at the meeting at the church last Saturday. You should have come."

LaShonda yawned and stretched. "Yeah. Wait, I thought you were too busy with your *new job*?"

I ignored her sarcasm. She always made everything more difficult than it needed to be. "Can I take a look at the letter you said you received where someone threatened to take away your house?"

She stared at me through the screen door for a beat before she pushed it open. I walked inside.

"Excuse the mess. I been busy too," she said with a frown.

The layout of LaShonda's house was exactly like Daddy's. But the two houses couldn't have been more different. Where Daddy and Ruth kept our house clean and in good repair, LaShonda's was the exact opposite. There was a hole about three feet wide in the living room ceiling that opened onto the wood joists. Laundry, paper, and toys were everywhere, on the sofa and chairs, on the table, and, of course, on the floor. The television was blaring the hoots and cheers from a morning talk show.

LaShonda's mother walked into the room from the kitchen. She was a short, round woman with a face full of moles. She was in her bathrobe too. And then it made sense why LaShonda was still in her pajamas.

"Hey, Deena! LaShonda told me you were back home. It's good to see you again."

"You too, Mrs. Duncan."

"Mama, you got that letter? The one about the house."

"Oh yeah. Let me get it."

Her mother hustled off down the hallway. LaShonda and I stood in silence. She turned and watched the talk show to avoid making small talk with me. And I was okay with that. A minute later, her mother returned and handed me the letter.

"Thanks." I read it. The letter was from an attorney in Savannah, and it explained that his client had purchased a share of LaShonda's house. The second paragraph contained near-identical wording to the letter Nell Drucker had received, except this time the amount was thirty-five thousand dollars—fifteen thousand dollars less than what they were demanding for Nell's house. And just like on Nell's letter, the "cc:" block at the bottom contained the name Bellar Homes.

"This letter only gives you about a week to take care of this."

LaShonda looked at me like she was irritated. "That's why I was trying to get you to help."

I sighed. Why was I even trying with this heffa? I took one of Sarah's business cards from my bag.

"Look, call this woman. She's with the Georgia Heirs Property Law Center, and she can help you figure out how to stay in your house. She won't charge you, but you need to call her today. I mean it. You don't have a lot of time with these situations. Okay?" I handed her the card. "If you want to keep your house, you need to call her right away."

"We will," LaShonda's mother said eagerly.

LaShonda took the card. She yawned again. "Okay."

I left the house and headed for my car. It was on LaShonda now. She couldn't say I didn't help.

"Hey, Deena!"

I turned around.

"Thanks," LaShonda said before she walked away from the screen door.

That was a nice gesture, but the cynical side of me figured her mother had forced her to do it.

I hopped back inside my car and sped off, praying Daddy or Roo hadn't seen me parked in front of LaShonda's house in the middle of the day. Daddy would ask me a bunch of questions, none of which I wanted to answer, and Roo would try to feed me. As I pulled away, headed back to the office, I was convinced Lester and Beau were behind this entire scheme. I just couldn't figure out how all the pieces fit together and why Holcomb and Delilah had been murdered.

Then the most horrific thought occurred to me. I'd accused Lester of killing the Gardners last night at the police station. I'd also told the police about Rae. If they weren't complete idiots, they would question Lester about the murders and mention Delilah's granddaughter. The fact that Rae hadn't already been murdered like her grandmother and uncle meant that Charlie Lester didn't know about her. If Delilah kept Rae in the dark about Lester, then perhaps she had kept Lester in the dark about Rae's existence. But if he found out about her, Rae would be as good as dead.

I drove straight to Rae's house.

CHAPTER 44

I hadn't responded to Rae's text from last night. I dialed her cell as I headed for her house. No answer.

I was standing on her front porch ten minutes later. I rang the doorbell. There was no answer. I nervously waited. Each second she didn't answer made my stomach queasy with unbridled fear that Lester had gotten here first.

I rang the doorbell several times in succession. I was just about to walk away when she peeped through the sidelight window, the same way she had that first day I met her. A couple seconds later, she opened the door, tying a red robe around her waist. Her braids were disheveled.

"I'm sorry, Rae. Did I wake you?"

"Uh . . . no. Is everything okay?"

"I wanted to talk to you about—"

Rae quickly put a finger up to her lips, indicating I needed to be quiet. "Sure, we can talk about that church bake sale."

At first, I didn't understand. Then she pointed toward the bedroom down the hall. Maybe Lester was here already. I mouthed the words *Are you okay?*

"I'm fine. I'm glad you stopped by. Come on in. Just give me a minute. Have a seat in the living room."

She hustled down the hall, the edge of her bathrobe flapping behind her. I sat on the sofa. The television was on and blared the same morning talk show that was on at LaShonda's house.

A few minutes later Rae returned. A tall, handsome Black guy with long dark locs pulled up in a man bun followed behind her. I was a little slow, but I finally put it together. I hadn't wakened her. I had interrupted her.

I watched them from the sofa as she walked him to the door. He leaned down to kiss her.

"I'll call you later," he said.

"Okay." She closed the door and joined me in the living room.

"I am so sorry. I didn't know you had company," I said.

"Who, Donte?" She flicked her wrist toward the door he'd just walked out of. "He's not company. He's just a little exercise I engage in every so often. You want something to eat or drink?"

"Um . . . no thanks."

"Come on, join me in the kitchen. I'm starving. *Exercise* always makes me hungry." She gave me a devilish smile. "And Donte . . . whoo, chile! I'm famished. So, who makes you hungry?"

I smiled. "That's none of your business." I was happy that we were joking, after the last time we were together and how we'd left it between us.

Rae scoped me from head to toe. "Hmm . . . you look like you haven't *exercised* in a minute, and I don't mean jogging either."

Rae was funny, but I decided to change the subject. "Listen, I want to apolo—"

"Uh-uh. I owe you the apology. Gran always taught me when you're wrong, you own up to it. I'm failing miserably at this whole adulting thing. And I'm rolling around in this house with memories of Gran in every corner. Some days are tougher than others. I didn't mean to act out on you the last time you were here. I know now you were just trying to help. I'm the one who owes the apology. I hope you'll forgive me."

We both stood there in silence. I admired Rae. This girl continued to display a level of maturity I was sure I still hadn't reached even though I was almost twenty years her senior. She was working, paying bills, and still healing with no one in her corner. At least after Ma died, I still had Daddy. In the silence, I thought about Ma's always admonishing me to help somebody else to help myself. I finally realized I wasn't doing this for Rae as much as I was doing it for me.

Rae walked to the kitchen sink and washed her hands. She opened the fridge and took out a food carton with Chinese letters on the side. "Donte always likes to order food but never eats it all." She grabbed a fork from the drawer and took a bite. "Yuck! This shit is gross." She dropped the carton in the trash and then removed a frying pan from the bottom cabinet. "I'll make us something to eat. You like salmon cakes?"

"Sure."

"Great." She smiled brightly. A few minutes later, she had water boiling for rice and was spicing up canned salmon.

I sat down at the table. "You haven't had any weird white dudes following you around lately, have you?"

"What?"

"Someone has been following me all over town." I decided to spare her the details of everything that had happened. I didn't want to send her into another meltdown like the last time I was here. Hell, I was surprised I hadn't had another one since this morning in the car. "I just wanted to make sure you were safe."

"No, I haven't noticed anyone. But are you okay? Who the hell is following you around?"

"I'm fine. It's not important. But I think I might have a lead on who stole your grandmother's property. But I need your help. Did your grandmother have a box of documents or important papers? Something that might be related to her owning property or rather selling it to a company called Empire Realty."

"Papers? Why you need to go through Gran's things?" She placed the lid on the pot of rice and lowered the flame.

"I think something really bad is going on with your grandmother's death. I didn't know her, but you did."

"I don't understand."

"Your grandmother and Holcomb were siblings. They're both dead and their property is in the hands of some dangerous people." I tried to tread slowly so we didn't get to a bad place again. I had a thin, unstable thread of trust going with Rae and I didn't want to break it. "I think Commissioner Lester had something to do with your grandmother's death, and Holcomb's too."

Rae stared at me for a moment. Then she turned back to the stove and gently placed the salmon patties in the skillet. The sizzle and pop from the fish drifted across the kitchen when she placed them in the pan. She walked over to the kitchen table and sat across from me. "So, you think that politician, the one Gran was dating, killed my grandmother to get her property?"

"I know it sounds crazy, but yeah. I just want to see if your grandmother had any paperwork that might prove his involvement with the property she owned."

"What kind of paperwork?"

"I'm not sure. Maybe something like mortgage documents or a sales contract. I want to see who she sold her property to."

"Gran said she didn't have a mortgage payment for this house. I assumed it was paid off. The few times I asked her about it, she said it had been taken care of."

"What does that mean?"

Rae shrugged and paced back to the stove. She turned the salmon cakes in the pan. "My grandmother was a complicated woman. She was very private and at the same time, she could be an open book. Generous to a fault. Giving people money. Always helping somebody."

"Who was she helping?"

"Neighbors, friends."

"But she never talked about her brother?"

"Nope. The first I heard of her having a brother was when you showed up at the door. But can I ask you something?"

"Sure."

"You know how things go around these parts. Even if you find out who killed Gran and that man . . ."

"Holcomb."

"Yeah, Holcomb. Even if you find out who killed them, what do you think will happen? Nothing will change. Gran and Holcomb will be just two old Black people who died, and nobody will give a damn."

"But that's just it. Charlie Lester did this and he's thinking exactly that. That your grandmother and her brother were just two old Black people nobody cared about. I think he wants us to give up. Then everything they were will be forgotten and their property will have been stolen. *Your* property was stolen."

For the first time, Rae perked up. "What do you mean *my* property was stolen?"

"That's what I've been trying to get you to understand. Somebody not only killed your grandmother, they stole from you. I think your family once owned that island property along with some other properties here in town. When they stole your grandmother and uncle's property, they stole that from you too. That was your inheritance. And you deserve to get it back."

"So, you think my grandmother's property was stolen and I can get it back?"

"Depends on what we find."

"Hmm . . . hang on." She removed the patties from the skillet and turned off the fire under the pan. The aroma floating through the kitchen had the most amazing combination of pepper and spices. I was surprised that she had the skills to whip up something so quickly that smelled so incredible. "Follow me."

I trailed Rae back through the living room and into a bedroom down the hall. She opened the door and stood in the doorway for a beat before she stepped inside. I could tell this was tough for her. I felt bad for making her relive whatever memories she was struggling with.

"This was Gran's room," she said.

As soon as I stepped inside, I smelled the perfume, a deep aroma of roses and patchouli. The same perfume I smelled whenever I ventured into the attic of the Old Victorian.

And cigarettes.

"Did your grandmother smoke?"

"Yeah, Newports. It's weird. I used to worry that someday she'd get lung cancer or something. But . . ."

Rae went quiet. I was a monster for making this poor girl trudge through all those memories of her grandmother. I just hoped I was doing the right thing.

The bedroom was neat but dated. It reminded me of Daddy's bedroom, with a huge ornate carved headboard and matching dresser. The bed was neatly made with a lavender satin bedspread. The dresser was covered with a doily and colorful little bric-a-brac. Taped to the dresser mirror was a picture of two women, one older and a younger one with a small girl between them. The little girl, sporting two shoulder-length pigtails with brightly colored barrettes adorning the ends of them, smiled widely into the camera with two missing front teeth.

I grinned. "Is that you?"

Rae walked closer and stared at the picture. "Yeah, I think I was about six in that picture. That was before my mother went into her own private hell on earth. She was really pretty. They both were."

I had to agree with her. "What happened to your grandfather?"

"I never knew him. Gran said she decided she didn't need marriage to make her a good woman. She raised my mother by herself. Tough lady."

I studied Delilah in the picture. She was dressed impeccably. A silk blouse and pantsuit. A beautiful necklace with a red stone in the middle of it. She looked like a Black woman who had some means. There were very few of those to go around in southern Georgia. Rae's mother was attractive in a pixie sort of way with dark curls and a dimpled smile.

This sweet little family of women had come apart at the seams from drugs, money, and murder.

Rae opened the top drawer of the dresser. She pulled out a green metal box. "This is the only thing Gran kept that had important stuff in it. I went through it after she died to find her insurance policy. But I don't think there's much here." Rae and I sat in the window seat, and she slowly opened the box. "I haven't been in here since Gran died."

She pulled out a couple documents. "These are just birth certificates for me and my mother. A death certificate for . . . The rest is a bunch of old junk."

"May I?"

Rae handed me the box. "Help yourself. I'm going to check on the rice. I'll be back in a few."

Rae was right. Beyond the birth certificates, the death certificate for Rae's mother, and half a dozen dog-eared obituaries from funerals Delilah must have attended, the box held nothing of any real value. There were a few bum lottery tickets, some old store receipts, and a few kid's drawings, probably made by Rae when she was little. I sat the box down on the window seat and looked around the room. I walked back over to the dresser and peeked inside each drawer. Just Delilah's clothes and unmentionables. Nothing.

I headed to the closet and opened it. Inside was an array of dresses, blouses, and pants. Hatboxes rose to the ceiling of the closet. Being in this room, looking through this woman's things, reminded me of trying to go through Ma's things after she died. Daddy had told me to take whatever I wanted. I was too broken up with grief to sort through them so I gave up trying. Eventually, Daddy packed up Ma's things and put them in the attic. One day, I hoped to be strong enough to venture up there and go through them.

I looked down at the floor at a gorgeous display of shoes, sandals, heels, boots, all size 7. Delilah was a "shoe girl." One pair in particular caught my eye. A pair of silver sequined heels. They were gorgeous. I bent down to pick them up. I wore a size 9. My feet hadn't been that small since middle school. As I placed the shoes back, I noticed a crack in the floor. I squatted down to get a closer look. The crack ran horizontally along the back wall of the closet. It was a panel of some type. I removed a few more pairs of shoes from the closet to get a closer look. I pulled my phone from my pants pocket and turned on the flashlight. As it turned out, the crack in the linoleum of the closet was actually the lip of an opening.

I tugged and managed to pull it up. Underneath was a space between the floor joists. There was something down there. I stopped. I had no right to go digging through Delilah's house like this, especially after the last time I was here. Rae was already suspicious of me prying through her life. But I had to know what was under here.

"Rae! Come here! I think I found something."

Rae came racing back into the room. "What?"

I waved her over. "There's something down here." She knelt beside me. I pointed the light toward the floorboards.

"What is that? A book?" She lifted it out of the hole. It was covered in dirt and dust. She sat cross-legged and blew off the dust. It was an old Naturalizer shoebox. I sat down on the floor beside her.

"What is this?" she said.

"Open it."

She glanced at me, then stared at the box for a few seconds before she lifted the cover.

Inside the box were five fat wads of cash held together by orange rubber bands.

"Oh my God, where did Gran get this kind of money?"

I just stared at it. All fifty- and hundred-dollar bills. "There has to be thousands in there."

"I know," Rae said. "But where would she get this kind of money?

She was living on a fixed income." She peered back inside the box. "Look! What's this?" She reached inside and pulled out a small stack of receipts and handed them to me.

They were tax receipts from the Georgia tax commissioner. All of them receipts for a parcel of land located on Boden Road, out on the island.

"I think your grandmother had been paying the property taxes on the land out on the island that Holcomb was living on."

"Really? So they really did own that property." She gazed back down into the box. "Hey, look at this." Rae removed a handful of letters with a faded pink ribbon wrapped around them.

"What's that? Love letters?" I asked.

"Oooh, maybe Gran had another secret lover," Rae said, grinning slyly.

I laughed. "Open one up. Let's hear."

Rae gingerly slid a letter from the stack. "Hmm . . . looks like it's from a soldier. It has one of those air force base return addresses." She slid the letter out from its envelope and began to read it.

My love, my angel Delilah,

I can't begin to tell you how much I ache to see you again. Thinking of you, remembering how it felt to hold you in my arms, is the only thing that keeps me going these days. I showed some of the fellas your picture. I know it made them jealous to know that I have someone so beautiful who belongs to me.

I was sorry to hear of your father's passing. He was a good man who loved you all deeply. I hope you and your family are coping well with the loss. Have you and Holcomb come back together after your last spat? I know that it can be hard with brothers. Me and Duke have our moments too. But we always find a way to come together, just like I know you and Holcomb will too.

Continue to love me and stay true until I can hold you in my arms again. I love you.

Always yours in love,
Jimmie Lee

Rae finished the letter and giggled. "Damn! This dude was *in love*."

I picked up the envelope and read the return address: *Mr. Jimmie Lee Wood*. I felt all the air go out of my lungs.

Rae stopped giggling and looked at me. "What's wrong?"

"Can I see the letter?"

"Sure." She handed it to me. "What's wrong, Deena?"

I looked down at the small, neat cursive letters. It was my dad's handwriting. "I think your grandmother's secret lover was my father."

"Wait! What?! Are you serious?"

"That's his name and this is my dad's handwriting. I'd know it anywhere. He was in the air force and he has a brother named Duke. Can I see the other envelopes?"

"Sure. Have at it. Apparently, Gran was something else, huh? Your dad. The commissioner." Rae got up from the floor. "I'm gonna go turn off the rice."

She headed back to the kitchen. I sat on the floor of Delilah Gardner's bedroom and read all twenty-eight letters. Each one of them heartfelt and spilling over with my father's love for a woman who was not my mother. He talked of his plans to return to Brunswick and marry her, the kind of life they would lead and all the children they would have. His letters were bursting with a fevered devotion to Delilah Gardner. But the last letter nearly broke my heart.

My love Delilah,

Why haven't you answered my last three letters? I find it so hard to concentrate on anything else. Each day is like an eternity of pain when I don't hear from you. Please answer soon so that I will know all is well and that you still love me. I cannot wait until my duty is over so that I can return to Brunswick, and we can be married. You will always have my heart.

Always yours in love,
Jimmie Lee

My father had planned to marry another woman. A woman that he loved deeply.

I never knew Delilah was such an important part of my father's life. I never asked questions of my parents. I always listened to their stories of meeting at church and dating. Neither of them ever mentioned that there was someone else before the two of them came together. Uncle Duke had joked about Daddy having a crush on Delilah before he went into the air force. But did my mother know of the depth of his love for this woman? Is this what she meant when she said things were complicated when I asked if she was Daddy's one true love? I had so many questions. Who was Jimmie Lee Wood, and what happened between him and Delilah? Why did she keep these letters if she didn't marry him? And what happened that made her stop writing to him?

I remembered the day Rae and I drove out to Holcomb's house on Old Farm Road after we learned Delilah was dating Charlie Lester. Rae asked me: *What would you do if you found out your mother or father had been keeping secrets from you?*

Now I understood how she felt. Perhaps it was not Ma's or Daddy's place to explain their past affairs to me. But maybe I might not have made so many mistakes if they'd shared their wisdom on navigating love and relationships.

Still, it troubled me that Daddy acted as if he barely knew Delilah the first time I mentioned her name. A woman he planned to marry. He continually warned me to stop digging into her death.

Why?

And now the truth has come to light. Deena knows of Jimmie's love for me. What she doesn't know is that I loved him as well. The rest is up to Jimmie to tell. The baby that neither of us had planned. The heartache that resulted. And all that lost love between us. I took his love for granted. I squandered it and I paid dearly because of it.

I lost the only man I've ever truly loved.

Fortunately, Rae and Deena know I tried to make amends for the mistake I made in losing Mama's house. I saved the island property. The tax man wouldn't take away our piece of the island as he'd done with our family home.

Figuring out how to learn from my mistakes—all of them—was my greatest life lesson. Unfortunately, it came too late in my earthly life.

CHAPTER 45

I left Rae's house with my head spinning. Why was Daddy so adamant that I not dig into Delilah's death if he was so madly in love with her? And how much did Ma know? Did Ruth know too?

I hadn't heard Ma's voice in weeks. I doubted whether I'd ever hear it again. But somehow, I was less anxious about it than I used to be. I loved her and she knew as much before she died. Maybe that was my consoling grace.

I was headed back to the office. I'd been gone long enough for people to ask questions. But something urged me to make a detour. I did and thirty minutes later I was crossing the bridge onto the island. Back to Holcomb's property. Back to where it had all started.

I'd stumbled onto his land two weeks ago and in doing so, I'd opened up a Pandora's box I didn't like the contents of. Strange men stalking me, trying to attack and intimidate me, and now love letters my father wrote to some woman half a century ago. Why was any of this happening?

I hadn't been out to the property since the day I discovered Empire Realty's For Sale sign on it. I pulled my car up to the edge of what appeared to be a new green silk fence that encompassed the property. This time there was a new sign to go along with it.

Coming Soon!
The Sea Spa
An All-Inclusive Luxury Resort
for Those Who Crave Indulgence
Hotel · Golf · Shops · Residences
A Medallion Development Property

Medallion bought Holcomb's property from Charlie Lester's realty company! Medallion was an engineering contractor. *What the hell?* Since when did they get into the property redevelopment business?

I stepped out of my car and walked a bit closer. Beyond the fence, there was an excavator and a few dump trucks parked on the property. All traces of Holcomb gone, as if he never existed.

"Deena?" a man's voice called from behind me.

Beau Walsh stepped over the short green silk fence and strutted up to me. "Now, this is a bit of a surprise."

I glanced from Beau to the sign and back to Beau again. I tried to quell the nerves that started to dance around inside me.

"Beau? What's going on here?"

"Remember that little pet project I told you Charlie Lester and I are working on? Well, here it is. The Sea Spa. It's going to be the turning point for Medallion. This is gonna be a game changer for the com—" He stopped talking mid-sentence and glared at me. "Why are you out here?" He chuckled and shook his head. "Now, I thought we talked about this back at the office. You ought not be poking around in matters that don't concern you."

"I don't understand. Since when did Medallion get into the redevelopment business? Medallion doesn't redevelop property."

"We do now. We're expanding the business. We've decided to build our own projects. Exciting stuff, huh?"

"Well . . . um . . ."

Beau grinned.

"So . . . Clare thinks this is the way to go? I mean, moving into property redevelopment instead of sticking to what the company does best."

Beau placed his hands in his pockets. "Clare has been distracted lately, you know what I mean?"

"Uh . . . no, I don't."

He hesitated for a moment. "I think Clare is focused on her next chapter. I don't know if she's really all that capable of deciding the future of this company. She's no spring chicken anymore. I don't mean that in a disrespectful way. It's just a fact. She's past her prime for a business like this. It's my job to make sure Medallion lives on beyond Clare."

Damn. This was the person she raised as her own son and brought into her business. Here he stood talking as if pushing Clare out of the company was part of his strategic business plan for Medallion. All this time, I thought Beau was an imbecilic jerk. I hadn't given him credit for being a worthless backstabber who didn't appreciate what Clare had done for him. Clare suspected Beau was up to something, and she was right. And the fact that he was working in concert with Charlie Lester made my blood boil.

"Well, I guess I'd better get back to the office."

"You just got here. Come on, let me show you how it'll all be spread out." He draped his arm over my shoulders and I cringed. "Over there will be the golf course. That will run straight out to the road back there. And straight across from us will be the resort, pool, spa, five-star everything. Deena, this is gonna be huge. Bigger than The Dunes, where I live. Nothing else like it on the southeast coast."

"Um . . . I'm sure it will be."

"This resort is going to be our flagship property, and we'll build more just like it around the country. We're scouting more property right now."

I felt lightheaded with the thought of what was happening. This was Holcomb and Delilah Gardner's land. Now Beau was standing on it, talking about plans to build a five-star resort, and the Gardners were dead.

"I'd better get back to the office," I repeated.

"Alright. I'll see you back there. Oh. Don't forget what we talked about. You stick to one thing and let me handle everything else." He laughed, a big ugly noise that made my skin crawl.

Beau turned to a couple men nearby, one wearing a suit, another wearing a hard hat. He talked animatedly, pointing all around. The three men smiled and laughed, excited about whatever plans they had for Holcomb Gardner's land.

I hustled off to my car and hopped behind the wheel. I had to sit on my hands just to stop them from trembling. Medallion's office had once been Holcomb and Delilah's family home. Now Beau owned it. The island property that had been in their family for generations, Beau also owned. Holcomb's blue house on Old Farm Road was up for sale by Empire Realty, aka Beau's little buddy, Charlie Lester.

Every single thing Holcomb and Delilah's family had worked for, the legacy their family had built, was now in the hands of a pair of charlatans like Beau Walsh and Charlie Lester. The ancestors must be crying from the heavens.

CHAPTER 46

It was almost four o'clock by the time I made it back to Brunswick. As I drove up to the Old Victorian, I noticed a couple TV news trucks parked in the circular driveway. Something must have happened. I parked in the lot. More cars than usual were there. Loud voices and laughter wafted all the way outside.

I stepped inside. The foyer and front rooms of the house were packed with people. Everyone stood laughing and holding champagne flutes.

"Deena!"

I stopped in my tracks, stunned into silence. Clare rushed up to me. In one hand she held a glass filled to the brim. In the other hand, she held a small brown dog with a shot of white fur over one eye.

Holcomb's dog.

This time, the dog sported a brand-new brown leather collar. From the front of it hung a shiny silver tag in the shape of a bone with the name Fig engraved on it.

"Deena! We tried to wait for you. Where've you been? Doesn't matter. Jennie, grab a glass for Deena."

"What's going on?" I said.

Clare kissed the dog on the top of his head. "What do you think of my new dog? Beau gave him to me." The dog licked her face, before he leaned in toward me. Had Beau killed Holcomb and stolen his dog to give to his aunt? *What the hell?*

Jennie hustled over with a glass of champagne and handed it to me. "It's the good stuff too," she said with a smile.

Clare tapped her glass against mine. "I just announced my run for Congress. The news stations picked up the announcement for the five o'clock slot. Nice, huh?"

I gave a weak smile. "Uh . . . yeah. Clare, I know this isn't the right time to bring this up, but did you know Medallion is planning a redevelopment project?"

Clare released the dog to the floor and brushed her hand through the air as if waving off the idea. "Beau's been talking about that for years. It's all rubbish. I think we should stick to what we do best."

An older, graying couple walked over and congratulated Clare before they said goodbye. Clare gave the pair air kisses before they walked out the front door.

"Clare, I think he has plans underway to do it."

"What?!"

Clare pulled me into the butler's pantry off the conference room. "What do you mean *plans underway*?"

"He's acquired a parcel of land out on the island. He's planning to build a golf-spa resort. You didn't know about any of this?"

Clare rubbed her temple. "Hell no! Are you sure about this?"

"I've seen it. It's out on Boden Road."

"Shit! I've been so focused on this congressional run that I've given him too long a leash." She hustled back to the foyer and slammed her champagne flute on Jennie's desk with a loud clink. "Jennie!"

The young woman hustled over.

"Where's Beau?"

"He was here earlier for the announcement but said he had an off-site meeting to get to," she said. "But Clare, you told me to let you know when Mr. Wagner called. He's on the line for you."

"Of course, thank you." Clare looked frazzled, the first time I'd ever seen her less than her normal composed self. "Jennie, track down Beau and tell him to get his ass back here and in my office right now!"

"Yes ma'am," Jennie said before she picked up the landline to call Beau.

"Deena, I have to take this call. Don Wagner is head of the party here in Georgia. I've gotta have his endorsement and backing to get any traction on my campaign. This call shouldn't take me more than half an hour. I'll find Beau after and get to the bottom of this. Thanks for the heads-up."

She scooped up Holcomb's dog and hustled upstairs to her office.

Part II
NIGHTFALL

CHAPTER 47

By the time I made it home from work, the first thing I noticed was the silver Range Rover in the driveway of Daddy's house. I knew that car. My heartbeat raced as I pulled up to the front of the house. There he was, standing on my front porch, with Ruth.

Charlie Lester.

I quickly parked and hopped out of my car.

"What the hell are you doing here?!" I yelled. I noticed LaShonda and her mother on the front porch of their house. They perked up when I yelled and stepped to the edge of the porch.

"Deena! I was in the neighborhood visiting some of my constituents and I thought I'd drop by. I was just chatting with your stepmother. Seems we go way back."

Ruth frowned. "You're no friend of mine, Charlie Lester. Deena, he said he wanted to see you, but I wouldn't let him in the house."

"Leave. NOW!" I said.

He looked at me like he felt sorry for me. "I know you've been under a lot of stress since your mother's death. Elizabeth was a really special woman."

"Keep my mother's name out of your mouth. Come on, Roo. Let's go inside."

I hustled up the stairs and grabbed her arm. Before we could make it inside, Lester blocked our path.

He narrowed his eyes on me, the same way he'd done outside the police station. "Deena, you're getting involved in things that are way over your head," he said sternly. "You don't know what or *who* you're dealing with. If I were you, I'd back off. Seriously. You don't want to play with these people."

"What people?"

"Trust me, dear, you don't want to know. They have the capacity to ruin this measly little life you're living right now."

"And if I don't?"

He chuckled and walked off the porch. Then, he took a step back and scanned the house. "Yes, I'd hate to see anything happen to you and your parents."

Another threat. I wanted to kill this guy with my bare hands. I wanted to scratch his fucking eyes out and choke the last breath from his body.

Ruth and I watched him drive off before we went into the house.

"That man is evil in a silk suit, Deena. I feel dirty just for having stood next to him. I wouldn't let him in the house. Oh goodness, I have to go burn some sage." She hurried off to the kitchen.

I stood in the middle of the living room, on the brink of screaming out in frustration or breaking down in tears. How did men like Charlie Lester and Beau Walsh get to live without consequences for their actions? And what people was I supposed to be afraid of?

Daddy walked in the house a few minutes later. "Hey, there's my little lawyer."

I just stared at him. I was rattled by Charlie Lester and now seeing Daddy reminded me of the love letters in Delilah's closet. I had so many questions. But I opted to keep them all to myself.

"You okay, baby girl?"

"I have a headache. I'm going to take a couple Tylenol and go to bed."

"Are you sure you're okay? Where's Roo?"

"She's off burning something in the kitchen."

* * *

A FEW MINUTES later, there was a light tap at my bedroom door. "Deena, it's me," Daddy said.

"Come in." I slowly eased up and sat on the side of the bed.

"Can I talk to you for a minute, baby girl?"

"Sure."

"I've never known you not to sit and talk to me, even for a few minutes, when we get home. Something's on your mind. Let me help."

"I'm fine, Daddy."

He sat down on the bed beside me. "No, you're not. Roo told me about that snake coming here to the house. Me and Duke will take care of him. He didn't get to you too bad, did he?"

"Daddy . . . it's nothing, really."

"I remember the first time you told me that, you were about twelve years old and LaShonda from across the street had said something untoward to you. Your mama told me you were in here sulking and refused to go outside to play. You remember that?"

I smiled weakly. LaShonda has always been the bane of my existence.

"I finally got you to tell me what was troubling you then. And I'll pull it out of you now too." He nudged me with his elbow. "Tell your old man what's going on."

"Life is a lot more complicated than LaShonda calling me dribble lips. There's a lot going on now and I probably need some time to think through it. That's all."

We sat in silence for a moment before Daddy chimed up. "I know how much you miss your mama. I miss her too."

"Do you?" His saying that out loud churned up a distaste inside of me. How dare he say that when his new wife of six months was in the kitchen burning sage and there was a stack of Delilah's love letters in Rae's house with his name all over them? I didn't want to be disrespectful, but he opened this up, not me. "You and Ruth married so soon after Ma's death. It just seems . . ."

"It seems like I moved on, huh? Deena, I haven't forgotten about Libby. I loved her. I still do. But I needed to move on from the grief. Roo helped me do that. And I suggest you find someone that helps you move on too. Trying to figure out how to re-create life the way it was when your mama was here is impossible. It's like trying to find dust in the dark. It's not ever going to be the same as it was when your mama was alive. But that doesn't mean it has to be bad either."

I didn't say anything.

"I ran into Howie downtown yesterday. When are you two gonna finally settle down and stop all this back-and-forth?"

I looked at Daddy. Surprised. Shocked, even. He didn't usually wade into relationship waters between me and Howie. That was Ma's job, and now Roo's.

"That's complicated too, Daddy."

"Matters of the heart always are."

There was another long stretch of silence between us. Finally, I figured if Daddy wanted to go there, *then let's go there*. "Why were you discouraging me from looking into Delilah Gardner's death?"

"What d'ya mean?"

"All my life, all you've ever done is help people. But with her and her brother, you've constantly told me to stop digging into this. Why?"

Daddy simply stared at me.

"I found the letters. The letters you wrote to Delilah when you were in the air force. I was at Rae's house. Delilah had the letters hidden in a crawl space in her bedroom."

Then, he leaned forward, his elbows on his knees, and stared straight out into the hallway. He didn't say anything for a long time. At first, I thought he would get up and leave the room.

"Hmph. I hadn't thought about Delilah since her funeral. And I was okay with that. Then you come home one day and mentioned her name out of the blue." He hesitated. "My, my, my. A lot of things happened back then. Things I didn't even tell Duke. I loved Delilah. At one time, I thought she loved me back. That story I told you last week about Club 115?"

"Yeah."

"I didn't tell you the whole story. That night when the fight broke out, everybody ran every which way. As I was running out the club, I found Delilah, trying to hide behind some crates. I scooped her up and got her out of there before the police came. That's how me and Duke got separated. I really did lose my left shoe, but I walked her home that night with just one shoe. I was smitten. She was beautiful. Smart. She knew so much about the island and our people. I felt smarter every time I was around her. But she told me we had to keep things secret, just between us, because she was supposed to be dating some guy from Savannah. Her parents wanted her to marry outside of Gullah. They thought it would improve her lot in life.

"Back then, there was two camps of folks. The ones that wanted to hang on to the old Gullah-Geechee ways. And the others who decided they wanted success, and that meant mingling in with the white folks, not talking in broken English, as they called it. A lot of folks in the second camp moved away up north or out west. Some of us simply moved to Brunswick or were pushed out. Delilah's parents were in the second camp, although they didn't go far. But they still thought their daughter could do better. Delilah loved her folks and I think she just wanted to please them.

"So, we'd sneak off and didn't nobody know we were a thing. We kept it secret from everybody. I hated it too. After I went into the service, she said she'd break it off with the guy and we'd get married. Didn't work out that way."

He shook his head sadly. I didn't interrupt this story.

"Who knows what happened. Maybe I was gone too long. Maybe I was just a plaything to her. Or maybe she just got restless. I don't know. Anyway, by the time I got back home on a leave, she was pregnant. It was the guy from Savannah her mama had wanted her to marry. He didn't stick around, though. Moved up north somewhere. Even though it wasn't my baby, I loved her. I offered to marry her."

"So why didn't you?"

"She turned me down. Said she wouldn't saddle me with somebody else's responsibility. Hurt like hell too. She was pretty strong to raise a child all by herself back in the 1970s."

"I'm sorry."

"It took me a good long while to get over her too. All that business about first loves . . . A few years later, I met your mama and I'm glad I did. If I hadn't, you wouldn't be here. Anyway, when you came in the house a couple weeks ago with all that talk of Delilah, it just conjured up all kinds of stuff. After I met your mother, I tried to tuck Delilah away like I'd never loved her. When she died, I went by the funeral home to pay my respects in private. I didn't even attend her funeral and for that I'll always feel bad. I should have. Like you said, things get complicated."

We sat quietly.

"I figured that night in Duke's shop, he'd tell you what little he knew about the Gardners and that would put an end to all this and I wouldn't have to think about Delilah Gardner anymore. I wouldn't have to . . . Anyway, that was a long time ago."

Finally, Daddy sat upright on the bed, looked at me, and patted my hand. "That's why you need to figure out what you gonna do about Howie. He has been working to become my son-in-law since y'all were in junior high school, even when you were married. He was always tipping around here, asking about you. He loves you. Trust me, I can tell." Daddy stood up from the bed. "Don't push away something good in your life. You might not get another chance to have it back. I'd better go check on Roo."

He left the room.

Deena talked to Jimmie Lee. Now we both know how much he loved me. My parents were wrong. I was too. Jimmie was the best thing to ever happen to me. He hated keeping secrets, but he kept ours. Even after all these years. And maybe now, Deena will understand how important it is to be with that young man who loves her.

But I'm still worried about her. There are evil forces all around her. I don't know if I can help her alone. Deena needs more than what I can offer. She doesn't know me. She still doesn't trust me completely.

I'm going to need someone else's help to protect her.

CHAPTER 48

The next morning, I was at my desk by eight. Knowing Medallion was redeveloping the Gardner property meant I was done with this job. Continuing to work here was like being at a party and sensing a shift in the vibe, knowing it was time to go. To work for Beau after what I'd learned—I wanted to do that about as much as I wanted to stand butt naked in the middle of the Golden Isles Parkway. I had to quit. But where would I go? I couldn't lounge around Daddy's house all day. My plans for buying my own house would be scrapped if I quit this job without another one. I needed proof of a source of income.

I pulled up the internet browser on my computer and started a search for another job in the area. That lasted for all of five minutes. I was kidding myself. There were very few legal positions in this town. I wasn't even working in a real legal job now. Maybe I could go back to Atlanta. Atlanta was big but maybe not big enough that rumors hadn't spread around town about my getting fired from the firm. The Black legal community was smaller than most people thought, especially in Atlanta. When Lance and I split up, he got all the friends and connections while I scrambled away to Brunswick to lick my wounds. Maybe that was a mistake. I'd made so many bad decisions.

I was on the brink of tears when I decided to do something instead of sitting at my desk crying. I pulled out one of Sarah's cards from the Georgia Heirs Property Law Center. I knew she was looking for pro bono lawyers, but maybe I'd call and see if I could talk my way into a full-time staff position. Before I had a chance to call her, Joe stepped inside my office.

"You left yesterday morning and we didn't see you until the end of the day. I thought we talked about this."

"I told Peg I had a doctor's appointment. Give me a break."

He eyed me suspiciously. "I told you, Beau is knee-deep in my ass about you not pulling your full weight around here."

I didn't respond.

Joe shook his head. "You've been warned. I came down here to tell you Beau wants you to work on a new project, which means he'll be watching you. I can't protect you anymore. I don't think Clare can either."

"What new project?"

"The Sea Spa project. Beau's taking the company in a different direction."

"I heard. I thought we were an engineering contractor. Since when did we get into the property redevelopment business?"

"Medallion doesn't pay me to make those decisions, so I have no idea. They don't pay you to do that either." Joe rubbed his forehead. "Look, I got two kids in college. All I know is that Medallion is doing this new project and Beau has become obsessed with it."

"What does Clare think about this project, because it seems to run counter to her philosophy for the business?"

"I told you, it's not my job to determine strategic direction for the company. It's not yours either. Anyway, Beau said you'd be really interested in this one. Something about you having a connection to the island. So, you can't screw this up. It means you're gonna have to be in here, *major* face time. No coming in late, wandering off during the day. Otherwise, I can't guarantee Beau won't fire you. Understood? I'll have Peg get you the files. Go through them and get me a memo on what needs to be done." He walked out.

Beau knew all along that I'd been looking into Holcomb's death and his property. This was a dig, his way of needling me about my involvement in the Gardner matter. But he had severely miscalculated my capacity to stand for bullshit. I didn't take it from anyone, especially from an evil and intellectual lightweight like Beau.

Helping him build on property that had been held by the Gardners for generations and then taken away from them? I wouldn't do it.

This is the hill I am willing to die on.

* * *

I STAYED IN the office well past quitting time, looking for another job and completing job applications, and I'd made some progress too. If the angels were on my side, maybe I'd have a new job somewhere soon. I left the office, but I didn't go home. I needed to talk to someone. Daddy and Roo wouldn't understand. And I didn't want to call my friend Bridget, because she usually turned the conversation into blow-by-blow updates about Lance and what an asshole he was. She meant well, but I had already gathered that information the hard way.

I drove around aimlessly until I found myself standing at the door of Howie's condo, a renovated pencil factory converted into lofts. I'd never been inside his place before and I was scared to go inside now. I was just about to knock when the door opened.

"Deena?" Howie smiled that smile at me. "What are you doing here?"

He was dressed in a pair of sweatpants and a Boston College T-shirt and holding a plastic trash bag. Even when he was taking out the garbage, he was fine. How was it possible for him to be this relaxed and handsome all at the same time? I quickly peeked over his shoulder, looking into the condo. I prayed he didn't have company.

"I'm sorry I didn't call first. Did I catch you at a bad time?"

"My door is always open for you. You know that. I was just about to take the trash out. But it can wait. Come in."

He tossed the bag to the side of the door. I stepped inside. The place looked like Howie, very manly and tasteful, embodied in expensive leather furniture, mahogany, and concrete floors. The view from his balcony overlooked East River and the Sidney Lanier Bridge and to the island beyond that. There was not a trace of a woman's imprint on this entire place.

"It's late. Is everything okay?"

"Yeah. I'm sorry to show up like this."

"Don't give it another thought. You want something to drink? Water, soda, a cup of tea?"

"Tea sounds good."

The entire place was one big open room. There was a large rice paper screen on one side of the room and I spotted the bottom edge of a king-sized bed behind it. I followed him over to the opposite side of the room where the kitchen was located.

As I stood at the island and watched Howie put the water on to boil, I finally admitted to myself what I had been denying since he walked into my office at Medallion Company. I had been in love with this man since the eighth grade but spent over half my life telling myself that I wasn't. Through his marriage and mine, I was in love with him. I think I had only accepted Lance's marriage proposal in the hope that he might replace Howie. He didn't, no one could. And now, I was secretly hoping from afar that Howie and I could be together, but I was too full of pride to actually work with him to make it happen.

Howie gazed at me and smiled. My face went hot like it always did whenever I caught him looking at me. And once again, instead of sending a signal to let him know that I wanted what he wanted, I punted. Instead of smiling back, I turned away to look around the room.

"This is nice," I said.

He smiled. "Thanks. I had a decorator. You know I don't have the skills to do something like this."

"Oh, I didn't tell you the good news. My offer on the house got accepted."

"Congratulations!" He winked. "You'll be close by."

After a few minutes, the teapot whistled. Howie grabbed two mugs and sat them on the island. I watched as he prepared chamomile tea for the both of us.

"What do you take? Honey, sugar, or artificial sweetener?"

"Honey."

"Did you just call me honey?" he said jokingly.

I smiled and shook my head.

"Oh, I'm sorry. I misunderstood. That's what you want in your tea."

"You are so corny. I bet you had to dust that joke off before you told it," I said with a grin.

Howie laughed and slid one cup toward me. I sat down on one of the leather barstools at the island and took a sip from the mug, letting the hot tea slide down my throat and warm me.

He took a sip from his mug and looked at me. "So, now that the pleasantries are out of the way, you wanna tell me what's going on that's so bad it's brought you to my place at nine thirty at night?"

"Clare Walsh has a new dog. She said Beau gave it to her."

"A new dog? Okay?"

"Holcomb's dog."

"What? Why are you so certain it's Holcomb's dog? A lot of dogs look alike."

"I know that, but this dog has some unusual markings. I'm certain it's his dog. The day I stumbled on his property, he had a dog. That same dog showed up in Clare's arms this afternoon. And by the way, did you know Medallion is no longer just an engineering contractor? Beau has purchased Holcomb's property from Charlie Lester and plans to build a golf-spa resort on it. This is in addition to Beau owning the house that used to belong to the Gardners."

"Okay, that might be a little more than coincidence."

"I'm pretty sure Beau is involved in the Gardners' deaths. I just can't figure out how."

"Let's slow down and think this through. Do you know if Beau bought the Old Victorian from Lester too?"

"Lester was seeing Delilah romantically and her friend confirms there was some sort of dustup between Holcomb and Delilah over the house. Maybe Lester knew about it and took advantage. According to Peg, Beau bought the house several years ago."

"Hmm . . . hang on." Howie left the island and retrieved his laptop from a desk across the room. We stood side by side at the island as he booted up. "Let's see if we can dig up who handled the transaction for the Old Victorian. What's the address?"

I rattled off the address for Medallion. Howie scooted down

some real estate rabbit hole on the internet and . . . bingo! He found the sale of the Gardner family house several years ago.

"It says here the house was part of a courthouse sale. Didn't pay the taxes on it?"

"Oh my gosh. She lost her family home because of taxes."

Howie stared into the computer. "It's sad."

"But what about the island property? When I first started digging into all this, I found information that said the island property was sold over a month ago. But Delilah was killed six months ago. How could she sell property she owned with her brother a month ago when she was dead?"

Howie nodded. "Hmm . . . maybe somebody killed her six months ago to get the property from Holcomb alone."

"Oh, wait!" I reached into my bag. "I found some files in Medallion's attic."

I pulled the folder from my bag and opened it onto the island. "This is a list of properties that Empire has been buying up in different states. I think they're using heirs property law to their advantage. They buy up portions of property owned by estranged family members and then force out the family members who remain on the property. I took a drive over to South Carolina."

"South Carolina? Damn! You are deep in this thing, huh?"

I ignored his remark. "I met a woman who might lose her home. Bellar Strategies, going under the name Bellar Homes, had their lawyers send the woman a letter threatening to force a sale of the property if she doesn't pay fifty thousand dollars. And trust me. From the looks of her and that house, I doubt she has that much money and the house isn't worth it if she does. LaShonda got the same letter demanding thirty-five thousand."

"Hmm . . . what's this?" Howie said, sliding a document toward us.

"I'm not sure. It came out of the folder marked 'Bellar' but I can't figure it out. It's just a list of names with contact info. Do you recognize any of these names?"

Howie scanned the paper and shook his head no.

"Maybe Delilah sold her portion of the land to Charlie Lester and then he forced Holcomb off the property. There is some connection between Charlie Lester and Beau Walsh, and it has to point back to that hedge fund you told me about. I cannot rest until I figure out what happened to those poor people. Ugh . . . why am I like this?"

Howie eased closer to me. "You're like this because you care. And there's nothing wrong with that."

"Daddy tells me I'm hardheaded and I shouldn't be digging around in this, but . . ." I looked up at him and then I felt the sting of tears welling in my eyes.

He pulled me in close. "Shh . . . it's okay. It's okay." He touched the small of my back and I could feel my heart speed up. That cologne again. Howie ran a soft thumb across my cheek, wiping away my tears. His hands were so warm and gentle, they made my skin quiver. Then, he kissed me. Just a little more than a peck. I didn't move. Neither of us moved until he pulled me in closer. I closed my eyes and sank into a deep blanket of firm muscle and soft breath. He kissed me again. This time longer, slower, deeper. Our tongues cautiously angling to find each other. I couldn't stop him. I didn't want to. The woody smell of his cologne slithered through my nostrils, enveloping me in its hypnotic scent. The taste of honey from the chamomile tea on his breath slid across my tongue. I had wanted him to hold me like this since the day he stepped inside my office. Everything inside my head told me that I should move away. But I didn't. Not this time. Because tonight, for the time being, this was just one old friend comforting another.

When we finally released the kiss, I didn't know what to say. We smiled sheepishly, and I won't lie, I wanted to do it all over again. He leaned in, but before we got the chance, we were interrupted. My cell phone rang. I dug it out of my bag.

Daddy.

"Hey, Daddy." I mouthed *sorry* to Howie.

"Baby girl, I need you to meet me over at Duke's place."

"Is everything okay?"

"Oh yeah. Everything's fine. I think me and Duke got some information you can use about Holcomb and Delilah. Come on over."

"I'm on my way." I hung up. "Sorry, I gotta go meet Daddy and Uncle Duke."

Howie looked at me with concern. "Is everything okay?"

"I hope so."

Howie gently stroked my arm. "You want me to drive over with you?"

"No, we can talk later."

Howie put his arms around my waist and kissed me again. "Please be careful."

"I will."

CHAPTER 49

It was after ten thirty by the time I turned onto the street where Uncle Duke's barbershop was located. Things were pretty quiet. And dark. The haunting silence and the pitch-black darkness of the sky crept into my bones.

I pulled up to the front of the shop. The Closed sign was hanging on the door and the lights were out at the front of the shop. Was this another setup by Charlie Lester? I pulled my cell phone from my pocket, but before I could dial Daddy's number I heard the front door open.

"Deena! Come on."

I slipped out of the car. "Uncle Duke? What's going on?"

He didn't say anything but threw up his hand in a motion for me to come inside the shop.

"Where's Daddy?"

Uncle Duke never responded. I stepped into the darkness of the barbershop. He locked the door behind me. I noticed a light coming from the back room.

I followed him across the shop toward the back room. He walked inside first. But I stood in the doorway, flummoxed by the sight in front of me. The card table that usually housed the Friday night bid whist games was folded up and stashed in a corner. In the center of the room was a single chair. And sitting in it—Charlie Lester.

His feet were tied at the ankles, his arms tied behind his back, and one of Uncle Duke's black barber towels served as a makeshift gag in his mouth. His suit was rumpled, and a huge, bright red knot stood out on his forehead against his mussed silver-gray hair. He no longer bore the pompous demeanor of a smooth politician as his eyes pleaded for rescue. And Daddy stood over him holding a gun loosely at his side.

"Oh my God! What the heck is going on here? Daddy? Uncle Duke?"

"Listen, baby girl. We found the commissioner out on the side of the road. Seems he had some car trouble." Daddy gave a crooked smile at Uncle Duke. "We felt obliged to bring him here and offer him some refreshments until we all figured out how to get his car fixed and get him safely on his way. It's pretty late, you know, and things can get dangerous out on a dark, deserted road."

"What are you two doing? Untie him."

"Nooo . . . that's not gonna happen, sweetie," Uncle Duke said. "Ya daddy told me this snake had the nerve to come over to the house, threatening you and Roo."

I sighed deeply. "This is not the way to handle things."

Lester nodded his head furiously, as if in agreement with me.

"Deena, this guy hired people to break into your daddy's house, to hurt you. He had some clown lying in wait to ambush you. You're family. My only brother's only child. I don't take too kindly to anyone putting my family in harm's way. Now, me and your daddy can take care of this with or without you."

I turned to my father. "Daddy?"

Daddy looked at me and calmly shrugged. "If you think he had something to do with Holcomb's and Delilah's murders, don't you think it's worth at least asking him a few questions before . . ."

What the hell?! I didn't even know Daddy and Uncle Duke anymore. "Ugh . . . okay, take the gag out of his mouth."

Uncle Duke snatched the towel from Lester's mouth so hard, it whipped the man's head back. Lester gasped to catch his breath. He glared at Uncle Duke.

"I strongly advise you to untie me. That's if you ever want to see daylight again."

Uncle Duke snapped the towel across the back of Lester's head, sending the man flying forward so fast he nearly toppled out of the chair.

I peered down at Lester. The knot on his forehead was still growing and the bloom of red blazed against his skin. "Why did you kill Delilah Gardner?"

"Go to hell, bitch!"

Before I had time to react, Daddy took the butt end of his gun and slammed it across the top of Lester's head. *Old men and guns!*

"Daddy!"

"Don't you *ever* talk to my daughter like that. Are we clear?" Lester's head lolled for a moment before he looked down at his lap. "Now answer her question," Daddy said.

Lester hesitated for a beat, then looked up at me. "I didn't kill Delilah. They did."

"*They* who?" I asked.

"Trust me, you don't want to mess with these people."

"What people?"

Lester went silent.

Daddy bent over and whispered into Lester's ear. "You want me to let this gun slip and fall across your head again? My daughter asked you a question."

"It's a company out of New York. Bellar Strategies."

"Keep talking," I said.

"I find the properties for them to buy. People that might want to make a quick sale."

"You mean Black people! Cash-strapped with nothing but their property. You prey on your own people."

"I get a good-sized bonus for every property I find for them. They buy them for their portfolios and then they sell them to other big companies or developers."

"And what happened to Delilah?"

Lester looked at Daddy and Uncle Duke. They stared back, Daddy still holding the gun. Uncle Duke leaned against the wall, one arm folded across his chest, casually picking his teeth with a toothpick as if he'd just finished a hearty meal.

"We were . . . friendly, and I convinced Delilah to sell her portion of the land. I promised her that her brother could stay on the property. But Bellar really wanted that property without him on it. We made plans to go to dinner on the island. She drove her car and left it at the park, like she always did when we would meet. At dinner, I told her that Holcomb might have to vacate the property. She got all worked up about it and said she wouldn't be responsible for her brother getting kicked off the land. She threatened to go to the authorities. Told me I had tricked her, and she was going to get a lawyer. I was able to calm her down but she demanded that I drive her out to the property. She said she wanted to tell her brother personally about his having to leave, said she wanted to apologize. I drove her out there. She got out of the car. Then this dark car drives by. He makes a U-turn and speeds past again, and hits Delilah and just kept going."

"So, how did they know she would be out there on the property?"

Lester lowered his head. "I made a call from the restaurant . . . One of their people must have—"

"You set her up and then left her out there to die? You didn't call the police?! What the . . . What kind of demon are you?"

"You dirty bastard," Uncle Duke said.

"You gotta believe me. I felt horrible. She was a nice lady."

"So, who signed Holcomb's body out of the morgue using my name?"

Daddy and Uncle Duke looked at me like I'd lit a torch and swallowed the fire from it. But neither of them said a word.

"They knew you were digging around in this thing. I asked a female friend of mine to go over to the morgue and use your name as the next of kin."

I could not believe what I was hearing.

"And then you sent your aide, Kyle Bowen, over to my house to break in?"

"They told me to scare you off. He was supposed to rattle you, that's all, but you broke his arm. That's when he sent some friend of his over to the Beaver Street house to meet you that night."

With every word Lester spoke, my head spun. "So, you're telling me some corporate bigwigs from a hedge fund are killing people to get their property? If you had Delilah's interest in the island property, how did Medallion get all of it? Holcomb said he'd never sell it."

Lester hesitated for a moment, looking between Daddy and Uncle Duke. "I turned over my paperwork to them like I always do. That's part of the deal. I told them that Holcomb still had an interest in the property. They said they'd handle it."

"You keep saying *they*. Who are you talking about?"

"I'm not sure. I just talk to a guy named Anton at the hedge fund.

But I don't think he's one of the financial people. He's rough. Uncouth."

"So, who's behind the hedge fund?"

"I don't know," he said.

Daddy slapped Lester across the head, with his hand this time. "Answer her."

"I'm telling the truth. For some reason, they really wanted that island property. The next thing I know, I get word from New York that the property's been sold. I didn't know Beau had bought it until the day I saw you at the office. That's when he told me about his plans for the resort. I just know whoever is behind all this is pretty dangerous. I tried to close Empire because I was tired of preying on my people in the community."

"Oh really?" Uncle Duke said. "Is that why you were over at the church last Saturday talking all that shit about people should sell their homes?"

"I don't like doing it. I started this business because I thought it would be legit."

"What does that mean?"

"I served some time in prison. Met a guy who told me he could help me open a branch of his real estate company here in Georgia. They were fine at first, but . . . I'm telling you, they won't let me stop or close the business. The last time I did . . . let's just say I spent a week in the hospital rethinking my choices. You better watch yourself." He glared at Daddy and Uncle Duke. "These two clowns won't be enough to protect you. Trust me."

This time Uncle Duke raised up from the wall he was leaning on, rushed across the room, and swung a backhanded slap across Lester's face, which immediately turned bright red.

"Name-calling ain't nice," Uncle Duke said.

"Uncle Duke!" I pushed him away from Lester. "So, you knew they killed the Gardners and you did nothing?"

"I'm so sorry. I loved Delilah. I didn't mean her any harm. I really did think they would let her brother stay on the land. I—"

Daddy walked around to the front of Lester's chair. "You didn't love her, you dirty son of a bitch."

Uncle Duke and I froze. It was the first time I'd ever heard Daddy utter a curse word in my entire life. Everyone went silent. The hum of the fridge was the only sound in the room.

"I ought to kill you." Daddy sneered before he pointed the gun at Lester.

Uncle Duke raced over to Daddy and pulled him away. "Easy there, Butta. Let's just take things slow."

"All three of you are going to jail when I'm done with you." Lester still had a little fight left in him even though, from the looks of things, Daddy and Uncle Duke had roughed him up pretty good before I'd arrived.

Uncle Duke chuckled. "Now, settle down there, Charlie Horse. The only one going to prison is you." Uncle Duke held up his phone to show that he'd been recording everything. "Deena, I could be wrong. You're the lawyer and all, but I think this man's been involved in a conspiracy to commit murder, fraud, and probably a whole bunch of other stuff I'm not smart enough to know about. What say you, Counselor?"

Lester's face went slack when he saw Uncle Duke's phone.

"If I were you, Charlie Horse," Uncle Duke said with a chuckle, "I'd keep my mouth shut about our little hospitality we extended to you this evening unless you want this recording to go to the FBI."

Daddy chimed up. "Maybe it's about time to take a drive back out to your car and see if anyone fixed those tires for you." He shook his head sadly. "Three flat tires. On an expensive car like that one. That's some really bad luck. I think you took the dangerous road home, ain't that right, Duke?"

Uncle Duke tossed his toothpick in the garbage can and smiled.

CHAPTER 50

Saturday morning, I got up early. Daddy got home sometime after I'd gone to bed. Heaven only knows what he and Uncle Duke had done with Charlie Lester last night after they left the barbershop. I was still reeling after listening to Lester describe how he'd driven Delilah out to the island and right to her death. Charlie Lester was evil incarnate.

I headed into the kitchen. The place was empty, and I heard the sound of sawing behind the house. I slipped through the screened-in porch and out into the backyard. It was a bright, crisp morning. Daddy was in the detached garage sawing wood. He had a John Lee Hooker blues song playing on the radio in the background. My stomach tumbled. Daddy always played the blues when he was angry. He said it calmed him down, hearing about how bad other people's problems were.

I walked up and joined him in the garage. "Morning, Daddy."

"Good morning," he said without looking at me or pausing his work. No "baby girl" greeting. Daddy was angry. He had every right to be with this bonfire of a mess that I'd dragged him and his brother into.

"What are you up to?"

"I'm gonna replace a couple floorboards on the back porch," he said flatly. Still no eye contact.

"What time did you get home last night?" I asked.

"Late."

"Did you and Uncle Duke flatten Lester's tires?"

Daddy kept sawing.

"Daddy?"

"Like Duke said, it can be dangerous out there. A random nail or screw on the road can wreak havoc on a tire. Or maybe he just had a slow leak. Who knows?"

"What did y'all do with Lester?"

Daddy didn't answer. He just kept sawing.

"Daddy, please talk to me."

He finally looked at me. "We took him back out to his car. His tires were still flat. Maybe he called AAA or hitched a ride. He's a big boy. I'm sure he figured it out."

"I'm so sorry I dragged you and Uncle Duke into all this."

"That guy came to my home and threatened you. He had men following you, trying to harm you. He scared the bejesus out of Roo." He shook his head slowly. "She's been burning and burying crap ever since he left here. If you think I wasn't gonna get involved in that, then you don't know me as well as you think you do. I will always protect the people I love and care about."

Daddy went back to sawing the plank.

"I'm sorry, Daddy. I didn't mean . . ."

He stopped sawing, stood upright, and looked me straight in the eye. "You're hardheaded, Deena! Always have been. Just like your mother. I tell you one thing, you nod and do the opposite. You go off to meet a demon like Lester in the dead of night and almost got us all killed! You think you're the only one who cares about these people? You're not. But there are consequences every time you go off half-cocked." He knocked off a bit of sawdust from the plank before he went back to sawing. "So, I guess I can't convince you to quit that job, huh?"

"You don't have to. I plan to quit on Monday."

"Good. Did you get something on your phone from Duke?"

"If you mean the recording from last night, yes. I saw his text this morning when I woke up."

"I'm not gonna tell you to take it to the police because you won't listen to me anyway."

"I know what to do with it. Don't worry."

He removed the plank and sat it against the sawhorse. He walked over and stood in front of me. "You heard the same thing I heard last night. That demon sat across a table from Delilah and broke bread with her. Then he drove her to the spot where he knew she'd be killed." Tears welled in his eyes. "Deena, if something happens to you . . . if I lost you too, that would be the end of me . . ."

I hugged him so tight I thought I might break his thin, fragile body. "You won't lose me, Daddy. I promise."

He removed a handkerchief from his pocket and dabbed at his eyes.

"I love you, Daddy."

He kissed me on my forehead, and I headed back inside the house.

* * *

Going to the police at this point would be useless. Detective Mallory didn't give a damn about the Gardners. Back in my bedroom, I pulled up Easter Prym's cell number. I was certain she would have some contacts that could help me. I typed a text.

> Take a listen. I need to get it to the FBI. It's Commissioner Charlie Lester answering a few

questions about Medallion and a hedge fund in NYC—Bellar Strategies. Can you help?

I attached Uncle Duke's recording and hit send.

Next, I called my friend Bridget back in Atlanta.

"Deena! You finally decided to pick up the phone. I didn't want to bug you. I've missed you. How are you?"

"I'm fine." My trademark response since Ma had died. "Actually, I'm not, but I'm getting better."

"That's good. It takes time to heal."

"It does. Listen, I need your help. Is your brother still a reporter for the *Atlanta Journal-Constitution*?"

"Yeah, why?"

"I think I might have a story he'd be interested in. There's something going on down here in the Low Country that I think needs some larger attention."

She called her brother, and we did a three-way call. I gave them an overview about everything that had transpired over the past couple weeks. Bridget's brother was hooked and agreed to meet me in Brunswick in a few days to discuss it further.

After I hung up with them, I went shopping at the mall. With Roo.

CHAPTER 51

By Monday morning, my plan was in place to bring down Lester and Beau and Bellar Strategies too. If Medallion had to fall as collateral damage, so be it. As the managing partner of my old law firm back in Atlanta told me the day he fired me: *You'll land on your feet, I'm sure*. So too would Medallion. My only regret was that Clare had been so nice to me. But she played Dr. Frankenstein to Beau, the Monster. He was playing fast and loose with her business and planning to kick her out of a company she started. It was up to her to fix the wreckage he had created.

I was nervous and jittery as I walked into the Old Victorian for the last time. I thought about what happened up in the attic. A fleeting thought crossed my mind: Maybe Delilah had been around this house the whole time, as a ghost or a guiding force, who knew? If she was here, in whatever form, I hoped she would help me this one last time.

I began cleaning out my office, removing the things I wanted to keep, including a picture of Daddy and Ma taken on their thirty-fifth wedding anniversary that I kept on my desk along with some Georgia Bar materials. I ran to the copier a couple times to make a few copies of the documents I'd lifted from the attic. Technically, these files were Medallion's property. My removing them, either in their original form or in copy, was "theft by taking" under the law. But I didn't care. These people had done much worst.

I still couldn't make heads or tails of some of the documents from the Bellar Strategies box. Random names. Employees? Investors? I made a copy of them too, in case they were important.

A few minutes later, Jennie called me from the front desk. "Hey, Deena. Beau wants you to come up to his office. He said it's urgent."

"Okay."

Beau didn't scare me anymore. Whatever the hell he wanted, it could wait. Ten minutes later, Jennie called again to tell me that Beau was insistent that I come to his office now. I waited another ten minutes before I decided I was ready to see him.

I tucked the last of my copies in my bag along with my other things. Now, I was ready to go to Beau's office—to quit. I knew he would readily accept my resignation since he'd wanted to fire me anyway. I decided against telling Clare. I knew she'd try to talk me out of it. It was best this way. Besides, I didn't particularly care for her putting me in the middle of their little family squabble. I was done with Medallion.

I headed upstairs to Beau's office. When I walked in, he was sitting at his desk, feet propped on top of it, acting very much like the pretentious wannabe executive he was.

He was on the telephone and signaled for me to have a seat. He proceeded to spend the next five minutes blathering into the phone with someone. Finally, I stood from the chair, removed my keys from my bag, and jiggled them loudly.

"Hey, buddy, look, I got something else to attend to here. I'll talk to you later." He hung up the phone, removed his feet from his desk, and stared at me. "You going somewhere?"

"As a matter of fact, I am."

"We need to talk."

"Your meeting. You go first," I said without an ounce of enthusiasm. Two weeks ago, I was terrified of losing this job. Now, I couldn't wait to be done with this place.

"I understand from Clare you had a little discussion with her about the Sea Spa project. If you had some doubts, why didn't you come to me directly?"

"Oh, sorry. My bad."

"My aunt and I have a difference of opinion on what's right for this company."

"Well, good luck with that."

He stared at me like he didn't recognize me all of a sudden. Maybe he didn't. When you no longer come from a place of fear, it can change your whole demeanor.

"From now on, when you have a problem with something I'm doing in this company, you come see me. Everything comes through me first. Are we clear?"

I didn't respond. I didn't care what the hell Beau or anyone else in this company did. He'd be in jail soon enough.

"And one more thing." He leaned forward on his desk. "I need you to stop sneaking around the office after hours and up in the attic digging through files. I want you to have all the resources you need to do your job. But from now on, you check with me first. Understood?"

"That won't be a problem going forward. Trust me."

He leaned back in his chair. "You need to make sure you are doing the job we pay you for. That means you spend your time doing legal work on Medallion's projects. Any other little side work you do isn't what we pay you for. Are we clear?"

"Actually, I'm not sure I know what you're talking about."

"Hmm . . . let me put it another way. People could get hurt when you're not attentive to what you should be doing. And any information you've learned about this company and what we do, you'd be wise to keep it to yourself."

Perhaps he'd had a little chat with his buddy Charlie Lester. Maybe Lester told him what happened Friday night at the barbershop while trying to get his car up off three flat tires.

This was yet another threat. To hell with Beau Walsh and his empty threats.

My cell phone rang. "Sorry, I need to take this call."

"Let that ring into voicemail. We're in the middle of a meeting and we're not done here."

"Trust me, we're done. I quit." I walked out of Beau's office and straight out of the Old Victorian.

CHAPTER 52

Fifteen minutes later, I pulled up to the law offices of Welburton and Harley. They were located in downtown Brunswick in a newly renovated building on Newcastle Street. I stepped inside an office filled with teakwood and low-slung furniture against a backdrop of white walls with precisely placed artwork. All of it gave the place a minimalist vibe. The receptionist directed me to a group of chairs while she called Howie. I didn't bother to sit because it would have taken me some extra effort to get out of furniture that low to the ground. A few minutes later, he walked into the reception area with a big wide smile planted across his face.

"Hey! Let's go take a walk." He turned to the receptionist. "I'll be back shortly."

I liked the way Howie interacted with other women in my presence—waitstaff, receptionists—pleasant but not lecherous. Not like Lance.

Outside, it was sunny. Brunswick reminded me of a sleepier version of Savannah, with its city squares and quaint downtown buildings. The blossoming crocuses and the bright pink-white color of the dogwoods starting to bud made everything pop. His building sat near a city square, and we decided to walk over to it.

"I talked to the paralegal this morning and took another look at that information you told me about. I found out that Empire bought

Delilah Gardner's share of the island property. I don't know how Lester convinced her to sell it for the pittance that she did. But once it was sold, Bellar's lawyers went to court and filed for a forced partition sale of the property. By that time, Delilah was dead, and Holcomb never responded to the petition. The land was sold to Medallion. Pretty fucked up. The Gardners lost a really valuable piece of property."

"I know. Charlie Lester told me. Apparently they killed her to keep her from warning her brother and fighting the sale."

"What? When did you talk to Lester?"

"It's a long story, but Daddy and Uncle Duke *convinced* him to answer a few questions for me." I shook my head. "They had Lester tied up in the back of the barbershop."

Howie threw his head back and laughed. "Damn! You don't play with the OG duo. I love them two dudes."

I told Howie everything we learned in the back of the barbershop. "Lester took her out to the property to talk to Holcomb, but not before he placed a call to one of Bellar's goons, who killed her. He said there's some powerful people behind Bellar Strategies. Whoever they are, they've got Lester spooked. He claims he doesn't know who they are."

"Hey, didn't you tell me Delilah left behind a granddaughter? What about her share of the property?"

"I guess whoever killed Holcomb and Delilah didn't know about her granddaughter. And Rae didn't know her grandmother had a brother so she wouldn't have intervened in the partition sale."

"Hmm . . . that would make the title on the property cloudy. Maybe she could file a quiet title action. But she'd have to show her relationship to Holcomb. And probably some evidence of how the land was passed down among the relatives."

We sat down on one of the iron benches in the square. "I checked with her and we found a bunch of receipts. Delilah was paying the taxes on the island property."

"Maybe that might help. I'll check it out," Howie said.

"Beau and Lester probably thought both deaths would go under the radar. Just two more dead Black people. One a mysterious hit-and-run and the other a loner drug head. How Lester can do this to his own people and live with himself is beyond me."

"Look, Deena, I admire your passion about getting to the bottom of this, but these people are really dangerous. If they're willing to kill two innocent people to get their property, maybe it's a little too risky for you to be chasing down the Gardners' killer. I'm just saying be careful, Deena."

We both sat quietly for a moment.

"Maybe we should change the subject?" Howie said.

I looked at him, not exactly sure what he wanted to talk about.

"That kiss Friday night. You left me hanging."

"I gotta go."

He gently grabbed my hand. "Not this time. Deena, please don't fight me on this. We've been in and out of some sort of relationship since we were thirteen. Two marriages and two divorces between us. What does that tell you?"

"It tells me I'm bad at picking my soulmate."

He chuckled. "I disagree. You picked right the first time. Your soulmate was just too boneheaded to see it. Look, I won't press you. But I will tell you, when you're ready, I'll be here." He leaned across the bench and gently kissed me. "Call me later and let me know if the granddaughter has any other information. I'd better get back to the office."

We stood from the bench, and he was still holding my hand. He smiled and gently squeezed it before he walked away.

Damn it, Howie.

Ma used to always say, *There's a lid for every pot and Howie Lawson is yours.* If she were here now, she'd tell me to go chase after him and tell him, *I'm ready now.* But she wasn't here, and I wasn't so sure I was.

CHAPTER 53

After I left Howie I drove over to Uncle Duke's barbershop. I peeped through the window and hoped Uncle Duke didn't have any customers or friends sitting around the shop. I stepped inside and the bell over the door jingled. The shop was completely empty.

"I'll be right with you," Uncle Duke yelled from the back room.

A few seconds later he walked in drying his hands with a paper towel. "Deena, sweetie! What are you doing here in the middle of the day?"

"I just stopped by to say hello." I took a seat in one of the barber chairs and Uncle Duke sat in the one across from me.

"I got the recording. Thanks. So, what happened with Charlie Lester after I left?"

"Nothing much. We took him back to his car and convinced him that if he fucked around again with you or anybody else in this family, the police would find him floating upside down in Dunbar Creek." Uncle Duke's stern expression told me there would be no further discussion on this point.

I let the matter drop.

"He wears five-thousand-dollar suits and drives a Range Rover. How many Black and brown folks live down in this neck of the woods drive a hundred-thousand-dollar car? Claims he flips houses. There aren't enough raggedy houses in Brunswick to flip and make the kind of money he spends. I always knew that guy was into something dark, but I didn't think he was hanging out with murderers. The only thing that confuses me is how somebody like Delilah would get involved with him. I woulda thought she'd have better taste. But them pretty girls always like the slick ones, huh?"

I didn't respond.

"And what's this business about somebody signing Holcomb's body out of the morgue using *your* name? And a car following you all over town?" Uncle Duke shook his head sadly. "Deena. Why wouldn't you tell us about this stuff?"

"I didn't want to tell you and Daddy because you'd worry."

"We do that anyway because you're ours. We're always concerned about your welfare, sweetie."

"Listen, I need your help again."

"Okay. What ya need?"

"How would someone move a trailer?"

"You mean like a trailer someone lives in?"

I nodded yes.

"I imagine you'd have to hire a hauler."

"You know any?"

Uncle Duke looked at me and smiled. "I just happen to have a friend. If my buddy's company didn't move it, they'd know who did. You need special equipment and not a lot of folks around here do that kind of work. Hang on, let me make a call. But you can't tell your daddy. You know you gave him a big scare. He really wants you to drop this thing."

"I know."

Uncle Duke nodded understandingly. "You're not gonna leave it alone, are you?"

I smiled back at him.

He picked up his cell phone and dialed a number. I listened patiently as he exchanged pleasantries and made the inquiry with someone on the other end of the phone. He grabbed a pen from his pocket, and I watched him scribble something on the palm of his hand as he held the phone between his ear and shoulder.

"Alright, thanks," he said before he hung up. "Here you go." He held out his left hand. "Here's an address. Ask for Mac. I let 'em know you're my niece."

I tapped the address into my phone. "Oh, I forgot. I wanted to ask you something. Remember when you said Daddy had a crush on Delilah Gardner? How serious were they?"

Uncle Duke scratched his head. "I don't think he ever acted on it. He mostly stood around making googly eyes at her. Maybe danced with her a couple times. But she was outta your Daddy's league. No offense. Why do you ask?"

I smiled weakly. "Just curious." Daddy and Delilah's secrets were not mine to share, as Miss Ophelia would say.

"Thanks. Well, I've taken up enough of your time."

I climbed down from the barber chair and leaned over and hugged Uncle Duke.

"What's that for?"

"For being exactly what I need whenever I need it."

He walked me to my car, and I hugged him again. I was blessed to have him and Daddy in my life. And Roo too. All these fierce protectors who loved me, girded me, and fed me with their wisdom. The ancestors would be proud of them.

CHAPTER 54

I headed for the address Uncle Duke gave me. It was on the outskirts of Brunswick, headed toward Darien. When I arrived, there was a small black and white sign affixed to a chain-link fence: Mac's Haulers. I turned into the opening, which led to a long gravel driveway off the street. My car bumped and bobbled over holes and pits in the gravel before I came to the front of a dingy-looking oversized shed. The sign above the door also read Mac's Haulers.

I looked around the lot. Dinged and battered cars and trucks were everywhere. I slipped out of my heels and into my Skechers I pulled from the back seat. The last time I'd worn them was when Holcomb had dragged me into the very trailer I was on the hunt for now. They still bore the mud and moss from his property.

I climbed a couple stairs out front and opened the door. An air conditioner anchored in the window cooled the makeshift office but made a loud rattling noise that caught me off guard when I stepped inside. Sitting behind a metal desk on one end of the shed was a large woman with strawberry-blond hair pulled into a messy bun and an ink pen stuck through the middle of it. She wore a red plaid shirt that her sizable breasts were nearly bursting out of.

Her eyes were bright blue, and her face lit up with a big smile when I entered. "May I help you?"

"Hi, my name is Deena Wood. I'm looking for Mac."

"You found her." She smiled devilishly, like she enjoyed throwing people off, that a woman should be sitting in her chair. "Are you Duke's niece?"

"Yes."

"What can I do for you?"

"I'm looking for a trailer that belonged to a friend of mine. I think you may have hauled it away. I'm just trying to locate it, maybe take a look inside." In just a couple weeks, Holcomb Gardner had gone from being a complete stranger who threatened me with a gun to my dead "friend."

Mac's demeanor changed. She scoped me from head to toe. "Hmm . . . where's your *friend*?"

"He's dead."

Mac went quiet. It was then that I heard the low twang of a country music song playing in the background and fighting to be heard over the air conditioner.

"Look, lady, I don't want no trouble. My place is on the up-and-up. Whatever you're into, I want no part of it."

"Ma'am, you are my last hope for finding out what happened to my friend. I think you may have hauled an old trailer from Boden Road out on the island a couple weeks ago. Can you at least tell me who requested the pickup?"

She stared at me for a beat before she turned and shuffled through a stack of receipts on her desk. She landed on one and stared at it for a moment. "Brian Mallory. Have a good day."

"Detective Brian Mallory?"

I knew there was something up with that guy. And then it all made sense. When I filed that missing persons report, I essentially alerted them that I was digging around into Holcomb's and Delilah's deaths. The only other person who knew Holcomb was in the morgue besides Monty, me, Daddy, and Uncle Duke was Detective Mallory, because I'd told him to check the morgue. The only way Lester could get a friend of his inside the morgue to sign out a body without my ID would be if a police officer was involved. And it was Mallory who'd ordered the haul of Holcomb's trailer.

Mallory was in on whatever Beau and Lester were into. He was helping them cover up their crimes. That's why he had so little interest in finding Rae when I thought she was missing and why he didn't put anything out to the media about Holcomb's disappearance.

I thought for a moment before I reached inside my purse and pulled out my wallet. I saw her glance at me with a side-eye. I pulled out sixty-two dollars. It was all the money I had on me.

"Look, I don't want any trouble either and no one will ever know I was here." I extended the money toward her. "Let me just take a look inside."

Mac glared up at the money. "I don't know you. I've never seen you before. But if you bring trouble to my doorstep, I'll be your worst nightmare. I don't care if you are Duke's niece. Are we clear?"

"Crystal."

She snatched the money from my hand and slipped it into her bra. "Take the path behind me and follow it to the dead end. The trailer is parked there."

"Thanks."

* * *

I FOLLOWED MAC'S instructions and prayed nothing would go wrong. My chances were pretty good considering Mac didn't want to be associated with a dead body. Of course, the real reason I didn't want any trouble with Mac was because she looked like she could kick my ass with one hand while sifting through the day's receipts with the other.

I made it to the trailer.

Holcomb's trailer.

The door was nearly hanging off the hinges. I carefully stepped inside. The place looked a sight with cabinets and drawers open and cans and clutter everywhere. A rat the size of a small dog crept across the table and I screamed. It ran off and it took me a minute to get my bearings. I looked down at the floor. Holcomb's dog's water bowl was empty and turned over. Either it had been a hell of a bumpy ride to get the trailer to this lot or someone had ransacked the place.

I walked over to the tiny bedroom at the end of the trailer. The mattress was askew and the bedcovers all across the bed and floor. I looked around, for what, I wasn't exactly sure. Taped onto the wall beside the bed was a Polaroid similar to the one Rae had given me. But in this picture, it was a younger Holcomb and a different Black woman. She was petite and dressed in a yellow floral minidress and a pair of brown platform shoes. Her hair was neatly pressed and hovered over her shoulders. Holcomb towered over her, so tall he had to stoop a bit to wrap his arms around her waist. They both looked into the camera with wide blissful smiles. This must be Holcomb's wife, Gracie, when they were younger. The wife that Uncle Duke told me about when I first asked about Delilah. They made a really attractive couple. What was she like? I thought about what Uncle Duke had told me in the barbershop about having a purpose. He had the barbershop. Daddy had Roo. And after Holcomb's wife died, maybe the island property had become his purpose.

I stood in the tiny space and closed my eyes. *What happened to you, Holcomb Gardner?*

And just like in the attic of the Old Victorian, I felt that weightless floating feeling again. I let it drift me away.

When I opened my eyes, the first thing I focused on was a stained tile in the ceiling, an odd brown pattern. Several tiles over from the stained one was a tile with a small bulge, not flush like the others. If Delilah was hiding money and love letters in her floorboards, maybe her brother hid his valuables around his house too. Holcomb certainly didn't strike me as the type to have a safety-deposit box at a bank.

I quickly straightened the mattress and stood on top of it. I poked at the bulge and prayed it wasn't a dead animal wedged under there. I shimmied the tile loose from the others and pulled it down. Stuck to the underside of it was a plastic bag tied with a knot. I peeled the bag loose and hopped down from the mattress.

I tried to undo the knot, which took some effort. I finally managed to get the bag open and pulled out the contents. Inside was a Ziploc bag with several documents inside. On top, there had to be at least a half dozen of the bright yellow flyers that everyone in Harristown had received, offering to buy their property. Holcomb had apparently saved every one of them he'd gotten. Below the flyers was a letter, almost identical to the letter that Bellar's attorneys had sent to LaShonda and to Nell Drucker in South Carolina, advising him of the impending sale of his property. Holcomb had obviously ignored the letters.

But the last document stunned me.

The paper was yellowed and a bit frayed but still legible. It was a deed for a parcel of land on what was then called Boden Trail. The land had been purchased from John Tilden by Farland and Julep Gardner in 1867, shortly after the Civil War. I imagined John Tilden had been a former plantation owner who split up his land into parcels and sold it to former slaves. It was just as Holcomb had said. This land had been in his family for generations.

I gently placed the deed and all the other documents back into the plastic bag and slipped it inside my purse. I headed out of the trailer, off the lot, and straight to Rae's house.

* * *

I DIDN'T GET an answer when I rang Rae's doorbell. She was probably at work, given the time of day. I sent her a text.

Found some info to help get your grandmother's land back!

I clicked off my phone. With the tax receipts we found in Delilah's closet and the deed I'd found in Holcomb's trailer, Rae might have enough evidence to file a court action to determine who rightfully owned the island property.

But that was only one half of the puzzle solved. I still didn't know the identity of the person who killed Holcomb and Delilah. I needed to figure out who was driving the black Ford Escape that had been following me all over town. Detective Mallory? And I still didn't know who was behind Bellar Strategies and orchestrating this scheme to take away so much from the people who could least afford it. A minute later, my phone buzzed with a text from Rae.

Just left work. Meet you at my house in 15

CHAPTER 55

I sat in my car in front of Rae's house waiting for her to come home. I pulled out my phone and scrolled through my email. There was an email from Lois about the inspection I'd need before closing on the house. There was another from Sarah Wheeler. She wanted to talk to me about the Georgia Heirs Property Law Center.

God, please let me find another job.

I was just about to open up Instagram when the phone rang in my hand. I didn't recognize the number. I typically don't answer calls when I don't recognize the number, but something inside me told me to answer this time.

"Hello?"

"Deena, it's Ellen Trainor. Is that you I see outside Rae's house?"

I looked up at Mrs. Trainor's house and saw her peeking through the blinds. Dusk was falling fast and the streetlights began to blink on. "Uh . . . yes, ma'am. It's me. I'm just waiting for Rae to return home. I hope I didn't alarm you."

"Oh no, dear. I just like to keep an eye open. You never know when some bad element is lurking."

Thank God for the neighborhood watch that is a seventy-five-year-old widow.

"I'm glad I have you on the phone, beloved. I was going to call you. I finally remembered where I saw that detective."

"You did?"

"Yes. I saw his picture in the paper. It's been a while, but I found the paper and his picture."

"Why was his picture in the paper?"

Mrs. Trainor chuckled. "He was in the society section, of all places. Looks like he gets around. He was at some swanky gala. I guess I didn't immediately recognize him because in this picture he's in a tuxedo. Mr. Fancy Pants."

I heard paper rustling in the background. *Hurry up and get home, Rae.*

"I tell you what. My granddaughter showed me how to take pictures with my iPad. I'll take a picture and text it to you."

"That'll be great, Mrs. Trainor." Every time I talked to her, I was mightily impressed with her tech skills. My phone buzzed again. It was an incoming call from Rae. "Mrs. Trainor, I have another call coming in I need to get. Just text the picture to my phone."

"Alright, sweetie. I will. You and Rae be careful out there, okay?"

"We will." I hung up and switched over to the call from Rae. "Hey, Rae, I'm outside your house. You on your way?"

"I'm calling because I figured out who killed Gran. The evidence is inside that house where you work."

"What?! What evidence?"

"Just meet me at your job." *Click.*

She was gone. I started up the engine and headed straight for the Old Victorian.

CHAPTER 56

I drove up the curved driveway at the front of the Old Victorian. The night sky was heavy with stars as if God had opened up the top of the universe and sprinkled silver sequins across the sky. The Old Victorian looked regal against the night background. I pulled my car up to the back of a black Ford Escape. The same car that had been following me. But I didn't see Rae's car anywhere. A knot the size of a grapefruit sunk in my stomach. I pulled out my phone and dialed Rae's number. No answer. I sent a text.

I'm outside. Where r u?

No response.

None of this was right. Then it occurred to me that the first time Rae had come to the Old Victorian she was concerned that she might have caused me problems by showing up at my job. She wouldn't have come here again.

My phone rang. *Howie.*

"Howie, something's wrong."

"I know. Where are you?" I heard anxiety in his voice.

"I'm outside Medallion's office. Rae told me to meet her here. She said there was some evidence inside the house proving who killed her grandmother. But something weird is going on. The black car that's been following me all over town is in front of the house and Rae's not responding to my texts."

"Listen to me, Deena. *Do not* go inside the house. I figured out what's going on with Bellar Strategies. I'm on my way."

"What?!"

"Stay inside the car and make sure your doors are locked. If anything weird happens, drive off and get out of there. I'm on my way."

"Okay."

I checked the car door locks and pressed them twice to make sure I was safe inside. My phone buzzed and I nearly jumped through the car windshield. It was a text from Mrs. Trainor. I opened it. Just as she said, she'd sent the picture from the newspaper. And there he was. Detective Mallory. He stood in the center of the photo, decked out in a tuxedo. And standing next to him in a sequined ball gown—Clare Walsh!

I dialed Howie's number. He picked up on the first ring. "I got a picture here and it shows that detective, Brian Mallory, and Clare together at some society gala."

"That's why I'm headed to you. I found out one of the officers of Bellar Strategies is Clare Walsh."

"What?!"

"Those names on that list you found, they're political donors, but some of them are really dangerous people. Deena, promise me you won't go in that house. Just drive away."

"I think they may have Rae in there. Mallory knows that Rae is an heir to the island property. They're going to kill her too. I have to get her out of there."

"Deena, listen to me. These are dangerous people. Some of them are tied to criminal money. I'm ten minutes away. Stay on the phone with me. Tell me what you see. Is there any activity going on in the house?"

I craned my neck. "Just a light on in the foyer." Before I could utter another word, a sensation came over me. It was that same warm floating feeling I'd had in the attic the other day. The same feeling I'd had in Holcomb's trailer. But this time, it was different. It was stronger and more distinct than it had been the other times. It was as if it were originating from within me instead of encircling me like the other times. I closed my eyes to steady myself.

"Deena? Deena?!"

I heard Howie's voice, but it sounded muffled, like it was a million miles away.

Deena, there's someone worse off than you. You have to go help her.

It was Ma's voice. *Her actual voice*. It was clearer than I'd ever imagined it in my mind on all those drives. This time, it was as if she were sitting right beside me in the car. And I started to weep. I cried because I hadn't lost her. She was with me.

"Deena, are you there?" I heard Howie ask just before I clicked off the phone.

We are all connected. Help one of those souls, Ma said again.

I knew what I had to do.

CHAPTER 57

I unlocked my car door. I stepped outside and slowly walked up the front steps. The light inside flickered once. When I opened the door I nearly fainted. Detective Mallory was standing inside the foyer with a gun pointed at Rae's head. She was one tough sister, though. Not a tear. Not a flinch. Nothing. She stood defiantly, reminding me of her grandmother in the old Polaroid she'd given me.

"Sorry, Deena. This asshole forced me to call you," Rae said.

"You. Shut up," Mallory said to Rae. "Come on inside, Ms. Wood. Close the door."

I stepped inside. The entire place was dark except for the lights illuminating the foyer.

"So that's your black car outside, huh?" It all made sense now. When I went to see Mallory about Holcomb's disappearance, one of the first things he asked me was if I was related to Delilah. He was the one who followed me from Holcomb's property that first day. "Listen, Detective, Rae has done nothing to you. Why don't you let her go and any problems you got, take them up with me."

"That's admirable to stick up for your friend, but it's not my decision," he said.

The detective turned slightly toward the staircase and yelled, "I got 'em both down here!"

I heard footsteps coming down the staircase. When Beau made it to the bottom stair, he smiled at me as if we were old school chums. "Hey, Deena. Glad to see you back. Now, I thought we had talked about all this. I told you people could get hurt, and here we are."

I didn't respond.

A few seconds later, I heard high heels on hardwood. Clare strolled down the front staircase wearing a pink pantsuit with an apple green silk shirt. Her gray bob grazed her shoulders as she descended the stairs. In her arms, she carried Holcomb's dog. The one she had named Fig but Holcomb called Trooper. When Mallory and Beau turned to watch Clare, I gave a side glance at Rae and mouthed the words *follow me and run*. She nodded slightly.

When Clare reached the bottom of the stairs, she stood still and gave me this sad, pitiful look.

"Deena, Deena." She shook her head like she was about to admonish a wayward child. "I am truly fond of you. I have been in your corner since the first time you stepped inside this house. I've tried to make sure you got every advantage. All I asked for in return was your support. I understand our mutual friend Commissioner Lester even warned you. But still you persist."

"I don't understand why you killed Delilah and Holcomb. You already had their land. Why kill them too?"

Clare smiled as she stroked the top of the dog's head. "You're a lawyer. You of all people know things aren't always that simple. Beau tells me that silly woman was going to make trouble for us. We found her brother living out there. And now, you bring in a granddaughter we've never heard of. I'm hoping this is the last of the Gardners." Clare looked at Rae. "You are the last one, right?"

Rae sneered at her. "Go to hell, lady."

Clare whipped her head back as if she'd never been told as much.

The whole scene would have been funny but for the gun pointed at Rae's head and the fact that I once considered Clare a friend.

"Deena, you've dug around into things you shouldn't have. Now, granted, my nephew has run amok." She turned to Beau and rolled her eyes. "Instead of letting me handle things as I'd planned, he jumped the gun. When you do one thing well, you stick to that thing. Now, I have to clean up this mess. Surely you can understand. I have a political campaign to consider, and the people supporting me will not want to have things sullied and dirty laundry aired to the public."

"So, you're more concerned with your political ambitions and political donors who are tied up in a hedge fund? So much so that you would kill innocent people to secure a seat in Congress?"

"God, you make it sound like I'm a monster. I'm just a woman who knows what she wants and knows how to get it. You'd be wise to take a page from my book. But instead, you've poked around into matters that are not your concern."

"You didn't have to kill innocent people to get their property."

"I didn't. Certain people got impatient." This time she rolled her eyes at Mallory. "Instead of heeding the advice of a smart woman, they chose to act impetuously. But enough with all that business. Detective Mallory is going to escort you two out to his car and you'll all take a little ride with him—"

Suddenly, a window slammed shut somewhere upstairs with such force that the windows in the foyer rattled. A few seconds later, another window slammed down. Clare, Beau, and the detective turned toward the staircase.

Clare's eyes widened as she turned to Beau. "I thought you said we were alone."

"We are. I'll check it out," he said.

Get the dog. Ma's voice again.

"Trooper! Come here, boy," I said loudly. The dog perked up and scampered from Clare's arms. I quickly scooped him up.

"Run!" I yelled to Rae.

We both took off running through the conference room, headed for the back door in the kitchen. I heard a gunshot behind us.

"You fool! Don't shoot that thing off in here," Clare screamed. "Lock the doors!"

I heard a loud long beep.

All the lights in the house flickered off and on. Then the floor literally rumbled under our feet. We both stopped inside the butler's pantry.

"Shit! What was that?" Rae yelled.

"I don't know. This way!"

We started running again. We made it to the back door just as the lock clicked. I pulled on the door. Locked. The alarm system was activated and had locked all the doors.

"Come on, this way," I said. We raced up the back steps to the second floor. I opened the attic door. "Go!"

Rae raced up the attic stairs. I closed the door behind me and caught up to Rae at the top of the stairs. The attic was dark. Then the smell hit me. Cigarette smoke. Perfume. And something else.

Gas?

I flipped on the lights. The voice was back. The same low chattering I had heard that first night I came up to the attic. But this time it was louder. Trooper barked and trembled.

"Who's that?" Rae whispered.

We both stopped.

That's when we felt the walls vibrate, like a pulsating sensation.

"What is going on in this place?" Rae said.

"Shh," I replied, leaning in to hear the voices.

"What are we gonna do now?" Rae whispered.

"Shh. Over here." Trooper whimpered in my arms as I held him tightly. I raced to the storage room at the end of the hall, with Rae right on my heels. "In here!"

We dashed inside the room and closed the door. "Help me with this table." Together, we pushed the table up against the door. But it was too short to wedge under the doorknob. Trooper was trembling in my arms full-on now.

A minute later we heard more footsteps. Mallory's followed by Clare's. Where was Beau? Was he up here too, hiding out, waiting for us?

"Ladies, let's go," Mallory said. I heard him going into the first room closest to the attic stairs. "We're gonna take a little ride."

Trooper began to whimper louder, still shaking like a leaf. It would be only a minute or two before Mallory made it to this room.

"Shh," I said again, trying to calm the dog. "It's okay, boy."

Rae stood against the wall and whispered, "What are we going to do?"

"I don't know."

Get out of this room.

Another voice gently whispered in my ear. But it wasn't Ma. I didn't recognize the voice. I stopped. I touched the walls again. The entire room pulsated as warm water slowly slid down the walls like tears.

Leave this room. This is my house, and I will protect you.

"We have to leave. Come on." I started to back the table away from the door.

"What are you doing?" Rae asked. "We can't go out there!"

"I don't think we're safe here. Let's go."

The lights flickered again. I held tight to the dog and eased through the door. Rae was right on my heels. We hustled to the end of the hall.

Go through the door.

What door? I looked around for a door. *What the hell?* Trooper scampered from my arms and ran up to a large bronze grate at the end of the hall. It was small, no more than four feet tall. He barked and scratched. I eyed the dog before I turned back to watch Clare and Mallory walking closer.

"There they are!" Clare screamed.

Mallory hustled down the hall toward us.

I tugged at the grate before it finally gave way. It was some sort of passageway. Trooper dashed in first.

"Go!" I said to Rae. She looked at me for a beat before she scrambled inside. I knelt down to climb inside too. I was halfway in when I felt something at my left leg. Tugging. Pulling. Mallory had grabbed my leg and was pulling me out of the small door. I kicked and shoved at him. My shoe came off in the process. And then . . .

BOOM!

A loud explosion behind me. Mallory released my leg and turned to Clare. "What was that?" he yelled.

"Shit!" I heard Clare say. "I think a fuse just blew. And where the hell is Beau? Get them out of there and I'll go see what's going on downstairs. And get my dog!"

The grate door slammed shut with a loud clang. Lights flickered on and off. The best I could tell through the flickering lights was that we were in some sort of secret passageway. Another storage area or a path to another part of the house?

"Look! Stairs over there," I said to Rae.

"Deena, what is happening? What is that noise?"

"I don't know."

The lights flickered again. The smell of gas permeated the small space.

Mallory was back, tugging on the grate at the opening that we had just come through. Then I heard a crackle and popping. Suddenly, out of nowhere, I felt the weirdest sensation, like someone pulling me by the waist.

"Rae!"

"Deena! What the hell is happening?!"

I scooped up Trooper and held on to him for dear life.

The force pulled me backward. The crackling sound got closer. The force was still pulling me, almost like it was lifting me from underneath my arms and dragging me down the stairs. Trooper whimpered as we were lifted and dragged.

BOOM!

A second explosion. This time noticeably louder. The entire house shook.

"Deena!"

Rae's voice was the last thing I heard before I went flying backward and out through a door at the end of the passageway. I couldn't tell whether it was from the unseen force or the explosion, but everything went black. When I opened my eyes, I was outside, on the side of the Old Victorian, against a row of azalea bushes. Trooper was still in my arms and trembling like crazy. I struggled to get to my feet.

"Rae! Rae!"

"Over here," she yelled a few yards from me. Rae was lying on her back, her arm bleeding.

"Don't move."

I heard a loud whoosh. By the time I stumbled to my feet, I

looked up at the house. It was engulfed in flames. I watched as the fire danced across the sides of the house.

Sirens wailed from a distance.

"Deena!" Howie ran toward me. "Deena, are you alright?"

I raced to his arms and started crying. "I'm fine. I'm okay."

"When you didn't answer me on the phone, I called the police. As soon as I pulled up, I saw sparks and heard explosions. I wasn't able to get inside. Every door and window was locked. Oh my God, I thought you were inside." We hugged and I was afraid to let him go.

We finally released each other and rushed to Rae. "Sit tight. Help is on the way," Howie said to her.

The sirens grew louder, and I saw red lights flashing in the distance. I turned back to the house, now fully engulfed in flames. Minutes later, the firemen seemed to appear out of thin air. They rallied around the house, shooting powerful streams of water onto the burning mass. The crackle and pop of the fire was loud, like Fourth of July fireworks. I watched as flames encircled the roof of the turret that used to be Clare's office. A few seconds later, the top of the turret crumbled into a heap of burning wood and crashed down through the house. And then, amid the red glow of flames and the rush of water from the hoses, I saw something rise from the house. I blinked a couple times to make sure I wasn't imagining it.

The form of a woman in a white dress slipped from the flames.

And then, a second form of a woman in a white dress.

Both images rose to the sky, before they disappeared behind a moonlit cloud.

What had happened in the Old Victorian?

My precious baby girl, Deena.

I've always been with you. I never left your side. I simply transitioned to a different plane. My love for you will never cease. You are a part of me, and I am a part of you. Nothing can ever change that.

Not even death.

And while my love continues, you are loved by so many people around you—your dad, Duke, Howie, and yes, Roo. She stepped in and saved your father when he was broken and at his lowest point. Just as I did when he lost Delilah. Remember, we are all connected. I am grateful to Roo for saving your father. You should be too. She only wants what I want for you—your happiness.

Continue to heal. I am here. Every time you remember a phrase I once uttered or think of a memory about me, I am with you. I am in the laughter you share with those around you. I am in the glow that blossoms in your face when you are excited. I am in the love you spread to others. That's why you must laugh again and most especially love again. You are blessed because you've found your soulmate.

My work on the earthly plane is done. Now, it's up to you to do the rest—find happiness with Howie, care for your father and Roo until their work is done, and continue to shine light where there is darkness, just as you've done here.

Even though I share space with the ancestors now we will always surround you and protect you. You don't need to strain to hear me because I am close. I am with you. Always.

Keep making me proud. I love you.

Ma

CHAPTER 58

Three weeks after Holcomb and Delilah's family home burned to the ground, Daddy, Ruth, and I watched the morning news footage of Charlie Lester being handcuffed and escorted from the Atlanta airport, where he was caught trying to leave the country. We sat in rapt attention, watching the television until the news story concluded. When it was done, none of us said a word. We simply basked in the hope that perhaps there was some justice in this world after all. Maybe it was fitting that Charlie Lester should spend the rest of his life in a prison jumpsuit, contemplating how his desire for wealth had come at the cost of Delilah's life and the destruction of his own community.

A few minutes later, I walked to the stairs at the back of the house, which led to a small attic space. I pulled the chain that popped on a single light bulb in the center of the attic. The pitched roof of the house barely left me enough room to fully stand upright in the tight area. I peered across a sea of boxes until I found the gray box Daddy had marked "Libby's Antiques."

I opened it. Inside were Ma's collection of antique tin cans. They were all different sizes and colors, some patterned, some with store brands and mascots imprinted on them. Some she used to store dry goods and fresh-baked cookies. Others she only brought out to decorate the house for special occasions. I touched each one and remembered every spot in the house where it had once been placed. I closed the box and took it downstairs.

Lois had sent me everything I needed for the new house, including the closing date, coming up in three weeks. I planned to take Ma's antique tins with me to my new house. I wanted something of hers to be there with me.

Always.

I didn't think I believed in ghosts and spirits. But I did believe in the ancestors. All those whose backs were bent but not broken, their brows coated in sweat. The ones who labored and loved and thought beyond themselves so that people like me might walk proud and without doubt into a better future.

I hadn't heard Ma's voice again since the night the Old Victorian burned down. I'd heard her voice in my car that night as clear as if she were sitting beside me. And now, I didn't. But somehow, it was okay. I didn't need to hear her to know she was with me. I'd learned from people like Mrs. Trainor and Uncle Duke and even Rae that grief is love, repackaged in longing and despair. But after the emptiness of it all wears off, the love remains.

I was at peace.

* * *

THE NEXT DAY, Rae sat in the front passenger seat of my car as I drove over to the island. Her left arm was bandaged and in a sling. Neither of us spoke a word the entire ride out to the island.

I turned off Boden Road and drove the car up to the edge of the green silk fence and parked. I glanced over at Rae. Her whole body was shaking. I reached over and grabbed her hand.

"It's okay," I said.

"I've never owned a thing in my entire life. I mean, nothing of real value."

"Well, you will now. Come on, let's go look."

We both got out of the car, the doors slamming shut behind us. I heard Trooper's sharp bark.

"Don't worry, little guy. I won't leave you." I opened the back door and Trooper tumbled out of the car. I'd bought him a new collar with his real name. He ran over to the edge of the fence and began to bark, his tail wagging furiously. He finally scrambled through a hole in the fencing and raced across the beachfront. He was home.

Rae and I stepped over the short fencing and onto the beach.

"The corporate bigwigs will try to tie you up in a bunch of legal nonsense, but with the documents and evidence we found, Howie says all this will be yours one day."

Rae looked at me and smiled. "I don't know what to say."

"There's nothing to say. What are you going to do now?"

"I know what I'm *not* going to do. I'm not selling it."

"Like I said, you've got some legal hurdles to hump over first. But yeah, this is yours along with that house we went out to on Old Farm Road. And a gas station that your great-uncle owned. And you'll have to find some way to pay the taxes on it or else you really could lose it."

"I'll find a way." She looked out onto the ocean and smiled. "Maybe I'll tell the Soul Food Station to find another cook and I'll open up my own place."

"Sounds like I hear culinary school in your future."

"So, what's gonna happen to that company you worked for, the one taking people's property?"

"You probably heard on the news that the two owners died in the fire along with the detective. They were tied to another company that's being investigated for fraud and a host of other things. Charlie Lester, the commissioner, was found trying to fly out of the country. He was caught and has been charged with manslaughter and fraud. Apparently, they've been taking the land and property of poor people, farmers, for years."

"So that means you don't have a job anymore?"

"I got a new job. I'm going to be helping other people like your grandmother who are at risk of losing their property. I'll be working for the Georgia Heirs Property Law Center. I start next week."

"Congratulations." Rae shook her head. "I'm so sorry my grandmother and her brother lost everything and never reconciled. But I appreciate you for what you did. You didn't have to do that."

"Yes, I did. I had to do it for me too."

We both stared out into the Atlantic Ocean. I remembered Clare's advice to me a few weeks back when she told me not to get swallowed up in the loss of what I used to have, to find myself among the ruins. She was right. I discovered I was stronger than I ever knew. Death. Divorce. Job loss. All of it hit me, hard, and I was still standing.

I heard a car pull up behind us. Howie. I turned and watched him bounce out of his car and walk up to us on the beach.

He leaned down and gave me a quick kiss on the lips. He slipped his hand into mine and I held on tight. I wouldn't let go this time.

Rae looked over at us with a sneaky little smile. "You been *exercising*, Deena?"

"That's none of your business," I said, and we both laughed.

Thank you, Deena. You saved my family and my family's legacy, and for that I will be forever grateful.

Sometimes, a bad decision can be the decision that saves your life. I destroyed my own home, a place I had become a part of, to save you and Rae. And I don't regret it for a minute. I lost my brother, Holcomb, because I once refused to acknowledge that I'd made a mistake. No more mistakes.

I foolishly listened to the wrong people and lost the only man I ever truly loved. People told me I could do better than Jimmie Lee. I later learned that was never possible. The truth of the matter is that Jimmie Lee deserved better than me. Fortunately, he found it in Libby. And I am grateful to your mother. She stepped into Jimmie's life and made him whole after I broke his heart.

Don't let that happen to you. Be with that young man you love. Put every misstep and mistake behind you. You deserve every happiness.

All the ancestors worked to bring you here again and give you what you needed—love. Never forget, we are the same people who were brought to this country in chains. We were strong enough to withstand ungodly abuse and resourceful enough to build homes. We are the same people who worked in bondage and built a house where the president of the United States lives. We smiled and rejoiced when one of our own was elected to serve and live there. And all that we brought to this Low Country land from Africa spread across this country when those of us set out to find a better life in northern and western cities. We didn't stop being Geechee just because we left. The land and water and fire of this place is within all of us.

It is within you, Deena. You are exactly where you are supposed to be. You are home.

So keep looking out for my precious Rae.

And now, just like the Igbo people, our ancestors, I'll fly home.

Delilah

AFTERWORD

A few years ago, I was sitting in my bedroom folding laundry and watching the evening news. A story came on that stayed with me long after the news report ended. I didn't know it at the time, but that story would become the genesis for this book. The reporter interviewed a woman about what happened to her when she applied for Federal Emergency Management Agency (FEMA) assistance to repair her home after Hurricane Florence damaged it. She was turned away, unable to repair a home that had been in her family for generations. The reason: a legal theory called heirs property.

Heirs property refers to a home or land that passes from generation to generation without a legally designated owner, resulting in fractured ownership divided among several living descendants in a family. This is an unstable form of ownership and historically has made it easy for developers to acquire property. If a developer can convince just one heir to sell their fractional share of the property, it can force a court-ordered partition sale of the entire property, even if the other fractional owners are against the sale. Additionally, when a person owns property with an unclear title, it is difficult to secure mortgages and loans or to access repair money to improve the property. All of this limits a family's ability to build generational wealth. Many people who own heirs property are land rich but cash poor—they have extremely valuable property but lack the resources to buy out the other owners or obtain legal counsel to assist in sorting out the clouded title.

Not surprisingly, heirs property is a significant problem in low- and moderate-income Black and brown communities and in poor white Appalachian populations and communities across the country. These communities typically do not have access to tax and estate planning services. It happens in both urban areas and rural areas. In Low Country regions of the south, most heirs property was acquired by Black Americans after Emancipation. Land that had once been deemed unsuitable because of its mosquito-infested marshlands is now in high demand by developers. Right now, in the state of Georgia, where I live, over $30 billion of generational wealth is lost in heirs property.

I wanted to document this plight and shed light on yet another system that perpetuates a cycle of haves and have-nots. I urge people to become knowledgeable about the value of their property and learn how to retain and grow their generational wealth. Seek assistance through nonprofits such as the Georgia Heirs Property Law Center and other organizations that offer property-related services. If you know people who may be owners of heirs property encourage them to seek assistance.

By setting this story in the Georgia Low Country, I found out that the rich Gullah-Geechee culture there is threatened by developers who are trying to use heirs property to scoop up land. My grandmother was born in Georgia. When I was young, my mother often said her family was Geechee. Unfortunately, I didn't take advantage of her knowledge and probe deeper into the culture while she was still alive, to my regret. But while researching this book, I met a distant cousin and learned of an heirs property involving some of my own family members. I also met some of the most wonderful Gullah-

Geechee people. I am forever in their debt for introducing me to this rich and vibrant part of my own personal history.

As I did in my other books, I write about issues and themes that make me think. Issues that make me examine how I can be a part of the solution rather than the source of the problem. I hope that by chronicling the heirs property concerns and the Gullah-Geechee culture in an engaging and entertaining story, I've made you think likewise.

ACKNOWLEDGMENTS

First and foremost, I thank God, without whom this life I live and this gift I am blessed with would not be possible. I also thank the ancestors who prayed and paved a path for me with their love and their literal blood, sweat, and tears.

Writing a book is hard. At least for me it is. And every time I start to think *Can I really do this?*, someone from my large and supportive village convinces me that I can. I am thankful to every one of them. My village includes my wonderful editor, Asanté Simons. As always, your wisdom and support are an indelible part of this book's entry into the world. Thank you to the terrific team at HarperCollins: Beatrice Jason, Tess Day, Kaitlin Harri, Virginia Stanley, Lainey Mays, Grace Caternolo, Liate Stehlik, Jennifer Hart, and Kelly Rudolph.

To my fantastic agent and friend, Lori Galvin. Thank you for taking my hand and leading me on the ride of my life. Huge thanks to my incredible team at Aevitas Creative Management: Allison Warren, Kayla Grogan, Ruby Rechler, Erin Files, Vanessa Kerr, Mags Chmielarczyk, Chris Bucci, and Esmond Harmsworth.

To my writing village: members of Crime Writers of Color, Karin Slaughter, Mary Kay Andrews, Joshilyn Jackson, Harlan Coben, Emily Giffin, Laura Zigman, Alafair Burke, Alex Segura (the carpool line has never been the same!), Lou Berney, Lisa

Unger, Hank Phillippi Ryan, Rachel Howzell Hall, Jess Lourey, Catherine Adel West, Sarah Weinman, Oline Cogdill, K. L. Romo, Molly Odintz, Julia Davis (yes, you!), and Brandi Wilson.

For the incredible people and organizations that gave me insight on the technical issues of the themes covered in this book such as heirs property, the Gullah-Geechee community, and the Georgia Low Country: Tamareeshi Geffrard, Gary Harris, Lillian Richardson, Michele Johnson, Cary Knapp, the Coastal Heritage Society in Savannah, Georgia, and the Georgia Heirs Property Law Center.

To all the booksellers, librarians, podcasters, bloggers, and readers: I can't thank you enough for your continued support of my writing endeavors. You are a gift to me.

I could not do this thing I love so much—writing books—without the love and support of my incredible circle of friends and family, including my sisters and brothers, both biological and in-law. I am so grateful to the best kids a mother could be blessed with, my three sweet peas: Alexandra, Mitchell, and Ashton. And for always, Anthony.

ALSO BY
WANDA M. MORRIS

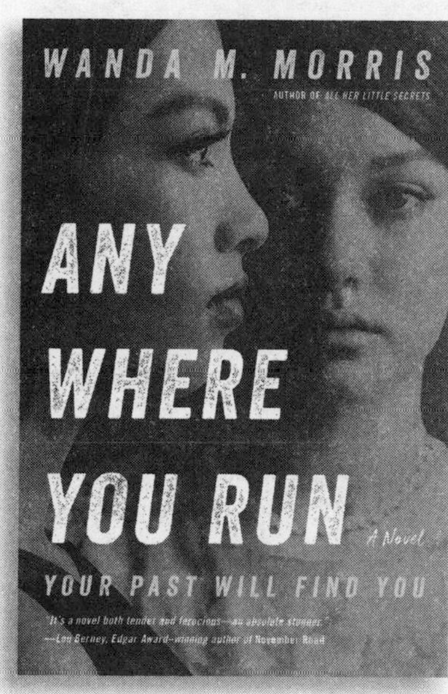

From the acclaimed author of *All Her Little Secrets* comes yet another gripping, suspenseful novel where, after the murder of a white man in Jim Crow Mississippi, two Black sisters run away to different parts of the country. But can they escape the secrets they left behind?

"*All Her Little Secrets* is a brilliantly nuanced but powerhouse exploration of race, the legal system, and the crushing pressure of keeping secrets. Morris brings a vibrant and welcome new voice to the thriller space."

—KARIN SLAUGHTER,
New York Times and international bestselling author

Discover great authors, exclusive offers, and more at HC.com.

MORROW